QUEEN OF THE BLOOD THRONE

Book Cover by Lao Lan, 2024.

Page edge design by Painted Wings Publishing Services.

1st edition, 2024.

Contents

SUGGESTED PLAYLIST

Still Here – League of Legends
I Choose Violence – Ramin Djawadi
The Return – CLANN
Game of Survival – Ruelle
Clockwise – Abbott
Afterlife – Hailee Steinfeld
You are a Memory – Message to Bears
Will I make it Out? – Tommee Profitt
If I Had a Heart – Fever Ray
Death Waltz – Adam S Hurst
Zombie – Damned Anthem

You can find additional Spotify playlists at *www.queensofmoirai.com/playlists*

ABOUT THE THREE FATES

The Fates, also known as Moirai, were the weaving goddesses that assigned destiny to mortals at birth. Their names were Clotho (the Spinner), Atropos (the Inflexible), and Lachesis (the Alloter). These women were often portrayed as the offspring of Zeus and Themis, while in some versions of the myth, they were portrayed as the offspring of Nyx. Each Fate had different tasks. Clotho created and spun the thread of life, Lachesis measured out its allotted length in hours, and Atropos ended it - cutting it short with a pair of shears or a knife. This is how they 'wove' a person's destiny.

Sometimes, the Fates were symbolized by time: Atropos (the past), Clotho (the present), and Lachesis (the future).

One – or all – of them can be seen reading or writing the Chronos, the book of fate.

Source: https://www.greekmythology.com/Other_Gods/The_Fates/the_fates.html

FOR MY DAUGHTER

The first Death was born among the stars, then wrapped in a blanket of sky.

Her hair resembled moonlight on snow.

Scholars said in her eyes, you could find all meaning.

Her creator Nyx, the Goddess of Night, was pleased. She'd built them to control man's destiny, to resolve the constant warring between Gods and man. Like most mothers, she did not understand how what was once beautiful could become ugly, nor did she know how monsters were made. This was her first mistake.

She nestled Death next to a being called Life and another called Time, and then considered her creations. Their futures.

After all this time I have come to believe that Death and I were not so different. In many ways, Death and I shared the same goal.

To be more than who we were.

As the descendant of Atropos, a Fate, your destiny is to kill. Ruthlessly and relentlessly, until you finally can bear it no more. Then your daughters should do the same. Bleak, unending horror... that is your purpose.

Will you willingly wear that black mantle upon your shoulders? Will you be an eternal enforcer, giving your people the blade instead of their freedom? I think not.

In these pages you will read how I, a simple thief, tricked them all. Death could not end me, and Time could not age me, because I'd found the answer. Know that it is possible, my daughter, to reject who others declared you to be. To refuse your future.

It won't be without cost. Each time I clawed my way out of the grave, I felt a little less like the person I had been. A little less capable of holding the shields that kept you safe, of keeping all these doors locked and our secrets guarded.

But I digress, daughter. Let us start this story at the right place: my beginning.

1

"Is it a boy?" My mother's eyes were closed.

"No, it's a heel," the midwife replied, yanking me from the womb by one ankle.

Much to everyone's surprise, clutched in my fist was a hand - my sister's hand. I gave a blood-curdling shriek, unwilling to leave her behind. Thus my first act was to save a life, pulling her along with me.

That might have been my first mistake.

"Twins. In there, head-to-head." The nurse had a perplexed look as she delivered a second daughter, pale and blue-faced.

Shell-shocked, my father watched as the nurse thumped his youngest babe with a fist directly in the chest, then cleared her airway with a crooked finger. My sister gave a pathetic mewl, and the midwife smiled with relief.

She smeared both our foreheads with the blood of a goat, then held us in each arm while my mother lay exhausted against the pillows.

"Two girls." The nurse was tired too. It'd been a long labor, thirteen hours. She frowned as she laid us on threadbare linens.

The cottage was drafty and cold, and the roof leaked when it rained. It was hardly a suitable place for pigs, much less a family to live in. There was only one crib, and it was less than sturdy.

My father, plain with lank blond hair and a sparse beard, scowled over her shoulder. "We can't afford two. We can barely afford one. Besides, aren't twins bad luck?"

"Nay. Twins are a double blessing from the Gods and the Fates."

"They look a bit different." My father peered at us in the firelight.

"With twins, one is always more hearty, another more clever."

You would think that my parents, hearing her words, would have decided that the stronger, better twin was me. After all, I'd been born first. I'd breathed easily. That would have been a reasonable response. But people, especially parents, are not always rational.

"This one is prettier. What do you think?" My father pointed at my sister.

My mother sighed. "I don't care. You know I would have rather had a boy to help out in the fields."

"Firstborns are always more loyal," the nurse said.

My mother spoke, contradicting her. "Well I've heard that children born feet first walk over everyone, and leap into things without looking."

There was a heavy silence in the cottage, the three of them holding their breath.

"She won't eat much. Nor take up too much room." The nurse's voice was kind; I always imagined that it was.

My father was angry. "Then let some other family have her. Give her to a woman whose child died."

"Sir..."

"If you leave her here, I will put her in the river." His face was hard.

"Are you quite sure?" The nurse studied our downy blond hair and button noses.

But my parents were not to be dissuaded.

So when the nurse gently pulled the door closed on that rundown cottage, my sister lay tucked into the crib under a threadbare blanket. I, the firstborn, was in a basket in her arms.

"I'll take you to Zeph. He will be thrilled. With those pretty eyes, who knows what is possible." She jostled me a bit as she dodged the mud puddles in the dark, and made her way into the town of Fidelisgrove.

Fidelisgrove was a crossroads of sorts. Witches and Fae, even the occasional minotaur – you never knew who would be passing through. It had no reason to be particularly popular, other than its location along one of the main roads of the kingdom of Moirai.

We were ruled by Lachesis, the Controller of Time. Our kingdom was called Kinkanali, which meant *Kingdom of the Reeds,* since there were many canals that stretched into the interior from the sea. Most of them were clogged with reeds and lilies, utterly unusable for trade, but a lovely place to fish and wade.

We had an inn, several drinking halls, three blacksmiths, tailors, four temples, a wishing well, and a marketplace where one could buy any sort of enchantment or potion. There was even a stone table upon which sacrifices to the Gods were made – usually when asking for harvest and the like.

Fidelisgrove lay in a bowl-shaped valley, which was quite perpetually full of smoke from the fires of its people. The breezes from the distant sea seemed to avoid it, and a single brown river ran through the center. There was a lake, quite large, where everyone went to bathe and drink and socialize, and as a result it was both crowded and dirty.

Like any town, it had its sordid underbelly. Thieves and petty tyrants, gossips, tricksters, and quite a few men who were cursed. Dark trade and restricted items could be bargained for or bought, and several merchants made a tidy profit on trafficking rare beasts and blessings from the Gods. And it was right in the midst of that underbelly our nurse traveled, to see a man who most feared, in a house called The Nightingale.

At the end of one of the darker lanes the Nightingale stood tall, with heavy purple velvet curtains covering its windows for privacy. A fancy gilded sign with a singing bird hung by the street - the irony being that this particular house welcomed anyone who wanted to sing.

That was, anyone who wanted to betray their master by telling their secrets.

Superficially, it was elegant. Discreet. If one looked closely, they might notice that the chimney was a bit crooked and roof tiles were missing in several places. The vines and flowers that grew along the side of the house rioted through the stones, and were covered in sharp thorns.

Any decent gardener would have cut them back years before. But then, any decent gardener would have quickly discovered that a charmed rosebush grows back in seconds and draws blood from anyone who hasn't been invited.

The green paint on the front door was fresh, and the door knocker was shiny gold. This was because anyone who came to the front door was surely a stranger. And strangers were always fooled by first impressions.

The nurse went to the side door, which was well hidden by vines and flowers. Once inside, she hung up her cloak and then made her way up a narrow staircase to the drawing room where the owner of the Nightingale was wide awake and waiting for her.

Zephyros Castan, leader of the most feared criminal gang in the city known as the Jackdaws, leaned back in his chair and stared at her with hooded eyes. "I task you with bringing me gossip and you lay a baby at my feet?"

"Look at that skin. The golden hair and green eyes. She will be a beauty one day. And if you teach her, she can trick every traveler out of his coin."

"One day! One day sixteen years from now! What am I supposed to do with her tonight and tomorrow? She is as useless as a potato."

He spit on the floor, barely missing the basket I lay in. He employed thieves, crooks, arsonists, hitmen, and those who did the jobs that most couldn't stomach.

He had no use for a baby.

The nurse, who had herself sewn up his wounds and spent too many nights in his bed, gave him a quiet look of reproach.

He shook his head. "You. You say you want a child. I say we'll make one eventually. Is this your way of forcing my hand?"

"Of course not." She was indignant. "I merely thought you might want a *lady* in your midst, someone who is not filthy and covered in fleas, for your more delicate jobs."

"I already have a lady in my midst," he murmured, and drew her down onto his lap to nuzzle her ear.

"I meant a *little* lady." She shied away from his kiss.

Zeph sighed. "She is not a lady; she is a baby."

"I rather like the look of her." She gazed down at the basket, putting one arm around his shoulders. "She looks like me, don't you think so?"

He scratched his head and peered down at the infant in the basket. Mostly the babe resembled a small troll.

"Think it over, spend some time with her. I will run to the market, and when I get back..."

"You cannot leave me here with this thing!"

"She's not a *thing*, she's a child, and you are quite capable. Surely the great Zephyros Castan is not afraid of a girl who weighs less than a loaf of bread."

He scoffed. "I'm not afraid of anything."

She touched his scarred face, the shiny skin drawn tightly white across his cheeks where someone had once tried to burn him alive and failed. "We could have a family, darling. She could be the start of it."

Zeph remained skeptical, begrudgingly accepting her kiss. He knew the streets better than she did; had seen the violence of Gods and man for too long. But he loved the healer, loved her kind heart and soft hands, loved her patience and loyalty. Even if he had not loved her, he still owed her his life many times over for all the ways in which she had saved him. If she wanted a baby - this baby - it suited him to give her whatever she asked.

"I'll think it over," he grumbled.

So the nurse left me in a basket at his feet, and Zephyros Castan sat in his chair and stared at me.

"You." He nudged the basket with a shiny black boot. "If you talk, I cut out your tongue."

Mute as a log, I remained still but alert.

He crossed his hands over his chest. "You run away, I shoot you in the back with a poisoned arrow."

I blinked, then yawned.

Zeph laughed. He hadn't seen someone so unintimidated by him in decades. The leader of the Jackdaws leaned over and scooped me up. He held me so he could see my face.

"I had a sister once. Beautiful. *Malheur* - unlucky - like you." He walked me around the room as he talked, speaking more than he had in years. "I might call you Malinda, the terrible beauty. What do you think?"

I, of course, had no opinion. Zeph carried on.

"Here is the fire. *Kenaz*." He held me a bit close and I squirmed, but did not cry. "First you will fear it. But someday you'll walk through it as I did."

Satisfied, Zeph settled back onto the couch, snatching the bottle from inside the basket. After he'd fed me, he placed me on his chest. "Don't cry. If you do, I'll give you away to the madame down the street."

Happy to oblige him, I fell asleep at once, exhausted by the long day. Zeph, pleased to have a baby asleep on his chest, began to think of the future.

We were both awakened by loud pounding on the door and the sound of men shouting. His men piled into the room, some bloodied, everyone talking at once.

Attack. Those bastards. They said it would send you a message.

Calmly, Zeph handed me off to one of the youngest members, who must have looked shocked to be handed a child.

"Get her out of here." Then, thinking better of it, he grabbed the thief's elbow before he could leave the room. "Find a bottle of milk. Feed her. Then put her in my room. Anything happens to her and I will kill you."

Stuttering, he did as he was told, even though he was a mere lockpick, not a midwife, and he'd never held a baby in his life.

Mavros, one of his most trusted men, came forward. He was holding a body.

"I'm sorry, Sir."

"I'll take her." With gentle hands, Zeph pulled the nurse to his chest, cradling her against himself. Her throat was cut wide open, her organs missing, a note nailed to one of her hands.

You take something from me, I take something from you.

Later that night a fire swept through a section of Fidelisgrove, wiping out several great houses. One of them, a fine brothel that many thieves frequented, was found to have just four victims inside, their hands nailed to the floor to keep them from escaping the blaze. Their bodies could not be identified, and the arsonist was never found.

As the sun came up, Zeph returned to his room to find me crying on the lockpick. Taking me into his smoke-scented arms, I stopped screaming immediately. Zeph dismissed the thief and sat down in the chair in the corner. Holding me up so the sun could shine on my face, his face grew thoughtful. Possessive.

He nodded slowly. "I suppose– I suppose you do look a bit like her."

2

Twenty years later.

"Well?" Smoke from a carved pipe wreathed his features - the shiny white scars, the dark curls cut close to his head.

I withdrew several coins from my pocket along with a golden ring, a heavy silver goblet, and a set of brass bells. I put them on the table between us.

Zeph pursed his lips. "It's not much," he said at last.

With a small shrug, I emptied my other pockets. "Travelers are becoming wary. There are too many thieves, and it seems they've been warned."

"Hmm." He put his pipe aside and inspected my small haul of stolen goods. For one day, it was not bad. But it was likely half of what I'd stolen a year before, and I was more clever and faster now.

"Here's your portion." He counted out coins from his own pocket, then slid them across the table toward me.

One third. Whatever he was paid for the gold, or the jewelry, Zeph split it with his thieves– a third for the house, a third for himself, and a third for whoever did the stealing. It was respectful of him...he didn't have to. But it gave him a reputation among the Jackdaws as someone who was brutal but fair, and many of them came to him willingly, wishing to serve a better master.

I put the coins into my pocket with a sense of acute relief. With every theft, I was steadily earning my way out of the Nightingale and Fidelisgrove. As soon as I had enough money saved, I would leave, and never look back. Zeph would let me, not just because I was the closest thing to a daughter he would ever have, but also because there were no prisoners here. Any of us could leave at any time and try to make our fortune elsewhere.

That was another thing that set Zeph apart from the other leaders. Though it did not win him friends in the higher ranks, he didn't view his thieves as property.

"You alright?" he asked, noting my somber mood.

"Just thinking." I glanced around the kitchen, the surfaces covered with dirty dishes. The Nightingale housed thirteen of us, and each meal generated an absolute mess. On the stove, stew still simmered in a large copper pot, and steam spiraled up from its surface. Spicy, earthy, with lots of meat - Zeph fed us well, mostly to make sure we returned.

"I should make friends with a witch. She can brew me a spell for luck. Maybe then I'd have more success."

His jaw hardened. "Don't dabble in that nonsense."

"I'm not." I shrugged with a faint smile.

Zeph had no respect for witches. He'd always said that the petty, amateur potion-making and curses were time consuming and temporary. That they were a waste of valuable herbs and money, both of which we had precious little of. Yet sometimes, *sometimes,* it did seem like those who dealt with the witches had just a little more time to escape, or found an unlocked door at just the right moment. Once or twice I'd seen one leaving by the back stairs, through the vines and flowers, made obvious by their blood red cloaks. So he couldn't be *that* against them.

"I have a surprise for you," he said and placed a small box on the table. "For your birthday."

I wasn't surprised.

"You shouldn't have," I muttered. He always remembered - it was a hard date to forget, since he'd gotten a child and lost his lover the same night. For him, it was the saddest day of the year, and for me too, since it represented the family we might have become instead of what we were.

Never one to wait, I unwrapped it quickly. Inside the box lay a set of dainty earrings made of hammered goblin gold, forged into runes.

Kenaz. Fire.

Isa. Ice.

They must have cost him a small fortune. "Wow," I murmured, eyes wide.

"You're a woman now," he said roughly. "With fire in your eyes and ice in your heart. Just as I taught you to be."

"Thank you."

I slid the gifts into my earlobes easily, turning my head this way and that. They were light, small, and high quality. No one could try to pull them out in a fight. He'd chosen well.

Suddenly overwhelmed, I kept my eyes on the box. Though he was imperfect and often cold, he'd done his best. He'd named me, cared for me and kept me alive, taught me everything he knew.

It was more than my real father had done.

Yet here I was, lying to him about how much I'd taken. Guilty, I debated whether I should just admit it right then. He wouldn't punish me; not if I told him the truth now, while we were alone. How all I really wanted was to leave, and have my own life, and not be a thief anymore. Even though he'd trained me well, I didn't want the world he'd given me. He might have understood.

Hesitant, Zeph placed his hand on the crown of my head and for a moment he simply paused, a small, simple gesture of affection. When I moved to speak, he had gone... and the emerald bracelet was still hidden in my boot.

I shared the tangerine room with another thief. Formerly a brothel, all the rooms were elaborately decorated with brocade wallpaper in various colors, sumptuous furniture, and chandeliers in every room. Mine was a lively shade of orange, which my roommate thought resembled yams or overripe fruit. The walls, bedding, and curtains were all the same shade, and the bed and wood trim was dark. My favorite thing was the beautiful, arched windows that overlooked the garden and the street. Stained glass roses adorned the top third of them.

The only downside to the room was that there was only one bed, and this I shared with Kirin, the only other female thief in our group. We were the same size, so she and I also shared our clothes.

This did not make us friends.

In fact, neither of us believed in friends. Too many times we'd seen a person leave this house and never return, and we'd both found dead bodies. Kirin was an orphan, purchased by Zeph when she was eight years old. Both her parents had been murdered in the night, though we never learned the motive behind it.

Instead of being friends, we were simply roommates, sometimes enemies or rivals, but definitely not friends. Most of the time, our preferred method of communication was either insulting or ignoring each other. Kirin usually did this via reading a book; she loved novels, stories of dragons and princes and love.

I preferred to practice knife throwing or walk in the rain.

"You'd be prettier if you'd smile more." Kirin peered at me as I toed off my worn boots by the door. "Those tight braids make your face look simple."

She'd gotten out a stack of playing cards and fanned them out on the bed. This is what we did on rainy afternoons, on the rare occasions when our coffers and bellies were full.

"As long as they don't make me look crafty or clever."

I unbraided my blonde hair and shook it out.

Kirin scowled. She knew all too well that it served my purposes better if everyone thought we were simple women with loose morals.

I sat down and crossed my legs. "I'll play, but please tell me you're not going to spend the entire time talking about the Fae in the woods."

"You're just jealous."

She dealt each of us nine cards.

A few weeks prior, Kirin had given her virginity to one of the Fae. It was all she could talk about, how the one who deflowered her had horns like a stag and a libido to match. She regaled me with how he'd given her a vision of a great tree and how they'd lain on a bed of flower petals. The vision wasn't real, of course - it covered a reality that was much less rosy. They'd lain together in a small narrow room in one of the cheaper inns.

Since then, she'd insisted on walking alone at night instead of with someone else in the group. I suspected that was because she hoped to encounter him again. She imagined that he would take her away and make her his bride.

It would suit her. Fae were remarkable in one aspect, which was their cleverness. Always playing games, they spoke in riddles, hoping to rope you into a bargain.

"I don't see why you had sex with a Fae," I told her. "If you're ever hoping to be married, most men expect a maidenhead."

"What do I care?" she asked. "I can always lie about it later."

I sighed loudly. For at least two years, Kirin had talked of getting out of the Jackdaws. The only way to do that, short of dying, was to save enough money to afford somewhere else to live... or get married. Kirin was pretty, with dark hair and large blue eyes and, despite her unsavory profession, many men were eager to marry her. In doing so, they hoped to make themselves a permanent friend to Zeph, that he'd regard them as some kind of adopted son.

In fact, I couldn't quite understand why she hadn't already said yes to one of them. Some were powerful merchants. Others were wealthy men looking for Zeph's favor - she'd even had an offer of marriage from a ship captain. Yet she refused them all, apparently preferring to share a bed with me.

"Are those new earrings?" she said suspiciously.

I had no reason to lie, so I didn't bother. "They are."

"Zeph gave them to you, didn't he?"

Shrugging, I re-shuffled the cards, laid them out again, and we continued to play.

"Maybe he hopes you'll sleep with him," Kirin sneered. "And you probably would, just to get out of here a little sooner. Even if he's all scarred up and double your age."

"Shut up," I said.

"Why? Truth hurts?"

Actually, the gossip hurt less than the truth. There was nothing between Zeph and me. Most of the time he treated me like a thief. Sometimes, however, he was unexpectedly soft. And his eyes lingered on me. He bought me gifts on my birthday, but no one else. No one knew why except for Phaedon and Mavros, who'd been there the night I arrived and the healer was killed. Everyone else in the house, and outside it as well, assumed we were lovers.

On my part, I would have preferred to call him my father. Sometimes, I dreamed that he was.

With a sly smile I was too familiar with, she laid out her cards on the bed. She won. Somehow, and I don't know how, Kirin always cheated at cards.

I might have argued it with her, but at that exact instant, I noticed a new ring on her finger.

"What's that?" Suspicion flared.

She pretended not to hear me. I leaned forward and gripped her hand in mine.

"Nothing," she tried to tug her arm away.

"You shouldn't lie," I said, turning her hand over to examine the heavy silver and obsidian ring. It had a secret compartment with poison in it. I'd seen it before, six months before, when I'd stolen it from a Eupatridae, one of the nobility, as they passed through Fidelisgrove. It was worth enough that they might send someone back to look for it.

"Maybe Zeph gave it to me."

"You took it from my closet." I frowned at her. "It's worth more than your life. You can't *wear* it."

"Then you should have kept a closer eye on it."

Kirin backed away from the bed, her eyes narrowed on me. She paused in the doorway, then smiled at me as she leaned down to pick up my boot. Then, before I could say anything, before I could *do* anything – she dumped the emerald bracelet into her hand.

"And what's this?" she sneered. "Been telling some lies yourself?"

"Put that back."

"Not a chance. You're lucky I don't go to Zeph now and tell him you've been skimming. He'd never trust you again. He's killed others for less, and he might have to make an example of you even if you are his favorite."

I couldn't move. Couldn't breathe. If she told him, he'd search my things, and he'd know that I'd been hiding a small trove for more than a year.

He'd know, for certain, that I had betrayed him.

If he cast me out, if he looked through my things and took all that I had saved… it would be years of work down the drain.

I swallowed hard.

"Please don't tell him."

"And what will you give me in return?"

"What do you want?"

"Half of your take. *Before* you show it to Zeph."

"He'd never believe it."

"That's your problem, isn't it? Just do what you do best. Lie."

I watched helplessly as Kirin pocketed the bracelet and strolled out of our room, humming a happy tune.

3

Dusk. Inhaling deeply, I closed my eyes and listened to the silence of the city. No one twittered, and the afternoon rain had rinsed away the stench of body odor and chamber pots. I perched on top of a roof, watching the last of the light fade and relishing the quiet before the streets filled again with people. In my hands, I held a bunch of herbs, ditch grass and yarrow, and these I wove into a small crown.

Phaedon sat next to me. He'd been a smuggler for Zeph longer than I'd been alive, and even though I didn't need him with me anymore, his presence was often a comfort.

"They say the prince of Kinver'i is looking for a wife. And he's coming here in a month. They'll all be dripping with jewels then, dressed up like birds for a feast."

"Yeah," I said. I couldn't wait. The Prince of Darkness was coming to Fidelisgrove, and when he did, every person in town would bring out their best... and I would happily relieve them of it.

Phaedon played with his rings - he had one on every finger, and plenty more at home. Each one represented a fight he'd won. That was why he was always sent with me; he was our best brawler. Zeph didn't need to worry I'd be overpowered if I were ever caught.

Not that that ever happened.

"They say Death and her son live in a castle of ice," Phaedon said. "Full of magical objects and diamonds big as a fist."

"Probably just a rumor." I glanced at his shaggy brown head tucked down, staring at his rings, counting them. He always did; I never asked why. He was a bit stooped, and his body wiry and scarred.

He's not always good, but he's a good man. That's what Zeph said. That's why he trusted him with me from the time I was small. In all my years I'd never had any cause to doubt him.

Overhead, the sky was streaked orange and purple. Everyone was having dinner now, home with their families. Soon, it would be night, and that was when I preferred to work.

Below us, the first of the revelers headed toward the pleasure houses, the inn, the drinking halls.

"You want to go together?"

"You know I work alone."

"And *you* know that Zeph insists I go with you if you are working near the pleasure houses."

The recent spat of violence between gangs, the tightening level of control of the city, the influx of travelers from new lands, some of which weren't exactly peaceful... There was always a new reason for Zeph to worry.

"Nothing bad has ever happened to me," I insisted. "And I've never been caught."

Phaedon frowned at the city below us, where the streets were dark but the buildings were lit by candlelight.

"I'll race you," he said finally. "First to have three coins?"

"Loser does the dishes?" Out of all our household duties, I hated that the most.

"Sure. Whoever gets back to the Nightingale first."

We shook on it, and then Phaedon hustled off, his steps quick and light. Meanwhile, I lingered on the roof.

Sometimes I won, so there was no reason for me to rush. Phaedon's face was too sinister, and anyone who saw him instinctively clutched their coins and hurried away. Unlike me, who could steal without being detected simply because no one expected it.

Unhurried, I watched the end of the sunset and wondered if Kirin really would keep my secret about the skimming.

"I'll have to switch rooms," I muttered. I couldn't have her continue to look through my things when I wasn't around, possibly stealing from my stash and undoubtedly spying on me.

If she intended to blackmail me - and she would - surely she'd know that I'd retaliate.

Not that it would matter. Zeph would cast me out, and I'd be without friends or shelter. All these years, he'd been my only family.

It was inevitable, I decided, that she would tell him. The only question was whether or not I'd still be here, or if I would leave before she spilled my secrets. It dramatically pushed forward my timeline, meaning that I'd have to leave sooner than planned.

The cobblestones were slick beneath my boots, a remnant of the afternoon rain that had doused Fidelisgrove in late afternoon. Casually, as if I didn't have a worry in the world, I strolled down the streets, looking for a target. Young, old, tall, short – that didn't matter. I was looking for someone who would be easy to take advantage of.

I shoved the hood of my cloak back and shook out my blonde hair. It was always a beacon to men, who I was either lost or easy. Lanterns flickered in the breeze, casting dancing patterns that gave life to the darkness. My eyes, accustomed to the play of light and shade, caught the staggered steps of a figure some distance away. Young by the look of him, his gait loose and carefree. Heading directly toward me.

"That one," I murmured to myself, a small smile playing on my lips.

He was laughing to himself, a merry sound that bounced off the stone walls and wound its way to me, meanwhile the light glinted off something metallic in his belt — a coin purse, perhaps.

My heart quickened, not from fear, but from the thrill of the hunt. Patience tempered my steps, each one dainty and unsure, as if I were lost but trying to fake confidence. This was the part I knew well — the dance between predator and prey.

As I drew closer, I could see the flush of alcohol on his cheeks, the carefree swing of his arms. He was blissfully unaware of the threat I posed, of the danger in his path.

"Oh!" I cried, stepping into the circle of warmth cast by a nearby lantern, letting its golden light drape over me like a shawl. My voice was soft, a velvet bell designed to snare his attention. "You scared me!"

He blinked, swaying slightly as he turned to face me, and surprise sketched itself across his features. "Evening, miss." His words slurred around the edges, but his eyes sharpened with sudden interest. "I'm sorry."

I bowed my head, letting my blonde waves tumble over my shoulders. "I was separated from my parents... The streets are a labyrinth in the dark and now I'm quite turned around. We were supposed to meet by the old fountain, but..."

I trailed off, letting the sentence hang.

His brow furrowed, the jovial spark in his eyes dimming with concern.

I stepped closer, allowing vulnerability to seep into my stance. "Could you walk me back? It's not safe for me to be alone." I locked my large green eyes with his, willing them to brim with an innocence I had not possessed in years.

The night and I both held our breath, waiting for the scales to tip.

"Alright," he exhaled, a reluctant smile tugging at one corner of his mouth. "I suppose it wouldn't be proper to leave a lady unescorted."

"Thank you, truly." My words were honeyed, my gratitude feigned.

His footsteps echoed alongside mine, each beat a tick of the clock, counting down to when I would disappear into the night. As we walked, I asked him good natured questions – how he liked the city, where he'd been. Nothing that would arouse suspicion. His silver pocket watch was gone from his waist in two minutes. He told me his name was Giorgios, that he and his friends were just passing through. He made jokes as we went along, and I almost felt sorry to poison him.

"Here," I murmured, pulling him toward one of the dark alleyways with a girlish giggle.

Obligingly, he followed, gripping my hand, touching my waist. Once we were in the shadows of the buildings, I leaned against the wall and tugged him close.

Sloppily, he ran a finger over my lips, his light brown hair falling in his eyes as he leaned down to kiss me. At the last minute, I turned my face and arched my neck so his lips drifted over the column of my throat, which he bit lightly and then sucked on. He undoubtedly smelled a lovely, floral scent there, a mixture of henbane and white poppy.

"Mmm," I cooed.

Encouraged, he continued– unwittingly inhaling, licking, and kissing the poisonous perfume on my neck.

I began counting the seconds. *Five, ten...*

Behind him, there was a low growl. We both froze.

"What was that," he murmured, his words slurred, which might have been the drink. Or it might have been the poison burning through his system.

"I don't know." My eyes were trained on a particularly dark section of the street where everything lay in shadow.

Slowly, excruciatingly so, I pulled out the blade I always kept at my waist. It wouldn't do much good against a large animal, but it would make me feel better. The noise came again - a low, menacing growl that made every hair on my arms stand up.

He turned, swaying on his feet as he put his back to me and faced the darkness. "Who's there?"

The thing growled again. It was obviously not some*one*, but some*thing*, and it did not seem friendly.

Stay and fight, or—

Run, my inner voice demanded.

I didn't stop to wonder about his safety. He was no one to me, and if I knew anything, it was that saving my own skin took priority over the life of a stranger.

So I took off like a shot, skirts flying, sprinting down the cobblestones, back toward the well-trafficked areas of Fidelisgrove.

In a flash the animal shot from the dark, quick and lethal. It didn't take long to realize I was being followed - loud, big, and not trying to hide its pursuit.

When I looked back over my shoulder, I saw it.

It was a Keres. Malevolent creatures, the Keres were a strange mix between a crow and a wolf. It had a head like a bird, but with a much longer neck; its chest was furry rather than feathered, and it had a small set of batlike wings.

I'd heard tales of them since childhood. Said to haunt the steps of the dying, sometimes they drank blood or attacked travelers from the shadows by the road. I ran faster, my legs pumping. Right, left, right - I lunged around corners, going deep into the maze of cobblestone streets. Here there was little light and few people. Most of the buildings were old and abandoned.

Suddenly I came to an unexpected and very unfortunate dead end.

An ominous silence settled over us as the beast walked toward me, its taloned feet digging furrows on the stones. Even the rats held their breath as they waited for my certain death. A growing panic gripped me as I stared into the creature's golden eyes, my gaze darting around the alley, looking for a way out.

"Why haven't you killed me already?" I muttered, palming the knife. "Come on."

Double eyelids opened and closed in a slow, serpentine blink.

I spun my blade, hoping the glint along the knife would fool the Keres into thinking it was bigger than it was. Keres had talons on their hands and feet, each with four claws. It definitely had the advantage in a fight, both in terms of strength, sheer size, and ruthlessness.

Briefly, I made my peace. If I was to die, no one would miss me except Zeph and Phaedon, and even them perhaps not very much. I had no friends other than the Jackdaws; my true parents didn't know if I was alive and did not seem to care.

The Keres leapt for me.

I quickly stepped aside and then whirled - my second knife hidden in my palm launching from my hand as I did so - and this knife stabbed it squarely in the chest.

Then I ran again. The blade didn't do much except arouse its wrath, but it was momentarily stunned just long enough for me to sprint into an open archway. The Keres was so close behind me I could smell it - like rotting meat and old eggs.

It swiped at me with one of its arms and its talons cut through the fabric of my black cloak. I tried not to panic. Panic would not help me, it would only make me stupid and slow. Making a split-second decision, I whirled, blade extended, and let the Keres slam into me. My blade sank directly into its left eye. Its scream was so loud that I couldn't hear anything else.

I wasn't fool enough to believe that would be enough. These short stabs would barely stall the animal, but it might give me enough time. I jerked away, hurtling toward who knew what. I'd lost my sense of direction in the labyrinth of dark streets in the underbelly of Fidelisgrove.

The Keres resumed its pursuit.

This was going to be a painful death. I jumped over the pile of garbage in a single leap, headed toward a ladder and a house with a red door.

When I'd almost reached it I stretched out my hands, but I felt the Keres' claws grasping at my cloak. Its heart was pounding so loudly behind me it sounded like hoofbeats.

"Help!" I screamed.

Not sure why, since there was no way anyone would reach me before I'd been sliced to ribbons. My voice echoed through the lane.

The Keres threw me to the ground, screeching like a harpy, its sharp beak snapping in my face. I tried to hold it off, grappling with its arms, its feet. I kicked it in the knee as hard as I could, ferociously pleased when I heard its bones snap.

It flailed away for a moment, shocked. Maybe all of its previous victims were less enthusiastic about staying alive.

I started crawling toward the door again, but the Keres latched onto my back, its talons digging into my shoulder as they sliced through my cloak and gown.

"No," I shrieked, as it slammed me into the cobblestones.

It pecked at the back of my skull.

With a final burst of strength I grabbed the last blade, the one I kept strapped to my thigh, and then rolled, exposing my belly, but slicing clean through the arm of the Keres.

In a fit of rage, it squawked directly into my face – its rancid breath making my eyes water.

Raising my knife again I tried to cut its throat, but it grasped my wrist in its beak and shook it, like a dog with a bone.

"Arghhh!"

I looked up into its golden eyes and its strange, bird-like face. As I prepared myself for the death blow I noticed a fine black mist flowing over the ground. The obsidian fog tumbled over the stones and dirt, over my boots, then covered my hands and face.

"What the hell?" I said.

Then watched as the smoky cloud rose up and snapped the Keres in half like a twig.

It fell over without so much as a chirp, landing half on top of me. I writhed uncomfortably, trying to get free, wincing from the pain of the gouges in my shoulders.

Overhead, the moon was shining. A man peered down into my face.

"You're a fool," he growled, by way of greeting.

"What?" I croaked, sure I was hallucinating.

Clad all in black, in a hooded cloak, he was likely a mercenary. Not the sort of person you wanted to be alone on a lonely street with, but I'd never been more glad to see him. With a square jaw and brown eyes so dark they matched his cloak, he scanned my face like he expected me to die at any moment.

"I said you're a fool. Everyone knows you don't run from a Keres." Biting, arrogant, he seemed more annoyed than anything else.

"Do I know you?" I muttered, wiping blood from my eyes.

"No. You don't. Can you stand?"

I struggled to right myself - as soon as I sat up, the world immediately spun. I shook my head slightly and my vision blurred again.

"I don't think so." I pressed my palm onto the cobblestone, hoping that it would stop the world from feeling as if it was inside a storm-tossed ship.

With a sigh of frustration, he held out a black gloved hand. I hadn't seen gloves that fine in my entire life. If I hadn't been feeling so terrible, I would have stolen them as soon as his back was turned.

I took it, and he hauled me to my feet.

"This is not the sort of place for a lady," he said, seemingly surprised.

"It chased me here." I flinched as I reached over my shoulder, then drew my hand away, covered in blood.

"You'll want to get that looked at," he murmured.

With a small groan, I limped over to the Keres and yanked my knife out of its eyeball with a soft plop.

"You might have been able to win if you'd had another knife on you," the man said.

"I only carry three." I wiped the blade off on the side of my thigh, soiling my red gown even more. Not that it mattered. The hem was shredded, and it was filthy as a kitchen rag. I'd have to burn it.

I looked back at the stranger.

Every angle of him was hard - the jawline, the straight nose, his sharp cheekbones. Coldness wrapped around him like a moat, and smoke snaked around his feet, then disappeared into the folds of his cloak.

He was currently appraising me, and his gaze dragged across my face, assessed my stubborn chin and tangled blond hair. Back behind him, a black horse twitched, impatient to return to their journey.

"Who trained you?"

A thief never gives up their secrets. "No one."

"That's a lie. No *lady* can fight like that."

We examined each other, two sets of sharp eyes shifting and inspecting. Perhaps he believed I was leading him into some sort of trap; I definitely felt the same.

I spoke first. "I wouldn't have imagined that the Prince of Darkness would be the sort of man to save a woman in distress."

He looked annoyed. "Who said I'm a prince?"

I pointed past his shoulder. "Your horse. That's a Tenebrix, which costs more to buy than most men earn in a lifetime. I don't know many men who can summon shadows, and your cloak does have the Atropos seal upon it, does it not?"

He frowned as he considered me. "I'm Melchior," he said finally.

"Obviously," I replied, and slipped my two knives back into the pockets I'd sewn into my gown.

Still lightheaded, I wanted to get back to the Nightingale as quickly as possible.

I started to walk away, but without warning, dizziness overcame me. I had to lean against the building to keep from falling to my knees.

"Easy," Melchior said, grabbing my elbow.

"I don't need your help." My tongue felt thick, and it was difficult to speak.

"Clearly."

I put my forehead against the bricks. *I'll just stay here. Until it wears off.*

"The talons have venom in them. It won't kill you immediately. It causes lethargy and then paralysis. Keres venom is an ingredient in many dark magic spells."

The Prince clicked his tongue. "Like this you'd be easy prey for just about anything, including any one of the men in this sordid town."

Without asking my permission, he scooped me up in his arms and walked toward the horse.

"Wha–?" I said with a tone of faint alarm.

He sat me on the back of the horse with ease, and then mounted behind me, placing his arms around my waist to hold me securely. As much as I might have protested, this was probably for the best, since I otherwise might have broken my neck falling headfirst into the dirt.

"Where to?" he asked.

I hesitated. I didn't want to give the Prince of Darkness directions to my home, and yet I had nowhere else to go. I was injured, my head was pounding, and if he was telling the truth, I'd be paralyzed soon.

"The Nightingale. It's an inn."

I blinked and tried to hold myself erect in the saddle. "I think it's that way." Overwhelmingly sleepy, all I wanted to do was lie down.

Sometime later, I opened my eyes and watched blearily as a thatch of vines curled toward him, their purple flowers reaching for his neck, and noticed how quickly his shadows shoved them away.

Stop that, they seemed to say.

Vines. He'd come to the side door, and we were home. As I watched them move, I wondered whether the bewitched flowers would admit him, or block him from entry.

I inhaled deeply. I was familiar with our garden; I'd explored it almost every day of my life. So I knew the exact smell of the trees and flowers, the herbs and moss. It was easy to tell which scent was his, because it was like nothing I'd ever experienced.

The prince was like a calming balm. Like winter mornings, like icicles on evergreens, like quiet, like hot tea in a wooden cup with a sprig of mint floating on its surface.

"Don't take this the wrong way," I said to him. "But I think I'm going to throw up."

Then, much to my horror, I leaned over, and vomited all over his fancy black boots.

4

Home. I breathed a sigh of relief as he carried me into The Nightingale. *Zeph will know what to do. He'll fix me.*

The prince had to duck under the bundles of herbs hanging from the wooden rafters, and he stepped over a basket of freshly picked vegetables from the garden. Not too gently, he deposited me in one of the kitchen chairs, stepping back to scan me.

"Stay still. Moving around makes your heart pump more, which spreads the venom faster."

I could feel that was true. With every movement, I was aware that the strange numbness expanded– my spine, my skin, my shoulders.

Listening to the silence, I looked up at him.

"I don't think anyone is here," I muttered. I had thought - no, expected - that Phaedon would have come back already. Or that someone would be here. I had no desire to be alone with the Prince of Darkness. "They're likely out working. They'll be home any minute." I tried to sound convincing.

"Where can I find the bandages? Yarrow?" he asked.

I shifted uncomfortably, my skin burning.

"Top cabinet on your left." I put my head down on the table and closed my eyes.

He certainly doesn't act like a prince. At least, none that I've ever heard of, I thought, as I listened to him move around the kitchen. He took water from the bucket, filled the kettle, placed it over the fire, then went through cabinets.

He paused, studying the shelves.

At one point I opened my eyes and saw him lean over a mortar and pestle to grind herbs. His broad shoulders strained the fabric of his black shirt.

"What are you doing?"

"Saving your life." He said it in a clipped tone.

If he was going to murder me, he would have done it already. Or he would have let the Keres finish the job.

I didn't speak again as he waited for the water to boil. It was all I could do to stay awake, slumped at the kitchen table, trying not to panic as the side of my face went numb.

When Melchior returned to my side, much to my surprise, it was not with a cup of tea but with cloth and hot water, a knife with the blade heated, and a pot of ...something that smelled like horse hooves and old grass.

"Let's take a look at those wounds," he said roughly.

I, with sweat dripping down my temples, still had enough of my wits to know that the other thieves could not find me half naked in our kitchen with a strange man.

Before I even replied, he used his hands to tear open the back of my crimson gown.

"For the love of Zeus," I muttered, my head jerking up, then rolling as I realized that I couldn't quite keep things straight anymore.

"Settle down. I'm not doing anything but cleaning and bandaging the wounds."

He brushed my golden hair aside, and I felt his eyes on me as if they were a touch.

"There's no one to clean these gashes but me. It won't take but a moment. So do you want to die, or do you want to let me help?"

I felt too sick to argue.

"Go ahead." I couldn't feel it anymore, but I supposed my back must look quite bad, given the talons on the Keres.

Gently, he ran the hot cloth over my skin, wiping away the dirt and blood, revealing several gashes, each the length of a finger.

"These will scar," he muttered.

Without warning, he poured cold liquid directly onto my skin. It felt like waves of fire cascaded across my back and I gritted my teeth so hard they might have shattered. I gripped the table, breathless with pain.

"Did you know," he said conversationally, "that a blood bond is part of the marriage ritual for the Fates?"

"I don't– I don't know anything about the Fates."

His hands were steady as he tended the wounds on my back.

"Well. As their descendant, I know quite a bit. There's nothing stronger than blood - blood magic, blood bonds, blood ties. When a Fate shares their blood, they share their magic. Forever."

I bit my lip as he pressed harder against the wound.

His voice distracted me from the pain, so I let him prattle on. He probably thought I'd be interested in marriage, interested in him, simply because I was female and he was a prince.

"You outran the Keres."

"No I didn't. It caught me."

Melchior dropped warm liquid into each gash, then salve. Gradually, I relaxed into his touch as the pain subsided.

"Did you study healing?" I asked.

"No."

He didn't elaborate. But he seemed familiar with the basics of nursing someone, of what things in our kitchen would be best for infected and venomous wounds.

His mother is Death. People are likely dying around him every day.

"Where did you get this scar?" he asked, his gaze lingering over an ugly white scar on the side of my neck.

I shivered, unnerved by his closeness. "Kirin. My roommate. We were pretending to be pirates."

"This doesn't look like mere play."

"It was a bit too firm."

After a brief hesitation, he lifted his hands. "Done. That will hurt for several days. And I don't recommend taking on another demon anytime soon."

Testing, I found I was able to lift my head and look around the room without my vision swirling. I blinked at him, The Prince of Darkness, sitting in the chair, across from me.

Studying my face.

I could now see that his eyes were not brown. They were onyx, like a night without stars. His hair was dark too, although it was impossible to say the exact hue because it was cut so closely to his skull that it was just a dusting. His eyebrows were stark, straight lines, making him look as if he were questioning me. And while previously I'd assumed he had a strong jaw, I could now see that his face was more like a heart. Not rectangular like most men I knew. His hairline dipped down in the center, softening him, making him far less intimidating than I'd originally thought. His chin had a dimple in the center, but not too pronounced. And his lips–

I openly stared.

I'd never seen a descendant of the Fates before. Depicted in books, on tapestries, statues and fountains. But in real life... he was certainly more attractive than any man I'd ever seen. Impassioned, I wondered who his father had been if the Fates often sullied their lineage with humans. Most likely his sire was another God— Apollo, perhaps.

The corner of his mouth twitched as he endured my overt curiosity. Obviously, he was accustomed to women ogling him.

"I need to put on a new dress... Can you close your eyes?"

At that, Melchior looked distinctly uncomfortable. Slowly, as if he were afraid I would stab him, he shut his eyes.

I skimmed his features again, then I stood, holding the shredded gown to my chest. With as much dignity as I could muster,

I fled the room.

I returned wearing one of Kirin's dresses. It was well-made, dark green with a black lace collar. She often wore it in the drinking hall, so I'd misted it with lavender water before coming down. I hoped he wouldn't smell the ale in its folds.

For a moment, I lingered in the doorway. Melchior was washing his hands in our sink. The bandages, the pot and the herbs, all of it had been tidied and rinsed and put away again.

"Do you want wine?" I asked.

"I don't care."

"Er... well...I'll just go and fetch it then."

In the cellar, I gave a tiny sigh of relief. Certainly, his manners were lacking. But he had saved my life, so I was obligated to offer him food and drink, or a favor of some kind. To not do so was to risk the wrath of the Gods.

I grabbed one of Zeph's most expensive bottles, a red Fae wine that was nearly black. But as I made my way back to the kitchen, I hesitated. His horse was tied just outside, his saddlebag and cloak across its back. Ignoring the twist of remorse, I sat the bottle on a small table... then exited the house through the side door, tiptoeing so he wouldn't hear.

I went to the garden. Like an arrow, I flew straight to the black mare. He'd tied her in the corner of our yard and she was happily munching on the fallen apples as if she hadn't eaten in days.

"Good girl," I whispered soothingly. "I'm just going to check something."

Happy to oblige, she nuzzled my hand, then resumed her grazing with a swish of her tail.

I wasn't exactly planning to steal something - not anything big at least. Melchior had saved my life. But I very much wanted to see what sort of wares a prince traveled with. After all, I'd never met one before.

With quick, deft fingers, I rummaged through the pack tied to his saddle. It was fine leather, black, buttery soft. It didn't have a scratch on it, almost as if he'd never used it before. Inside, I found a velvet pouch, which jangled happily as I lifted it.

Goblin gold. At least thirty pieces.

Enough to feed our house for a month, longer if the weather remained fair.

I couldn't resist dipping my fingers into the bag, fingering the snowflake shaped coins.

It must be wonderful to be a prince. To wake and have gold flowing from everywhere, a crown upon your head.

I rubbed my fingers over the symbols engraved upon them - the hourglass, the thread, the knife. The symbols of the ruling families of Moirai controlled every aspect of our lives. More than queens, the Houses of Atropos, Lachesis and Clotho were Fates - they controlled Death, Time, and Life, and without them, who knew what our world would be. Melchior was more than a prince, he was the son of Atropos, and he'd spent the last hour cleaning my wounds.

What a strange night this has been.

Pursing my lips, I weighed the coins again.

A month, Malinda. A month's worth of food. Would he even notice it was gone?

"Find something you like?" Melchior drawled, stepping out of the shadows.

Surprises didn't faze me; they added to the thrill of getting caught, and getting away with it. Tonight was no different. Smoothly, I flipped a knife into my hand as I dropped the bag, the coins spilling over the grass at my feet. Before Melchior could shift to grab them, my blade was at his throat.

"It's not what it looks like," I said.

He cocked a brow at me. "I'd say it looks like you're robbing me."

I pressed the blade against his skin and saw a drop of blood bead along the tip.

"You bleed red, Prince of Darkness."

"Most men do."

"You are not a man, though, are you?" I challenged.

He blinked those dark eyes at me and I became aware of the shadows gathering at my feet, of the icy cold hands creeping up my legs, up my bodice. One of the shadows grasped me around the throat.

Then it squeezed.

"Truce?" he asked, as I pressed the knife a little closer.

The shadows hissed, and one tugged at my hair. Begrudgingly, I realized the shadows could probably snap my neck faster than I could cut his.

"Fine," I ground out, and pulled the knife back.

The shadows vanished, collapsing into nothing in an instant.

"A handy trick, that." I rubbed at the skin of my throat, which was now several degrees cooler than the rest of me.

Kneeling at his feet, I swept the coins back into the pouch. When I stood again, the prince held out his hand. Reluctant to admit defeat, I slowly placed the bag in it.

He leaned closer, mere inches from me. I'd never been scrutinized so carefully before, and my eyes skimmed over his stubbled jaw, his lips, his eyelashes.

"You faced the Keres and nearly won," he said. "I saved your life, and you attempt to rob me for my kindness. Anything else I should know about you?"

"Zeph says I'm a masterful liar and should have never been born."

He continued to study me in that strange, disconcerting way of his. Utterly still. "Do you need money so badly that you're willing to slight the son of Death?"

"Are you going to kill me for it?"

"Not today." Melchior looked around the overgrown garden, then at his bloody cloak and gloves. "I wouldn't want to spoil our thoroughly enjoyable evening."

I blushed.

He touched the bridle of his horse. He was just seconds from leaving. Leaving, with a purse full of coins - and there was no way he could possibly spend them all. I was much more desperate than he; I could play upon his sympathy for a damsel in distress.

"Let us make a deal," I said hastily. "You give me the coins, and I'll give you anything you ask for."

"That's a bold offer." Melchior considered my face, tipped up toward his. "You don't have anything I want, Malinda."

"Then take me with you." Unfazed, the words were out of my mouth before I could stop them.

"With me?" Melchior raised his brows, genuinely surprised. "You can't be trusted. You'd steal my coins given the first opportunity, and probably my horse as well."

He was a smart man- of course I would do exactly that. It pleased me that he realized it... Most nobility were oblivious idiots, indolent and useless.

I curled my fingers into a fist, then placed it over my heart. "I swear I won't try to rob you again, if you take me with you."

"And you think I should trust your word?"

"Yes."

It looked as if he were actually considering it. "You don't know where I'm going."

"I don't care. I have no preference."

Melchior was silent for far too long. It made me nervous.

"If you won't take me with you, give me some of the coins," I begged. "I'll trade you something in return."

"What do you have, besides cheap stolen trinkets? Thirty gold coins in a brothel would buy me weeks of many women, not just one."

"Been to many brothels have you?" It was an appallingly rude question.

The corner of his mouth twitched. "I haven't, actually."

Weighing the coin purse in his palm, he considered me. "You'd give me anything I want?"

"Within reason. I won't kill myself for it."

Those onyx eyes found mine. "What if I asked for a kiss?"

A kiss?

"Didn't you just say you could get far more in a brothel?"

"I'm curious. I've never kissed a thief before."

I hesitated. Not that kissing bothered me, I kissed men to steal their purse all the time. I did not exactly want him to know that, however. I'd also never kissed a prince before. It seemed like a bad idea. Still...

To confirm our bargain, I repeated it. "I will kiss you. And then you will give me the bag with thirty gold pieces?"

"Thirty-seven," he murmured, his expression intense.

Thirty-seven! I screamed inside. If I kept it for myself, it was a huge sum. This would mean I had enough to leave Fidelisgrove, enough to book a passage on one of the pirate ships that went all the way to the southern isles. I would have enough to fly on the back of a dragon and wear fine shoes.

I should pretend to think it over. To hesitate.

Haltingly, slowly, I slid my hands up his chest. There they were small, compared to his broadness. "Softly?" I asked.

"However you like," he replied.

I gave him a quick peck. "There. A kiss."

"I've kissed my own hand with more enthusiasm." Melchior frowned. "Surely you don't feel that was worthy of thirty-seven pieces of goblin gold?"

"Fine." I eyed his lips. "I'll just imagine you're someone else."

He smirked. "Do what you must."

I thought of the scenes Kirin read aloud, the ones that made me red-faced, and then what she'd told me about the Fae. I thought of Theon, the man I'd wanted since age twelve, who never looked at me twice because he was in love with Kirin for nearly as long.

The garden was still; the flowers moved gently in the breeze. As he waited, his hands drifted to my waist.

I licked my lips nervously and stared up into his face. Obviously, I had kissed other men at this point – many. He was richer than any of them. A descendant of the Fates. His mother was Death itself.

Don't be a coward, I told myself. *Yes, he is a prince, but he's flesh and blood too isn't he?*

Even if he were made of cobwebs and nightmares, he has thirty-seven gold pieces.

You can do anything for that amount of gold.

His expression was calm. But underneath, I sensed a snapping curiosity, expectation, and something strangely angry. As if this kiss were meant to *prove* something to himself, though what that might be I couldn't imagine. In any case, it didn't matter - I wanted those coins and I would have them. So I shifted my hands to cup his face, to angle it so that I could reach his mouth.

Full and lush, his breath smelled of tea and wintergreen—

A deep voice rang out in the garden, chilling me down to my bones.

"Get your hands off my daughter."

Zeph, with his horribly scarred face and a sword, stepped out into the moonlight.

Daughter. He'd called me his daughter. Not his favorite, not his second, not a street rat. *Daughter.*

It made me feel even worse for what I'd just suggested, that the prince take me with him, as if I were a captive. As if I'd been poorly treated. As if Zeph hadn't been my savior many times over.

Seething with hostility, he stared at the Prince of Darkness, ready for battle. "What are you doing here?"

"Leaving," he said.

"We were only talking," I began.

Melchior's eyes skimmed across my features as if he were seeking the answer to a riddle. Angling his body, he stood between Zeph and I. He pressed the bag of coins into my hand as he stepped back. "Take them," he whispered. "And leave this place."

His thumb ghosted across my cheekbone, as if he were wiping away a tear, or a smudge of blood. I blinked up at him, my thoughts muddled. Perhaps he'd misunderstood; maybe he thought I was abused or held hostage.

I couldn't ask. He'd honored our deal... even though the kiss had been interrupted.

Within a beat, he had mounted his horse. "I would say goodbye, but we will meet again."

Clicking his tongue, he tugged at the reins. Not exactly sure why, I reached out and touched the toe of his boot. It was in the stirrup, easily within reach. He paused, then gazed down at me.

"Be careful," I told him. "You wouldn't want to meet your Death in the woods."

Melchior's eyes narrowed. "That might be the most ironic thing anyone has ever said to me."

Then, wordless, he rode away as I fingered the small fortune he'd left with me. I turned to face Zeph.

"Who was that? And what was he doing here?"

I made my way across the garden, limping slightly, wincing as I moved. "Melchior. The Prince of Darkness."

He eyed me. "What? Why was he here?"

"He saved me. A Keres attacked while I was with a mark in a dark alley, and he had to bring me here."

"A Keres in Fidelisgrove?" Zeph looked skeptical. "And you were going to kiss him as his reward?"

I held out the bag of goblin gold. "He offered this in exchange."

Zeph took the bag and silently counted the coins. "Thirty-seven pieces of goblin gold for a single kiss?"

"He's a fool," I said with a shrug. "It wouldn't be the first time; Gods fall for mortals all the time."

"Don't insult the house of Atropos. Fates are far more powerful than Gods." He turned and stomped back toward the side door. "You never know when they'll show up and ruin your life."

"I doubt they know I exist."

"Kissing one of their sons is a hell of a way to stay anonymous."

He had a point. I followed him inside, brushing the vines and flowers out of the way.

"Regardless, I didn't kiss him. You interrupted."

"Well that's unfortunate. One of the most powerful beings in Moirai, and you've attracted his interest." Zeph took a seat at the kitchen table. "What did he say to you when he left?"

I bit my lip. "He said we'd meet again."

5

My days returned to the monotony of waking at sunrise and robbing from the rich, punctuated by chores and errands for Zeph. To my intense annoyance, I occasionally found myself thinking about the Prince of Darkness. Especially when I counted his coins, most of which Zeph had allowed me to keep.

Meanwhile Phaedon returned, shocked to hear how my evening had gone. "You've had so many brushes with death. And a handsome prince to rescue you."

"I wish I'd seen him," Kirin mused. "He sounds so dashing."

She would have accused me of lying if Zeph hadn't corroborated my story.

"Tell me again what he said in the garden," Kirin pleaded.

"Do I have to?" I sighed.

"There's nothing else to do," she replied.

"There's sweeping to do," Alistair called from the other room. "And hanging clothes on the line!" He and six other Jackdaws were in the living area, playing cards.

"Malinda! The bread!" Kirin jumped up from her seat at the table and ran to the fire.

I'd charred the loaf to a crisp.

Sighing, I set to work scraping away the burnt bits – we didn't have the luxury of being able to throw it away.

"What was the exact shade of his eyes?" Kirin asked.

Midnight. Onyx. The underside of a raven's wing. Everyone knew that Atropos and her sons had black eyes. "Unremarkable," I answered.

I'd set my goal at fifty gold pieces - with the coins from Melchior, I nearly had enough. Even after giving Kirin part of my stash as payment for her to keep her treacherous mouth shut, I had enough.

"I have excellent news," Zeph announced, as he entered the room. "The Prince of Darkness is staying at the rectory." To his credit, he didn't even look at me as he said it. He searched through the cupboard, evaluating our food. From behind, he was handsome - well built, muscular. It was only his face that was so terribly marred, like a ghoul with the white and pink mottled flesh.

"I'd like to go pay him a visit," Kirin said, grabbing a handful of peas and shelling them into a large copper pot.

"Perhaps he values his privacy," I muttered.

If I knew Kirin at all, she would be sneaking down the stairs come nightfall.

She rolled her eyes. "He's a man looking for a bride. He is essentially *inviting* women to throw themselves at his feet."

"Melchior is not a normal man," I told her. "He's the son of Death."

"I wouldn't say he's *looking* for a wife," Zeph told her. "Atropos wants an heir. Whoever of her two sons marries first, his wife will be queen."

"Queen temporarily," Phaedon said, rolling his eyes.

"What?' Kirin and I spoke in tandem.

"The Fates never truly step down from their thrones, they are immortal. They only let their heirs occupy the throne for their mortal lifespans. Some of their offspring live longer, but they are never truly immortal."

"So once their offspring die, most of the time the Fate retakes the throne and restarts the bloodline." Phaedon continued for the sake of Kirin and me. "They only step down if they are bored...or murdered."

"Which is irrelevant." Zeph easily took back everyone's attention, "With the Prince here there will likely be other nobles and wealthy individuals traveling and staying with him. As always, if you get caught, the consequences are your problem."

With that, Zeph grabbed an apple and headed upstairs to his study. The chatter in the kitchen picked up once more, everyone discussing how much they might make off of the Prince and his entourage.

"If he picked me, I'd be Queen of Kinver'i." Kirin gazed out the window, daydreaming.

I didn't much care for Kirin's imagination, nor did I particularly want to imagine her married to Melchior.

"Being the queen of Kinver'i sounds terrible," I said. "Rule a kingdom with Death herself watching over your shoulder? Everyone else telling you what to do? Awful."

"Well then you can spend the rest of your life stealing, covered in dust and goat hair, wearing these cheap gowns."

I bit my tongue. I wanted to control my own destiny. See the world. Have freedom and adventure. I didn't long for a heavy crown, shackling me to a dull prince and his children.

I put the bowl of peas aside. "A throne would give responsibility and children, a people whose expectations you would never meet, and probably a husband who is a tyrant. Little else."

"What a pessimist you are." Kirin furrowed her brow. "I'm glad you don't want him for yourself. I wouldn't want to compete with you."

She was being insincere. There was no competition between us, because she always won. At least where men were concerned.

I glanced out at the garden. There was still picking to do, and I would bet two gold coins that Kirin had given up halfway.

"What of his brother Julian, the Prince of Blades? Is he also coming to Fidelisgrove?"

"Not that I've heard." I poured water into a cup and gulped it down.

Kirin was confident. "I'll make Melchior fall in love with me. How hard can it be?"

How hard indeed. "He'll never marry a thief." I continued to shell peas. "And if I recall correctly, most of the children of the Gods end up dead. I'm sure Fates are the same."

Later, as we elbowed our way through the crowded streets of Fidelisgrove, a sense of anticipation fluttered in my chest. I wore a fine red dress and my golden fire and ice earrings. Kirin, meanwhile, completely ignored me, and strode toward the rectory.

"We're just going to see if we can catch a glimpse of him."

The windows were latched shut, despite the sweltering heat of the day.

Almost immediately, sweat gathered under my breasts and at my temples, and although I fanned myself, I could feel my golden hair curling and frizzing.

There were at least two hundred women here with the same idea. All strolling around, attempting to look bored, their eyes glued to the door of the rectory.

"He's not going to come outside," I told Kirin. "It's hot as Hades, and there are too many people. It's a mob."

She stamped her foot.

My eyes flicked to the mosaic that ran along one building in the town square - the Three Fates, Lachesis, Clotho, and Atropos each held a magical item as horses and demons churned around them. Atropos - his mother. I'd never really looked at her before. Platinum-haired, dark eyed, absurdly tall and thin as a wraith. Like a star plucked from the night sky.

"Let's go back to the Nightingale," I suggested. "It was a good idea, but there's no way we are going to see him."

Kirin's eyes were glued to the curtains - she'd seen them shift slightly. "Are you going to look over the crowd?" she muttered this from one side of her mouth.

"Of course."

"Leave some for me then."

I gave a short nod, and then the two of us split up - her hoping she would find the Prince of Darkness, and I with the intention of robbing several of the women.

It only took me a few minutes before the hidden pockets of my gown were nearly full. Satisfied, but vaguely disappointed, I headed back toward the Nightingale.

With a sigh of relief, I entered the house. It was dark and cool, and infinitely preferable to the heat of the day. Immediately, however, my idea of sitting around in peace was torn apart - I heard the sounds of men arguing from the living room.

"Zeph?" I said, and poked my head around the doorframe.

My mentor was sitting on the couch, smoking his pipe. Despite the heat, he had on a crisp white shirt and a jacket, plus his pants and boots.

I immediately recognized Melchior, even though his back was toward me. He was dressed all in black.

"You're home." Zeph gave me a tepid half smile. "Won't you come in?"

Tilting my head, I took a step into the room - inhaling deeply. I smelled him. Evergreen. Winter. Suddenly I noted how the room was darker than it should be, even with the sun shining outside. Melchior glanced over his shoulder and then turned to face me.

"Malinda."

"You're here." I couldn't fathom why he would want to come back to the Nightingale.

Melchior was watching me again in that strange way that made me feel as if he planned to crack open my head and sort through its contents.

"You look tired," he said. Bottomless midnight eyes searched mine. Fates eyes.

"I am tired," I admitted. The cuts on my back from the Keres still bothered me - in their healing, the skin had drawn tighter, making it difficult to sleep.

There was a pause, as if he searched for words.

Zeph filled the silence between us. "The prince has come to make you an offer. I have listened to what he has to say and I think you should consider it."

The blood drained from my face. I licked my lips and lifted my eyes to his. "What offer?"

Keenly, he eyed me, and came to a decision.

"This is my sixth trip. My mother Atropos has lost patience. If I come home without a bride, my mother will choose one herself. You can easily imagine how much I would hate that to happen."

"So you have to find someone immediately."

"I've already found her." Melchior's black eyes were like an abyss as they held mine.

I glanced past him, at Zeph, who appeared strangely sad. As if... he'd lost something. As if he were in pain.

Confused, I shook my head. "Zeph?"

"He means you. You're his choice."

I laughed. "I'm not marrying you," I told Melchior, before I could talk myself out of saying it.

"Duly noted."

"This is ridiculous," I replied. "You barely know me."

Melchior leaned against the desk behind him. "How many female thieves do you think there are in Moirai?"

At least two in this house.

I pursed my lips. "I couldn't say. I've never left Fidelisgrove. But I don't know what that has to do with it."

Melchior considered me. "Do you have any other special skills besides thievery, being stupidly brave, and that ability to run like the wind?"

"I'm a fair lockpick." I ran my tongue over my teeth.

"That you are." His eyes skimmed my body, and I got the distinct impression that it was no longer lockpicking we were talking about. "And you're decent with a blade."

"These aren't skills that make me marriage material."

Melchior nodded. "I'm not asking you to marry me."

"You aren't?"

Zeph spoke up. "The prince isn't looking for a bride. He's looking for a thief."

"What?"

"You'll find and steal a magical object for me. I'll pay you handsomely for the trouble, and it likely won't take you very long."

It took me a minute to understand him, despite his plainspoken command. Melchior, Prince of Darkness and son of Death, was asking me to come home with him, as ... a personal cutpurse?

I settled into a chair facing him, my pockets jingling as I sat, though Melchior remained standing. He periodically paced the room as he spoke, a strangely nervous behavior.

"Your father assures me you can steal anything."

Father. My eyes darted to Zeph, who was watching me with an intent expression.

"Do you think he's right?" Melchior asked me. "Or is he biased?"

"He's right," I said slowly. *Soon.* I'd been planning to leave so soon.

"Come home with me. To Grace Castle."

"I can't," I could see Zeph begin to massage his temples from the corner of my eye.

Melchior was not a man that people said no to.

"Why not? What will you do instead? Stay here, saving one coin a month, waiting until you're forty before you set off on your grand adventure?"

Zeph spoke. "Melchior wants you–"

"Do I have any say in the matter," I interrupted, "or am I simply to cater to his whims?"

Melchior cleared his throat.

"It would be an honor to serve Atropos. Most people in your position would be thrilled," Zeph said smoothly.

"I am not most people." I shook my head. "I don't want to do this. I want to be *free.* I want to travel south and make a real life."

Melchior snapped. "What if your destiny is to accompany me?"

"Someone else can have that destiny," I said stubbornly. "I don't want it."

"What is it that you want?" Zeph asked, looking at me as if he'd never seen me before.

"Money. Freedom."

"Ten thousand gold pieces," he said abruptly. "That's how much I'm willing to pay."

Holy Gods. It'd taken five years to save the amount I had, and almost all of it came from him. And he was offering... My mouth was dry.

Ten thousand.

I licked my lips.

It was more than someone like me would earn in a lifetime.

Ten thousand gold pieces.

Danger had a high price. I glanced at Zeph; instead of looking elated, it was as if he were standing beside my grave.

"What do you need stolen?" My palms itched, and instead of scratching them, I clenched my fists.

"Does it matter?"

I didn't know. Maybe it did. But for ten thousand gold coins, I was willing to steal almost anything. Yet a keen sense of foreboding filled me. Call it intuition, or the witch charm under my pillow, but something in me knew that if I left with him, I would never see Zeph or the Nightingale again.

"I'm not the right person for the job," I told him. "Find yourself someone else."

Zeph looked disappointed.

Melchior pursed his lips. "If you would just..."

"Good evening." Kirin strolled into the room with a coy smile as if she hadn't been listening outside the doorway. "And you are?"

"This is Melchior, Prince of Kinver'i and son of Death. Your Highness, this is Kirin." She gave a little bow, flourishing her hands. I caught the quick look in her eye - speculation, then recognition, as she scrutinized the stranger whose presence cast shadows that danced across the floor.

If Melchior was surprised, he didn't show it. Instead, he accepted her bow graciously, and his gaze skimmed over my roommate. She was dressed in an elaborate golden gown with a black corset, and her dark hair was down, tumbling in loose waves.

"Charming," he replied, his voice a melody of midnight, unnervingly serene.

"Why would someone like yourself come calling here at the Nightingale?" she settled onto the velvet couch, fluffing her gown so it fanned around her and emphasized her small waist.

"I require a thief for a rather delicate matter."

"Well then, you're in luck. Delicate matters are my specialty."

The silence that followed her claim was thick, layered with expectation. Zeph cleared his throat, his annoyance like the strike of a match in the dimly lit room.

"Kirin," he said, his voice low but echoing with authority, "the Prince of Darkness has come with a proposition for *Malinda*."

She tossed me a dismissive look. "Why her? She's not even the best thief we have."

I couldn't argue– I wasn't. Mavros was still better than me, although I knew Mavros would die before leaving Zeph, or the Nightingale. As long as I'd been alive, he'd never spent even one night away from his bed.

"I'm only interested in Malinda." Melchior's expression was unreadable, a mask of calm indifference.

"But she's not interested." Kirin twirled a strand of her hair around one finger.

She probably meant to look sultry. But her smile was all wrong, twisted in strange ways, that made her look manipulative and evil, instead of enticing.

Averting my gaze, I stared at the shadows pooling at his feet and recalled how they'd gripped my neck.

Zeph glared at her. "Leave us. This was a private audience."

I waited until the door closed behind Kirin before speaking again, even though I knew her ear was already pressed against the wood to hear every word.

"What about the other Fates, Lachesis and Clotho? Or your brother, The Prince of Blades? Couldn't they help you?"

"Who says they aren't?" Melchior took a sip of wine. "I need a thief, Malinda. Come with me, and I'll make you richer than you've ever dreamed."

Ten thousand pieces of goblin gold was an unimaginable sum. Despite my misgivings, I found myself considering his offer more seriously.

"Who would I be stealing from?"

"My mother."

Aghast, I stared at him for full ten seconds. Zeph began to laugh.

His mother was one of the Three Fates. Death. Atropos the Unyielding. She could kill me with a simple thought from the other side of the kingdom. If she ever found out it was me, I'd live the rest of my days with a target on my back. Melchior planned to steal from Death herself. I decided that he was clearly insane.

"I'll show you out," I muttered.

"Will you at least consider–"

"No." I interrupted him. "But thank you for the kind offer."

As we walked to the front door Melchior addressed me. "I'm staying at the rectory. If you change your mind, come see me."

"I'm not going to change my mind."

"Yes you are."

He was infuriatingly confident. But he didn't seem arrogant; he did not gloat. He simply seemed sure, as if he knew my mind better than I did.

When I returned to the drawing room, Zeph was still there.

"What?" I huffed as I plopped down onto the couch next to him.

"Never thought I raised you to be a fool, Malinda."

I bristled. "You raised me to know when something is too good to be true. His little project would be a painful way to die, and I'd rather keep my head."

Zeph blew smoke toward the ceiling.

"You taught me to fear The Fates. You taught me history. You made me learn words like *machinations,* for Gods' sake."

"Aye, I did everything I could to prepare you."

"Prepare me for what? Him?"

Zeph's brown eyes leveled with me. "You're really going to refuse him?"

"His mother is Death!"

"So? How many times have I defied Death?" He rubbed his knuckles across the scars of his face. "I've been burned, stabbed, shot, trampled, hung, drowned... yet here I sit."

"Maybe Death was busy doing other things." I picked up his goblet of wine, sniffed it, and went to take a sip.

Zeph plucked it from my fingers and sat it down on the table, out of my reach. He didn't like me drinking. He said it dulled the senses, that it made good thieves sloppy and stupid.

"Perhaps Atropos is losing her touch. You help Melchior, and the House of Atropos owes you a favor. It's not just about money–"

"It's about reciprocity," I finished. "I know, I know."

Reciprocity was a core value of the Jackdaws, of Zeph. It was the only honor thieves had, the idea that you repaid every kindness, favor for favor, a life for a life.

Melchior had saved my life; I now owed him.

"I don't want you to be like me. I don't want you to stay here, stealing and pilfering until you are too old and ill to manage it. Yes, you must repay your debt to him... but has it occurred to you that this might be the last thing you ever steal?" Zeph leaned forward, putting his elbows on his knees, his gaze intent.

"If Atropos kills me, then yes, it would be the last thing," I told him.

"It's an opportunity. You play this game right; he'll make you his queen. You play it decent; he'll make you rich."

"You want me to go with him. And steal for him... be his cutpurse." Incredulous, I studied his scarred face. "You want me to seduce him."

"If you don't like him, leave." Zeph puffed his pipe again. "Or take his money and kill him, keep whatever he wants stolen for yourself."

"Ah. there's the man I know and love," I quipped.

Love. I'd said the word; I couldn't take it back.

Zeph swallowed. Cleared his throat. His eyes watered. He looked away, past my shoulder, toward the door.

I couldn't look at him either. It felt as if I'd eaten something spicy, and my mouth puckered.

"He saved your life, Malinda. You owe him. There's no question what you should do."

Slowly, I nodded. I could steal anything. I would have the ten thousand gold coins. Zeph would be proud. I would have escaped my circumstances - I'd be a rich woman, in control of my own destiny. If Melchior became a problem, or attempted to imprison me, I could kill him.

"Fine. I'll do it," I said at last.

"Then go on. The Prince of Darkness is expecting you." Zeph shooed me from the room, still unable to meet my gaze.

6

She was insane. Her problems were not my fault. I had been struggling in the same house, under the same rules for even longer than she had.

I scrambled to my feet before she lunged at me again. I grabbed the knife, tried to pry it from her hand. Then Kirin stepped backward and her heel caught on the longer part of her dress. She tripped, falling backwards, me falling with her.

I screamed as I felt the knife plunge into me and my nails slid across the stone wall of the bridge. I caught myself before going completely over the ledge, but Kirin's body kept falling to the water below.

The last thing I saw was her tumbling down, down, down, her eyes still open, trying to determine if she'd succeeded in killing me.

I slid down against the side of the bridge, warmth spreading across my abdomen.

"Oh," I muttered, feeling light-headed.

I just needed one second to get my bearings. Just a moment to close my eyes and grit my teeth through the pain. Just one.

When I regained consciousness, I was lying on the bridge, alone. With a groan, I rolled over onto my side. Dimly, I heard the river beneath the bridge. For long minutes I just sat and breathed, feeling my way through the aching pain in my abdomen.

She stabbed me. I pressed my hand to my stomach.

With a grunt of pain, I forced myself into a sitting position. The wound on my stomach felt like a hole had been punched in me – I'd bled through my gown. I didn't know how I would manage to walk home to the Nightingale, but I would live.

"What was she thinking?" I muttered. "Trying to kill me like that."

Whimpering from the pain, I forced myself to stand. There was blood all over my gown, my waist, the ground beneath me– and the knife glinted from the stones where it lay.

The pain was blinding at first, but eased fairly quickly.

She'd merely grazed me. Nothing life threatening.

I glanced down, into the water, over the edge of the stone bridge. "Wake up, you selfish bitch," I called down to her. "I'm not carrying you home."

She didn't reply. Her head and chest rested on a rock while the rest of her body bobbed in the water against a collection of boulders, her gown fanned out around her.

"Kirin?"

A cloud parted overhead, and the moonlight shone down on the bridge. I could see Kirin's blue eyes were open. Up and up, she gazed into the heart of the moon. Unseeing. Dead.

"This is *not* my fault," I muttered. "You tried to kill me. You started it. You tripped over your own stupid dress and fell off the bridge." It was true she'd often made my life hell, but many happy memories had Kirin in them. We shared a room for years. I would have felt sorry for her death, and nearly did, except...

I'd never expected her to raise a weapon against me.

I took a deep breath. I had never been one to panic, especially not in the midst of committing a crime.

"You'll disappear. I'll say it might have been the Fae. The ones you're always pining after. Maybe they took you, you had no choice but to go."

I stared down at her body. No.

There was a better plan. With the water, and the river, I didn't need to make up a lie. I needn't say anything, because no one would ever find her. She'd be carried to the sea, away from the village.

When I was younger I hiked along its banks for a long distance, at least a day. There was nothing but forest. No people, no one to see what might lurk in its depths. If Kirin drifted downstream, it was likely she would simply disappear.

I shivered again convulsively. Not from cold, but from adrenaline.

Liar. Thief. Murderer.

But not impatient. Not irrational. Calmly and quickly, I considered the alternatives.

I couldn't bury her, because someone might see me dragging her from the river. Then there'd be no hope of explaining it as an accident.

If I retrieved her body, there would be too many questions. And it was possible, indeed likely, that I'd be given a rough time... maybe even sent to the mines. Thieving was one thing, murder was quite another. Even Zeph could not protect me, if I were accused of murder.

I peered over the side of the bridge. Kirin's body still stubbornly floated on the surface.

Sons of Zeus. There's no way someone won't see her.

I tried to compose myself. I needed to think and act logically. Most likely, I would have to go down to the bank, wade into the murky waters, and find something heavy to weigh her down. But as I scanned the river's edge, all the boulders were too big to move and the rest was mud and debris.

My throat felt as if there were a hand around it, strangling all hope.

Closing my eyes briefly, I tried to think of a better solution. If Kirin wouldn't float along out of sight, nor sink, I'd have to pull her out and do something else. Hide her somewhere.

When I opened them, however, I noticed Kirin had continued to drift away. It was a fast-moving current, so if I was going to retrieve her, I had little time... but she was quickly heading downstream. I eyed the body and considered it.

Later, this river widened, forming rapids and waterfalls. If her dress snagged on a tree limb in the next five minutes, or if she drifted toward the bank instead of staying in the center...

Don't think like that, I admonished myself. *If all goes well, she'll be far from Fidelisgrove by daybreak.* It would take weeks to find her, if anyone ever did. By then, her body would be unrecognizable.

I knew. I'd seen the bloated bodies of drowned people before.

Now she couldn't tell Zeph about my skimming, and she couldn't go with the prince.

It was a miracle that no one had come upon us, that no one had come to investigate our argument, that the river was swollen from recent rains. *No. Not a miracle. An opportunity.*

Wincing, I pressed my palm to the wound in my side. The pressure lessened the pain.

Behind me, someone spoke.

"Well, well. This is an unexpected twist. The little thief is also a murderer."

The last person I was expecting was Melchior, yet it was he who stepped out of the shadows of the trees. He must have watched the entire thing.

" ."

"The first ones always are." He smirked.

Irritated, I turned away from him to watch Kirin's slow progress downstream.

Beside me, Melchior stood silent as the church bell chimed in the distance. Six hours until sunrise. I'd been unconscious much longer than I realized.

"This feels like a dream," I admitted. "Or a nightmare."

The prince glanced at me, a flicker of curiosity in his eyes. Then he leaned back against the railing of the bridge.

"What are you doing out here?"

"I don't know," I admitted. And I truly didn't.

"Were you coming to accept my offer?"

Checking the water surreptitiously, I was relieved to find that her body had continued to drift away. "Do we have to talk about this now?"

Melchior pursed his lips. "Why delay? Were you coming to see me or not?"

Still I hedged.

"I have to go back to the Nightingale," I announced. "To tell Zeph."

"And then what?" he said.

I turned toward him. I'd been running to try and reach him. To say yes to him. There was no real point in denying it.

"I found you on the bridge because I was coming to see Zeph," Melchior said. "To tell him again how important this is. Because I've chosen you, yet you've refused me. I hoped he would force you."

I pulled my eyes from the river, irritation biting at me.

"Force me?"

"To say yes, that is."

I knew a desperate man when I saw one, and whatever it was he wanted, Melchior wanted it badly enough to leave his kingdom, seek out the seedy underbelly of a wasted city, and he'd found me. He would likely be willing to pay *more* than ten thousand coins, as Zeph said.

What are you waiting for? a voice hissed inside my head. *Don't waste the opportunity.*

Perhaps the task would be easy. Quick and simple. Even if it wasn't, when I succeeded, I'd have more gold than almost everyone in Moirai. Enough to buy myself my own ship, my own castle, my own land.

"What is it that you want?" I asked. "What jewel am I supposed to be retrieving?"

Melchior hesitated.

"You might as well tell me now, while we're alone."

"The Eternal Slumber. Have you heard of it?"

My mouth fell open. "The mask? Death's mask? You want me to steal her mask?"

"I do."

I was so shocked I almost couldn't process it. "That's crazy," I finally said.

The Eternal Slumber was Fae-forged, its magic keyed to the owner. Atropos, his mother, already had considerable power as the Controller of Death, but with the mask she was able to walk among the living without being seen, control the shadows, travel great distances... Rumor said that it was made of obsidian and the fingerbones of Ares, the God of War.

"No one can steal the Eternal Slumber from Death."

"Except you."

Momentarily speechless, I just stared at him. He was insane. Or delusional. Both.

Melchior seemed suddenly angry; he clenched his jaw as he looked out over the river. "Unless you don't think you're good enough?"

It didn't make sense. I was nothing, no one, a petty thief in a grim town. Still, I needed the money.

"Atropos wants to rule it all - to kill the other Fates, to get revenge against the gods, to rain destruction upon Moirai until we beg for Death."

I was skeptical. "How do I know you aren't lying? And that this isn't a clever bid to steal your mother's power? So you can be king?"

Melchior shrugged. "What do you care? Isn't one Death the same as another?"

Good point. Dead was dead, and it didn't much matter which ruthless villain delivered the final blow.

"I need an answer. Do we have a deal?"

Steal a valuable, rare object from one of the Fates. Join the Prince of Darkness. "And if Atropos kills me first? What then?"

Melchior smirked. "I'm not going to let that happen."

No one could defy Death once her mind was made up. No matter what Zeph said, I'd always believed that the only reason he was still alive was because his entire attic was full of magical objects, random bits of luck. He carried a piece of mirror that was said to deflect Death, rendering its owner invisible.

He didn't believe it, of course, but that hadn't stopped him from buying it. Or carrying it wherever he went.

"I'll go," I said at last. "And for ten thousand gold coins, I'll steal whatever you want."

"And do you have any other conditions?" Melchior's dark eyes gobbled me up. He was eager, far too eager, for me to say yes.

"Actually, I do," I muttered, and then winced as I moved my hand away from my waist. "I'll need you to heal this."

His lips twisted in a sneer. "Blood on your hands and injured again, Malinda. This seems like a recurring theme."

I hoped it wasn't. In the last week I'd already been injured more times than I had in the last two years, and in the Nightingale it was often said that misfortune comes in threes.

Below us, Kirin's dark hair spread in a black halo around her delicate features and her skin glowed in the starlight, an ethereal demon struck down by the Gods. Melchior and I watched, alone in our thoughts, as she drifted into the night.

7

I'd never seen snow before.

At first, it was exciting. Novel. I grabbed handfuls and tossed them in the air; I tasted it; I laid down and let it drift on top of me. But after traveling for a week, I would have been happy to never see the icy mess again.

Serrated peaks surrounded us like jagged teeth, their white crests glinting beneath a brilliant blue sky. A shiver coursed through me, though not from the cold—I had grown numb to the freezing wind at that point—but from the sheer drop that teased my peripheral vision.

"You're missing the view," Melchior said as his horse, Caerwyn, picked her way along the narrow mountain ledge.

My eyes were tightly shut as I gripped his waist, not daring to look. "You can tell me about it if you care that much."

He sneered. "You can face a demon but you're afraid of heights?"

"I'm afraid of *falling,* and from here, we'd most certainly die."

"A strange statement for someone heading on horseback toward Death herself... Come on. Open your eyes. You'll likely only see this once."

No – if I was lucky, I'd see it twice - coming and leaving. But I didn't bother pointing that out. Not really trusting him or Caerwyn's footing, I squinted through my lashes at the landscape around us.

With utmost caution, I allowed myself a quick glance, and oh—the world unfurled before me. A tapestry woven with sapphire and pearl, diamond and stone. I caught my breath, then peered around at the dazzling landscape.

Pristine. Vast.

Snow-capped mountains reached toward heaven like great fingers, and clouds rolled by almost close enough to touch. Not a village, not a single puff of smoke or scent carried on the wind. It was as if the world consisted of just us two, and the incredible blue of the sky.

"Where are we?" I fought to keep my eyes up, instead of looking down– just a little sliver past the narrow path Caerwyn plodded along was nothing but air.

"Kinver'i." His tone was snappish, as he'd been ever since we left.

His kingdom. The land of snow and ice. Huddling down into my cloak, I buried my face against his broad back again, my teeth chattering.

Anytime I asked a question, he either dismissed it or answered in one-word replies. At first, I'd barely noticed–my thoughts were occupied with leaving Zeph and images of Kirin's body drifting down river. But once I put my feelings aside, his clipped responses and silent treatment seemed strange. We slept side by side each night and yet he couldn't manage a civil conversation with me.

My grip was like iron as we gained elevation, terrified that I would simply slide from the back of the horse and roll down the mountain.

I really hated the cold... but I hated heights even more. My back ached from tension and the awkward position of holding him tightly, trying to stay on the horse.

To distract myself, I made conversation. "Tell me more about the Three Fates. My education wasn't exactly thorough when it came to the, uh, more *refined* subjects."

Or, more accurately, anything that Zeph deemed to be a waste of time.

"The infamous sisters of Time, Death, and Life definitely weren't included."

"They aren't sisters. They were made by Nyx. As far as I can tell, they've always hated each other."

"In all the stories, it sounds like they were best friends."

Melchior gave a short laugh. "If they were together for more than an hour, they would have killed each other."

"How long has your mother been Death?" I found myself asking.

"Always. Thousands of years. Since the dawn of man. Longer, even."

"When did it fall apart? And why did she leave the three-seated throne?"

"So many questions."

"I've never met a Fate before."

His black eyes flicked over the landscape, as if he were checking to see if we'd be overheard. "I suppose you'll find out eventually... so I might as well tell you now."

"The story goes something like this: the Three Fates were not friends, but not yet enemies, when Atropos met a man in a wood named Tassos. She was supposed to take his life; his time was up. And for some reason, I no longer remember why, she decided not to kill him."

His lips twisted in a wry smile. "Of course, the man did not take the additional time he was given and become a saint. Instead, he murdered a man, changing his destiny and putting various other threads off course. Lachesis, the Controller of Time, was furious – she'd have to reset time backwards, and at that point she was much more interested in sharing her evenings with Bacchus and Apollo."

I didn't know what he meant by *threads*, but I didn't want to interrupt.

"Lachesis said she'd cut his time short, that Atropos should go and take his soul. Do it right this time. But he'd already evaded her once, and this time when she went to claim him, she found that Clotho had been lured to him.

Lured.

"My mother says Clotho was always the curious one, poking her nose where it didn't belong."

"Zeus and Nyx were angry. Atropos failed to fulfill her duty, not once but twice. So they struck the man dead, wrenched the flesh from his bones and burned him alive."

It seemed typical of the gods to punish man for the failings of their creations.

"Did Atropos love him? Is that why she spared his life?"

"I doubt she's capable of love." Melchior looked out, toward the snowy landscape of Kinver'i. "So, I don't know why."

"Regardless... he tricked them. He'd evaded Death twice, tricked Time, and married the source of all Life. *The Fates can be tricked.* It was an astounding discovery, especially for them."

"Why were they so surprised? Gods are manipulated by humans all the time."

"I suppose they thought Fates were infallible. Immune." Melchior seemed reluctant to continue and lapsed back into silence.

"Why did you say yes to my offer?"

Ignoring the height once more, my eyes scanned the horizon. I couldn't tell if he actually cared about the answer or if he was just trying to distract me.

"I don't suppose you'd believe me if I said adventure and novelty."

Melchior gave a dismissive, half-hearted laugh. "Not really."

"Thrills, thievery, and goblin's gold?"

"Ah. So it was only the money you wanted." Melchior flicked the reins, urging his horse onward.

"What else could it have been?"

I sensed his distaste, and for some reason, this goaded me into revealing more than I otherwise would. "I've been saving for a while. Hoping to leave Fidelisgrove and make my way south."

"Why?"

"I don't know. To have a normal life? To set up a shop of some kind or work in a tavern. Anything, really."

Except being a thief.

"And your family? How do they feel about your plans?"

I frowned, looking out into the blinding landscape where the sun refracted off every white surface. "They didn't care if I lived or died, so they surely won't care about any *plans.*"

"Is that how you ended up at the Nightingale?"

I gave a brief nod. "My family turned on me for no reason at all."

He should know the type. In fact, he was exactly the sort of family I'd had. Planning to steal from his own mother in order to make himself a king. Disloyal. Selfish. So much for *family.*

When he broke the silence, it was as if he could read my thoughts. "You think I'm like them."

I made a half-hearted shrug. "I don't know your motives. Or your intentions."

It wasn't a real answer. It was a true but irrelevant fact. Zeph had trained me well, in the art of conversation with liars, thieves, and murderers.

Melchior didn't press further. Instead, he let the horse have free rein and she carried us forward, through the jagged mountains, toward the forests beyond.

We didn't arrive at the camp until well after dark, and at that point I was crusted with frost and frozen down to the marrow of my bones. A fierce gale whipped through the mountain trees and I huddled against Melchior, trying my best to cover every inch of my face with my cloak. When I glimpsed light ahead, the feeling of relief was palpable. I couldn't wait to be warm and off the horse.

Since he was a prince, I'd first expected a bed. Good food and drink. Perhaps even servants to welcome us. But with Melchior, I was sadly disappointed. The prince preferred to travel in secret, to sleep in the woods, and he didn't seem to eat or drink very often.

He didn't concern himself with my comfort, nor even inquire how I was doing. Within just two days, my expectations were drastically lowered.

After sleeping out in the open with only his shadows to protect us, I was thrilled to see a small camp, with one dilapidated tent huddled next to a sputtering fire. There was a smell of food on the wind, with a burnt, smoky odor.

I was ecstatic.

As my eyes scanned the clearing, I noted a single traveler seated there- a man, tall, with hair so brightly orange it might have been a piece of the sunset. He looked up as we entered the clearing, tensing as if he expected trouble, then relaxed as he recognized Caerwyn and Melchior.

"It took you long enough," he groused, not rising to come greet us. "Did you crawl through Moirai?"

Melchior dismounted gracefully, then raised his hand to help me down. "This one took some convincing."

I ignored his offered hand and hopped off the back of the horse.

"A girl? I thought you were looking for the best thief in Kinver'i."

Melchior frowned. "And this is she. Malinda, this is Fenix. He's a forger."

Fenix. The name suited him. Tall, thin as a wraith, with that uncombed mop of unruly tangerine hair and golden eyes, the Fae male very much resembled the birds I'd seen depicted in history books. He shifted so quickly that his movements were a blur. In his palms he rolled about two golden orbs, like small balls of lightning that could not burn. He handed one to me skeptically, careful not to touch my skin. As soon as it landed in my hand it sunk into my palm and a glow faded up my arm. Immediately, a burst of warmth flowed through me, thawing my body from fingertips to toes, which were likely frostbitten. I let out a sigh of relief and awe, and watched Melchior do the same beside me.

"Thank you for that," I said.

Fenix stared at me as if I were covered in spiders. "Sit and eat."

I was ravenous, and even if the food didn't smell great, it would be hot. Soon I was perched by the fire, wrapped in a large fur provided by Melchior, clutching a wooden bowl and spoon and eating a bitter brown soup that tasted almost as bad as it smelled, but filled me just the same.

Fenix spoke first, his golden eyes fixed on the two of us. "Before we walk into the lion's den, perhaps you could explain your latest thinking on the plan."

I nodded emphatically. Certainly it would help if each of us knew exactly what was expected, and what we'd be facing when we arrived in the House of Atropos.

Melchior set down his bowl.

"Tomorrow, we will complete our journey. We'll travel separately, of course. Malinda and I will arrive before noon, Fenix just before sunset. Once inside," Melchior continued, "I will announce us, and inform my mother that I've finally found my bride."

In theory, it was straightforward. Everyone would think we were betrothed, I would steal the mask, then vanish. Simple, clean. The only wrinkle in this plan was that I would have to play the part of the Prince of Darkness's betrothed *convincingly* until we found the mask. I would have to meet and interact with his mother as if I wanted to be the next Queen of Moirai and rule next to Melchior, without arousing her suspicion or wrath.

"And what's your cover story?" I asked the red-haired Fae.

"I'm a migrant, traveling for better work so I can send money back home for my wife and son." Fenix scowled in my direction, baring his teeth. "Staying in much poorer accommodations than you will be."

Hopefully not the kitchens. I grimaced. His cooking left much to be desired, and I didn't want to face Death and dysentery.

"Fenix will be making a forgery of the mask, so that Atropos won't notice hers is missing." Melchior set his bowl aside.

"And the plan?" I asked.

"Has several problems." Fenix scowled at me. "Atropos uses the mask of Eternal Slumber often. So the timing is an issue. She hides the mask, and Melchior doesn't know where it is."

"You don't know where it's kept?" I swung toward Melchior. "Then how..."

"Once you know where the mask is," Fenix said, "we'll have to make it past her guards, which I assume there are several. Then we'll need to replace the mask with the fake. A very convincing fake, which I'll create after we arrive."

The blood drained from my face.

"At least tell me you've seen the original," I said.

"I have," Fenix answered. "It is not terribly complex."

I cleared my throat. "So... we don't know where the mask is, we don't know how we're going to get it, and we don't know if our forgery will pass visual inspection." Blowing out a long breath, I cursed internally and wondered if it was too late to back out.

Fenix looked offended. "It will be a perfect copy."

I raised an eyebrow. "How do you know? How can you be sure?"

Fenix bared his teeth in a grimace that passed for a smile. "Because I helped to make the original. And I'm here because I regret that my father gave it to Atropos."

So that's his motive, I thought. I couldn't help but glance at Melchior– I still didn't know his.

"What about after we've stolen it and she has the forgery in hand? Then what?"

"We'll be gone. We can't hang around waiting for her to kill us."

"And what will you be doing?" I asked Melchior.

"I will remain at Grace Castle. With the mask." He avoided my gaze, as if some part of his answer was a lie. "Once I have the mask in hand, you are free to go. What happens to me afterward is none of your concern."

As long as I had the money he promised, I didn't much care what the Prince of Darkness chose to do.

"And you have no idea what could be guarding it?" I drew the fur closer around my shoulders, trying not to let the alpine chill touch my skin.

"None." Melchior's voice was low, almost flat.

"We should assume its location is warded with dark magic." Fenix added a branch to the fire, and it crackled. "And guarded by bloodthirsty creatures."

Long ago, I'd come across a bear that had been attacked by a troll. It lay in ribbons, shredded. Not for food, but for fun.

I stirred the cold soup with a frown.

"How do we avoid being caught?" I asked. "Or, rather, when we are inevitably caught, what should we do?"

"If you are caught by Atropos, you will die. So I recommend not letting that happen." Melchior's face was near unreadable in the darkness.

"But what if we do?"

"*You won't.*"

Any plan – even a good one– could still go wrong. Any number of things could happen, and then it would all fall apart. Fenix and Melchior exchanged looks, some silent conversation happening between them.

Fenix prodded the fire. "If that should happen, we will do our best."

Do our best?

"That's more wishful thinking than it is a plan," I began.

Melchior interrupted me. "All you need to worry about is your part. Find the mask, and when I tell you we are ready, steal the mask and give it to me. Nothing else."

I glared at him.

"So there is no real plan. In case one of us is killed by Atropos before stealing the mask." Annoyed, I crossed my arms over my chest.

Fenix eyed the two of us.

Unable to help myself, I yawned. It had been a long night, followed by a long day, and I was exhausted. Even if the tent contained nothing but a blanket, it would be enough.

"We'd better get to bed. We have an early morning." Melchior stood and started toward the tent. Stretching, I pulled the fur closer – I was more than willing to remain here, by the fire, at least until he was asleep. Then I wouldn't have to endure the awkward silence between us as we lay side by side in the dark.

"Not that it's any of my business, but if you're going to tell Atropos you're engaged, shouldn't you pretend to like each other?" Fenix broke a stick into pieces, then tossed them into the fire.

"Tell him that," I replied. "He's been about as friendly as a mountain troll."

It'd been days and Melchior hadn't opened up. He acted like I was a major inconvenience. I'd been as friendly as I could, under the circumstances. Yet I also knew that if we continued the way we had been, convincing Death that he'd *chosen* me as a bride and fallen in love with me was laughable, if not impossible.

"I'd be in a better mood if I didn't have her thrashing around, keeping me up all night." Melchior suddenly said from across the clearing, his expression sour.

Fenix shrugged. ", you don't seem like a couple in love to me." He gave me an appraising look. "If he brings home a woman without title nor wealth, without magical bloodline, and he's not in love with you – you're dead. Atropos will see through it right away."

"I'm not the problem!" I protested. "It's him. He's been awful. Barely polite."

Melchior's face might as well have been a blank page of parchment.

"Anyway, do whatever you want. I'm sleeping in the woods. The tent is for the two of you." Fenix cracked his neck and stood. "Keep your weapon close."

Without saying goodnight, the Fae male stood and strode across the clearing, his long strides and quick steps eating up the space until he'd vanished into the wood.

As he did, I noticed a small movement. An owl peered back at me from the branches of an evergreen. He blinked several times. He'd been listening the entire time, blending into the tree line. None of us had even noticed him.

"Come on then," Melchior said. "Come sleep in the tent."

With him. Sleep in the tent with him.

Confused, I stared at him for a long moment. He was noticeably tense, fists clenched, eyes narrowed.

"Why do you seem angry?" I asked. Surely he had considered the fact that we'd have to pretend to like each other at some point, yet Fenix's words put him even more on edge.

"I'm not."

"Yes you are." I shook my head, amazed at his obstinance. Did he really hate sleeping next to me that much? I'd shared a room my entire life. Until I was thirteen, I'd slept in a room with two other *male* thieves. Certainly, it was no hardship to sleep in a room with me. Time seemed to stretch as we each waited for the other to speak. When he didn't, I cursed to myself softly.

"I can try not to move around so much."

Melchior scowled. "Fine." He held up the tent flap. "Now come on."

I was hardly in the mood to argue. My back ached, my hands felt stiff.

We each slept fully clothed; it was too cold to do otherwise. I settled in next to him, several inches between us. After a beat, Melchior pulled his large, warm cloak over the two of us. Lined with fur, it was much warmer than mine.

"You know," I said, after a long silence. "Fenix has a point. I have nothing to offer the throne: no money, no land, no influence. You'll either have to pretend to love me or come up with some far-fetched reason why I would make a good match."

"I know that." His tone was clipped, cold.

"If you don't, we won't fool anyone, much less one of the Three Fates."

"I said, *I know that.*"

"Alright. Great." I chewed my lip, worrying. We would be arriving tomorrow– tomorrow– and we could barely manage a conversation. I was going to pretend to be in love with the son of Death, and try as I might, I couldn't remember a time when I'd been in a more dangerous situation.

8

"Avoid Julian, if you can," Melchior reminded me as Caerwyn plodded along, her hooves cracking through the snow. "And try not to make Atropos angry."

"You said that already." I shivered uncontrollably, vibrating from the cold. Around us was a wilderness so vast, it felt like we were the only people in Moirai.

All I wanted was for us to arrive at Grace Castle. No matter how terrible it was, even though Death herself sat on its throne, I just wanted to be out of the frigid wind. If only I had more layers, if only I'd worn a warmer cloak.

"I will pretend to be enamored with you, and you with me. Meanwhile, you'll be scouring the castle, looking for the mask. Not to steal it, but to get its location. Once the forgery is ready we will know exactly where to retrieve it from."

Melchior had been lecturing me for nearly two hours. While I was grateful for his body heat, I wished he'd stop talking. Just so I could think.

My chest was flush against his back, which radiated warmth, my face pressed between his shoulder blades. My arms were wrapped around his waist, hands exposed. We were much higher in elevation, and the mountain air was thin. Each breath was a knife slicing at my lips and nose with its sharpness.

"Don't be alone with her. Remember: she's Death. She was made to lure you, to seem like a friend. Death will whisper that she alone has the answers."

"Does she have the answers?" I asked.

"Maybe. But whatever they are, you don't want to hear them."

On and on, he continued. We were finally headed downhill. Several times, the horse stumbled, and I clutched at Melchior's cloak.

The deeper we went into his territory, the more obvious it was that this was a place that had never seen summer. Every tree bore the weight of snow, boughs snapped or sagging like weary limbs. Everything smelled of pine and frost. Here and there, I noticed deep crimson berries that had fallen to the ground. They resembled blood drops on a white veil. I shuddered.

Here, in his realm, sounds were swallowed whole.

The seconds crawled by. Desperately cold, I burrowed into Melchiors back. My hands burned.

He glanced down. "You should have brought gloves."

Obviously. I hadn't been able to find any. Even if I had, they wouldn't have been warm enough to matter. I'd never seen snow, much less been in temperatures this cold.

With a long-suffering huff, he guided my hands under his cloak, beneath his shirt, against his bare skin.

I gasped. He was so warm to touch. Like a roaring fire. He hissed as my icy hands flexed against his stomach, slid along his ribs. I didn't even apologize, didn't care if it was unseemly or inappropriate. Without gloves, my fingers were so frozen that they might snap off.

I would have given anything for hot tea, a bath, the baking sun... an oven.

Much later, he cleared his throat, rousing me from my reverie.

"We're here."

I poked my head up and peered over his shoulder.

Emerging from the snow just ahead were two stone pillars, each carved into the shape of a gargoyle. They supported a large iron gate. As tall as two men, these gates were flung open, revealing a castle in the distance. Restless, Caerwyn pawed the ground, eager to return to her warm stable and a large bucket of oats.

Sitting up a bit straighter, I gazed up at the House of Atropos. My new home, for now... though it was the sort of place where one was likely to be murdered.

Made of indigo stone that was neither blue nor gray, the rock that formed the castle was a strange blue-black. Obsidian flags flew over four formidable towers, and snow covered most of the steep slate roof. It looked ancient.

Cruelly beautiful, it was not a castle as much as it was a fortress, meant to withstand thousands of enemies at its door. A desolate gloom hung over the entire area, and the mist that wreathed its towers added an ominous, eerie feeling.

Despite it being midday, the clouds and the gray made it seem like twilight; the towering evergreens cast everything into deep shadow. Grace Castle hardly seemed like part of Moirai– instead, it was more like something out of a dark fairytale. A place built both to keep people out, and to keep them in.

It was probably haunted. All manner of ghouls and foul creatures might lurk inside, serving at the feet of Death. The hairs on my arms prickled, and I rubbed myself restlessly.

Melchior pulled the mare to a stop on a small knoll, so I could get my bearings. Off to our right, restless waves crashed against a rocky shore. Here the sand was graphite gray, and smelled strongly of metal and smoke. The waves were oily, the color of charcoal.

"What do you think?"

"It looks like there might be a family of gorgons sleeping inside."

Melchior rolled his eyes. "Does that mean you want to turn back?"

I huffed. He truly didn't know me at all. "I'm not that easily scared off."

My gaze skimmed over the stone balconies and arched windows. Though not exactly hospitable looking on the outside, surely there would be fire, warm food, hot water... and piles of blankets.

I pressed my face into his back again. I'd seen enough, and my lips burned from the wind.

He tugged at the reins, meaning to go on, but I placed my hand over his.

"Wait."

A sudden foreboding had come over me, inexplicable, but I wanted to leap from the horse and run back in the direction we'd come. As my eyes traveled over the castle once more, they spotted movement. A shadow along the balcony - tall, with platinum hair, unmistakable. Atropos was exactly like her pictures in books.

"Your mother is watching us," I said.

Melchior's head tilted to the side as he studied the castle. His eyes lingered so long that I wondered if Id been wrong.

"It's her." His voice was soft, barely a whisper in the wind. "On the left. The third-floor balcony."

"Do you think she'll be convinced?" I asked, when the tall figure disappeared back inside. "That you're in love with me?"

"No." Melchior said coldly, then spurred the horse forward. "I don't."

Melchior escorted me into a sitting room where the silence was so profound it felt like the room had never been spoken in. Everything was black - the walls covered in black silk, the settee a midnight velvet color. In the corner, a black cat lounged on a black cushion, stretching its claws. And in the midst of it all, Death waited to receive us.

As welcoming as a black widow, or a sip of poison. She lifted her eyes to us as we entered.

"You're back. And you've brought a woman with you." Her voice was velvet draped over a sword, rasping.

"Mother, may I present my future wife. Malinda Castan, of Kinkanali." His fingers were tightly entwined with mine. The three servants in the room all stared, and one of them - the one holding a kettle - was slowly pouring tea onto the table.

Atropos didn't bat an eyelash. Instead she inspected me, layer by layer, toe to head. Wrapped in a black fur coat, wearing a long dark gown encrusted with diamonds along the hem, she looked every bit like the Controller of Death I'd imagined. Her hair, long and flowing, was white-blonde. Like a shaft of moonlight. Easily a head taller than me, she was a lush figure crafted by the Gods with the sole purpose of enticing men to their doom.

"What a pleasant surprise," she murmured. Her lips were dark red, thin and unsmiling.

"A pleasure to meet you," I said as I stepped forward, then bowed deeply.

Don't let her intimidate you, Zeph had said. As if it were possible that one wouldn't be intimidated being in her presence. One of the Three Fates stood before me, a creation of the Gods.

Atropos scrutinized my face, my gown, my figure. She eyed my cheap, muddied boots. I had no illusions - I was a young girl with windblown blond hair and red cheeks, and little else to recommend me. She circled around me, examining me from all angles.

"You are not dressed appropriately."

"I apologize. It was a long journey, and I could not bring much." I fought to keep my voice steady.

"There is more dirt under her nails than elegance in her bearing." Atropos turned to Melchior. "Wherever did you find her?"

I flinched, but his face was marble as he replied. "West. A village called Fidelisgrove."

I tried to draw strength from his resolve, my stubborn chin leading the way.

Atropos raised a perfectly sculpted brow. "And you chose *this one?*"

Melchior gave a curt nod.

"Well, this is inconvenient. Since you've had many fruitless bride searches before, and I wasn't sure if you'd return with one, I took the liberty of sourcing a potential."

Melchior, to his credit, did not seem surprised. "And where is she?"

"Downstairs. Of course."

Melchior's eyes flickered with some emotion I couldn't place. "I'm sure you've made her accommodations pleasant."

Atropos smirked. "I always aim to make guests feel wanted."

As a chronic liar myself, I was easily able to identify when others lied. This statement was most certainly not true. Whoever she was, undoubtedly she'd be beautiful. Though likely, far less adept at thievery.

"I look forward to meeting her," he said after a beat. "With your permission, I will show Malinda the castle, and then bathe. It's been a long few weeks."

Atropos stared at me, her speculative gaze as heavy as a chain around my neck. "Of course. I hope I'll see the two of you at dinner."

I spoke up. "We would love to-"

At the same time, Melchior declined. "We're quite tired. I believe we'll dine alone tonight."

I shot him an annoyed look. I wanted to begin acquainting myself with the castle immediately, not dine alone with him.

Atropos' eyes narrowed. "I'll amuse myself in other ways, then."

Melchior all but dragged me from the room. We strode through dark corridors, his fingers painfully gripping my arm. With interest, I glanced into cavernous, empty spaces, one after another -

A library with hundreds of books lining its shelves, warmed by a cheery fire crackling in the grate;

A room with silver flooring polished to a mirror-like finish;

Halls with large stained-glass windows depicting scenes of war and death. Flickering candles provided dim light in the darkest corners, but did nothing against the bitter cold that permeated his home.

"What now–"

He whirled to me and held up a hand to still my tongue, and gave a faint shake of his head. *Not here.*

While he unlocked one of the doors, I watched an enchanted tapestry bolted to the wall. Its characters moved, the figures in it lurching drunkenly as they ran from a shadowy blur. My fascination turned to vague dread as I watched the tiny threads re-enact their own gruesome deaths.

Melchior held open his bedroom door and gestured for me to enter. As I did, a wave of warmth hit me - a fire already burned, and likely had for some time. A white fur rug, laid in front of it, beckoned. With simple furnishings of dark walnut and blue, golden lamps cast a warm glow on both sides of the bed. Despite its large size, the room felt cozy, inviting, even. Beyond the bed and fireplace I could see a long balcony through arched double doors overlooking a field of snow. It was a welcome refuge.

Sighing with relief, I went immediately to the fireplace, then stood as close as I dared, letting the blaze warm my frozen bones.

Coldly furious, Melchior pulled off his gloves and set them on a long dresser, then tossed his cloak over the back of the chair.

"I can't believe she brought a woman here for me to marry," he muttered. "As if I would ever accept her choosing on my behalf."

Melchior pulled the stopper from a heavy silver decanter, then poured himself a goblet of clear liquid. "Drink?"

I shook my head no; I preferred to keep my head clear when on the job. "What do we do now?"

"For tonight? Bathe, eat a good meal, sleep. Proceed as planned."

He took a long sip of whatever was in the cup. He gestured at a heavy black door across the room, its iron handle shaped like a scythe.

"Your room is just through there."

I stared at the door. "Our rooms adjoin?"

"I thought you might feel safer that way. Just in case something tries to murder you."

It didn't exactly inspire confidence.

I eased through the open door and into a dim, empty room decorated in red. A plush red rug, and red velvet bedding dominated the center of the room, along with a wide fireplace. There was also a small desk, a pair of mostly empty bookshelves, and an ornate silver mirror. It seemed recently cleaned. I wondered if anyone else ever used this room, like one of his lovers... assuming he had some.

None of my business. I'm here to do a job: get the gold and leave.

The windows... I stepped closer, peering out into the gray day. I could see the ocean. White-capped waves pounded against stone, undulating and ceaseless. My heart stumbled - once, Kirin and I had talked of running along the sea, of swimming naked.

It was nicer than anywhere I'd ever been. Kirin would have screamed and thrown herself onto the bed, reveling in the luxury of having so much space to sprawl. Now I had it all to myself, and found the feeling... uncomfortable.

A creeping cold seeped through the stones, and it was silent as a tomb. I shivered violently a few times as Melchior entered, then lit several tall candles. He struck another match and lit the kindling in the fireplace.

"Do you want tea? I'll summon someone." He didn't wait for me to answer, but rather went to a small box inset into the stone wall. Inside, there was a simple string - he tugged it. To my quizzical look he said, "It rings a bell elsewhere in the castle. A servant will come."

Overwhelmed by it all, I sat down on the bed with a thump, then looked blindly around the room. When a servant appeared, Melchior ordered food and drink for the both of us. I tried to ignore the curious, speculative look that she shot at me.

A few minutes later, he handed me a mug of hot tea brought by a completely different person.

Gratefully, I took the steaming mug and felt its warmth all the way to my aching bones. We'd ridden through snow for so long - all I wanted was to sleep, with as many blankets as possible piled atop me.

He stood stiffly, staring down at me. "Go to bed. You have two days before I expect you to begin looking for the mask."

He left, then returned a moment later with a large fur blanket. "Here."

It was the blanket from his bed. Catoblepas hide. Plush, soft, of deepest onyx. I rubbed it against my cheek. At the Nightingale, our blanket had been simple, thin. I'd never had anything as lovely as this, nor had any need for such a heavy fur.

Seemingly not knowing what else to do with himself, Melchior left, closing the door firmly behind himself. As soon as I was alone, I slipped out of my clothes and into the bed, between its crisp cold sheets. I watched the roaring fire until my eyelids grew heavy, drawing the black fur close around myself.

Briefly, I tried to imagine what Kirin would have done. She would have slept in his bed; teased him and kissed him and had sex with him. He probably would have preferred her.

But as tired as I felt, I couldn't sleep. It was likely the sounds. The crackling of the burning wood, the dull roar of the sea against the cliffs, the howl of the wind in the halls. It was easy to imagine it as a league of demons, banshees or harpies patrolling the halls. I rose and crept to the door that separated us. After the briefest of hesitations, I put my ear to it. Nothing.

Grabbing a slip from my bag, I quickly shimmied into it. I turned the handle softly, then eased the door open. Peering into his room, I was surprised to see Melchior asleep. He'd been reading in bed. I tiptoed forward, studying him, primed to bolt if he stirred.

He was on top of the covers.

I stood there, torn, knowing I should go back to my room, but not being able to... as if some unknown force pulled me to him. I stepped closer, closer.

The Prince of Darkness was beautiful. Like a god. Or, more accurately, the descendant of one. I watched him for a long time, studying his features in a way I would never do if he were awake. He'd been exhausted, and was deeply asleep, with his head tilted back. The long pale column of his throat was completely exposed. Vulnerable. His dark lashes fanned against his skin, his sensual lips slightly parted. The golden light of his lamp shone onto his chest as he slept against the headboard, shirtless. My eyes trailed down, lingering. He had a faint white scar shaped like a crescent moon on his collarbone, and the faintest dusting of dark hair that began at his navel, and went down, toward the band of his pants.

I'd seen enough. Slowly, I crept back to the door and then shut it quietly behind me.

9

"Your bath is ready, milady," murmured the maid, giving me a low curtsy before she left.

Milady.

I wandered into the bathroom barefoot.

"Wow," I gaped, staring at the counter.

Laid out in the morning sun was a series of small silver bowls, each one full of a different scented oil.

I sniffed each one. Lavender and rose petals, sea salt and cinnamon, orange peel and sage, myrrh.

The heavy bowls were decorated in pastoral scenes, and perfectly matched a clawfoot tub that took up a corner of the room. Full of steaming water, it was big enough for three.

Outside of the tall arched window, the waves broke on large boulders, foaming and sparkling.

Certainly it did not seem like staying here would be any great hardship, taking scented baths and being waited on.

Liberally, I dosed the bathwater with cinnamon and rose. Then I sank into it gratefully. At the Nightingale, I'd taken baths only once per week, and never with hot water.

Sighing with pleasure, I submerged myself to my chin and hummed a little tune. I washed my hair with a thick bar of rose-scented soap, and sat until the water was tepid—letting the water warm my weary bones. In my bedroom, on the mantel, the clock ticked.

A third woman, this one garbed in a deep blue, entered the bathing room without knocking. Shocked, I covered my breasts with my hands. "Do you mind?" I demanded.

"I'm here to take your measurements." She eyed me speculatively. "We'll need to have your dress ready for the ball tonight."

Ball?

Intrigued, I exited the bath and stood wordlessly in front of the mirror in nothing but a pair of underwear.

The seamstress put a tape around my waist, my arms, then counted out my height.

"You're quite muscular, for a woman," she muttered. "And your hands are calloused."

Her eyes were sky blue, with flecks of silver, and her skin was unblemished porcelain. She couldn't have been more than twenty, which meant we were roughly the same age.

"What's your name?" I asked.

She hesitated. Most likely, it wasn't proper for her to converse with me at all. "Ilya."

"I'm Malinda."

"I know who you are." She stared at me speculatively, then went to the wardrobe. "Let's see if this one fits."

I stood, silent and awkward, as she helped me into a severe black dress and then did up the long row of buttons on the back.

I felt her gaze on the scars left by the Keres.

"So he did rescue you? And cleaned your wounds?"

She seemed awed. Probably, like most women, she thought he was the most handsome man she'd ever seen and was dying to bed him.

"He did," I said curtly.

Something about her reminded me of Kirin. Not her appearance, but her way of being - how she carried herself as if she were assured that the world owed her more than what she had been given, and that she was going to seize it at every opportunity.

I flexed my shoulders in the gown. It was too small, wrapped across my chest like a second skin. It also itched terribly, and I tugged at the hips.

Checking my reflection in the silver mirror, I frowned. "It's hideous."

"Even though black is the house color, he prefers women in red."

"Who?"

"Melchior."

"So?" I replied, not caring what he preferred. Then, seeing the surprised look on her face, I quickly realized that I'd better be a lot better at pretending to be in love with him. "I mean to say, he says he likes me in every color."

A myriad of emotions flickered in her eyes; she opened her mouth, then shut it firmly.

Resigning myself to the dour black gown, I selected a simple silver ring from the drawer stuffed with jewelry. "What time is the ball?"

"Seven."

"Wonderful." I couldn't wait. I'd be surrounded by gold and jewels, and purses full of coin.

Quickly, Ilya neatly braided my golden hair, coiling it around my head like a crown.

I caught her gaze in the mirror. "Thank you for helping me."

"You're welcome," she murmured.

When she was gone, I admitted to myself that I could have been nicer. As a woman my age, she was my best opportunity to make a friend inside the castle, and she might have ideas on where the mask might be hidden.

Next time, I promised. Next time, I will be more social.

I knocked on the door between our rooms - but Melchior wasn't there. Therefore I took the liberty of thoroughly going through his belongings, carefully checking for loose stones, hidden passages, secret compartments, peepholes... anything he might surprise me with.

He was my employer, we were in a fake relationship, and I needed to know as much as I could about him.

Very quickly, I discovered the chair by his fireplace had a false seat, and hidden within it I found a grimoire, an ancient book of spells. The cover was clad in red dragon scales, the pages gilded.

"Strange," I muttered, turning it over in my hands. The pages were primarily in elvish, which I luckily knew because Elvish scrolls often contained instructions to treasure. I glanced through a few of the spells and was shocked to see they were primarily focused on death - necromancing, poisoning, soul bonding, curses.

Putting it aside, I continued looking through his things, moving from the nightstand to his wardrobe, a large closet with two chests full of crowns, jewels, coins, and all manner of objects. Almost everything he owned was the same color - black - and emblazoned with the crest of the House of Atropos.

Slowly I inhaled, and my nose was immediately flooded with Melchior's scent - skin, sweat, pine, something like leather and parchment. As if he'd been reading books in the woods. Inhaling deeply against one of his fur lined cloaks, I admitted what a nice scent it was.

"Who are you?" a loud voice demanded.

The woman's face was tight with disapproval. "Stealing from the Prince?"

"What?" I said, dropping the cloak. "No. I'm his... betrothed."

"He's back with a bride?" She studied me with a critical eye. "I don't like it. He's been gone for two months and didn't even tell me he'd returned."

"We've only just returned. I could–well, tell him you came by to see him."

"Nilensi."

I held out my hand. "Malinda."

Understanding dawned in her eyes, and she gripped my hand fiercely. "So you're Melchior's thief, come to take the Eternal Slumber." Her smile widened. "Welcome."

She was in on it, whatever his plan was. "I'm not *his* thief. I'm *a thief,* who he has hired."

Nilensi's teeth were perfectly white and even, and she grinned. "I'm one of Atropos' witches. Nice to meet you. Now...Where is Melchior? Atropos' advisors are meeting in the west gathering room to discuss trade difficulties with the Mer. They are expecting him."

"I don't know where he went," I admitted.

"Hm. Well, I'd just have to return and tell them that he's wandered off again. He often does, they won't be surprised." She continued to look at me in such an openly curious way that it unnerved me.

"Did you need anything else?"

"No. I'll be going. See you soon."

The witch left, in a cloud of perfume that smelled faintly of poison, smiling again.

I waited until I was absolutely sure she was gone, her footsteps completely faded away, before I darted back to my room.

Hours later, Melchior strode into my room without knocking.

Dressed in elegant black clothing and wearing a heavy silver crown studded with black diamonds that made his face even more coldly beautiful. He hadn't shaved, so there was a dusting of dark hair along his jaw.

"Are you ready?"

"You tell me." I turned to him and his eyes widened.

"You look..."

"Amazing. Incredible. Magnificent," I finished for him, preening before the silver mirror, glancing over my shoulder. The body-hugging red gown was backless, open all the way to the base of my spine, flagrantly showing off the pink scars from the Keres. Its sleeves were red lace, the fabric coming to a point just over my knuckles.

The ruby earrings I wore sparkled like nothing I'd ever seen.

"Who picked this dress?" I asked. "It's unbelievable."

"I did."

I arched my brow and gave him a skeptical look. "Really?"

"In that dress, anyone would look beautiful."

I couldn't decide if this was an insult or not; I didn't care much if it was. Right then was the most beautiful I'd ever been, my hair piled on top of my head in elegant braids, my eyelashes darkened, my lips reddened.

And I smelled amazing, like cinnamon and honey.

He's a liar, I thought, gazing into the tall, gilded mirror. I'd seen plenty of women in my life, having visited the brothels of Fidelisgrove to collect information and dues for Zeph. And right now, I was prettier than any of them.

"It's for shock value," he explained. "Everyone will be staring at you, wondering who designed the gown, how much money I spent on you and how extravagant our wedding will be instead of wondering why I am betrothed to someone who offers nothing of value to the kingdom."

His harsh words couldn't bring down my good mood.

"You don't want me to be inconspicuous?"

"Never." Melchior angled his head, studying me.

Pursing my painted red lips, I glanced down at the floor. Shadows pooled at his feet, like servants eager to do his bidding. They blended perfectly against the stone, the dimness of the room, but I still noticed.

"Do those things follow you everywhere?"

"Things?" He looked down. "Ah– no. They *are* me. A spell I've been working on for a while."

One of them caressed my ankle and, unable to stop myself, I kicked it away.

His arm was warm as I took it, tucking my fingers into the crook of his elbow. We made our way downstairs, toward the chatter of many voices and the clink of goblets. The long hall was decorated with black banners, each one adorned with the crest of the House of Atropos – a knife, a skull, a tree without leaves.

"Are you nervous?"

"Should I be?" I'd been pretending most of my life to be someone I wasn't... usually for money. This would be no different.

I gripped his arm a little tighter.

"Don't let her intimidate you."

When we entered the main ballroom, a gaggle of people - both male and female - descended upon Melchior like a well-dressed swarm of locusts. Each of them wanted his time, his attention, his favor.

There were several jeweled necklaces I would have liked to steal.

Some of the women eyed me with overt hostility, as if they themselves had expected a proposal from him at any moment. The intensity in his gaze never wavered as he held court, his razor focus flickering from one person to another, assessing, splitting his time equally among them.

"You and your brother toy with hearts as if they're mere trinkets," one of the women trilled, her voice carrying through the room. A brunette, her jaw was almost as large as her breasts, which she was showing entirely too much of.

Melchior gave a tight smile. "Do we?"

I stayed at his side, a silent, red-feathered bird, awed by the decor and the food. The room was decorated in onyx and white and silver, and I counted six crystal chandeliers overhead. Servants scurried through the crowd carrying silver trays, laden with fruit and meat and cheeses. The ceiling high above us was domed, tiled with pearl and pewter. As I studied it, one of the stone statues moved.

"Is that... Is that a gargoyle?" I asked in wonder.

Melchior leaned close, his breath tickling my ear. "Unfriendly little beasts. They only pretend to be sleeping when you look at them."

The crumbling little monster scowled at me, then turned its back, stretching wings that were no bigger than my shin.

I clapped my hands with delight, and Melchior tugged me close, smiling. In front of the others, he was a doting man, feigning affection flawlessly. His fingers brushed against mine as he handed me a glass of wine; his hand lingered on my back as he introduced me to lords and ladies.

Intent, steady, his black eyes met mine over the rim of his glass. "Enjoying yourself?" Melchior asked.

"Immeasurably." I held the glass, but didn't drink it. "You?"

"No." Melchior offered a mindless smile. "I hate these."

I surveyed the room again. "For being in the House of Death and Darkness, these folks sure are friendly."

"Atropos would gladly cut their throats, and may at some point, but until she does, they will fool themselves into thinking Death can be bought, convinced, or compelled to be their ally."

"Would she do that? Offer immortality?"

"She's Death. On her list of potential outcomes, making people live longer wouldn't make the highlights."

"I didn't think she seemed that bad."

Beside me, almost unnoticed, a servant moved with silent grace, his presence an unobtrusive shadow.

"More wine?" he asked, hovering at my shoulder. "It is a delicate vintage from the west, unsung, but far more beautiful than anything else in the castle."

"I don't drink," I snapped, tired of being asked.

"I would, if I were you," said a masculine voice. It was Fenix. Our eyes met briefly as he poured more wine into my goblet with flourish.

"Thanks," I muttered, eyeing the liquid in the cup as if it were poison. I looked back to find Melchior watching. "What?"

"You don't drink?"

"No. Dulls the senses. If I need to fight or flee, better to not be drunk."

"Ah." He took a sip of his own wine. "That's smart."

"Isn't it?" I sat the untouched wine down on the table next to me, and when I turned back toward him, Melchior leaned close and tucked a strand of golden hair behind my ear.

"It is. You'll need to be on your guard. To trust nothing and no one."

I met his eyes. "And what about you? Should I trust you?"

He chuckled. "I wouldn't. Nothing in this house is as it seems."

I swallowed hard.

"Don't be fooled, Malinda. People are terrified of us for a reason."

Us. Atropos... and himself.

Melchior glanced over my shoulder, and his demeanor completely changed.

"Gods. My mother is heading this way. Don't turn around."

I did anyway.

Atropos was indeed striding across the room, a woman trailing close behind her. Looking tragically nervous, the girl was wringing her hands. She might have been eighteen, but I doubted it. Dressed in a vivid yellow gown with an enormous citrine necklace, she was unmistakably out of place in the House of Atropos. Like a daffodil in a burial pit.

She must be the other potential bride.

"Son. You remember Demitra." Atropos' smile was forced, completely artificial.

Demitra, for her part, was studying the instruments of death tacked onto the walls with a horrified expression.

Melchior took her hand, civil and charming and princely. Demitra commented on the food, the warmth of the room, and the terrible weather. I barely heard her. I'd sized up the girl in less than ten seconds, and determined that she was here against her will. She had no desire for Melchior, and was eagerly awaiting his rejection.

In short, she was a terrible match for him, but she was a fantastic distraction for me. If his mother were focused on convincing Melchior and forcing the two of them together, I'd have more freedom to explore the castle. I would have welcomed a horde of women instead of just one if it meant finding the Eternal Slumber even one day faster.

I silently rejoiced that once I left, I'd be ten thousand coins richer.

Meanwhile, while in his mother's presence, Melchior's expression morphed into something cruel and cunning. An impenetrable mask without a shred of warmth. For the first time, I felt a little afraid of him. I shivered as he drew me tightly to his side.

"They're calling us to dinner. Come on."

Gripping my elbow, he steered me toward a long table where, much to my horror, I was seated across from Atropos, with Melchior right next to me.

Servants bustled around us, serving several different types of meat, bread, and fruit. Thankfully, Atropos did not say much. Instead, she stared at me with such oppressive silence I thought I might actually die.

My eyes kept going to the scythe propped behind her chair, knowing that she'd killed people with it, half-afraid she'd suddenly grab it, swipe it over the table, and take my head.

His words rang in my ears. *Don't let her intimidate you.*

I considered my next steps carefully. I couldn't make an enemy of her. I could not insult her, yet I was afraid to seem weak or unworthy.

Never ask a question that you don't already know the answer to. That's what Zeph would advise me, if he were here.

"Tell me more about the other Fates," I said finally, forcing myself to sound friendly. "Were you like sisters? Were you friends?"

Her black eyes lifted; she was unnaturally still as she considered me. "You realize most people would be speechless with fear in the face of Death."

And who could blame them, I thought.

"Yet here we are, drinking wine," I replied, a sly smile twisting my lips.

The other guests around us had gone silent, awaiting my doom.

For some reason, Atropos responded.

"Clotho, I did not much mind. Lachesis is a whore." Her gaze held mine. "You'll meet them eventually, I'm sure. Lachesis can't resist interfering."

Next to me, Melchior carefully unfolded his napkin.

Atropos took a drink from her goblet, then wiped her lips with one finger. Her nails were shiny, slick.

"My son tells me you killed your sister," she said. "Is that true?"

I didn't know why he'd told her. But I had no choice but to trust Melchior's judgment - he knew his mother best. If her believing I was a murderer helped me make friends with Atropos, I was willing.

"She wasn't my sister."

"An enemy, then?"

"A roommate." I didn't give her any further information, and Atropos, catching onto the game, leaned back in her chair.

A flurry of activity and murmuring caught my attention and I glanced at the doors.

A man entered, a man I could only assume was Melchior's brother, the Prince of Blades.

Raven-black hair fell into his eyes, combed carelessly, and a gruesome scar went from the right side of his mouth all the way to his ear, making him look as if he were permanently smiling on one side. Taller and broader, his demeanor was harsher, colder, and full of deadly assurance.

He was not handsome.

Fear welled in me, quick and irrational and complete. Everything else diminished to a mere pinprick:

The scent of fragrant tea and flaky pastries on the long marble table,

fresh fruit in the bowl, honey dripped over it,

the fire crackling with warmth,

fine silverware and china, etched with motifs of thread, spindle, and scissors.

All of it faded to nothing next to him, Atropos' youngest son, who dropped into the chair next to her with a sneer.

"So this is she," he drawled, as he considered me from across the table. "My brother's betrothed."

Intently, he studied me. His eyes were not black, but a strange blue green. And while their color was completely normal, I'd never before seen such violence in a pair of human eyes. It was as if someone had taken the idea of ruthlessness and honed it to a fine, sharp point.

"Aren't you going to introduce me?" he asked Melchior.

Melchior cleared his throat. "Malinda, this is my brother Julian."

They were nothing alike. This might have been because they had different fathers, or something much more fundamental; that even the universes of lightning that drove their cells were controlled by different Gods.

Atropos seemed amused as she watched our exchange.

Julian stared at me as if he were a cat planning the demise of a helpless baby bird wandering aimlessly between his paws.

A servant - Fenix - served me a portion of baked fish, flaky and golden.

"How are you liking Grace Castle?" Julian laid a jeweled knife on the table.

"I'm not," I replied coldly, putting on my persona as Melchior's future bride.

Julian laughed.

"Later, if you like, I'll show you more of the castle... you shouldn't go poking around without an escort. You might end up dead."

An invitation, but also a warning. "I'd be honored," I lied, while also hoping like hell he wasn't planning to throw me in the dungeon and murder me.

Atropos watched us, silent as a shadow. Behind her was an intricate tapestry of a black dragon battling a urn. The fabric rippled in the dim light, an unwilling witness to our conversation.

Finally, her gaze was so unsettling, so relentless, that I had to raise my eyes to hers.

"What?" I asked innocently.

"No matter how fetching you may be, you cannot marry him."

I completely agreed with her. She was right – no one would ever believe a Prince of Darkness would fall for a thief. His potential mates were likely demi-gods, offspring of Artemis or Athena.

"You think you could please him? Satisfy his needs?" I felt Melchior shift beside me.

The idea of satisfying his needs made me shudder.

Luckily, I was accustomed to lying my way out of tense situations. I had to show her I wouldn't be intimidated.

So I arched a brow at her and reached over to Melchior. Giving him a smoldering look, I trailed my hand down the front of his shirt to the band of his pants.

Glancing over my shoulder, I blinked my eyes at her, vivid green without a hint of fear, and said, "I'm quite sure I can please him."

I leaned into him as his mother watched, a lover's smile ghosting my red lips.

Demitra choked on her drink, sputtering red wine onto her dress.

Melchior, quickly catching on, kissed the shell of my ear. He, too, could play this game.

Atropos had to have the last word. "If you leave now, I'll allow you to live."

"Darling..." My voice was sultry, just a touch too loud. "Your mother wants us to leave."

"But isn't it *our* party?" he murmured.

Then, before I could say anything else, his mouth was fixed warmly on mine in a long, slow kiss. I wasn't the kind of person who would kiss in public, particularly not the kind of kiss that smoldered and swept you away.

Make them believe it.

As we kissed, he trailed his fingers down my arm, straight down to my lap to where the fabric gathered. Then his fingers fanned over one hip, a hot brand that sent shivers of anticipation cascading through me.

I tilted my head, my focus entirely on him. He tasted like Fae wine and ice. *Guaranteed to make a thief sloppy, and stupid.*

The tip of his tongue flicked against my lower lip and I reacted, my hands tightening on his shirt as I kissed him back.

It was several seconds before I drew back, needing to catch my breath.

"That should do it," he murmured. "We've scared them off."

"Oh?" I breathed, my eyelashes fluttering.

Atropos had retreated, leaving the dining table. Her shimmering black gown trailed behind her as she crossed the polished floors, her stride angry.

I took a sip of wine from Melchior's goblet. "Leave now, and I'll allow you to live. That's what she told me."

He smiled, and I noticed his mouth was redder, due to my lipstick. "It's good advice. Maybe I should tell her the same."

10

In the days that followed the party, Melchior seemed dedicated to pretending I didn't exist. I did not go in his room again, and unless we specifically needed to appear together, we did not speak.

This suited me fine.

I was here for a job, not to be friends.

My first priority was to begin scouting the castle and determine all the potential places Atropos might store the Eternal Slumber. Most likely, Melchior said, it would be within reach. Personally I doubted she would leave it anywhere where it would be accessible. It was too valuable.

Taking a pen in hand, I grabbed one of the pieces of parchment and began to make a list.

Entry, throne room, keeping room, dining, kitchen, larder, pantry, armory, bake house, solar, great hall, drawing room, kitchens, servants' passage, dungeon, cellars, several studies, card room. On and on, room after room, I attempted to list every possible place in the castle where the mask might be. If I checked one room per day, it would take me… I did the sum in my head.

Eighty days.

"So much for leaving quickly," I muttered to myself.

"How many libraries are there?" I asked Melchior.

"Five."

Dutifully, I wrote it all down.

I began my search with the other rooms alongside mine. This was purely a matter of convenience - I doubted the mask would be in any of the vacant bedrooms along our corridor. Room after room of opulence, most decorated with heavy, carved furniture, velvets and silks in a rainbow of colors. Gold clocks sat on mantels, endlessly ticking, with no one to ask them the time.

How many bedrooms can one family need? I thought crossly. Although, I supposed, it was a good thing there was no one near Melchior and me, thus lessening the risk that they'd overhear our conversations.

Directionally, there were mountains to the north, a flat field to the west, the sea in the south, and then endless forests to the east. This made it possible, if there was a window, to glance outside and see where I was. *If,* because the castle did not have nearly as many windows as I expected. There were four towers, north, south, east, and west, accessible via spiraling staircases of dark blue stone.

One long corridor after another, but every few feet or so, a servant stopped me to smile pleasantly, asking me if I needed help.

"Are you lost?"

"Can I get you something to drink?'

"No, no thank you," I'd say politely, which seemed somehow like the wrong response.

If I heard heavy bootsteps, I dove into the nearest room and hid, hoping no one would enter. This helped me avoid running into Atropos, who I dreaded seeing again.

Occasionally, however, I found a door that was shut tight. When that happened, I'd look around, ensure no one was watching, and then take my small lockpick tool from my pocket. None of the doors posed any problem– I quickly found my way inside.

I carried on.

There were jewelry boxes with tarnished bracelets and jewels as large as an eye. Bookcases full of leather and dragon bound volumes, none of which had ever been opened or read. I skimmed through these too, ensuring that none of the books were decoys with hidden compartments.

It was all very excessive. Atropos had so much wealth, there was no way to appreciate or catalog it all. I should have been happy about this - no one would notice if I stole something. There were often multiples of things and, surely, if she had five, she wouldn't mind if there were suddenly only four.

And yet... I realized that stealing from Atropos did not sound very appealing. If she did suspect me, or somehow found unexplained items in my room, I would miss out on the larger prize.

It wasn't worth it to steal a small gold ring when ten thousand pieces of gold were mere days away.

When I felt ready to give up for the day, I returned to the fourth floor of the northeast wing, to a small library that faced the mountains. It was one of five, and considerably less grand than the others. Cozy, decorated in emerald green, it was well worn and comfortable, with a fire going. It was my favorite room so far.

Of course, I glanced at the book titles emblazoned on the spines. There were spell books and potion books, history tomes and guides to magical beasts. There were books about humans and Fae, gods and their love affairs. There were multiple books about Moirai and the Fates.

I grabbed one of the books from the shelf at random - a faded grimoire wrapped in black fabric, held closed by a silver clasp - and settled onto the couch.

From here, I had a view of the mountains. It was peaceful outside, the snow softly falling. Next to the windows was a map of Moirai, taller than I was, bolted onto the wall.

Fidelisgrove was drawn with a small flourish.

My village. My home.

I wondered what Zeph was doing. If Kirin's body had been found. He hadn't written to me yet, though I had no doubt that he would.

Opening the grimoire, I thumbed through the first few pages.

Συνταγές για το σκοτάδι και την απόγνωση

It was Glossa, the language of the Gods, and though I didn't know it well, we'd been taught the basics. Zeph insisted that I was tutored, and there'd been several who lived in the house over the years. Mostly to prevent us commoners from signing away our lives in magical contracts, Zeph believed that education made his guild better than the others.

I sat down in a chair close to the fire and began to read.

"Complete Faithfulness?" Frowning, I studied the handwriting and the drawings.

This grimoire had probably been stolen from the northern witch covens – several years before, their sacred places had been ransacked by the Fae, and most of their magical tomes reappropriated. This one was similar to the others Melchior kept in his room.

He did say that Atropos practices magic. And she has several witches here in the castle, including Nilensi. I continued to read through the pages with interest.

I'd never seen so many spells in one place, particularly dark magic such as this. Briefly, I thought back to all that Zeph and Kirin had ever told me. About how anyone could do magic, as long as they said the spells correctly and had the right ingredients.

The book was currently open to a spell on how to entrap a soul, making the person unquestionably loyal to only its beholder.

"Strange," I mused. Though I could see how useful it would be, it seemed unnecessarily cruel to bind someone to you via taking their soul. In all my days of thievery, I'd never heard of anyone stealing a soul.

"What's that?" Atropos asked. Soundless, she'd crept up on me like a ghost. *Close enough to touch.*

I nearly dropped the book. "Just a book I found." I snapped it closed, then gave her a pained smile.

Dressed in typical black, although this gown was oddly designed, as if it'd been shredded with a knife. There were hints of silver underneath, pale, to match her unbound hair. Today, her lips were darker, nearly purple.

"Can I help you with something?"

"No." It was as if she were looking through me.

The silence between us stretched and yawned, profoundly awkward. I fidgeted with the elbow of my dress, then played with the rings on my fingers. Then I re-opened the book and tried to focus on the words. Meanwhile Atropos simply stood there, waiting for something, though I didn't know what.

"Why are you here?" she finally asked.

Did she mean in the library? At Grace Castle? With Melchior? There was only one of these that I could safely answer.

"Reading passes the time. There's not much for me to do here, apart from eating lavish meals and wearing expensive gowns."

"You think royal life is dull." Atropos didn't leave. Instead she came and sat next to me on the far-end of the couch, close to the fire.

I glanced over at her from the corner of my eye. I couldn't quite make sense of it. She hadn't murdered me or insulted me, and it'd been almost two minutes. Was she trying to *befriend* me? Get to know me? I decided to hope for the latter.

"The book is pretty interesting," I said, scrambling for things to talk about. "It appears to be dark magic. I saw a spell on how to retrieve souls, or separate them from the body. You know all about that though."

"I do." Her eyes narrowed as she glanced over at the thick book in my lap.

Another long silence simmered.

"Do you love my son?" she suddenly asked.

If I hesitated, it would be all over. "Yes," I lied, with as much vehemence as I could muster.

"I loved someone once. It was a mistake." Her voice was hard. Cruel.

Was she trying to warn me off or show a shred of common experience, extending an olive branch? Curiosity gnawed at me, eager to uncover some bridge of humanity between myself and his mother. I decided to start with a grain of truth and see how she'd respond. "Melchior mentioned someone. His name was Tassos, right?"

Atropos clenched her jaw. "He was killed by the Gods. I tried to bring him back to life. I failed."

It was ironic–Death was upset about someone's dying. That she would attempt to bring them back to life was even more so. Still, I didn't want to waste the opportunity, if it even existed, to win her favor.

"I saw a spell in here," I tapped the page. "To bring back the dead. Or at least, I think it would. It's a little complicated, and my knowledge of dark magic is not very good."

When she didn't respond right away, I found myself babbling. "I think you'd need a real witch to do the incantations."

"Anyone can do magic, as long as they have the spells and the ingredients. No witch required." Atropos seemed disinterested.

The crackling fire provided the only sound that dared to intrude upon the heavy silence that enveloped us. I glanced at her and was surprised to see vulnerability etched onto her face, along with something else... sadness.

"It couldn't hurt to take a look." I held out the grimoire.

Atropos eyed the book with skepticism. "Fine. Let me see it."

She grabbed it with long, pale hands, then thumbed through it, her eyes skimming the pages. She paused here and there, frowning.

"What do you think?" I finally asked.

"These are unlikely to succeed. It's been too long, and most of these require ingredients that aren't available here."

"Oh." Unable to hide my disappointment, I frowned.

Atropos glanced over at me. "May I borrow this?"

"It's your book," I replied. "Or at least, it's in your library."

There were more, and it was no more interesting than any other. Why shouldn't she have it?

Room by room, every nook and cranny, my thieving hands rifled through the House of Atropos. I eventually discovered several trap doors, hidden compartments, three safe boxes, two secret passageways, a dusty trunk with a carnelian and diamond necklace inside–nothing notable until I journeyed down one particularly narrow servant's passage in the north wing and found myself standing inside of a well-lit bedroom. Nearly the entire wall consisted of arched windows, facing the mountains. There were no curtains.

The bed was ridiculously wide, and wrapped in silver filigree and scrollwork so profuse that it was almost ugly. But the bed was the least of my concerns once I noticed what was in the corner– a cage. A *human* cage. Iron and heavy, and big enough for a grown man to sit in.

Thank the gods it was empty.

Slowly I made my way into the room. It smelled like old blood and men's cologne, herbs and leather. On the desk was a collection of knives, none of them shiny, all of them dull and used.

I recognized them based on their hilt. It was Julian's room.

With a sense of profound dismay, I glanced around. I couldn't just leave. I needed to go through every crevice and look for false boards or hidden places and see if there was anything here. Of course, I doubted that the mask would be here. But there might be other things that would be useful.

I had to be quick about it, because I had no idea when he might return.

As speedily as possible, I checked the walls for hidden nooks. Then the bookcase for hollow fakes. I checked under his chair for a hidden compartment like the one in Melchior's room.

But there was nothing.

Nothing but that strange coppery scent in the air.

Julian was most definitely hiding something... and that something was most certainly dead.

I scratched my head and slowly turned, my eyes skimming every surface.

Where are you?

Nailed to the wall behind his bed was a tapestry, a pastoral scene with hounds and demons. I lifted the corner and was not very surprised to see a door embedded in the wall of stone.

I tried the knob.

It was unlocked. Telling myself not to be a coward, I turned it and opened the door. This revealed yet another passageway. Unnaturally quiet, and completely dark. I waited for several long, tense seconds. If this was a trap, I was doomed. But my instincts told me that the room beyond was empty, holding only a dead body. So I headed into the corridor calmly, trying not to make a sound as I slid my knife from its holster at my waist.

It led to another room, but inside was a pile of body parts and bones. I covered my nose to keep from gagging at the stench.

Sleeping squarely in front of that pile was a dog. Or rather, *not* a dog, but a Laelap.

Made of pure gold, Laelaps were dog-like, and often used as guards. With razor sharp teeth and quick speed, they could catch most intruders. In fact, it was a Laelap who had protected Zeus as a child. Loyal and unrelenting, they could track anything, even over incredible distances. Zeph had once given one as a gift, though it was so long ago I couldn't remember why.

Its crimson eyes shot open and I froze in the doorway.

"Good puppy," I murmured shakily.

With a low growl, its hair rising on its neck, the shimmering beast got to its feet.

I began backing down the corridor and the dog took one step, then two, toward me.

Whirling, I sprinted toward the door. The Laelap was immediately in pursuit, barking viciously and loosing an unearthly howl.

Thankfully I didn't have far to go.

But something strange happened as I ran - the light from the open door seemed to move and get further away. Almost as if the passageway was expanding beneath my feet. Spelled.

Razor-sharp teeth unexpectedly grasped the back of my calf. I didn't even think. I lashed out and stabbed deep into the Laelap's neck, shoving it backward.

I kept running, my now blood-covered knife still in hand, reaching the door within seconds. I pounded through it, then slammed it behind me just quickly enough for the beast to slam into it face first.

Winded, I leaned up against it, breathing heavily.

That hadn't gone well.

I glanced around in a daze, grateful not to find Julian lounging in the bed with that deranged smile on his face. I lifted my skirt and tried to see the gashes - twisting awkwardly to get a good view. As best I could tell, there were several deep lacerations, all of which were bleeding badly. With a soft curse, I untied the ribbon from my hair and wrapped it tightly around the wound.

Making sure there was no blood on the floor, that nothing else was disturbed, I limped back to my room. And as I did, I said a prayer to Nyx that Laelaps bites healed quickly.

ΠΡΑΚΤΙΚΈΣ ΣΤΗ ΝΕΚΡΟΜΑΝΤΙΚΉ

PRACTICING NECROMANCY?

Resurrection spells, a cornerstone of necromantic therapeutics, exhibit a high degree of unpredictability and inherent instability. Clinical observations have noted that subjects restored through these spells frequently exhibit cognitive deficits, displaying behaviors and characteristics significantly divergent from their premortem state. Emotional volatility should be expected.

During the resurrection process, the soul undergoes morphological alterations, including fragmentation and partial reconstitution. This phenomenon is hypothesized to result from usage of suboptimal or adulterated alchemical components during elixir synthesis, or errors in the incantation and spell-casting protocol. Specifically, the precision of verbal components in spell articulation is crucial; deviations result in a spectrum of unintended pathological effects.

Post-resurrection, tissue decomposition will accelerate. Progressive decay can be inhibited through periodic administration of rejuvenation serums or freshly formulated resurrection potions. The efficacy of these treatments in halting or reversing necrotic processes is a subject of extensive research. Frequent infusion of blood has also been observed to extend the functional longevity of subjects.

11

The next day, a maid came to my room and invited me to the Forum - Atropos had specifically requested that I attend and sit by her side. I couldn't help but feel triumphant.

At Forum, citizens gathered to make their complaints to Atropos. As their ruler, and as a Fate, she was expected to mediate disputes, offer advice, and make decisions regarding land and water and livestock. It all seemed very trivial for someone who was created by a Goddess, but it was a tradition spanning hundreds of years. In fact, some brought their newborns to see the Fates in hopes that they could beg for a long life or a happy destiny.

And she'd invited me.

It was a step in the right direction.

"I'd love to," I told her. I could feel Melchior's judgmental gaze through the open door.

He waited until she'd left to speak. "You shouldn't go."

"Why not?"

Melchior prowled toward me, his expression so intent and cold that for a moment I felt afraid of him.

I stepped back.

He paused, noting my nervousness.

"It isn't what you think. Typically, Forums are... unpleasant. I don't think you're ready."

Unpleasant. My mouth twisted and I looked away.

"It isn't a fucking tea party, Malinda. She's Death. She kills people. Daily."

"Oh really? I hadn't noticed." My voice was almost a hiss. "If you think I'm so incapable, why did you bring me here?" I didn't back down, my chest nearly touching his.

"I don't think you're incapable, I think you're unprepared. And that you don't understand the risk you're taking every time you even speak to her."

"This whole job is a risk."

"Yes, which is why I told you to limit your interactions with my mother as much as possible." His face was mere inches from mine.

"Why are you so concerned? I'm a thief, *your* hired cutpurse. I know what I'm doing." My heartbeat was a loud roar in my ears.

Melchior's expression rippled. "I suppose you do." He assumed a tight, practiced smile. "You should of course do whatever you think is best."

"I usually do." Ignoring him and his scowl, I went to get ready.

I followed my escort through enormous indigo pillars carved into the shapes of skulls and twisting flowers, noting that someone had set out white and black urns full of winter roses, white and scentless as snow.

We entered the throne room from a set of large iron doors that were more than double my height and as thick as my arm. Due to the sea of people inside, the guard paused, waiting until there was a lull to escort me to the front of the room. This gave me plenty of time to take it all in.

The ceiling was high - as high as a cathedral, which amplified the conversation and general noise.

At the front and center of the room was Atropos' throne - the Blood Throne. I watched in horror as it gurgled, its empty seat bubbling. Rivulets of blood leaked down its legs onto the dais like a crimson river.

She sits on that?

I tried to hide my expression of disgust, but couldn't stop myself from staring. It was neither functional nor beautiful, and it could not have been comfortable, so it seemed it's only purpose was to terrify her citizens.

Which, I had to admit, seemed effective. As I gazed over the crowd, I noticed that several others were also studying the throne, with varying looks of revulsion.

Behind the throne hung the banners that depicted Atropos' crest – scissors, a blade, a tree without leaves. Stark, cruel, with jagged edges... It was so different from the banners I'd seen in books for the Three Fates– a spindle, an hourglass, and the scythe, all wrapped in the threads of time.

For the briefest of moments, I wondered how it was possible that Atropos didn't miss it, at least a little. The life she'd left behind. In the past, she'd ruled from the three-seated silver throne, Life and Time by her side. She'd been surrounded by elegance and opulence, instead of being cast out to the frozen north.

Over the room hung the vaguely sweet, metallic scent of blood from her throne. This was co-mingled with the scent of fire and ash from the four fireplaces constantly burning, which was the only way to keep the great stone room warm.

Beneath my feet, the floors of the throne room writhed. I stared down at them as words appeared and disappeared, shifting as if they breathed. Reading several, I realized quickly they were prayers, sent to Death. I wondered if Atropos read them or ever answered them.

"Come." A guard beckoned me forward.

Trying to hide my misgivings, I gave him a gracious smile and made my way up to the dais. Another servant scurried to provide me a chair, which he placed to the left of Atropos' throne. Once I was seated, one by one, the visitors paused - stopped talking - and gaped at me. I tried to ignore their curious gazes, to not pick my nails or swing my feet or chew my lip.

Thankfully, it was only a few seconds before Atropos entered, straight and proud and cruelly beautiful, her moonlight hair falling to her waist. She was clad in a black gown with a long train that spilled across the floor like ink, contrasting sharply with her porcelain skin.

She settled onto the Blood Throne - the strangely alive, hideous, blood-creating throne - and I couldn't help but wonder if it felt like sitting in a mud puddle. It must have been enchanted, however, because somehow Atropos remained perfectly dry.

I watched as her fingers dripped red from where she'd swirled them on the armrest.

Meanwhile, the crowd had taken their seats and quieted, giving me a chance to look them over more carefully. Most were finely dressed, though the styles varied greatly. There were flowing gowns, strange warrior outfits, silks and doublets, and also Fae who were nearly nude.

Melchior was nowhere to be found. I supposed he didn't want to attend; after all, he'd strongly discouraged me. He hadn't said what he was doing instead.

The first audience began. It was a centaur who, quite eloquently, requested that the human farmer whose land encroached upon his forest be killed. Not slowly or painfully - he wasn't hoping for cruelty - but simply because the farmer's livestock consumed too much water, and his dogs kept killing the river sprites.

Atropos listened closely. "How soon would you like him to die?"

"Immediately."

She was impassive, regal. Her onyx eyes missed nothing.

"Would it not be better for his livestock and dogs to die, rather than the farmer?"

The centaur blinked. "I suppose it would."

"Then you do not need me. You and the other Centaurs have my permission to kill as many of his animals as needed. If you require assistance, you may request the help of the Keres or the Naiads."

She was rejecting a request to kill not one, but many things. It was fascinating to watch, and an entirely different experience than living with her. I almost couldn't believe it was the same person.

Melchior appeared a second later, standing just behind me, his tall, imposing figure suddenly too close. He was a perfect Prince of Darkness, sly as a shadow, silent as moonlight.

"I thought you weren't coming," I said crossly, glancing up. I hadn't yet forgotten our argument about attending.

"I changed my mind," he said curtly.

Uncomfortable, I squared my shoulders and stared straight ahead, determined to ignore his presence.

Forum continued.

Fae, mortal, mythical beasts that spoke strange languages... an hour, two hours. All came before Atropos and she answered. Behind me, Melchior stood unmoving, almost as if he were frozen, like his jaw was carved from the icicles that hung from the roof.

It was all fairly boring, until one of the woodland Fae came forward with a complaint.

Tall, willowy, he moved with a quick grace as he stepped in front of his queen. His eyes, a piercing shade of sapphire, held the depth of forest pools. His silver hair was held back by a leather band, and his shirt appeared to be made of autumn leaves. Years were etched into fine lines that webbed like delicate frost patterns across his skin.

"Atropos," he began, his voice resonating with a courage that belied his station, "I am Elonde, one of the elder Fae, and I stand before you to relay the grievances of your people."

As if on reflex, Melchior squeezed my shoulder. I felt his flinch, his sharp intake of breath. To use her given name was deeply disrespectful, and surely a Fae of his stature and age would know that.

"Speak, Elonde," Atropos said flatly. "And let your complaints be heard."

"The grievances of Kinver'i are many. Our lands are seized, our homes taken, leaving many in dire straits. The taxes are too high, and our sons are taken for service to you. A great many never return. But this is not the worst of it, and today I raise our objection so that you might hear our request." A hush fell over the room. Whatever Elonde was about to say, the crowd braced themselves.

Atropos waited; her face impassive. The only hint of her impatience was how she rubbed her index finger on the arm of her throne. Slight, subtle, but a tell, nevertheless.

"We have heard whispers that the Fate Atropos has lost her powers. Only Fates or their chosen heir may rule Moirai and its kingdoms; if you have no power, you are no longer one of the Fates."

A heavy silence fell upon the room, the audacity of the accusation shocking the audience.

Her eyes bore into him but Elonde continued. "If you are no longer a true fate, you must abdicate the throne."

Atropos began slowly tapping her finger, blood splattering with each tap. *Click. Click.*

"Where did you get your information?" Atropos asked, her face carefully expressionless.

"The Fate Lachesis has written a letter to Lord Lorcan."

"I see. And you're going to believe my enemy?"

I held my breath.

Melchior grip tightened on my shoulder, as if to steady me.

"Well... what choice do we have, without sufficient demonstration?" He looked around for supporting faces but found none.

He'd still never addressed her as his queen. He'd come to ask her to step down. Perhaps he hoped that Lachesis might take her place, and Atropos would be neither Fate nor ruler, cast out of her castle.

I decided right then that whatever his intention, Elonde was a fool.

Atropos, with cold, measured grace, rose from her throne. The room held its breath as she approached Elonde the Fae, his defiance now replaced by the realization of his imminent end.

I wanted to flee - I wanted to run from the room. I started to stand.

Melchior's grip on my shoulder tightened. "Do not close your eyes. Do not faint," he hissed under his breath, holding me in place.

"The Fae would like a demonstration of my power," Atropos told the audience. "As his queen, it would be generous of me to grant his request."

She turned back to Melchior and me. "Son. I'd like you to assist."

His fingers flinched against my shoulder, but when I glanced up at his face, Melchior's expression was cruel, unfeeling. Eager, even. "As you wish." With one hand, he unsheathed the sword at his side - I hadn't even noticed it.

"You have stolen my time, and my patience." Atropos stepped toward the Fae. "You have said a vicious lie to my face, and to my citizens."

"The penalty for theft is cutting off your hands." Atropos gave a beatific smile. "And the punishment for lying is your ."

Atropos drew a slender, gleaming pair of shears from beneath her robes. A gift to her from Nyx, the Goddess of Night, these might be the same scissors I'd seen in tapestries depicting her...the one she allegedly used to cut the thread of life.

She held them up to the light, as if she were marveling at their magic.

"Hold him," she commanded.

Melchior did. With controlled, fluid movements, he grasped Elonde. Despite the fact that Fae typically were incredibly strong, Melchior subdued him easily.

As we all watched, Atropos cut out the tongue of the Fae. Blood sprayed everywhere, including on her black gown, coating the jewels at her neck, the gold laurel crown that rested in her hair. She laughed as Elonde screamed.

Laughed, and the maniacal combination of her cackling and his shrill shrieking was something I would never forget. When she was done he writhed along the floor, like a butterfly that had been stepped on. Leaking and flapping, and desperate for the misery to end.

"Now his hands." She peered down at Elonde. "Without your hands, without your tongue, you have nothing. No magic. No way to make a living. No way to tell your lies."

Melchior's sword sliced through the air in a wide arc, twice. Elonde screamed. Once his task was done, Melchior's eyes were on the wide windows, the snow falling outside. He didn't even glance at the Fae male weeping at his feet.

The throne seemed to undulate towards the pooling blood of the Fae, thirsty for more.

Atropos picked up one of his hands and pressed it to his chest. "Elonde the elder Fae, you shall suffer and live out your days without end. Keep this as a reminder of your treachery." The other hand she picked up and examined carefully. "I'll feed this to my hounds."

Wordless, the audience stared at Elonde as Atropos returned her throne. Ignoring them all, she smiled at me. "Shall we break for lunch?"

12

"Is it true?" I demanded, as I trailed after Melchior down a windowless hallway, still reeling from the events at Forum. "That Nyx revoked her powers, and Atropos is no longer a Fate and her powers have been revoked by the Gods?"

Melchior hesitated, but then gave a short nod.

"So the Fae wasn't lying. She broke the rules and they punished her... was this because of Tassos?"

Irate, I realized that he'd omitted these details when telling me about his mother. Intentionally.

"There had better be a good reason you didn't tell me," I demanded. "Because it would have been nice–"

"*Shhh,*" he hissed as he spun to face me. "Be quiet. Do you want the whole castle to hear you?"

I glared up at him. "How has she deceived everyone for so long? How can she still kill people? How—"

Melchior shook off my hand. "She has the *mask*, remember? The one you're supposed to steal? Without it, and without her dark magic, she'd have no power at all!" With a frustrated shake of his head, Melchior turned away, striding down the narrow corridor.

Oh. Well. If I stole the mask, he'd have her power. But—her dark magic must be powerful, if she'd been able to convince an entire kingdom...

Belatedly I realized he was leaving me behind. I dashed after him, down the twisting corridor.

"Where are we going? This isn't the way to the dining room."

"My personal study."

It was a tight squeeze, and at times I felt the sides of both walls brushing my arms. The air was stale, as if the passage was rarely used.

"In case this isn't obvious: don't break anything, don't steal anything, and don't touch anything."

"I won't–"

"*Anything.*"

He turned, and lifted the edge of a tapestry, revealing a door. Melchior drew a knife, and swiftly cut across his palm.

Blood welled, and he then pressed his hand to the center of the door. The print glowed red, pulsing, before sinking into the wood.

"What are you doing?" I asked.

He shook his head faintly. "You don't know a blood enchantment when you see one?"

A moment later, there was a loud click, and Melchior pushed inward, revealing a large room.

"Ladies first." His expression was hard, clenched jaw and cold, obsidian eyes, but also tired. Very likely, Atropos had him killing prisoners in the dungeon at odd hours.

Eager to explore the room, I slipped past him, noticing the wounds already closing on his hands. I made a mental note to ask about the blood enchantment on the door later.

Several cauldrons bubbled in the center of the room and the witch stirred one of the iron pots. Not even a single shaft of sunlight pierced the dimness, as there were no windows. I had to strain my eyes to see, despite the candlelight. The entire place was clean. Herbs hung from nails along the walls, each bunch labeled with a careful hand. There were racks of vials, a shelf of grimoires, overstuffed couches and stacks of parchment.

But I jerked to a halt when I saw the Fae Elonde sprawled out on a table, blood pooling on the floor underneath him as Nilensi doused the stumps of his wrists with a potion.

There was a leather belt in his mouth, likely his own, for him to bite down on to keep from screaming.

Melchior brushed past me. "How is he?"

"How would you be?" Fenix stood over Elonde, furious, his hand on the Fae's shoulder.

"You should have let her kill him." Nilensi set aside the cup and then checked Elonde's wounds again. "A Fae without his tongue or hands might as well be dead."

"Can you reattach the hand she let him keep?"

"I don't know yet."

Melchior looked down at the book that lay open on the table, his eyes moving rapidly across its words. "Fenix. Do you think you could create a bracelet quickly? From silver?"

Though he surely wanted to rage and argue, Fenix bent his head.

Abruptly, Melchior returned to me, where I still stood frozen in the center of the room. He took my hand in his. "I'll be taking this," he murmured, slipping the heavy silver cuff embedded with onyx off my wrist.

He tossed it to Fenix, who easily caught it. "Melt that down. It needs to fit tightly against the skin."

While Fenix was using his hands to soften and reduce the cuff to a new silver bracelet, Nilensi and Melchior were muttering over the grimoire, arguing over ingredient modifications.

Shaking her head, Nilensi frowned. "It won't work."

"Trust me."

It took only a few minutes, and she passed him a small bowl of salve. Melchior took it, and leaned over Elonde, whose eyes were dazed from pain.

"Is that bracelet ready?"

"Yes." Fenix came back, and handed the newly forged band to him.

Quick, efficient, Melchior spread the salve over the bleeding stumps. Then, he held up the bracelet, and pressed it to his lips.

"*Na xana kollísei.*" I barely heard the whisper, but as Melchior spoke, shadows slithered and wrapped themselves around the silver, then sank into its surface. He breathed into the metal.

Eyes wide, I watched as he slid it into place on Elonde's wrist, then set his removed hand there, pushing it lightly into place.

Elonde, tongueless, screamed against the leather belt.

The shadows twisted and spun around his wrist until they formed a small hurricane, whistling and ruffling my hair.

Then they exploded in a small puff and vanished.

Fenix and Nilensi did not seem nearly as shocked as I was.

Melchior leaned over again. "Can you move your fingers?"

Elonde's brow furrowed, forming deep wrinkles. But his index finger moved, and then his thumb.

Fenix nearly collapsed with relief.

"I'm going to give him a sleeping draught," Nilensi told Melchior. "He needs rest."

Meanwhile, Melchior wiped his hands on a cloth towel. He could feel me staring, and finally turned to face me. "Say it."

"You healed him."

"As best I could, yes."

"But you're the son of Death. You're the one who mutilated him. Why even bother?"

His jaw kept clenching and unclenching, as if he wanted to shout at me. Finally he said, "I do the best I can. If she orders me to kill them, I do. If not, I repair what I can."

"But..."

"Leave it, Malinda. You wouldn't understand."

I scowled at him. "I might understand if you'd bother to explain."

Once Elonde was asleep, Melchior stood by a large candelabra, his silhouette backlit by the flickering light, casting long shadows over the stone walls. On the tabletop directly in front of him was yet another book - as far as I could tell, whenever he wasn't assisting Atropos in murdering their citizens, he was reading. Now I understood why - he'd been looking for *medical* spells to undo the harms he had done.

Each of us gave our updates in turn. Fenix had been assigned to the kitchens, which suited him fine. He preferred food to people.

Nilensi gave me a questioning look. "How's the scouting?"

"It's been a week, and nothing," I replied. "But I've ruled out all of the most obvious places."

"Just keep looking." Nilensi didn't seem worried. She and Fenix were confident that any day now I'd find the mask– once it was in our grasp, we'd all be leaving, our pockets full of gold.

I frowned. The team might not be bothered, but I was. Every morning, I woke up confident that this would be the day. By nightfall, I returned to my room empty handed with only cobwebs in my hair and dust on my feet. Often, my searches were derailed by servants appearing, and I would skulk away, or pretend to be lost.

Besides being frustrated, I was starting to doubt myself. What if I didn't find the mask? What if accepting Melchior's deal turned out to be the worst choice I'd ever made? After seeing that innocent Fae mangled, I was under no illusions. If we attracted her attention, if we angered her or displeased her, Atropos would murder us. Melchior might even be the one who did the honors.

"What were you working on today before we came in?" Melchior asked Nilensi. "Smells like poison."

I inhaled deeply. "Belladonna and white poppy," I replied. "With apples." I looked at Nilensi. "Planning to slip something in Atropos' breakfast?"

Nilensi gave me an appraising look. "Julian, actually. I don't like him sniffing after my skirts and lurking in the halls."

Silently pleased, I agreed with her. Melchior's brother would be a problem; I could sense it. The sooner we dealt with him, the better.

Melchior studied me. "How is it that *you* know so much about poisons?"

"It passed the time. But I prefer perfume rather than putting it in the food."

"My father taught me," he said, answering my questioning gaze. "From Luminora. He served Atropos, for a time."

At the other end of the worktable, Fenix had begun the delicate task of crafting the duplicate mask. It was manual work, and his fingertips glowed white as he shaped the metal. Every now and then he consulted a stack of drawings next to him, lists of runes and symbols. Drawn with painstaking precision, it was all he would have to guide him– at least, until I found the original.

Even incomplete, with it still taking shape, I could imagine how I would feel to turn and find someone behind me... wearing it. Crafted from pure obsidian, it was heavy, sinister. The design was of a skull, with bones made of pearl. Flecks of diamonds and other materials made it shimmer ever so slightly, and faintly, I could see vines, or thorns, chiseled where the mask would meet someone's hairline.

This mask must be identical, not only in appearance, but in essence. Any flaw, any deviation, and all our efforts might be for nought. Craftsmanship wouldn't matter if Atropos sensed the deception.

They worked in silence, Nilensi adding ingredients to various cauldrons, Fenix shaping the mask, Melchior reading his book, Elonde now sleeping peacefully. I was the only one with nothing to do.

"What if we don't succeed?" I broke the silence. "What if Atropos can tell it's a fake?"

Fenix dipped his fingers into a bowl of serpent's blood and stroked it across the face of the mask. It amplified magic, and it often coated everything made by the Fae. "Oh, she'll know it's fake," he said. "I'm more worried she'll realize that before putting it on, or before we have a chance to get out of the castle."

"Nothing is ever certain." Nilensi ladled some of the purple-silver liquid into a vial.

"That's not reassuring." A born skeptic, I had little faith in the plan. After Atropos donned the fake and discovered it didn't work, as before, we'd have minutes to escape the castle before she killed us all.

I watched Nilensi stir the cauldron with a rhythmic precision that was almost hypnotic.

Sweat dripped from Fenix's temples. Paler than usual, red hair wild, his coppery eyes studied me. "The original took nearly a year to make." His hands glowed as he traced over the obsidian. "I will have however many days it takes you to locate it. So I say, do not hurry. The longer the better."

The door scraped open behind me and I whirled, fully expecting Julian or Atropos to emerge from the shadows, scythe in hand. Instead, it was a small, dark-haired child dressed in a neat black uniform. A small drop of blood dripped from the end of his finger tip.

"Mama?" he asked.

"I'm here." Nilensi continued to stir one of the cauldrons.

"Who's that?"

"My son Nico. He's a servant in the castle. Atropos seems to favor him."

I frowned. An errand runner for Death. The boy was far too small to be working in such a dangerous place. He couldn't have been very old, and he had wide hazel eyes that were much too innocent to be in the presence of Atropos.

I watched as he went to Melchior, who affectionately ruffled his hair – an uncharacteristic gesture for him.

It's none of my business. She's his mother. She'll look out for him. I cleared my throat and addressed Nilensi. "Since you're more familiar with the castle than me, do you have any ideas? Guesses?" I could steal anything, but I had to know where it was.

Melchior replaced one of the grimoires onto his bookshelf and grabbed another. "As I recall, I'm paying you for your guesses and ideas."

Gritting my teeth, my frustration bubbling, I plopped down into the worn-out armchair beside the fire. On the table within reach was parchment and a pen, and I wondered if Melchior ever wrote letters.

As if he could sense my discomfort, Melchior smirked at me. He'd rolled up his sleeves, with the top two buttons of his shirt undone. Unlike me, who was visibly sweating and with my hair already escaping its braid, he was cool and unbothered, despite the heat of the room.

"By the way, Demitra left yesterday."

"Did she?" I continued to study the paper. "Was she scared away by your radiant personality?"

Fenix snorted; Melchior scowled.

Nilensi spoke up. "That's too bad. She was one of the only friendly people in the castle. Pretty, too."

Fenix coughed. "You sound like you're trying to matchmake him."

I caught Nilensi's eye. "I thought she seemed almost normal."

Fenix scoffed. "Her being normal would immediately disqualify her for marrying into the House of Atropos, as you two surely realize already."

The corner of Melchior's mouth quirked. "Regardless, she's gone. My mother only was interested in her as a potential match because she seemed expendable and unthreatening."

He didn't laugh, though I could tell he was amused. it was one of the few times I'd seen him without a frown. Most of the time, he was angry, disinterested, and dismissive. Sometimes he was cruel and murderous. Always, he seemed remote. Untouchable. As if he were walled away in ice.

It was probably purely self-preservation.

Drawing my paper from my pocket, I scanned the parchment. I'd drawn a bold, dark line through each place I'd already checked. Thorough. Meticulous. I was left staring at just a much shorter list of rooms, the first of which stared up at me.

Atropos' bedroom. If it were in her room, she'd have it close to her. Ready to use.

There were other options of course. Yet, I didn't think it was wise to save all the most dangerous locations for last, as they were the most likely place the mask might be.

"Her bedroom, eh?" Fenix said from behind me, making me jump.

Hastily, I refolded and put the paper away. "It's more likely than anywhere else."

Nilensi drummed her fingers on the table. "As long as Atropos is elsewhere in the castle, the odds of being caught in her room are fairly slim. If you have to check there eventually, why not just get it over with?"

That was just what I planned to do.

13

I jiggled the key in the lock and then held in a sigh of relief when I felt the click and the handle turned. My silk slippers were utterly silent. As I eased into the room, the chiffon trail of my black gown flowed across the floor. Melchior slipped in after me, then gently closed and locked the door behind us.

Silence. So much silence in these rooms.

Her bed was neatly made, the sheets pristine and tight across the mattress.

The walls were clad in ebony silk. It probably cost thousands to build and furnish just this single area. The fireplace was large enough to stand in, carved with skulls and flowers. One wall held nothing but weapons of torture - axes, scythes, knives, and all matter of sharp instruments I couldn't even identify.

I nearly screamed as I saw, from the corner of my eye, a man in the corner. Startled, I leapt toward Melchior, clutching his arm. It was only a statue - a life-sized, fully nude statue of a winged Fae male, its cock proudly erect.

"Weird," I muttered, as I studied the figure. There were splashes of blood all over it, including smeared handprints, and there was no way to discern what she might be using it for... but the iron shackle that extended from it suggested that she might be using it to tie her victims to, or at least, chain them up to prevent them from wandering off.

Melchior visibly shuddered.

Driven by pure instinct, I proceeded to check various places in the room. The shelves first, the hidden desk drawer, the secret compartment behind a tapestry. Slowly and methodically, I worked, my ears tuned for the sound of footsteps outside.

Nothing.

Nothing.

Where are you? What am I missing?

"Do you think it's in here?" I asked Melchior.

He shrugged his broad shoulders. "Not really. There are no guards."

I went to the massive bed. I checked under the white pillows, under the mattress. Still nothing. I let my eyes roam over each wall, all the objects I could see. I tapped my foot.

It just isn't here. There are other rooms, perhaps she hid it there–

Shifting, I decided I would go look elsewhere, even though... I scanned the floor. Maybe there was a loose board, a hidden compartment.

My eyes narrowed. "Surely not," I said aloud.

There was a white fur blanket piled on the floor next to the bed, half under it. It was the only item out of place, the only thing not perfectly folded and tightly creased.

Carefully, I leaned over and picked up the blanket with one hand. Underneath, now in plain sight, was a grimoire.

It was the one I'd given her in the library.

The clock on the mantel clicked ominously, off-cadence and irregular. *Time to go.*

The feeling was so strong, it might as well have been someone tugging at my shoulder. Or someone shouting in my ear.

I turned, startled, and scanned the room–

"What?" Melchior asked. "What did you hear?"

"Shh," I said to him, scanning all the corners of the room.

There was nothing.

I glanced down at the book again. Every fiber of me screamed that I should take it with us. That Atropos should not have it. But if we took it back, she would likely notice its absence. She would wonder who had been in her room and taken it..

With an irritated sigh, I tried to recall its contents. This was one of the darker ones, with spells for souls, necromancy, memory loss, plague, and various poisons. Carefully, I recovered it with the fur blanket.

I was still debating whether I was making the wrong decision when we heard a key in the lock.

My eyes darted here and there, looking for a safe place to hide. But Atropos' room didn't have a servant's passage, it didn't have a balcony. We couldn't escape out the window, could we?

The door was opening. The amount of time we had to decide and do something became ever smaller - whatever we were going to do, it had to be now. Panicked, I shifted from one foot to another, my mind skipping from one idea to another.

"Come on," Melchior hissed, pulling me toward the bed.

"What are you..." I watched, open mouthed, as The Prince of Darkness dropped to the floor and scrambled underneath his mother's bed. A moment later, his shadows reached out and grabbed my ankle. Shaking them off, I realized that I didn't have time to debate or argue. The door was swinging open.

So I dived under the bed myself, then clapped my hand over my mouth to keep myself from breathing too loudly.

Someone entered the room. From this vantage point, I couldn't see much beyond Melchior's face. His eyes were tight, narrowed, as we waited. Both of us listened as footsteps approached. Heavy. Thudding. *Heavy.*

Death's footsteps were the steps of a shadow, a knife in the dark. Atropos was like a ghost. I'd never heard her, not even once.

Yet these moved with a sense of purpose, each step echoing in the silence. Boots. *Men's* boots. It was very poor timing.

Surely they'd look under the bed. Then, they'd see us, and we'd have either a lot of explaining to do or we'd both be dead. I licked my lips and looked at Melchior. He, too, held his breath.

A voice spoke, undeniably male. "Do you have everything you need?"

"I do. Your last trip was very fruitful," Atropos replied.

"Of course. I aim to please." I didn't recognize his voice; I was certain I'd never heard it before. Deep, gravelly, with a faint lilt – perhaps it was one of the Lords from the party.

"I've missed you."

"And I you."

The sound of kissing followed. And not a chaste peck, but loud, wet, sucking sound.

I glanced quickly at Melchior, who was baffled at first, then mortified.

His mother.

Our eyes met. I tilted my head and blinked three times. *Can you believe this is happening?*

Melchior bit his lip and shook his head. *No.*

"The book," Atropos said, her voice laced with authority. "Is it still here?"

"It is." A male hand appeared along the floor briefly, moving the blanket, then scooping up the grimoire.

Overhead, there was the sound of pages turning, and then a muttered incantation. I couldn't make out the words; I wasn't sure if Melchior did either.

"Get the bones."

Next to the bed, I heard the drawer of the table open, a shuffling sound, as the man retrieved something from the drawer.

Above us there was a groan. The sounds of movement, a gown being removed... it hit the floor next to the bed. Next to me, Melchior closed his eyes with a pained expression.

I gave him an awkward grin in response. Death and her lover were just above us, and they were clearly in the midst of something intimate. With each whispered endearment or sound, our eyes would meet. I nearly laughed, and Melchior wore a furious look that said he expected me to stay silent and serious.

Without warning, the movements above us grew increasingly aggressive, frenzied. The bed groaned and creaked, its ancient wood frame sounding like it would cave in. It seemed as if there was an ocean above us, and we were the fish underneath, watching and listening as the boat rocked and tossed on the waves.

My face heated, and I kept my gaze on the stone floor. I began clenching my fists, wondering if it was possible to make myself deaf simply by wishing for it.

"Put it in me," Atropos ordered. "Now."

I bit my tongue, both curious and ashamed. Certainly, I'd never heard anything like this. I made the mistake of looking at Melchior, and he was staring at me. His eyes were darker, and they burned into mine.

The man overhead gasped, groaned. Melchior's eyes held mine as he reached forward, slowly and soundlessly, to brush the hair away from my face. His fingertips touched my skin as if it were made of butterfly wings, as if he might take away the very thing that enabled me to fly–

And came away red.

My eyes widened, and he gave a subtle warning with his fingers over his lips. Then he touched my head again, and I flinched as I felt a single drop of blood roll down my forehead, down the side of my nose. I brushed it away.

Had I hit my head when we'd crawled underneath? There was more, more, and I had to wipe it away to keep it from blurring my vision.

Melchior's eyes drifted up, toward the mattress, where the two above us were moaning... and he grabbed my arm. Tugged me toward him. I struggled silently against his grip, until I could tilt my head back and look up.

To see a knife blade plunge through the red center of the wet mattress.

I flinched and cringed against him, and we both watched as the blade came through again. The man gasped, a rattling, raw gurgling sound. The bed was sopping, dripping down onto us... and Atropos gave a low, sensual chuckle.

She kept on long after he was dead, pleasuring herself, and she used his dead body. I didn't want to think about it.

Do not panic. Do not scream. Do not breathe. Do not vomit.

I put my hand over my mouth, just in case it decided to rebel. And I stared at Melchior, and prayed that we both would make it out of this bedroom alive.

It was hours – *hours* – until Atropos left. And in that time, I could do nothing, and say nothing, only curl tightly against Melchior and watch the widening circle of blood on the floor, listen to the steady *drip, drip, drip.*

Melchior closed his eyes and waited for the time to pass, stoic and patient, while I sweated and doubted and inwardly went through phases of disbelief and panic.

At some point I nodded off, my body unable to endure the constant tension and painful silence. Or I fainted, because I'd been trying for so long not to breathe. I awoke to Melchior shaking me gently, his lips near my ear.

"She's gone," he whispered. "We need to hurry."

He went first, making sure that the room and the hallway were clear before I exited, the two of us then walking - not running, as I would have preferred - back to our rooms. We went to Melchior's, and he locked both doors as soon as we were inside.

"Did you see who it was? Did you recognize his voice?"

Melchior paced. "No. I couldn't see. It was too dark, and I didn't... I'd never heard his voice before. He could have been anyone. No one."

"There was so much blood," I muttered. "Too bad she didn't cut his throat; he would have died faster."

I swiped at my forehead, where the man's blood had caked and dried upon it. I'd never felt so violated, as if disgust was a word that had been chiseled deep into my bones.

"I can't believe she did that," I said, still reliving every sound of the man's demise, how Atropos had continued to pleasure herself–

"Believe it. I told you she's ruthless."

"This is a nightmare. Am I dreaming?" The words slipped out.

Rolling his eyes, Melchior yanked his bloody shirt off and dropped it on the ground, then went into his bathing room.

Meanwhile, I went to the window and drew aside the heavy velvet curtains, rubbing the rich blue velvet between my fingers as I stared at the landscape. The sun would rise soon, and the sky was beginning to lighten. We'd spent the entire night hiding under Atropos' bed. My back and head both ached.

Sighing, I leaned my forehead against the cold glass, letting it cool my feverish skin. If that was what Atropos did to her lover, for fun, what would she do to me if she discovered that I planned to steal The Eternal Slumber?

It'd been another week of fruitless searching. Despite the images in the books, I hadn't found the mask. *Think.* Inside – inside a butterfly beat desperately against the cage of my chest. My reflection was a distorted shadow, an echo of my shape. What point was there in having a thief who had nothing to steal? Or searching for an object that could not, would not be found?

Subtle light began to fill the room as the sun rose, painting the sky with streaks of pink and purple. In the early dawn light, my gaze lingered on the evergreens, on the path that went north toward the crypts, the gates just dark silhouettes.

Melchior was annoyed as he called out to me, over the sound of running water. "You just have to keep looking. It's here; I know we will find it."

"What if it's not in the castle? I've gone through almost every room, and it isn't here."

Melchior exited the bathing room and stepped toward me, now bare chested and shoeless. "Let me help you, and don't go it alone. You'll be much less likely to die if I'm with you."

That was likely true.

"In the meantime, you'll want to shower all that blood off."

Disgusted, I glanced down at my gown. I already knew that much of my hair was matted together, sticky.

"Here." Stepping close, he took a warm, wet cloth, and wiped my forehead, then my cheeks. "You look frightful."

"Like a war-lord after the siege." I closed my eyes as he cleaned my eyebrows, my nose, then my chin.

"Ha." Patiently, he wiped the blood away. Just as he had when I was injured by the Keres. His hands were gentle, steady. The hands of a healer.

My eyes fluttered open, and I gazed up at him.

Instead of his usual coldness, or annoyance, or his detached disdain, Melchior's expression was wistful. Curious. His right hand rested lightly on my shoulder, his fingertips on my bare skin.

He felt my eyes on him. "What?' he asked, still intent on his task.

"Your mother just killed someone."

"She's killed multiple others while you've been here. You'll grow accustomed to it."

"Did you?" I hoped not.

"Did I what?"

"Grow accustomed to it."

"Eventually. Everyone dies. Some faster than others, some more painfully than others. Very few deserve what the Fates decide, but the Gods gave them that right."

"If you think everyone dies, if you're so accustomed to it... why do you bother healing people?"

Our eyes met, and Melchior paused. Slowly, he lowered his hands. "If you want to leave, I understand."

It wasn't an answer, which was typical of him. I sighed, a release of my pent-up frustration. "I don't want to go. I just want to find the mask, give it to you, and get paid. As quickly as possible."

"Good. I don't want you to go either." He handed me the bloody cloth and grinned. "It's much more interesting with you here."

I laughed. "Yeah?"

"Mmm hmm." Melchior flopped down into his chair by the fire, opened a grimoire, and began to read. My eyes skimmed over his long, tall form, his hair which actually was not black, but a dark mahogany brown. Barefoot, wearing only brown pants, he didn't act like royalty, or a descendant of the Gods. He could have been a thief. Or a farmer. He might have been normal, except for his excruciatingly princely face.

The clock on the mantel chimed, then clicked. *Click. Click. Click.* It made my eye twitch.

Shaking my head, I returned my gaze to the windows, to the snowy landscape outside. My eyes went wide, then narrowed, as a cloaked figure moved through the field toward the crypts. It wasn't exactly the sort of place someone would visit at dawn, and I wondered which of the servants it might be–

Her gown slithered through the snow like an old poisonous snake.

Take the shovel and cut off the head.

It was Atropos.

She turned and glanced back at the castle. Scared she might have noticed my face staring down at her, I jerked away from the window... then looked out again a second later.

"Where's she off to?" I murmured.

"Who?" he asked.

"Your mother. She's skulking about in the field."

"Ah. She's either burying a heart, which she likes to do after murdering someone, or, visiting the crypts again. She goes every day. As regular as clockwork. Though I don't know why she bothers."

Open-mouthed, I glared at Melchior with such hostility that he paused.

"What?"

"You didn't think to mention that she visits the crypts *daily?*"

He shrugged. "Most likely she's going to see Tassos, to make love to his bones. Or whatever it is she does when they're alone. You saw the statue in her room."

Yes... I had. "So Tassos is the lover who the Gods killed, and then they revoked Atropos' power because of him?"

"Correct."

He was probably right. She was going to visit the bones of her lover. It'd been hundreds of years since he'd died, and yet she still pined for him. It made sense, and yet...

"Then whose bones are in her bottom drawer?" I asked. "If Tassos is in the crypt, who's in the nightstand?"

"How would I know? Could be anyone."

"They might be his."

Melchior shrugged, unconcerned, but my mind was spinning. Atropos defied the Gods for Tassos. Lost her powers because of him. Turned against her only friends, lying and scheming against them. She sacrificed everything she possessed for him.

She hadn't loved him, she'd been obsessed with him.

Most likely, she'd keep his bones within her reach, not so she could remember him, but so she might grasp them in her hands and reassure herself that he was still there.

I whirled to Melchior. "What if the Eternal Slumber is in the crypt? Instead of inside the castle?"

"Then that would be bad."

"Why? It'll be easier to steal, if it's not somewhere easily observed. She's rarely there; we could figure out her schedule. I could go out tonight even–"

"That's where she keeps her more dangerous items."

I turned back to him, a pained look on my face. "That's true of the entire castle."

"Which is why you won't be going without me."

I crossed my arms. *Which is why I would be going, later, as soon as his back was turned.*

14

I took yet another bath, scrubbed away the blood from Atropos' dark deeds. Afterward, I laid down on my bed in a towel. I was so tired, running on so little sleep and food... it felt as if I were a knife, sharpened until my edge was a line too thin to see. I closed my eyes, just for a moment...

Suddenly there was an agonized scream in the corridor that ripped me from slumber.

Melchior threw open our door.

"I have to go. Stay here. Do not come out." He eyed me, laying on the bed, still wrapped in a towel. "Do *not* come out."

Before I could say anything, he'd fled the room.

I stood dazedly staring at the spot where he'd been standing, bleary with lack of sleep. Whoever was in the hall was most definitely being murdered. Painfully.

Yet I'd be damned if I was just going to lay here and let it happen. The instant I heard Melchior's shout in the corridor, I leapt from the bed and threw on a dress.

Stay, he'd ordered me. *As if I were some sort of dog.* I wasn't his, he had no right to order me around like a servant. And surely, I wasn't intending to sit politely in the bedroom, missing all of the action. Curiosity simmered in my gut as I ran down the hallway, past door after door. Immediately after I turned the corner, I froze. There was a wide trail of blood leading down the stairs, across the landing, and toward the throne room. It looked as if one of the maids had mopped with red paint.

Atropos dragged a gorgon by one arm - the snakes of her hair were vivid green, hissing and spitting venom, and there was a strip of fabric covering her eyes. Dressed all in black, Atropos had a smear of blood across her cheek, and her hair hung long and loose, like shafts of moonlight that flowed to her waist.

Julian, following close behind Atropos, grinned at me. "Come to join the fun, Malinda?"

Melchior stepped between us, as if he could shield me with his presence alone. "Can't you two keep your toys in your own room?"

Julian chuckled. "Hasn't anyone ever told you that it's the thrill of the chase?"

Unruffled, Melchior put his hands in his pockets, then examined the floor with a vaguely disappointed expression. "You're always so sloppy, brother. It's inelegant."

"Ah, but I prefer brute force and bloodshed. Visceral enjoyment."

The gorgon moaned, and I visibly flinched, jerking my head toward the windows. That way, I wouldn't have to watch.

"Are her screams bothering you?" Atropos purred in a low voice. "I can easily make them stop."

I flushed, my cheeks stained scarlet as I pressed myself against the marble banister. "No, I... wasn't complaining."

"Malinda. Go back to my room. I'll be there in a moment." Melchior didn't so much as glance in my direction, keeping his back toward me. "Once I've helped my family clean up their mess."

He didn't need to ask twice.

I ran back to the bedroom, slamming the door behind me. Then I collapsed on the floor, hugging myself tightly, forcing myself to inhale, gasping.

The screaming downstairs resumed. I put both hands over my ears, trying to block it out. It felt as if the air was burning through my lungs, like my heart might explode out of my chest. *Do not cry. Do not.*

I kept trying to breathe, panting. *I'm going to die here.*

As I listened, they mutilated a gorgon, with their bare hands, for entertainment. Inhaling and exhaling too quickly, cold sweat beading along my temples. Panicking. What chance did I, a fragile mortal, have against them?

Outside, it was abruptly silent. I tried not to think about what that meant. A few minutes later, Melchior threw open the door. "Idiot. I told you to stay here. When will you start listening to me?"

When he saw my face, my position on the floor, his hard expression faded. He crossed the room, kneeling down in front of me. "Calm down. Malinda. You have to calm down."

Gently, he gripped my shoulders, stopping me from rocking back and forth. "You're safe. I'm here." The warmth of the fire, and his hands, slowly registered. Anchoring myself to the sound of his voice, I counted to ten.

One. Two. Three.

"They killed her. For no–no reason–no purpose. For sport."

Melchior blinked. "They always do."

I gripped his hands in mine. "I'm going to die. They are going to kill me—"

"No you aren't. You're going to steal the Eternal Slumber, I'm going to give you ten thousand gold coins, and then you're going to take a ship south. You're going to live a long, happy, normal life. Just the way you always wanted."

"How can you stand it?" I squeezed his hands so tightly, my nails probably cut into his skin. "How can you live in this awful place with them and still stay sane?"

Melchior brushed away the tears still running down my cheek. "I never said I was sane."

I dropped my head onto his shoulder and leaned on him for a long moment, trying to regain control of myself.

Melchior stilled, then after a moment, pushed me backward.

"We aren't friends, Malinda." Disdain hung over him as he jerked his arm away. "Just because I don't like seeing you hysterical doesn't mean you can presume to touch me."

His eyes were obsidian, cruel and unfathomably cold. He was so full of animosity that I was startled, yanking myself backward as if I'd been burned.

Like he hated me.

I couldn't think of any reason that he would even dislike me, other than I had been trying and failing to find the mask for far too long. Or he regretted choosing me instead of another thief. But no, that would just be annoyance.

The expression on Melchior's face was hatred, seething animosity.

And I hadn't done anything to deserve it.

The world felt like it had suddenly turned over, and the easy comfort I found in his arms was replaced by fear.

His face twisted as he kept looking at me, as his eyes searched mine, then fell to my lips, because he expected me to say something angry in response.

I found my voice. "Fine. No problem."

Melchior stood and stalked over to the fireplace. Then he leaned against it, bracing one hand on the mantle. "If you believe that the mask is most likely in the crypts, we can go look for it. Together."

Together. After he'd just given me a look that promised he'd knife me in the back. I glared at him. "I'll go alone, thanks."

Melchior blinked, and I could have sworn that I saw a flash of hurt on his face. "No you won't. Absolutely not."

"Tonight while you're at dinner with your mother. Atropos will be distracted, and I won't have to spend another meal pretending to be in love with you."

"And how will I excuse your absence?"

I shrugged. "Tell her I have a headache. Female troubles. Or that I drank poison. I don't care. Make something up."

"I would rather you wait, so that we can go together." Melchior cracked his neck.

I realized that most likely he was worried I'd take the mask for myself, then sell it to one of the traders as a forbidden magical object. On the black market, it'd likely be worth thirty thousand gold coins. Maybe more.

"I prefer to work alone. Having you with me will only slow me down." I forced myself to pull out my silver knives, to inspect them to see if they needed sharpening. "If you want to help me, distract Atropos. Besides, the crypt might hold nothing–"

And then he'd have another failure to count against me.

"I insist," he replied. "We go together, or not at all."

Clicking my tongue with annoyance, I protested. Melchior, true to form, argued every point I made. At last, with no other recourse, I decided to lie. To fake my agreement, just to shut him up, even though I had already decided exactly how to handle the situation.

I walked back into my room. "If we left now, we'd have the mask before Atropos sits down to her soup."

"After dinner," Melchior ordered. "Together."

"Fine." I tossed back over my shoulder. "We can go after dinner. Though I wish I could skip it. I'm not in the mood to face Death twice in one day."

He was scowling as walked into his bathing room. As soon as he was out of sight, I snuck to the door between our rooms and softly closed it. I'd have to move quickly, if I was going to go to the crypts, retrieve the mask, and be back before he realized I was gone.

15

Any good thief will tell you that the key to not being caught is caution. I, a good thief, would also tell you that it's better to work alone. The more people involved in a crime, the greater the chance of getting caught.

If Atropos discovered me wandering around the crypt, it would be better if Melchior wasn't present. Then, I could claim to be exploring, or to have heard a noise, or even say that a servant told me there was a secret passage and she'd requested me down there. But if *he* were next to me, it'd be obvious that we were looking for something.

Besides, I would rather him not be there. His attitude and demeanor was so hot and cold, it made my head spin. I didn't know whether he'd be friendly or stab me in the back—some days it was definitely the latter.

I slid on two of my favorite rings - one had a jagged blade as its stone, ideal for shoving into an attacker's eye, and the other the ring Zeph had given me, the one with a secret compartment full of poison. I armed myself with three different knives, tucking them into various places beneath my gown. I started to walk out of my bedroom, but as I did so, a faint sense of discomfort filled me. I studied the door between mine and Melchior's room.

I'd lied to him, and soon he would know it.

I wasn't seen by anyone as I ducked into the corridor that led to the bowels of the castle. Like a ghost, I crept through the castle and down the stairs, toward the side door that would put me on the path to the crypts.

I was constantly on the alert for the sound of Atropos' voice, or the tap of a maid's shoes. I brushed past locked doors, lovely, empty rooms.

Once outside I proceeded through the icy landscape in the direction of the crypts.

As I entered, I glanced up at the sinister statues guarding the entrance. Easily double my height, proud, cold faces stared down at me. Armed with a scythe, they were ominous reminders of who owned the ground under my feet, and what she'd do if she knew I were here.

I carried on.

There were several crypts to choose from, all perfectly blending into the snowy landscape. Each was an elaborate house of marble and stone, smooth and white in the moonlight. With a furtive glance to make sure I wasn't observed, I studied them, trying to decide which might house the mask.

Skulls, flowers, minotaurs, and Pegasus– each had columns and carvings that were wholly unique, the only way in which they were similar is that they were half buried by snow. The fifth was unremarkable, traditional, plain in comparison to the others other than a pair of scythes carved into either side of its front door.

I couldn't dawdle - it was a beautiful, clear night, with a large moon, which meant I could easily be seen from the castle. It was colder than anything I had ever experienced, and I was standing in a gown and cloak, shivering.

"Just pick one and get it over with," I grumbled.

The crypt with the Pegasus ended up being the closest, so I walked up its stairs, sliding on a layer of ice, watching the icicles that hung from its eaves as if they would snap off and impale me.

There was no light. Not a candle, not a moonbeam, nothing.

Thankfully, I'd expected this. I brought a candle from my pocket, and a match, which I struck using one of the walls. It flared, guttered, and then caught the wick.

The Pegasus crypt was full of junk. Stacked against the walls were all sorts of items - furniture, weapons, music instruments, baskets, urns, vases... it wasn't a crypt at all, but some sort of eternal bizarre storage room.

To my relief, there were no coffins, no dead bodies wrapped in gauze. I wandered around, considering the items, looking for anything of value and scooping it up out of habit more than interest.

Across the room was a set of stairs that went down into the void. I snuck a look over my shoulder at Grace Castle. Several windows glowed, and I could hear the sound of servants talking.

I continued forward, cautious not to trip over my own feet or the hem of my gown. My hand ran along the wall, and I realized after a few steps that there were inscriptions chiseled into them. It wasn't anything I could read. As I neared the stairs, I heard the sound of a faint click–somewhere down there, something moved.

Steeling myself, drawing my knife, I descended. My footsteps were whisper-quiet on the marble. The candle cast trembling shadows; try as I might, I couldn't stop the faint tremor in my fingers.

When I came to the bottom, there was a long hallway, with rooms on either side, and then another set of stairs down again. Lifting the candle in front of me, I went left first, the walls white as the pages of a book. Each room led to another, all empty. It was meant to entomb an entire family, and instead held nothing but air. Some of the walls held drawers, the fronts made of bronze. I studied these, and debated tugging at them to see if there were people inside.

A loud *bang* from another room tore my attention away from these. Something heavy had fallen, perhaps, but then I heard the sound of quick footsteps.

I didn't dare blow out the candle. So instead, I stepped into a corner and waited, desperate to see if anyone would come.

After a few minutes, when no one did, I slowly made my way back to the main hall and the stairs. The rooms on the other side of the hall beckoned. Atropos herself might be in there, making her way toward me... yet still my feet carried me forward.

Until I saw her.

A woman.

Slumped against the wall of the crypt, seated on the floor. Her legs were stretched out in front of her and her head was tilted back. As if she were sleeping, except for her face. Her skin hung in red ribbons, dangling like fringe. Shredded. Unrecognizable.

"Hello?" I whispered, holding the candle toward the mangled body.

She was dead. Long dead, by the look of it. Days at least.

I drew closer, wondering.

Wondering.

Her right eye was closed, as if she were sleeping. But the left was gone, plucked out, leaving an odd sort of hole. There was so much blood caked on the front of her gown I couldn't tell what color it had been. It might have been gold brocade.

She was wearing a necklace.

Heavy, expensive, it was fashioned like a collar. With square cut chunks of citrine. With a gentle finger, I reached out and touched it. Not to steal it, just to feel the cold metal, to make sure I was really seeing it...

Because I recognized this piece.

At the party, the day we arrived, when I'd walked into the ballroom.

"Melchior said you left. You went home."

My eyes scanned the ruined face, the meat and bones of the skull. I couldn't see anything of the shy woman I'd met, of Demitra. But it was her. I was sure.

Stunned, terrified, I stepped backward, wanting to put some distance between the dead woman and myself –

And she grabbed my wrist.

I dropped the candle and it continued to burn on the floor.

"What in the hell?" I shrieked, scrambling backward, trying to jerk away. The knife I'd pulled clattered out of my hand.

Then that thing - the undead, rotting corpse of Demitra, lunged after me.

How she moved solicited a very loud scream from me. Demitra staggered as though her veins were full of mud, her neck bent at an unnatural angle. Her one eye remaining was open and rolled up so that only the whites of it showed. No matter who else might be down here, I was beyond caring now.

I ran from the room, flinging the door closed, but Demitra lurched after me, her teeth chattering and clicking, her bony hands grabbing at my cloak. A flurry of incomprehensible sounds followed, and a slash of fear cut through me– maybe I wouldn't be able to outrun her.

That smile pushed me over the edge and I shrieked again as I scrambled up the stairs.

I stumbled multiple times. At one point, I felt her hand around my ankle, and the smell that wafted toward me was sickening. I kicked her in the face as hard as I could, screaming.

There was no way someone wouldn't hear me.

In the main room, Demitra caught me, throwing me toward one of the walls. I landed with a sickening thud, my arm suddenly burning with pain as I toppled into the pile of random objects.

When I pulled myself back up to standing, however, I realized there was a scythe propped there. It must belong to Atropos. Taking it into my hands, I whimpered. My shoulder might be dislocated.

Demitra's head craned from side to side as if she were underwater, rolling on the tide.

"Come get me," I said, holding up the wickedly curved blade, hoping I'd know how to use it.

So when she lunged at me with a low growl, I anticipated it. Still, I shut my eyes, expecting to just die as she overpowered me, to feel her teeth in my neck. But my grip on the scythe kept her at bay - only just. It was the only thing keeping her from killing me. Demitra snapped and shrieked, her mouth just inches from my face. The half-moon silver blade I held cut deeply into my hands, and blood ran onto my chest.

Gasping, I tried to push her off, but she was too strong. That flayed skull with dangling skin was all I could see, the delicate features gone. Slimy black liquid dribbled out of her mouth and splattered onto my chin when she howled in malevolent joy. With her one rolling eye, Demitra glared at me. In it, there was madness more profound than anything I'd yet found in the House of Atropos.

I did the only thing I could do.

Biting my lip through the pain, I gripped the blade tighter and then rotated it, until the sharp edge was up, and then I let Demitra shove herself upon it. As she did, the narrow edge sliced deep into her neck.

The thing screamed. I screamed too, spitting as I did, trying to keep my mouth empty of the revolting juices that sprayed into my face.

Drenched in gore, I entered our rooms. In a flash Melchior was on me, inspecting me, his forehead knitted with worry.

"Where have you been? I told you not to go alone. Why are you covered in blood?"

"It's not all mine," I said flatly.

"Whose is it?"

I realized that probably I shouldn't sit down in his chair. Anything I touched would need to be burned. So I stood still, pressing my ruined hands to my belly to staunch their bleeding.

"Remember how you cautioned me about Atropos' pets?" I glared at him. "Well. I ran into an old friend of ours. Only she wasn't exactly happy to see me."

"Old friend?" Melchior made a quizzical face. "Who?"

"Demitra."

Melchior shook his head. "How is that possible? I saw her leave."

"She didn't make it very far." I swiped at my eyebrow, only to discover that I had a chunk of her face stuck in my hair. "She's dead. Although not completely dead. It seems that Atropos killed her. And then, I suppose, brought her back to life."

"I don't understand," he said.

"Necromanced. Whatever you want to call it." Limping, I walked into my room, leaving our door open so he could follow.

I had to get out of these disgusting clothes.

For the second time in the same day, I peeled off a bloody gown and turned on the bath. Melchior hovered just outside the doorway as the dress dropped in a heap at my feet. I was so filthy, I didn't even care if he saw me naked.

Stepping into the bath, I hissed. It was always too hot, but this time I didn't mind its heat, and slumped down, shivering. Bruised and pissed off, I tilted my head back and let the water rinse the blood away.

"Did you find the mask?" Melchior asked, keeping his back to me.

"No. Of course not."

I exhaled and inhaled, shifting my shoulders, feeling all the injuries.

"Did anyone see you?"

"A half dozen servants. Although, none of them seemed keened to chat." I picked bits of flesh out from under my nails.

He cursed softly. Then, pensive, he studied the stained glass windows.

"I wonder what she's thinking," he mused. "Trying to raise the dead. Necromancing is messy business, and usually the ones you bring back are unstable."

I sat up, leaning on the edge of the tub, and watched him. Melchior was now re-arranging the jars on the counter, looking at the scented powders. He seemed determined to look at everything in the room but me.

Maybe he thinks he'll turn to stone, I thought wryly.

"I don't think she's trying to raise *everyone,* but one particular one," I told him. "Tassos. And she never would have been able to manage that if I hadn't given her the damn book."

"Don't blame yourself."

"Why not? It was my mistake." I pressed the heels of my hands against my head and then grimaced, opening my eyes to look at the large gashes across my palms.

The cuts ran directly along the headline, which I'd always been told was weak. I supposed the scar would fix that. Now I'd have a vivid, red slash reminding me not to be stupid, instead of Zeph and the elderly palmist in Fidelisgrove.

"You should have Nilensi heal your hands. She's faster than I am."

I leaned my head back against the tub and sighed."I'll go after I'm done."

Melchior cleared his throat. "I have other bad news."

"I tell you I discovered a dead but yet-still-alive woman, last night we overheard your mother murder someone. How much worse could it be?"

He shoved his hands in his pockets. "Atropos wants us to be married. Immediately."

The water dripped from the silver tap.

One.

Two.

Three.

I reached fifteen before he continued.

"Apparently you've made quite the impression. She'd like us to get started on giving her a grandchild."

"Hm. As if I would allow her to get her murdering hands on our babies."

Melchior coughed as if he were choking. Blocking him out, I slid down into the tub, submerging myself entirely, holding my breath as I went under.

I'd never intended to marry anyone, even though Zeph had always claimed it would happen. He'd expected me to seduce the prince, but that had sounded far-fetched. I preferred to work alone, to *be* alone. I didn't want children. Didn't want to tie myself to a family. Lie, steal, cheat, kill... I'd always been willing to go very far for the sake of a scheme. Kissing, even sex. But I'd never considered *marriage.*

In the silence under the water, I felt myself slowly suffocating.

I came up for air at the last possible moment, emerging with a gasp and a splash. The bathroom had stained glass windows, and I sat for a while trying to figure out which gods were depicted on them. I didn't know nearly enough about Gods and monsters to survive in this place.

Melchior was still there. Watching. Waiting. Effortlessly elegant, unbothered and unscathed. He'd sacrificed nothing, he'd never been in any danger. Because I'd gone alone.

"Was this part of your plan?" I asked, suddenly suspicious.

"Which plan? What do you mean?"

"You wanted to convince her that we were a happy couple. Did you know she'd expect us to marry?"

As soon as I said the words, I regretted it. Of course his plan wasn't to *actually* marry me. I'd simply taken too long - he'd probably expected me to find the mask within days, and then be gone. If I was caught, she'd kill me, and he wouldn't have to pay me the ten thousand gold coins.

"Nevermind," I said. "Just tell me what happens."

"It's a standard marriage ceremony, for the most part. Our hands will be bound with red ribbon. We'll take a blood oath. I'll place a crown on your head. Then we'll kiss and it will be over."

"What about our wedding night?" I asked flatly. "Surely we have a consummation ceremony."

He was quiet for far too long. "I don't know."

"Am I supposed to fuck you, or fake that too?"

"I said I don't know, Malinda."

A sob rose in my throat; I refused to let it out. "You expect me to just endure it."

"No– no, I don't expect you to endure it."

"Then what? You don't have any kind of plan. No distraction, no dark magic, no easy way out?"

Melchior shook his head. "It's a bed with sheer curtains. What do you expect me to do?"

I couldn't have sex with him. I simply could not. Melchior didn't love me. He didn't even *like* me.

My gaze dropped down to the shadows at his feet, which shifted and fled from the firelight. He'd used those shadows to kill people. Dozens. Possibly hundreds. All in the name of Atropos.

"You don't have to look so panicked," he sneered. "Afterall, you're a thief. A liar. A murderer. Yet you can't manage one time with me?"

"I don't want to..." my voice cracked faintly, and to my horror I found I couldn't finish the sentence.

His expression wavered, something indecipherable flickering in his eyes. "So you won't do it."

I gave a hollow laugh. "I– I'm not... I don't know."

Melchior pressed his lips together. He looked strangely lost, as if he hadn't been the one pressuring me into marrying him a moment before.

Irritated, I realized I was letting my emotions get the best of me. I was putting my feelings ahead of logic. Speaking before I thought things through. It was the exact opposite of how I should handle the situation.

Bowing my head, I rubbed my eyebrows and considered.

If I left, I would go back to the Nightingale. Zeph would take me back, he would not even ask for an explanation. I still had the coins from before, I would simply return to my previous life. Without those coins, I would be back to thieving. Achieving a better life, a *normal* life, would take awhile longer... but it was possible.

If I stayed... I had to marry him. I hadn't found the Eternal Slumber yet, and there was only so long that Atropos would believe we were *deeply in love* and yet didn't want to get married. A fake marriage would keep me alive a little bit longer, long enough to find the mask.

Plus, if I was his wife, it would give me some protection. And a title. Wealth. Even after I stole the mask, once I had the gold coins, I'd still have that title.

It was obvious what I should do. Even if it hadn't been, I didn't have any alternative. Short of giving up and going back to Fidelisgrove, marrying Melchior was the best course of action.

"I'll do it," I said, in a tight voice. "But we have to figure out the wedding night."

ΑΘΆΝΑΤΗ ΠΊΣΤΗ

COMPLETE FAITHFULNESS

Ingredients

Cordis fidus canis - Heartblood of a loyal hound

Solani folia, septem - Nightshade petals, seven

Cinis ex pergamena desiderati iuramenti - Parchment ash of desired oath

Pinna corvi media nocte evulsa- A raven's feather

Tres guttae triae proprium sanguinem - Three drops of the caster's blood

Ramenta ferrea, unum - Iron shavings, one teaspoon

Preparation

In a cauldron, combine heartblood and nightshade petals. Stir counterclockwise with raven feather. Slowly add the ashes of the desired oath, ensuring dissolution into mixture. Finally, three drops of caster's blood

Incantation

per sangvinem fidelivm, et de flore noctis tenetor;
cineres promissionis, noctisqve potentiae.

Recipients will be pliant and biddable; ideal for loyal soldiers.

16

I did as he suggested, seeking out the witch Nilensi to have my hands healed. Normally, I would have simply wrapped them and gone on with it, but with those deep cuts on both palms, bathing, dressing, and even eating was painful. I wouldn't be able to get married with them looking like this.

Not sure if she would actually be able to provide relief, I went to her rooms, which were located in the north wing of the castle, closest to Atropos.

You'll know you're in the right place when you reach the door with a raven's wing pinned to it, Melchior had told me. I scoured the halls, looking for the proper place to knock. When at last I found it– a black door with a black raven's wing nailed to it, skeletal and with half its feathers missing–I was shocked to see Atropos had just pulled it shut behind her.

Drawing up short, I quickly ducked back behind the corner, then hid in a nearby alcove. I prayed that she hadn't already seen me.

A few seconds later, Death hurried by, clad in her customary black gown, reeking of old flowers, and I held my breath and stood as still as a tree for a full minute after.

"What was she doing here?" I asked, as soon as Nilensi opened the door.

"Who?"

"Atropos. I saw her leaving," I said, while at the same time, I realized what a ridiculous question it was. As Atropos' favorite witch, of course she would be here often.

Yet Nilensi seemed to debate herself. As if she were nervous about Death's visit to her door. If only for a moment, she considered how to reply.

"She just wanted me to look at a spell she found. Nothing unusual." She licked her lips. "Why are you here?"

I held out my hands, palms up. "Melchior sent me. Hopefully you can heal these."

Gingerly, she unwrapped the bandages from my hands, and her long braids swung down to tickle my wrists.

"Sit," Nilensi ordered, then clicked her tongue as she inspected the clean but deep cuts across both palms. They were still bleeding bright red– the skin around the edges was pink, and a bit too warm.

The witch left my side to gather ingredients from a wall of blackwood cabinets and shelves, studying vials and boxes, sometimes sniffing them before she put them back. Her bookcases and tables held several grimoires, in every shade and topic, including one bound in metal, with a ruby embedded in its cover.

"How'd this happen?" Nilensi ground up some items with a mortar and pestle made of stone.

"It's an exciting story. I checked the first of the crypts and found an unexpected guest." I took a tall chair next to a work table littered with small boxes, three cauldrons, jars, urns, and all manner of other strange objects.

"Demitra was chained to a wall, dead. Yet also, not dead."

I watched the witch's face carefully.

To my intense dismay, she didn't look surprised. Instead, there was a flash of guilt, uncertainty, then resignation. She blinked her large, almond-shaped eyes, and said nothing as she sprinkled powdered herbs onto my open hands. She then dripped a cold, clear liquid on them.

I dropped my eyes to her robes, a beautiful swirling pattern of emerald green and gold, and tried to mask my sinking sense of dismay. At the very least, Nilensi had known about Demitra and not told us. She was not completely trustworthy.

It didn't bode well for me or our plans.

Briefly, I wondered if Atropos had given Nilensi the grimoire from the library. If what she'd done was ask her favorite witch to *test* its effectiveness on some poor, hapless victim– and when Demitra announced her intention to leave, that made her the best candidate. If Nilensi wasn't the *reason* for Demitra's awakening.

Nilensi began to lightly massage a thick, foul-smelling salve into the cuts on my palms, and I hissed.

"It burns," I muttered, keeping my eyes lowered.

"As it should. These are getting infected."

There was a long, uncomfortable silence as she worked the medicine into my wounds.

"So... it seems Atropos is necromancing members of the castle." I announced this with a questioning tone, trying to see if I could bait Nilensi into telling me the truth. Or at least, revealing a little more.

"Indeed." Her face was smooth, as calm as a lake.

"You know what I'm thinking? If we're going to be up against Death and the undead, then I want protection."

Nilensi pursed her lips. "What sort of protection?"

"There's no reason for me to be wandering the halls of Grace Castle, purely mortal, with only a knife and prayers. I'll be damned if I end up dying here," I told her. " I want to be able to walk away when we're done. I'm sure you can think of something."

"It'd be dark magic you're asking for."

"Whatever it takes." I knew she was capable, as was Melchior. "Nico is warded and protected. Why shouldn't I be?"

Nilensi cleared her throat. "I expected you would do it yourself. Or Melchior would. Protection spells are not complex."

I felt a slight, telling tremble in her hands as she held my own.

Growing up in a place like the Nightingale, I'd seen all kinds of unsavory characters. Frequently, the sound of hammering on our door woke me in the middle of the night, when some wayward soul came to our front lawn. They were all desperate to see Zeph and to spill their secrets. I'd heard more lies than I could count, watched hundreds of card games full of bluffs and cheats.

I'd even been down in the basement with Zeph, where I'd watched thieves beg for their lives, claiming that it wasn't *they* who sold him out.

It must have been someone else.

They would never.

Though each man's tells were different, there was no stench stronger than guilt.

Nilensi was lying.

17

On the morning of my wedding day, I strapped a knife to my thigh with white ribbon while I propped my foot on the bed.

That was how Melchior found me, my entire leg exposed, tying a bow. His eyes widened as his gaze traveled along my bare skin to the tip of my satin shoes. “May I ask what you are doing?”

“In case I have to kill anyone, I want to be prepared.” I knotted it tightly around the top of my thigh.

I let the fabric of the gown fall back in place.

“You’re in blue. On our wedding day.”

“Am I only allowed black? I thought it would be nice to wear something different.” Ilya had chosen light blue. Not white nor black, not silver nor gold – sky blue. She told me that even if my marriage to Melchior was a farce, there was no reason to not look like a queen. Reluctantly, I’d agreed, then let her handle everything.

The seamstress had outdone herself, crafting the loveliest gown I’d ever laid eyes on. Ethereal, floating, blue chiffon fluttered down to the floor, with a train that stretched behind me. Small diamonds crusted the bodice and hem. Tiny sleeves drifted off my shoulders, and the neckline plunged between my breasts, forming the shape of a heart.

It was exquisite, feminine. Worthy of Hemera, Goddess of the Dawn.

Undeniably, it was the most beautiful thing I’d ever worn.

She'd selected sapphire teardrops for my ears, ones that shone with fire every time I turned my head, and my golden hair was studded with tiny diamond pins, each shaped like a small star.

Melchior seemed temporarily at a loss for words.

"Which crown should I wear?" I studied the dresser, which now had two rows of glittering headpieces.

"Whichever. Every crown has its own weight."

I trailed my finger over the edges of a silver one topped with amethysts. It was lovely, but wouldn't match the gown.

"Excited to be a princess?"

"Probably as excited as you are to be my prince."

He studied the sky-blue gown again, holding his tongue.

The clock struck five. Our wedding was in the great hall. We'd have to be going soon. But it felt like my feet were glued in place.

The winter sun streamed in, waning as night approached. The smell of evergreen and firerose filled the air. Grace chapel was full of guests, all of whom watched me. I squirmed uncomfortably and wished it was already over.

The invitees were citizens, royalty, merchants, and advisors to Atropos. In this room, I had no friends, no parents, no family, and no title. Everyone was a stranger. I felt their judging eyes upon me, feasting like vultures on my unease. I hid my calloused hands behind my back and lifted my chin.

Ten thousand gold coins.

An unimaginable sum, but was it worth my soul? Was it worth it? I'd gone from stealing a mask to marrying a man I barely knew. He'd saved my life, so now I owed it to him... but was he worth dying for?

Feeling panicked, I scanned the crowd. I spotted Nilensi and Nico first. Both mother and son eyed me from the pews, their faces grave and worried. This– me *actually* marrying him – was not part of the plan. There was no reasonable way to refuse and no excuse Melchior could make that would sound adequate, so it was happening... but this change was only going to yield more complications.

Atropos arrived. She was suddenly next to me, like a dark stain had risen from the rug. Clad in a black and gray gown, Atropos resembled a sword, sharp and long and dangerous, coldly beautiful and well-made.

"This reminds me of the wedding I was meant to have," Atropos mused.

I smiled faintly and said nothing. The pins holding my crown dug into my scalp, painfully, and I imagined blood running down onto my neck.

Melchior entered the chapel. As tradition dictated, he walked to me, down a long path between the hundreds of guests. Clad all in black, his face was perfectly expressionless as he approached Atropos and me. With his pale skin, he looked as if he were carved from marble. His eyes betrayed nothing, and were without even a hint of warmth.

Atropos held out her hand. After a brief hesitation, I took it. Her skin was ice, her nails long and pointed. I didn't flinch.

"Does Fate recognize this marriage?" asked the historian, dutifully copying the details into a thick, gilded book.

"I do."

Her obsidian eyes held mine as she leaned forward and brushed her lips over my knuckles. It was all I could do not to tear my hand from her grip and run from the room.

Atropos bound our hands together with red ribbon, wrapping it around and around, to symbolize how Melchior and I would be forever tied to one another, our destinies entwined.

The tradition was ceremonial only, not real. And yet... Apprehension tightened his features, and each time he spoke, his words were tense. Clipped.

The tips of our fingers were pricked by Atropos, her white teeth flashing a smile as she pierced my skin with a blade. Melchior and I pressed our fingertips together wordlessly, and I asked myself again how I'd gotten here. If this was really happening. Or if, somehow, I was still in my bed at Fidelisgrove, trapped in a nightmare.

"I, Melchior, take thee Malinda as my wife. To protect, love, and honor, until we are parted. This is my solemn vow, given freely."

By Death – until we are parted by Death. He'd omitted the words at the end of the vow.

I repeated the words back, my voice so soft that there were murmurs in the back of the room.

"You may kiss your bride." Atropos stepped aside.

Melchior cupped my face and leaned in, then pressed his lips to mine. I expected quick. Cold. Unfeeling and loveless. But no.

He brush his lips over mine, then lingered. An urge for entry, a hint of demand underneath. Control, mastery. My cold lips warmed under his, and I felt some of the starch leave my shoulders as I melted under the onslaught. His tongue touched mine, and suddenly my heart jumped.

He backed away.

Not that I'd ever expected anything, but I'd certainly expected less enthusiasm.

Swallowing my doubts and the sense of doom that coursed through me as I smiled at the crowd, I interlaced my fingers with his and stepped down from the dais. Once more, I scanned the audience, hoping for familiar faces. I found Ilya's, and she gave me a teary half smile. Despite how little we truly knew of each other, she had become a friend.

Atropos had organized a huge dinner, with dancing, and celebrations. There were at least double the number of people who had been at the ball, and everyone wanted to congratulate me, to speak with me, to comment on my marriage. Melchior took it in stride, but the sheer number of women who tried to speak to me or touch me quickly became overwhelming.

Every step, I was being stared at, judged. Some kneeled. Some kissed my hand. Others tried to touch the hem of my wedding gown, or my golden hair, for luck. It was overwhelming.

"Wine?" asked a servant.

"Please." I gulped the overly sweet Fae wine, and then asked for an immediate refill. Hopefully, it would help me relax. On my third glass, the curious looks, the stares were more bearable. After my fourth, I could almost pretend that I belonged here; that people weren't whispering how

Melchior had married an unknown, a princess from a faraway kingdom, the daughter of a God.

I was none of these. But they - my new people - didn't know that.

When it was time, I followed him upstairs.

With deft hands, the maids turned down the bed and scurried away, shutting the door on the music and the guests still downstairs. The shuffle of feet behind the wooden screen along one wall filled me with alarm.

A short distance away, just as he'd warned, there were no less than ten witnesses. All huddled behind an ornate screen, fashioned with peepholes. Watching us. The bed had curtains, thank God, and the room was dark but for the fire and a single candle. Yet still, it was more than enough light to know what was happening.

What would happen.

Melchior unhooked his cufflinks, toed off his boots, unhooked his baldric, and began unbuttoning his tunic.

I had to look away. Outside, it was a clear, starry night. Quiet, with a fresh layer of snow.

When he was shirtless, Melchior came to stand behind me, and put his hands on my shoulders. His touch was light.

"Pretend they aren't there," he said loudly.

As if that were possible.

He turned my body to face him, then removed my crown, taking the diamond pins from my hair. I couldn't look him in the eye, too sure that there would be only cold and ice.

The guests held their breath a few feet away.

I would endure it.

Melchior took me by the hand and led me to the bed. Then he slipped between the curtains and I followed. Melchior carefully arranged the sheer fabric behind us, making sure not even a sliver remained to peep through. It reminded me of making a tent of the clean sheets when I was small. Shutting out the sunlight, making my own world.

They could still see the outline of us, straining their eyes so that later they could claim they'd seen my naked body, covered in snakes or strange markings that could only come from demons.

"I'm going to take this off." Melchior gestured at my gown.

Wordless, I nodded. Then he lifted the fluttering blue wedding dress over my head, put it off to the side, dropped it through the slit in the sheer curtains. This made clear to our audience that I was naked.

I trembled from the cold of the room, from the feeling of a dozen gazes creeping over me. Thoroughly embarrassed, I now sat naked in front of him. He didn't look at me - he never did. When I'd been in the bath, in a towel, all those times he'd never really looked, and he didn't now. He didn't care; he felt nothing.

"Lie back," he ordered, his eyes fastened to some invisible point over my left shoulder.

I did, and stared at the fabric over our heads.

I flinched, nearly yelped, when I felt his hand slip up my leg, up my thigh. Melchior silently slipped the knife from its sheath.

As I watched, he took the knife and made a cut across his palm. Then, his eyes on mine, he placed his palm squarely between my legs - on the bed beneath me. Carefully, he smeared the blood from his own palm.

Proof. He was giving them proof of my virginity. Just in case I wasn't.

Melchior moved quickly now. He set the knife aside, then removed his pants.

I didn't look. I didn't want to see him naked. I studied the ceiling again, waiting. Then, covertly, I felt as he slid a sheet between my legs, over my stomach, up over my breasts.

Covering me. Putting a barrier between us.

If we hadn't had an audience listening to our every word, I would have thanked him.

Then he laid atop me, settling between my legs, and kissed me. His weight pressed me into the mattress, but it wasn't wholly unpleasant.

He eased back a few inches, and I could feel his questioning gaze. Waiting for me to give him a signal that I was alright, that he could continue. Briefly, with my eyes closed, I nodded. My lips pressed tightly together.

I made a small sound of surprise when he claimed my mouth.

His hand cupped my jaw, and Melchior swallowed my gasp and ran his tongue along the curve of my lip.

It was alright. It was not terrible. I could do this.

Carefully, perfectly controlled, he kissed me again.

Melchior's tongue brushed against mine, and his mouth widened.

After a minute or so, I kissed him back. I'd done this before, of course. So, I kissed him a bit harder, the way I thought he might prefer.

At first, he seemed surprised. Then, when I continued, he slid his hands up into my hair and tugged. Exposing my throat.

His mouth traveled along my neck, down to my shoulder, and he sucked and nipped along my skin. Every thought eddied from my mind and I let out a small sigh of pleasure. It'd been such a long time since I'd really kissed someone, and he was very good at it–

I'd definitely had too much wine after the wedding.

I felt his hardness between my legs as he settled against me again. Trying to smother the feelings simmering under my skin, I held myself rigidly and tried to not show any kind of physical reaction.

But I bit my lips.

An act. It was only an act. The sheet was there– saving me.

I arched my neck, giving him more access, and Melchior immediately nipped his way down, to my collarbone, to my shoulder.

His fingers he threaded through my own, then anchored my hands into the bed with his.

Despite months of being near him, I'd really only viewed Melchior as dangerous. Coldly beautiful. Not as someone I desired.

But now...Heat bloomed through my entire body as the weight of him bore down against my ribs and breasts and hips. I writhed against him - not to encourage, just to get a little closer - but the outcome was only to rock my hips against his. Horrified, I clenched my teeth and turned away, holding in a small moan.

Melchior paused. He lifted his head. Then he thrust against my core.

I was aware of how my hips immediately tilted forward to meet him, my answering gasp.

He did it again.

Then again.

It had to look convincing. The audience would see the shadows of us, and he had to seem as if he was really having sex with me. I had to seem like I was enjoying it.

I stopped clenching my legs together so tightly, letting them fall open slightly, so that when he thrust again, it would persuade them.

The sheet was old, paper thin. And I felt his shaft, the head, pressing against me, felt it–

He knew how responsive my body was.

"You feel amazing," I whispered, brokenly. I probably wouldn't have admitted it, but I had drunk several glasses of wine after the wedding, and I never drank. My face flushed, I shifted under him, trying to find the right angle–

Melchior squeezed my hands, and pressed his face against my throat. There was no danger that I might look at him. But I knew it was just the same. The intensity of his eyes, his lips, his sharp jaw, his slashing eyebrows – those dark irises always studying me, questioning, as if he were trying to figure out some question without asking me directly.

"Don't stop," I said.

So he continued.

Each thrust it felt like would enter me, would go slightly deeper, but never more than the barest amount. It was maddening.

The sheet kept his skin from mine; it kept him from being inside me. It needed to be burned on a pyre in effigy. It needed to be shredded by claws.

With my eyes still screwed closed, I slid my hands up along his chest. Up his neck, to his face. To trace his lips. I'd wanted to touch them, to see if they were as soft as they appeared. These parted as if I'd asked, and I slipped past, into his mouth. He sucked on my finger, and I felt his teeth. He bit down lightly. Not enough to bleed.

When a whimper escaped my mouth, Melchior increased his pace.

Yes, God yes, more–

When he leaned down, closer, I turned my face so that our lips crushed into each other, our tongues meeting again.

I'd never felt this way before, like I would scream if he wasn't inside me soon.

The delicious friction and pressure was enough and not nearly enough. I imagined what it would be like. If he meant it, if he weren't holding back. If he would just snatch the damnable sheet away.

I gave up trying to hide my physical reactions completely, relinquished the pretense of control. Instead I threw myself into a fire I didn't know existed, and didn't care to rein in.

Repeatedly, our pelvises met as he pushed against me.

"There," he whispered against my mouth, and his thrusts became more forceful and slower. His breathing shifted, and I kissed him harder, wanting his tongue against mine.

My arms tightened around him and I could feel the clench of his muscles under my hands, the intensity of his focus, his body–

He came in a sudden rush. Shuddering, his mouth on my throat.

Damp spread between my legs, across the white fabric between us.

We were both still. He pressed his forehead against the damp skin of my neck, inhaling and exhaling. With my right hand, I stroked his back. Comforting him. I didn't know why I did it.

Those who remained tittered, whispered among themselves.

I'd forgotten they were there. The reality of what had just happened washed over me. Fake or not, he had come. A crowd had been here to witness it.

With a frustrated groan, Melchior rolled over onto his back, looking up into the canopy.

I couldn't look at him. Unable to help myself, I sniffled, and I felt two hot tears slide from my eyes.

I felt his eyes on me, then he sighed. Melchior sat up and began putting on his pants. A few moments later, he threw aside the curtain. He exited the bed, then strode across the room and left.

Outside, the evergreens were silent. Bright stars shone in a blue-black sky. A lone elk snuffed, its breath fogging in the cold air. I began to cry in earnest.

The audience quietly filed out, casting furtive glances back at the bed as they left. Atropos, the last onlooker, quietly turned away.

18

When I awoke, I was still in the golden room, the curtains closed around me, completely naked. The sheet was still in place. The clock on the mantel ticked - it was a little after one in the morning. The fire burned low, mostly embers.

Now I was married.

It'd only been three hours since we'd entered that chamber, and yet–

It felt as if the foundation beneath my feet had cracked. I'd lived alongside him for months, and never thought anything like that was possible. I talked to him every day, ate my meals with him. Despite my reservations, we'd started to grow closer. I'd seen him as a friend, certainly nothing *more,* despite our charade.

It must have been the wine.

But when he'd looked down at me, when Melchior had touched me... I exhaled softly as I recalled how he'd parted his lips and how he sounded when he–

Stop thinking about it.

I could not. Even though he hadn't really even touched me, even though he hadn't had sex with me.

We're physically compatible. That's all. It didn't mean anything more.

I sat up and listened. Judging myself alone, I hurriedly yanked on the blue wedding dress, which was balled up on the floor. Furtively, I tiptoed from the room.

The corridors were lit by candlelight, strangely deserted. Tiptoeing down them, I tried to be soundless– I didn't want to meet anyone along the way.

When I finally reached our rooms, I dove into the familiar furs and hugged the covers around myself, squeezing my eyes shut.

Married.

And when he'd been on top of me–

I twisted the sheets between my hands.

If only there was a way for me to never see him again.

Instead, in just a few hours, probably at breakfast I'd have to face him again. Would we be expected to act married? Would we share a room from now on? Would we... would he want to or expect to have sex?

I glanced at the door that lay between our rooms, closed and foreboding. What if he wanted to talk about it? Should we? I did not want to, and I wasn't sure I could.

I watched the firelight on the ceiling, letting it all sink in, and inhaled slowly.

Exhaled and counted backwards from one hundred.

Then again.

I didn't have to talk to him - I didn't have to say anything. There was nothing to say. We had agreed to get married and to pretend to consummate the marriage, and we'd done that.

My heart slowed, and I stopped feeling the twist of panic in my belly. As my mind cleared, I analyzed the situation again.

I was married to the Prince of Darkness, son of Atropos.

I was.

There was no point in trying to pretend otherwise.

Mentally, I knew there was nothing wrong with this. Hundreds, perhaps thousands of women had lined up to become his bride. It was not the worst thing that had ever happened to me, it likely wouldn't be the worst thing that ever *would happen to me.* And yet...

I couldn't reason my way through what had happened in that bed.

He'd told me, more than once, that I was plain. Inelegant. He'd been cold and rude and dismissive. He questioned my ability and my judgment and my character, and often he seemed determined to push me away.

Yet when I'd been underneath him–

I stared at the ceiling. Tears slid from the corners of my eyes, down my cheeks, along my hair. I smeared them away.

I'd been alright during the wedding. He hadn't been unkind. He hadn't been disinterested or aloof. So even though we weren't in love, or even particularly friendly, the wedding had been uneventful. But then–

I flushed faintly. Maybe I just hadn't been emotionally or physically prepared for the chemistry between us. The sense of connection. Now that I knew, I'd be on my guard for it.

Rolling over onto my side, I stared out the arched windows into the night. It was snowing again. It was always, always snowing, It made me feel trapped.

There was no reason I couldn't talk to him about it. Maybe he was as bothered, as surprised, as I was. That was likely why he'd left so quickly.

For a moment I imagined that he would come knock on the door. Or he wouldn't knock at all - he seldom did - and instead he'd sit on the edge of the bed in silence until I had no choice but to talk to him.

It's fine, he'd say. *It meant nothing.* And he'd be right.

I closed my eyes with a long, weary sigh, and then...

Someone knocked on my door.

Shaking my head slightly, I was shocked to see that it was morning - the sky was an angry gray, and swirls of snow buffeted the doors of my balcony.

Hurriedly, I put on a robe, and rushed over. The door between Melchior and I was still closed. He hadn't come during the night, and I supposed I'd fallen asleep.

"Melchior's gone," Nilensi said as she stepped into my room, her arms full of parchment, envelopes, and an assortment of packages.

"How do you know?"

"I found this in his study." She dumped the mountain of items on the bed, and then handed me a folded piece of parchment.

My hands shook slightly as I opened it. There was no way to know what he might say.

I'll return soon.

"Is this all?" I stared at it in disbelief.

"I'm sure he'll be back in a few days." Nilensi began sorting the items on my bed.

"I know that."

"If you know, why do you look so wounded?" The witch arched an eyebrow at me.

Frowning, I sorted through the pile of items. Correspondence, invitations, congratulations, wedding presents.

"How do so many people know already? Am I expected to reply?"

"Of course. You're a princess. You must be properly polite."

She settled herself into the chair at my desk and took out a clean piece of parchment.

"I don't really want to do this right now," I began.

"Too bad. There are about a hundred more downstairs, and if you don't start, we'll never finish."

"Why start at all?"

"Because it's expected of you. And if you don't, Atropos will likely wonder if you're not taking your role seriously."

Right. Of course.

I picked up the first box, and begrudgingly opened it to reveal a golden crown made of gilded laurel leaves.

Nilensi made notes. "And who is that from?"

My gaze flicked through the card inside. "Ares. God of War."

"Lovely. We will reply graciously and tell him how you've always admired his ability to crush his enemies, and that you hope for his continued blessings."

I rolled my eyes.

The next box stank. I shook it, then sniffed at it. It smelled awful, like an old goatskin, left half full of milk in the sun. Even Nilensi seemed surprised when the brightly decorated box revealed a small, withered human eyeball.

Revolted, I turned away.

"You should keep that. Good for potion making. Who is it from?"

"Trafalagar?" I didn't recognize the name on the card.

"Ah. Leader of the Trolls of Zinbirith."

"Never heard of him," I muttered.

"Yes, well, don't tell him that. He's very easily offended." She started a new thank you note.

"Why betray Atropos?" I asked suddenly. "If you've got a good position here, and she trusts you, why bother?"

Nilensi should have expected the question. Nervously, she scratched her wrists. "She killed Nico's father. Dragged us here against our will."

"Oh. I didn't know."

"I don't like talking about it." She bowed her head, her black braids falling down into her lap. "For the first month, she kept us all in the dungeon. The only reason she let us out was because I agreed to make potions for her. By then, my mate was dead, my son very nearly."

"So you're hoping for revenge."

Nilensi looked me directly in the eye. "I'm hoping to kill her, yes."

After we were done with the presents and congratulatory letters, Nilensi and I went to the library.

I went through every grimoire, noting the spells which I found most promising. Surely something in their pages would help me; or might shield me from Atropos. Whether invisibility, stealth, luck... Anything would help. I piled the grimoires on my bed, reading until my vision blurred and my back ached from huddling over their pages. I read six different histories of the Fates.

When I finished, I went back and carefully tore out the pages I thought I might need the most, assembling them into my own collection, a strange mix of spells and incantations that gave me hope. Repeatedly,

I found my eyes drifting back to the closed door. Melchior had not returned.

Later that evening we huddled in the secret room, our first meeting without Melchior. Outside, a fierce snow storm raged, the gale whistling through the cracks in the indigo stones of Grace Castle. And although our room was warm and cozy, I shivered.

Fenix brought more news– three of the servants had been declared missing, assumed lost to the winter storm.

"What do they think happened to them?"

"Oh, you know. They wandered too far from the castle and froze to death."

"In this weather, that's probably true," Nilensi griped. "No use in having a search party unless you want more people to go missing."

I worried about Melchior. I didn't know where he'd gone, or why, but I hoped he wasn't out in the forest. Shoving the thought aside, I reminded myself that he was a descendant of the Fates, that he'd decided to leave, and that he could take care of himself.

"On a different topic, I need to have a book bound," I told the two of them.

"I'll do it." Fenix replied. He was seated by the fire, smoking a pipe. "What's in it?"

"Spells. Curses. Random things."

"You're collecting dark magic? Interesting."

"Collecting won't matter if you don't practice," Nilensi muttered, looking over her cauldron. "You have to say the words precisely as they are meant to be read."

I watched her, my elbows propped on my knees. "Can you teach me? Teach me how to do the spells and incantations?"

Nico, playing with the carcasses of a pair of dead spiders, glanced up through his dark curls.

"Why not?" Nilensi asked. "It's not as if I have much else to do."

"Just so we're all aware, you wouldn't need magic if you'd just find the mask." Fenix grumbled at me.

It was true.

"I don't know where it is. I've looked everywhere in the castle."

"Then maybe it's not in the castle," Nilensi said.

I told them about my theory about the crypts - how Atropos kept the bones of her lover beside her bed, and visited the crypts everyday.

"Well," Fenix said, "This morning I saw Atropos emerge from the minotaur crypt wearing the mask. I'll bet that's where it is kept."

Nilensi and I both turned to him. "We need to search the crypts for the Eternal Slumber."

"As soon as the forgery is done, yes."

"How much longer?" I asked.

"Soon. Maybe a day."

I started to say something, but just outside the room there was a shuffling groan, then silence. We all froze, words dying in our mouths, waiting to see if someone would attempt to turn the handle. After a long moment, it moved on.

"Atropos calls the undead *Cullen.* They who were killed, but not reaped." Nilensi whispered the words.

No longer alive but not quite dead. I thought of Demitra and shuddered.

"That would explain the number of maids that have gone missing," I replied. "Where is she keeping them? Do you know?"

Fenix kept his voice low. "Likely the dungeon. Or the crypt. But I'm not willing to go down there and find out."

I wasn't either. I'd had more than enough of the undead already, and it'd only been the one. I glanced at Nilensi, who appeared to be deeply uncomfortable with our whispered conversation.

She licked her lips nervously as she donned a pair of dragon-hide gloves. She knew far more about the undead than she was telling us. As Fenix and I sat silent, she carefully dosed the interior of the Eternal Slumber with drops of a silvery potion. These immediately dissolved, sinking into the metal and then disappearing. "There we are... One dosage. I'll add more later."

It was an intricate and stunning work of art. Just looking at the mask gave me chills, and my heart raced with a strange mix of anxiety and anticipation.

"I still feel that the eyes need to be narrower," Fenix murmured, more to himself than to anyone else. "And those symbols along the cheek should be carved deeper...they are not just decoration. They're integral to the enchantment."

Hypnotized by its beauty, I reached to pick it up.

"Don't!" Nilensi cried, and I jerked my arm backward. "Not without the gloves."

Nico, playing with a wooden toy in the corner, scowled at me as if to say, *fool*.

Nilensi had wrapped the boy in so many protective enchantments that his skin sometimes glowed like gold. I envied him – not just because of his mother's love, but because the boy was the most protected thing in the castle. Most likely, even if Atropos herself tried to cut his throat, he'd slip away unscathed.

I could use that. If only I had the spells.

"When should we go?" I asked Fenix.

"Unless you plan on staying here, *princess,* as soon as possible. I'd rather not end up in pieces, or rotting around this castle for the next fifty years."

"So we continue?" I asked. "Even without Melchior?"

"We have to. There is no other reason to be here."

"What will you do with the original? The real Eternal Slumber?"

"Destroy it." Fenix gulped down a goblet of cold water and wiped his mouth and beard with his hand. "We don't want anyone else using it."

"Was that what Melchior asked you to do?"

"He never said."

He never said? To me, that meant Melchior planned to keep it for himself, perhaps to take Atropos' place as Death.

"Mama? I'm hungry." Nico tugged at Nilensi's sleeve.

"Can you get him something from my bag?" She pointed to a satchel in the corner.

I rummaged through it, then handed Nico a bit of bread that had been wrapped in brown paper.

"We should go back to our rooms," Nilensi said. "Separately. We can discuss the plan again later."

Silent, Fenix and I nodded.

Melchior did not return by dinner. And whether that was because of the storms or because he was avoiding me, I couldn't say. With a lack of better things to do, I spent much of my time thinking of him, replaying our interactions, and dissecting the things he'd said.

I hated to admit it to myself, but seeing him was part of my daily life, and even though we hadn't meant those vows, I was now his. He left so abruptly I didn't know how to process what had happened on our wedding night, and I didn't dare talk to anyone else about it.

Still... I missed him.

At a loss, I realized that whatever feelings he might have, they were too complicated for me to understand. Melchior's behavior before our wedding and at the consummation had been so strange. There was something *off* about Melchior's motives, not just around the mask, but around bringing me here, specifically. I still didn't know why he wanted the mask at all - both his reasons and his plans were a complete secret.

If he wanted to escape Atropos, he could have just left and never returned. He didn't seem interested in using the mask– in fact, Melchior didn't seem interested in killing. He only did so when Atropos asked him to, and even then... I recalled how he'd healed Elonde instead of letting him die.

Shoving through his door, I vainly hoped to find Melchior there. If he were, we could talk through whatever I had said or done, and come to some agreement on the fake marriage and how we were going to handle it. Maybe we'd let things go a little too far on our wedding night. But it didn't need to be a big deal. It wouldn't happen again.

The room was empty and cold, the fire snuffed out.

Unable to stop myself, I lay down on his bed. It still smelled of him, and I buried my face in his pillow and inhaled.

Now I'd married him, despite all these unanswered questions. I was as ignorant about Melchior as I had been on the day we met. I still barely knew anything about him, and I couldn't even begin to understand what motivated him.

More importantly I was starting to wonder if I understood what motivated *me.*

Was it ten thousand gold pieces?

Or the thrill of stealing something from Death?

Was it simply making Zeph proud, and proving that I could be more than who I had been?

Was it because Melchior had shown me kindness, one of the only people in my life who ever had? Because I felt like I owed him?

Whatever it was, I hadn't been thinking about the mask. I'd kissed him and touched him, and the act itself... I hadn't anticipated how it would affect me. How much I wanted his touch, to feel his skin against mine. To hear his breath hitch when I kissed his neck. All of that was just physical, of course.

Against all odds, maybe I liked him. Liked the Prince of Darkness. Sometimes I even felt that he was somehow a kindred soul, a light in the dark. Despite his hot and cold behavior and secrecy, despite his awful mother.

I rolled onto my back and stared up at his ceiling. It was probably for the best that we hadn't really had sex. If I was this conflicted about merely touching him, I couldn't imagine how it would feel if I had true feelings for him.

After another hour of waiting, when he still did not return, I forced myself to my feet and went back to my room to read.

DISCORPORATION SPELL

Spiritus, a corpore disiungo,
Per alas noctis, per umbras mundi,
Hanc animam libero, vincula frango,
Per hoc potio, fata recondi.

AFTER DOSAGE, SOUL DISASSOCIATION OCCURS WITHIN TWO HOURS. THIS WILL BE VISIBLE IN THE FORM OF A GRAY THREAD, TYPICALLY FOUND AROUND THE FEET. THREAD CAN BE GATHERED AND STORED.

19

I've always thought bad things don't happen on sunny days. For some reason, when a new day dawned with a bright blue sky overhead, and the air was warm and breezy, it seemed like everything would go my way. There were no ominous clouds and no gusting of frigid wind beating at the windows, and the light on the ocean made the water look a lovely sapphire instead of inky gray... Despite Melchior's absence, I felt hopeful.

Off to my left, a flock of noisy crows roosted on the parapet, squabbling in the unexpected warmth. Behind me, lying on my bed, was a velvet bag.

Fenix's forgery.

I pushed it from my mind as I regarded the waves, breathing deeply the scent of salt and sea. It'd only been two days, but his absence grated on me. He was clearly avoiding me, questioning his decision. I didn't believe he was on an errand, nor did I think he was captive in the dungeon. He just didn't want to see me.

Which was fine.

Pushing him from my mind, I focused on the plan. Today, I would go get the mask. I'd find the mask in the crypts, swap the real one for the forgery. If I dressed and left now, I'd likely be back before dinner. I had everything I needed.

There was time for one last prayer to Nyx before going back inside. The fire was crackling, the curtains were drawn back, and it was warm and cheerful. I watched the flames licking at the logs and wondered if I was stalling.

Don't get yourself killed, Nilensi told me, when she'd delivered the forged mask sometime after midnight.

It was stupid, but I'd held onto a vague, ridiculous hope that he'd appear and demand to know what was happening. Surely we wouldn't carry out his plan without him. I wouldn't face whatever monsters waited in the crypt, alone... would I?

I felt a sinking sense of doom as I tied the velvet bag to a ribbon which I looped around my neck like a collar. This would hold the Eternal Slumber in place under my cloak and gown. Difficult to reach, but it would keep my hands free. Just in case there were more Cullen in the crypt, and I needed my knives. I was just walking into the bathing area when behind me, I heard the sound of the door creaking.

I whirled and found Melchior standing in the center of my bedroom. Clad all in black, his hair wild, as if he'd been raking his hands through it. He smelled as if he'd been drinking and sleeping in the woods, like tree bark and snow and wine.

"You're back," I said, after a lengthy pause.

He looked me up and down, as though inspecting me for injuries.

"I am."

No apology. No explanation.

He wasn't dead. He wasn't injured. He hadn't been cursed or disappeared into an abyss or been kidnapped by Cullen, not eaten by gargoyles.

He reeked of alcohol. He'd been in a brothel, for all I knew.

I felt torn between a desire to cry and punch him in the face. I bit the inside of my cheek, fighting to hold in all the furious things I wanted to say.

You disappeared. I didn't even want to marry you. I certainly didn't want to have sex with you with a bunch of onlookers. You made me do it then abandoned me for it. Why are you doing this? Why do you even care? Is this all so that you can become king?

I didn't say anything.

Whatever this was between us was, he'd done it to us both. He'd found me, he'd brought me here, and now he'd irrevocably tied us together. At that moment, I resented him so intensely I felt like bludgeoning him to death.

"I just wanted you to know."

My jaw tightened. "I'm not sure why you think I would care."

Melchior gave a thin smile. "I consider it appropriate to inform my *wife* that I've returned."

My wife.

I gave him an answering scowl of my own. "I would consider it appropriate to tell *your wife* that you were leaving ahead of time."

I scanned the room, making sure I hadn't forgotten anything. My knives were tucked into the pockets of my gown, the mask was tucked securely under my arm.

"Now if you'll excuse me. I have other things to do."

He caught my arm. "Where are you going?"

"Funny. I thought we were the sort of couple who doesn't share details like that."

Yanking my arm away, I rushed out of the room, fully expecting him to catch me in the hall.

But he didn't follow.

I made my way down the stairs, through Grace Castle. As if I had nowhere else to be. As if there wasn't a forged mask nestled below my armpit. As if the dead wandering around me were none of my concern.

Grace Castle's corridors were quiet, nearly empty. However, they weren't completely empty. There was a Cullen sitting in the corridor.

Undead. Rotting. Its strange yellow eyes peered up at me, and then it returned its gaze to its ankle, which was falling apart. It picked at the loose, gray flesh, then ate it. Idly.

What in the name of Zeus? I hurried by, convinced that it would lunge after me while my back was turned.

"Do *not* panic," I muttered to myself. "Those ten thousand gold pieces are almost within your grasp."

Now that we knew where the mask was, within days, I would leave this wretched place, richer than anyone I'd ever known. From there, I could do anything. Be anyone. Buy my own castle, far away from Melchior and Atropos.

I pushed open one of the arched side doors and stepped out into the bright world. The stone walls, with their deceptive promise of security, fell away behind me and I breathed a sigh of relief. It was a beautiful day, the kind that filled my chest with hope—like a thousand butterflies were caught inside, beating against my ribs.

I hadn't been outside in the sunlight in so long. Taking deep, heady inhales of the fresh air, I headed down a well-worn path. Snow snapped and cracked beneath my leather boots. The air carried the scent of burning wood and evergreen, of mulled wine and cider. I would have liked to linger, hiking around the castle, if only to pretend that I didn't have to go back inside. To let my skin soak in the few rays of warmth.

Ahead, the graveyard loomed, an expanse of silence and stone that seemed to call out to me. You would think that entering a graveyard would make someone feel dread, but my heart was noticeably lighter the instant I made it through the gates. The walk here from the castle was open, without any place to hide. The fact that I'd made it this far proved that the Cullen weren't on a mission to kill me.

Not yet anyway.

If they had been interested, Cullen could have snatched me off the path, dragged me back into the castle, or snapped my neck. Instead, the Cullen I saw left me alone, shuffling along on their various errands with their strange limping walk. Teeth chattering, vacant eyes... not dead, but certainly not alive.

Focus.

My fingers traced the hilt of the dagger hidden beneath my cloak, a small comfort against uncertainty. With every step, the adrenaline surged stronger, as if I could feel the rush of blood through my veins, like a drumbeat urging me on.

As I threaded between tombstones and toward the crypts, the tiniest bit of optimism buoyed my steps. Now that I knew what to expect, and I was well-armed and emotionally prepared, I didn't think that retrieving the mask would be too difficult. All I had to do was get into the crypt, retrieve the mask, and replace it with the forgery. From there, all the other details would take care of themselves.

"Malinda," a voice called out behind me, smooth as silk and twice as dangerous. "Wait!"

For a moment – an idiotic, ridiculous moment – I thought it might be Melchior. That he'd come after me, and now I wouldn't have to do this alone.

Julian emerged from behind an angelic statue, his smile lopsided and his ocean-colored eyes gobbling me up. I realized he was much taller than I'd thought, and more muscular. He grinned at me, and I noticed immediately the reek of ale. His dark hair was slicked back, wet from a recent shower.

"Julian," I greeted coolly, tucking a stray lock of hair behind my ear as I assessed him.

Would I be able to reach my knife in case I needed it?

He stepped closer, his presence now impossible to ignore. "I saw you from the window. You seemed in quite a hurry," he observed, a sinister note underlying his words. "One might think you're eager to join the dead."

"Perhaps I'm just escaping them," I retorted, forcing lightness into my tone. "Or have you not noticed the halls of your castle?"

"It does seem a bit changed since I was here last," he admitted.

"Not for the better." I hoped Julian would admit he didn't like Cullen either, and be an ally.

Julian tilted his head in feigned sympathy. "Do they bother you?"

I met his gaze, searching for the intent behind his scrutiny, aware that I shouldn't be completely honest, but also that he would probably sense a lie.

"Yes," I conceded, letting the word hang between us, thick with unspoken implications. Our conversation felt like a dance on the edge of a cliff—one wrong step and I'd find myself plunging into an abyss. He was far too close, and I needed to make sure my secrets were kept carefully guarded.

"Would you like me to protect you from them?"

He looked at me with a lasciviousness that made me shudder.

"I'm a man who believes in reciprocity. If you're good to me, I'm good to you." His blue-green eyes held a strange glint, and I didn't really want to think about what he might mean. Or what his definition of good might be.

"You know, Malinda, I think the atmosphere has improved since I was here last. You're here; Melchior's not." Julian's voice had the smoothness of silk, but it was the sort that suffocated if wrapped too tightly.

"He's back," I replied, eyes narrowing as I read his intentions. "He's upstairs."

"Ah, then we'd better make this quick."

He stepped closer, and I could smell the earthy scent of moss and stone clinging to him—a reminder of graves and secrets. Still I tried to smile politely, to pass it off as non-threatening.

"What do you mean?" I took a cautious step back, feeling the warmth of the sun on my shoulders.

"I'd like to show you something. It just might be *exactly* what you're looking for."

I feigned disinterest while my heart raced. "I'm not looking for anything."

"Aren't you?" There was a sick triumph in his smile as if he'd already won some unspoken game. "I've stumbled upon something... intriguing. Something I believe you'll find particularly interesting."

"Is that so?" I kept my response noncommittal, though curiosity gnawed at me.

"Indeed. But words do it no justice. It must be seen. Held. *Worn.*" He gestured to the nearby skulls crypt, its door like a maw ready to swallow us whole.

"Worn?" A cold shiver traced my spine. Now I was certain; he knew where the Eternal Slumber was. Despite my better judgment, I was intrigued, and it showed on my face.

"Come. I'll show you." Julian's hand closed around my arm with unexpected force, his fingers biting into my flesh.

Considering his hand, I knew I had moments to make a decision. I could pull away and insist on going back inside the castle. I could wait and see if he left, then make my way down into the crypts.

Or I could investigate, and see what this item was.

"Fine," I agreed. "Show me."

Julian leered at me, though I couldn't be sure if that was due to the strange scar around his mouth or just the general feeling he gave me.

He whirled away, tugging me along behind him as he navigated the headstones, striding toward the crypt with the columns of carved skulls and thorns. Next to it sat the crypt with the Pegasus sculptures, their wings spread wide... and I wondered if anyone had found Demitra's decapitated body yet.

"Are we going in there?" I asked, desperation seeping through my words.

Julian urged me toward the crypt. "Trust me," he murmured, his deep voice velvety. "You won't regret this."

I most assuredly would. I already regretted it, and we hadn't yet entered the door. Every instinct screamed at me to flee, to run and hide, to escape him now while I was still in the daylight. But I had this realization too late, as Julian had already opened the door to the skull crypt and hauled me inside.

The dank chill clawed at my skin and I twisted, trying to jerk my arm away, but his grip was a shackle I couldn't break. I wished desperately – desperately– that Melchior knew where I was. Or, even better, that it was him here with me instead of Julian. Even if Julian bore me no ill will, I had no desire to face whatever might lurk in these rooms with him by my side.

I had no reason to believe he wouldn't readily sacrifice me, just so that he could have the mask. Perhaps I was bait, a distraction, so that he would have a chance at stealing it for himself.

And now, because of my own stupidity, I had no choice but to go with him.

"It's just a little further," Julian coaxed, his tone incongruously gentle.

I'd already gone too far. Alarms went off in my mind, my skin crawled as he steered me into the darkness. Our footsteps heavy on the marble stairs, overly loud in the empty space, Julian firmly gripped my arm and took me down into the abyss.

Away from the light.

20

Water dripped.

I tried to remember what happened, but it was a blank. At some point, I'd struck my head—or Julian had hit me. Gingerly, I felt the place where it throbbed; my fingers came away damp with blood.

He hadn't killed me. Not yet.

That, most likely, was not the goal. The goal was for us to be alone. Down *here.* I woke up alone, without Julian, but I knew he'd return. It was possible he thought I was dead or dying, and more likely that he'd been interrupted and called upstairs. Perhaps he intended to keep me prisoner indefinitely.

There were no windows, so no sun nor moon light. No way to tell how much time had passed. It might be day or night. No torch lit the corridor of cells. I didn't like the dark, but I was sure that I'd like being his captive even less.

My wrists were chained to the floor with cuffs bolted to the stone, with enough give so that I could touch myself, but little else. I could do nothing but lay here, face up, unable to see anything.

Slowly, I explored with my feet, stretching as far as they could reach. Dreading the moment I might find bones or some rotting corpse. In the worst case, I thought I'd find a filthy chamber pot. But I found nothing, almost as if the cell was completely empty. Nothing but darkness within its four walls. Not even a piece of straw to pick a lock.

I couldn't search with my hands. There wasn't enough give in the chain. But it wouldn't surprise me if he'd taken my knives. Thankfully Zeph's poison ring was still on my finger. At least I had that.

Soon Melchior would realize I was gone. Although perhaps he'd think I was avoiding him, or that I'd rather be alone. If only I'd waited and he'd been with me. If only I had mentioned where I was going. If only I'd never come to this wretched place.

It felt like ages before I heard the first sound - the screech of door hinges, then footsteps coming nearer. Out in the corridor, a torch flared as it came into view – he slid it into an iron holder and it cast an eerie orange glow over the cell.

My stomach clenched in fear as I watched him turn a key in the lock, open the door, and saunter in.

"Forgive my absence. I went to get provisions for our time together." Julian held up a knife, some food, rope, and a scrap of red lace.

"I'm very excited to spend time alone with you, Malinda."

I faked courage I didn't feel. "You aren't going to get away with this."

Julian laughed. "I already have. My mother encourages this sort of thing. No one else cares."

I shivered as he loomed over me, pressing my back against the stone. I didn't want those big, clenching hands on me.

"Now nothing will interrupt our fun."

Julian fell to his knees.

His fingers dug into my shoulder and gripped so tightly I couldn't pull away. I could smell the sour on his breath - Fae wine, and body odor, something coppery.

"Here we are," he said, and then took a firm hold of my gown and yanked downward, ripping the cloth asunder.

I screamed.

"Hush now." Julian slid his hand under the fabric and squeezed my right breast painfully, twisted my nipple between his fingers. "These are incredible, aren't they?"

He exhaled slowly, his eyes closed, like a child opening a coveted gift.

Then he leaned over so his body was atop mine. He tried to kiss me on the mouth but I snapped my head away and his mouth lips on my hair instead.

"When I first saw you sitting at that dinner table I wanted to fuck you right there. I always tell my brother it's not who is first that counts, it's who is *last.* I intend to be the last man you ever have, Malinda."

"You're insane."

"Really? I know what you're doing. I know how my brother plans to dethrone Atropos. How he hired you to help him do it. You have the face of an angel, but the heart of a snake. And if you want me to keep your secrets so my mother doesn't flay you alive and serve you as a meal..."

He shivered with anticipation. Slowly, he pulled my dress up beyond my thighs. I kicked and writhed, trying to escape him, shouting for help.

"Shut up," he said calmly, slapping me across the face. My vision swam along the edges, blurred, and folded in on itself.

"I can't wait to see what you're wearing under all this black," he growled. "The maid said Melchior likes red, so I hope you don't mind me going through your drawers."

I started crying as he caressed me, his breath hot and putrid on my neck. Panic coursed through my veins, but I had no time to process it. Julian was on top of me, biting my neck, his knees forcing my legs apart. I couldn't think; I couldn't focus.

My cries were muffled and useless. I struggled against him, my mind racing as I tried to come up with a plan to escape this nightmare, but I knew I was completely at his mercy.

I cut my hands open on the hard edges of the stones, ripped my nails trying to find something to hold onto. To hit him with.

"Be still," he ordered.

I felt his hands tearing, shoving at my body. In a flash of inspiration, I pretended to return his kiss. Then I bit his cheek. Hard. Harder. Until a chunk of his flesh was in my mouth, sopping and bleeding and dribbling over my lips like raw meat. I spit it at him.

"You bitch!" His fist slammed into my throat and squeezed.

My head lolled back as he jerked me forward. "I'll make you regret that. I'll leave you here for days."

I cried out but couldn't move, held fast by the iron manacles that locked me to the floor.

His hands crawled over me like hairy spiders, and I began to cry. If I didn't stop him... I shuttered my emotions, closing them into a box that I locked and shoved to the very back of my mind.

Do not panic. Do not cry. We have to act. We have to be quick. Like Zeph taught us.

Zeph!

I suddenly remembered the ring on my hand. He said to use it whenever I was in trouble, whenever a man wouldn't let me go. That it should only be used in emergency situations. This, I decided, was definitely an emergency.

Quickly, I thumbed at the compartment on the ring. It was meant to be opened with a flick, so I dug my thumbnail under its edge and pressed upward. I didn't know if it was a poison powder or liquid or a pill, but I immediately pulled my hand close to my face, with a vague hope that somehow I could get my fist inside of Julian's mouth, that way he might inhale or lick the poison that lay inside the ring.

It was not a well-thought out plan.

Nevertheless, the ring sprung open helpfully, and a small object fell out. It dropped onto my face, and I tried to catch it– hoping that it was a poisonous pill to spit into Julian's mouth. To do that, I figured I would have to pretend to kiss him.

However, the second that the item touched my face, it began to move.

Not like a pill or a powder... but like a living thing. Some sort of insect, with tiny legs.

Startled, I shook my head. And the bug, or whatever it was, scurried across my cheek and my lips, then leapt onto Julian's face.

"Argh!" he shrieked. "What in the Gods was that?!"

I couldn't answer, because I didn't know what it was.

Julian gasped. A sharp, painful inhale. I couldn't quite see because it was still so dark, despite the torch, but I saw him scrape at his own throat. Like he might want to take a knife to it and let out whatever it was that just crawled inside him.

Did it burn? Did it creep up his nose?

"Get it out!" Julian screamed, suddenly lurching away. "Get it out!"

He clutched at his head, digging his fingertips into his hair. "Out out out out–"

Dragging his fingernails down his face, clawing at his own skin, I watched as flesh peeled away, furrowing.

He pitched forward, landing hard on his knees, his screaming going from high pitched to guttural, until he fell forward face first onto the stone and then began scraping his face along the rock. First his forehead, then his nose.

I turned away, and he clutched at my leg. "Get out!" he screamed again.

Shaking uncontrollably, I held my breath until he finally stopped kicking and struggling. Until he was still.

Then, as I watched in shock, the small creature crawled out of his ear. Light purple, with a vivid green blob for a head, it closely resembled a caterpillar. Tiny, cute, inconsequential. It scuttled toward me, and even though I flailed away, it walked straight onto my hand and settled back into its seat - squarely in the poison compartment of the ring.

I glanced over at Julian, who was unquestionably dead.

"Good job," I said to the bug.

"And good riddance," I said to Julian.

"Diamonds and glass," Zeph said as he inspected the ring I'd stolen. "Not many can tell the difference, but this is a well-orchestrated fake."

"How?" I asked. "It looks real enough." I took it from the wealthiest man in town.

"Powerful people are easy to fool. They believe they control everything, that because they have wealth and title, no one would dare deceive them."

He handed it back to me. "Keep it."

"What for?" I'm sullen, unsatisfied.

"It's still beautiful, and those who would judge its value will always be wrong."

I walked through the woods and golden light streamed through the leaves. Daffodils grew by the brook and a blue and white butterfly perched on a stone at the water's edge–

I remembered the dream when I woke up. A few steps away, Julian's body formed a small mountain, like a crumpled pile of laundry. He thought he was too powerful to lose, yet he had.

With every ounce of strength I possessed, I pulled at the chains. I tugged and begged and twisted, and still both of my hands remained bound. My wrists were slick with blood, yet I could not pull them free.

I cried for help as loudly as I could, repeatedly, until my voice gave out.

No one heard.

I was trapped.

Trapped here in the crypt, with no way to escape.

Here and there I slept, dipping in and out of consciousness like it was a pool.

Periodically, I heard strange clicking sounds. Like someone had brought a clock into the dungeon and sat it in the corner. Someone wanted me to know I was running out of time; they were counting the seconds until I starved to death, until I gave up.

Seconds, minutes, hours; they bled together, punctuated by my screams.

It had been a mistake to come to the crypt, to implement the plan. But someone would come. Melchior or Atropos, Nilensi or Fenix. Someone would realize where I was, and they would come find me. They would remove the chains from my wrist that tethered me down here in the darkness. That was what I told myself, those first few hours.

When no one came, I couldn't quite believe it. Surely someone had noticed that I was missing. They'd known I was going to look in the crypts, wouldn't they conclude that maybe I was trapped? Wouldn't anyone try to find me? Julian claimed that Atropos had sent him to the graveyard – that's what he said. I didn't know why he'd lie, but he didn't seem like the sort of man to tell the truth, either.

I supposed it was fitting- I'd always been apart, unloved, unwanted. In some ways, dying alone was expected. To keep myself company while I waited, I talked to Zeph as if he were there. As if he could still give me advice, or rescue me somehow.

You play your cards right, he'll make you his queen.

How right he had been, and how wrong. I was now married to Melchior, but far from a queen. I was chained to the floor, beaten, and was probably going to starve to death before anyone found me.

I rattled my chains and screamed for help again.

"Can anyone hear me? Hello! I'm in here!"

Eventually, Melchior would come looking for me.

I fell asleep and dreamed of our wedding night, and in my dreams it went much differently. *I love you. I long for you. You're beautiful.*

Maybe if I had not been so distant and untrusting, we might have had a chance. The barest sliver, buried in the darkest recesses of my heart, believed in him. Trusted that Melchior would come. I waited, holding onto that hope.

I turned my head toward the door of the cell and saw a torchlight. Unblinking, I stared at it until it seemed as if the shadows around it formed a man, and the man reached out a massive hand and took hold of the bars.

There was utter silence, like every sound had been sucked from the room and cool darkness washed over me. It felt like rain. Then footsteps. I thought I heard them so many times, and every time was a lie. No savior.

Just the silent oblivion of the dark, and my own heart echoing.

21

"Pick her up," said a soft, feminine voice. It was Ilya. "Get her inside."

Warm hands slid over me, lifting me easily into the air, and a rough voice whispered into my hair.

"I'm here. I've got you."

Melchior cradled my body against his chest. I blinked up at the towering mist, and slowly it fell away to reveal the jaw I knew, the cold black eyes that always followed me around the room. I began to sob before he'd even left the cell, clinging to Melchior as he stepped over Julian's body.

It was night. And the moon, glowing white, burned my eyes. Melchior was cloaked in shadows, obsidian mist wreathed his shoulders and fell to his feet, surrounding him like storm clouds. "Ilya," I said brokenly. "How did you know where to find me?"

Her sweet voice never answered.

Melchior's face was hard as he carried me through the snow, back into the castle, up the stairs to our room. Scrapes on my back throbbed with every step. Even breathing was agonizing, from the bruising on my ribs and chest.

Overwhelmed with relief, I twisted my hands into any part of him I could touch– his shirt, his cloak, his shadows. He was alive; I could see him and feel him and know that we were both still alive. One tear, then two, misted my eyes.

They rolled down my face.

Then I was crying, sinking. I fell apart too fast to hide it, with wretched, uncontrollable sobbing. He did not say it would be alright, he did not ask me to feel better.

I cried and cried, raw despair leaching out of me in wave after wave.

Melchior put me down on the bed and fell to his knees, ripping off his gloves and cloak. His face was twisted with fury as he took in my condition, the shredded gown, the bite marks on my chest, the bruises on my ribs and throat.

Kneeling next to the bed, he used his fingertips to draw a series of symbols across my skin. They glowed red as they seeped in, and I gasped as an astringent burning began in my chest. Intent, his gaze skimmed my legs, my arms, down to my bleeding fingers where I'd torn off several fingernails.

White with rage, Melchior healed those too. He was steady handed, even though his voice shook with anger every time he spoke. "It's alright. I'll take care of you."

With my eyes, I begged him never to leave me again as he cleaned all the blood off me.

He drew me a bath, then carried me into the steamy room. I smelled like piss and blood, and it didn't seem to bother him at all.

Melchior stripped me nude without comment, tossing the mask onto the counter. Then he deposited me in the water. "Do you want me to go–"

"Don't leave." *Please,* I silently pleaded.

He waited as I sat in the steaming water, letting its warmth wash me clean. After the water drained away, Melchior dressed me and put me in his bed. I traced the pillowcase with shaky fingers. It was silk. It smelled like him. I curled into a tight ball, trying to force myself to stop shivering.

Sometimes food appeared. Melchior fed me calmly, patiently, and then I went back to sleep. I couldn't be sure if he left or stayed, but it seemed that whenever I opened my eyes, Melchior was holding my hand, threading his fingers through mine. I listened to the clock on the mantel, the hands sweeping across the face.

When I came back to the surface of myself, it felt unfamiliar. As if I'd lost track of time, like it had wandered off into the woods and I didn't know which way to get home.

Melchior was next to me, his back against the headboard, reading another of the grimoires. He felt me studying him via the golden glow of the lamp.

I could see the tension in his jaw and the hard line of his mouth, the stillness he forced upon his body.

"Are you alright?"

He didn't say *I told you so,* or *I told you not to go without me.*

Maybe that was why.

Slowly, I leaned over and pressed my lips to his. Soft. A brush. I lingered, then he sighed. Despite his obvious hesitation, I pressed closer. I wanted to lose myself in his scent, in his taste. To reassure myself that I was still here, still alive, and so was he.

I kissed him. I wanted to feel his weight on me again. So I tugged him on top of me, slid my fingers into his hair. My body knew him, and I dampened, ached, yearned for him.

"Undress or I'll do it for you." My voice rasped. I hoped he wouldn't argue.

Melchior stilled, then drew back. I opened my eyes and acknowledged what I was saying. His gaze, searing and silent, burned a path to my soul.

"Please." I trailed my hands up the front of his shirt, seizing on the buttons, starting to undo them. "I need you to."

And I did. I needed him to anchor me, to give me something, anything, that was warm and meaningful. I thought he would say yes.

Shaking his head, he pulled away. "That is the last thing you should be doing."

My hands were still on his chest, some of the buttons undone, and he was telling me no. I twisted the cloth of his shirt in my hands.

"Why? What's wrong?"

I could tell he wanted me; that much was obvious. Why wouldn't he just take me, when I was here, in his bed, offering?

Melchior sat up, and the cold air between us was like a burn across my skin. His expression was bitter.

"Is it because of what happened?" I asked. "Because of Julian?"

"What? No. We just... I'd rather we talk first."

Talk?

I'd married him, and he could barely stand to touch me. I tried not to let his rejection hurt my feelings; told myself that there were much bigger things to be upset over. It didn't matter that he didn't want me. That we could talk. I sat up in the bed, across from him. "How did you and Ilya know where to look for me?"

Melchior sounded distinctly uncomfortable when he answered. "That's not her name. Your friend Ilya the seamstress isn't real. Or rather, she is, but... It's Lachesis. Using a false name."

"Lachesis helped you find me? The Controller of Time?"

"Yes."

Open mouthed, and eyes wide, I was flabbergasted. "She's been here the whole time, pretending to be a seamstress?"

"Apparently."

"She was at our wedding," I said, shocked. "I saw her in the crowd... Wouldn't Atropos recognize her?"

"Lachesis can enter points in time and witness them without others noticing. She can freeze time for everyone but one person, or speed it up. Those things are well within her abilities."

In stunned silence, I digested his words. If what he was saying was true, then Time was the most powerful of the Fates. Life and Death were merely there, like a pair of bookends, but time was everything in between them, twisted or straight, backward and forward. Manipulating every minute.

"Why would she care?"

Melchior shifted, brushed a spec of lint off his pants. "She has a strong interest in keeping you alive."

"Why? What's so special about me?"

At last he answered. And when he did, the words were not what I expected.

"She wants me to be happy."

That didn't make sense either. "Why would the Controller of Time care if you're happy?"

"Because." Melchior gave a deep sigh. "Lachesis was my lover."

"Your what?" I stood, my head spinning. His words were only half of the truth - I felt it in my bones. Like a house built on sand, it stood well enough until there was the slightest breeze. Something in me itched and I went to stand by the window. I needed fresh air. The room felt small and hot, and I wanted cold.

Melchior followed me, leaving the bed. "Before you, my only meaningful relationship was with her."

Was. Past tense. Still, it felt like I couldn't breathe. Like some invisible thing squeezed me tightly, held my heart captive.

"When?"

"It started when I was eighteen. She came here to check on Atropos. We... It wasn't a good idea, but I didn't have many of those back then. I was too angry, too violent. And she was kind. It's most likely because of her that I'm not a violently insane."

Every time I inhaled, it felt as though a knife flayed my insides.

"Does Atropos know?"

Melchior was adamant. "Of course not. She'd kill us both if she did."

An understatement. If Atropos knew Lachesis was regularly in her house, in a relationship with her son... I couldn't imagine what she would have done. Whatever it was, there would be lots of torture involved. She wouldn't let either of them die quickly.

"It was Lachesis who started me on the path of the grimoires and learning dark magic. I was mostly drinking, wasting away. I didn't know what to do with my life, but I didn't want to be like Atropos."

"So, Lachesis helped you dig out of the abyss." She gave him a reason to be a better person, crafted him into a *good* person. For some reason I didn't feel like thanking her.

Melchior nodded. "She's the one who told me about my mother having the mask made, and how her powers had been revoked. Until then, I didn't even know– didn't realize she'd lost some powers, gained others. Atropos kept everything secret. Not that I would have necessarily noticed."

He'd loved her. I could hear it in his voice. *He'd loved her.* And I'd been under him a few minutes ago, begging him to have sex with me. I could have died of shame.

I swallowed over the lump in my throat. "So that's why you don't want me." My voice cracked faintly.

"I never said I didn't want you." His words were stern.

True, but he'd never said he did, either.

"The last time I saw her was three years ago. She showed up in my room, near hysterical. She'd skipped ahead, examining my future. She thought it'd be *our* future, so she used her ability to control time to go forward through my entire life."

Melchior took my shoulders and turned me to face him.

"She told me about you. How you were going to face a Keres in an alley, and I was going to step in and save you. And that I would sit in your kitchen. She made quite a big deal about how I touched your bare skin, when I didn't even know your name."

He took a deep, shaky inhale. "I told her that wasn't true. I would never do that. I would never touch another woman because I only loved her. But she had seen it. She screamed at me... Described our wedding night to me in graphic detail."

Melchior gazed intently at my face, his eyes searching mine. "She had it all written down, page after page, in a Chronos. She gave it to me, just to prove she was telling the truth."

I felt myself pale. "You didn't tell me any of this."

"Would you have believed me?"

Probably not. Especially not when we first met.

His dark eyes skimmed over my face. "For a long time, I hated you. Even though you were just a girl when I found out, a thief in a random city... It ruined the only bit of joy I had. Lachesis shut me out after that, refused to see me, refused to talk to me. I wrote to her of course. Berated her for inspecting my future, then pleaded with her to come back, apologized for things I hadn't even done yet."

Oh.

"I see." I couldn't help but notice the bitterness in his tone. And truthfully, I didn't blame him. Melchior had so few people in his life. No friends. No family other than Julian and Atropos, who were unhinged murderers. As a result, he was silent. Withdrawn. Always carefully controlled. He rarely — maybe never — touched other people.

"Was she... that is... your only... I mean..."

"Yes. She was. At that point."

He'd been alone here, trapped in this castle, year after year... But not completely alone. For much of it, he'd had Lachesis. And then he'd lost her, because she'd seen his future with me.

"So that's why you were so strange when we met. Like you knew me, acting as if you hated me." Sullen and withdrawn, yet interested by turns, cordial and then like he wanted to never see me again.

"I've read about our relationship too many times to pretend that I don't know anything about you."

"And you didn't tell me."

"No."

I swallowed. Tried, and failed, to find more words.

"I didn't see her again until the week before I met you. She told me it was now, now, I had to pack and leave right now, or else I wouldn't be there in time to save you. I was drunk. So I told her to manipulate it– to have Julian rescue you, or a neighbor, anyone. I said I didn't care, that I hoped the Keres ripped you apart, and she laughed. She called me a liar and vanished."

And then he'd come. He had come to rescue me. Because he'd been too alone, or too curious, or because he'd lost so much for me that it would have been stupid to let me die.

"Did you see her again after I got here? After we met?"

"I didn't even know she was at the wedding until you asked about the woman in blue, and then you wore that blue dress– it was familiar, her style. I didn't know she was your Ilya. I just assumed you were trying to make friends. That you were lonely."

Maybe I had been, but Lachesis had simply taken advantage of it. She suggested I wear blue - not because I should, but so it would remind him of *her*. Then she sat and watched me marry him.

And clearly, it had worked. He had thought of her the entire time.

"You went to Lachesis after our wedding night." It wasn't a question. Somehow I knew he had, and the betrayal of it felt like someone hollowing out my bones with a spoon.

"I needed to speak with her." His tone was clipped, cool. As if he were announcing that it might rain.

Even though I knew it, to hear him admit it was shocking.

Bewildered, I gave a ragged gasp and turned away from him so he couldn't see my face. He was alive, and he'd come back, and he'd saved me from the crypt. But Lachesis was still the one he loved. He didn't want me. He might have left me there to die, if she hadn't forced him to save me.

It felt a little like I'd been stabbed, like I was wounded, flailing and dying and wanting to be as far from my attacker as possible. I suspected he was still lying to me, even though I didn't know why or about what. Despite my skill for deception, I found myself unable to pretend anymore. He'd gone and stayed with *her*. I tried desperately to hold in all the rage I felt, putting it behind stone walls.

It shouldn't bother me. Our marriage was fake. Every kiss, every kindness, none of that was real.

Yet somehow–

Melchior waited for me to say something else, but I couldn't. I couldn't. At some point, in our efforts to convince everyone we were a couple, I'd convinced myself. I'd almost been raped by his brother; an undead woman had nearly ripped me apart, a mythical dog had chased me down a magically expanding corridor, I ate almost every meal sitting across from Death, and now I was rapidly realizing that I'd fallen in love with him.

My chest constricting, I gave a hollow laugh. I'd played my part so well that I'd convinced myself. The tension, the dinners, the secret glances, the kisses, the wedding. A ridiculous game, a ploy intended to trick his mother… a lie that, in the end, I had believed.

"Get out."

"Malinda."

"You *abandoned* me here to go have sex with someone else."

"I would never–"

"You think I'm nothing, nobody, a useful fool. Now that I've tied my life to yours, you think you can just exploit me as you please?" There was nothing but this feeling of betrayal inside my chest, the lash of despair.

"Of course not. That's not what's happening."

I stared at the floor. "Did you ever even intend to steal the mask, or was that just a lie to get me here?"

"What?"

"You have no problem lying and manipulating me to get what you want. You took me away from my home, from *my life,* just so you could see if I would live up to her journal entries? And now what? What was the point?"

He stared at me, his face twisted with anger. "Why?" He bared his teeth, snarling. "Because you're my destiny. My wife, even though I've never had any choice in the matter."

"Then don't be with me!" I threw up my hands in frustration. "If I'm so terrible, why did you go through with it? If you hate me so much, why bother saving me? Why come back at all? You could have stayed with Lachesis and left me to die, why didn't you?"

"I don't know!" he shouted. "I don't know why!"

My stomach flipped. "On our wedding night, when–when we—"

"I don't want to talk about that."

"Oh really? Is there a point when you will look at me and be honest?"

Melchior's head snapped toward me. "You want to talk about it? Fine. Let's talk about how every time I even came near, you had to have another glass of wine just so you could face the horror of being my bride."

He stalked forward, closing in on me. "You don't drink, ever, because you prefer your emotions unclouded and your reflexes sharp, but not on *that* day. No, at our wedding, you were doing whatever you could to brace yourself."

I paled. It felt as if he'd doused me in cold water, and I couldn't–didn't– know how to respond.

"I suppose you didn't think I'd notice how you flinched. How you closed your eyes so tightly. Right?" Sneering down at me, his eyes were cruel, unfathomably cold.

"Am I attracted to you physically? Of course. You're beautiful. You're cunning. But I must admit, it does dampen my enthusiasm somewhat to know that you'd let me do anything if it meant getting my gold. So forgive me if I didn't feel like facing you immediately after, and if I don't want to talk about our so-called *marriage*."

Melchior spun and walked out, leaving me standing by the fire while I fought back tears.

22

As much as I wanted to sleep, and forget his harsh words, I couldn't. All I could do was stand and stare helplessly at the door between us, dreading our next interaction. Desperate to put some distance between us, I went to the chandlery, where all the candles in the castle were made.

"Let there be light," I whispered, as I lit several of the yellow beeswax candles, each one giving a small bit of fragile illumination. There were hundreds in the large room, piles on tabletops, thin ivory ones that tapered in various silver candelabras. Some were thick as my thigh, with wooden wicks rather than cloth, clearly meant for outdoor use.

Once I had enough light to see, I studied the room with a careful eye. It was long, with several fireplaces. There were molds of many sizes, stacked neatly on shelves, and easily a thousand candles. It smelled comforting, a heady mix of honey, straw and wax, and the faint scent of salt and flowers.

Out of habit, I checked the walls. There were no secret doors, nothing hidden behind tapestries, no item out of place.

"What am I still doing here?" I muttered to myself. I should have left already; when it became apparent I wasn't going to find the Eternal Slumber, I should have gone. But I hadn't... and he was wrong, it wasn't about the gold, it was about—

Well. Pride, maybe. I couldn't bear to admit that I'd been beaten, bested. That was what it was, wasn't it?

I stared down at the marks on my wrists. They'd eventually be scars, but for now they were just raw and red, the places where Julian had chained me to the floor. It felt as if there were a cold weight inside my chest, like that singular part of me was already a corpse. There was a dull ache, a sense of emptiness. I'd never understood him, and now it felt like whatever moments of happiness I'd had were lies.

The relationship between Lachesis and Melchior, *former relationship,* shouldn't matter to me. It shouldn't. But it did. Once upon a time, I'd walked into this house of Death feeling optimistic - not because I was stupid, but because he had been with me. Before he'd left me for Lachesis and then not come back.

Now I felt like I couldn't trust him or her. They had both deceived me in much the same way.

Of course Atropos needed to be stopped. There was something rotten, something corroded in her. She wasn't worthy to be a Fate. She should not lead this kingdom, nor any other. She shouldn't decide the future, or the endings, of any of us. But there was no reason it had to be *me* to play the hero. I wasn't a knight, not a soldier. It wasn't as if I knew how to handle any of it, and now—

Watching light and shadow play through the room, I hugged myself tightly and watched the candles flicker.

Suddenly, the golden flame of the nearest candle sputtered and a shroud of darkness swallowed its luminescence in a hungry gulp. My heart clenched as I turned, shadows clinging to my skin, to face the silhouette that had materialized among them.

"Melchior?" My voice barely breached the silence.

He emerged from the shadows and our eyes met, held. His hair was wild, his eyes frantic.

"I woke up and you were gone," he said. His shadows poured over me, inspecting me, confirming I was still in one piece, checking for wounds. Confirming if I was untouched.

"I'm fine," I told them, then him. "I'm sorry. I just wanted to check something. I couldn't sleep."

"...You're fine." His breath caught. "You are sorry–"

He reached for me, then clenched his hands into fists instead.

Something about that movement captured my attention; I'd done it so many times myself. Every time I wanted to touch him and didn't, I fought my instincts to show how I cared. And suddenly I realized how worry and relief showed so clearly on his face. He'd woken up and I was missing. He thought Atropos had taken me. He'd sent the shadows to look for me, not knowing what they would find.

"Well then. I'll just... leave you to it." Melchior heaved a sigh of relief.

"Wait."

The silence stretched between us, heavy with words unsaid.

"Melchior," I began, my voice as unsteady as the heart in my chest. "Tell me why you left. Why you went to her."

"Because of you, obviously," he said bitterly. "Because of our wedding night."

"I only did what you told me to do. You said we had to get married."

His gaze was like the surface of a pool of ink. "You made it very clear that you didn't want to. That marrying me was repugnant. Once the ceremony was over, you were drinking heavily just so you could tolerate my touch."

"No." I had to look away. "That's not what it was."

"Well," his voice was clipped, "you hardly looked at me."

"I was nervous."

"To be with me.The Prince of Darkness! Son of Death." His mouth twisted with disgust.

"To be with anyone."

His expression was guarded, and for a moment there was nothing—no sound, no movement—as if the universe itself had paused to consider those words. Then, slowly, deliberately, Melchior erased the distance that separated us.

"Then you won't flinch when I touch you?" Sliding his fingers along my jaw, he tilted my face up toward his.

My jaw trembled. I exhaled softly as he rubbed his thumb across my lower lip.

But I didn't cringe away; I didn't scream or cry. Instead, I gazed up at him, and watched his expression slowly change from challenge to softness. There was a silence punctuated only by the soft sound of wicks burning as we stood together in the candlelight.

He stroked my cheek, thinking.

My words tumbled forth like he'd dragged them up from the depths of the sea. "You're in love with someone else."

Melchior contemplated me for several seconds before he spoke. "Every second, of every day, I live in fear that something will happen to you. That you, with your stubborn, ridiculous obsession with independence... will do something idiotic. Without me there. That I won't be able to save you."

"Really?" I swallowed nervously. We were mere inches apart. "What about Lachesis?"

"What about her?"

"You went to see her. Right after our wedding night." *To sleep with her.*

"Only to apologize. To tell her she was right."

"About what?" I couldn't think, not with his finger on my lips, not when his eyes looked at me like that.

"That I'm in love with you, and had been since the moment we met."

"Oh," I mumbled.

An instant later, his mouth was on mine. Soft. Intimate. Sensual. Like a dream. More gentle than I imagined he could be.

I tightened my grip on his shirt and kissed him back, deeply, desperately. It was like a dam burst... and I was willing to drown.

He wrapped his arms around me, crushing my body against his.

His hands slid down and up my back, then he tangled his fingers in my hair and his lips found my mouth again. He deepened the kiss, his tongue touching mine until I was gasping for breath. Insistent, demanding,

Melchior started kissing along my throat, dragging his teeth and tongue down my skin.

His other hand tore open the laces of my nightgown, tugging, pulling, releasing me from the confines of fabric. My nipples hardened as he palmed my breasts and rubbed a thumb over one peak.

I ripped open his shirt, tearing off several buttons in the process; he shoved my gown down, past my hips, until it fell and pooled at my feet. He kissed me ravenously, like whatever lock he'd had on his emotions, the key had been turned. The candles around us, with their small yellow light, burned away his restraint.

With a sweep of his arm, he cleared the tabletop, wax and scent jars and tools scattered to the floor, their clattering sounds muffled by the pounding of blood in my ears. He sat me upon the cold, hard wood.

He explored and exposed, grinding himself against me.

I wrapped my legs around his back, pulling him closer. I arched into him and lifted my hips as his mouth lowered to my breast and sucked, his tongue flicking against my nipple. Harsh.

"Melchior," I gasped, his name a talisman against the dark.

I slid my hand into the front of his shirt and ran my fingers over the smooth skin of his chest, then pulled him closer to mine. He wrapped his arms around me and our mouths fused together again.

"Stop me." He sounded like he'd swallowed a mouthful of sand.

Instead, I jerked his pants open. His groan went straight to my head, making me feel as if I would burn down the castle just to have him inside me.

I'd never felt like this before. I definitely did not intend to simply get up and walk away. Sliding my hands up his body, I studied Melchior's face. We were going to do this, and I suspected that once we did, we'd be unable to turn back.

I wasn't afraid, and I should have been. My self control was hanging on by less than a thread as he paused at my entrance, as his gaze wandered over my breasts, my belly, the thatch of hair at my thighs.

"I want you," I said softly.

Melchior released a shaky breath. He hadn't said yes, but he hadn't said no.

He had to do something, *now,* because the desire pumping through my system was so overwhelming that I didn't know what to do.

"Mine. If we do this, you're mine. Once I claim you..."

"Just fuck me," I snarled, tilting up my hips. I was going to die if he didn't bury himself in me, with fast, punishing strokes.

Finally, he slid all the way in with a long, guttural groan.

My head fell back, against the table, my hair spreading out all around me. I moaned from the friction, from the feeling, from the sensation of pleasure and pain. His hands guided me, lifting me, widening my legs.

"You look like a fire goddess, a siren." Melchior sank deeper. "I don't want to hurt you," he rasped.

"You aren't."

It felt like I'd waited my entire life for this, and there was no room for anything else. Beeswax clung to the air, a rich and earthy scent that melded with the smoke, with the scent of us. My core was a low, slow burning ember, and every movement he made stoked a fire.

The angle of his movement, the intensity of his gaze... I dug my fingernails into his shoulders, anchoring myself as his pace slowed. He kissed me again, and his breaths shifted into something calm, deeper.

We were bathed in candlelight. Warmth. Everything else was cold in comparison.

"Oh god." I felt unbalanced, precarious, like I might fall–

Then Melchior thrust fast, harder, and the pressure inside me finally broke. I cried out as my body clenched around him, as he found his own release. The feel of him inside me, marking me, gave me a strange pleasure. Although I immediately wondered if he would regret it, if he would pull away and tomorrow treat me as he had before.

For a long time neither of us moved, my face tucked into his shoulder, his lips against my throat. Slowly, I slid my hand over his back, tracing raised scars I could feel but not see. I kissed his neck, then bit it lightly. We were still joined, so I felt his response immediately.

I reached up and touched his cheek and he pressed his face against my hand. I might have thought the gesture sweet, but Melchior's gaze was possessive. Ravenous.

I kissed him again. We didn't speak again until much later, as we lay on the floor in a pile of our own clothing. The candles had burned low, many of them completely used up.

"Next time, let's find a bed," I murmured.

Melchior chuckled against my throat. Then he rolled off me, pulling me with him until I lay on his chest. He smiled, smug and sleepy.

"Who would have guessed I'd fall for the orphaned thief with the pretty green eyes."

I kissed him and raised an eyebrow. "You think my eyes are pretty?"

"Better than. Your eyes are what the sea should be, sunlight striped blue and green."

"I can't say I've ever heard that line before."

"I've been thinking about it for a long time."

I traced a heart on his chest. "You're a prince. A descendant of the Fates."

Melchior ran his hand gently down my back. "And you're a princess."

"I am no one. I come from nothing."

"You're meant to be with me."

"I think I knew after our wedding night. When I woke up and you weren't there... I looked for you. Wanted you."

"You have me." He looked at me as if I were the only woman in Moirai. In the world.

I hoped it was true.

Content, sleepy, I listened to his heart beat. "You know what I realized in the crypts? We don't have to steal the Eternal Slumber. We only have to *convince* Atropos that we have stolen it, and provoke her into putting on the fake. After she's dead, we take the throne."

"Can we not talk about this now?" Melchior asked.

"I don't see the point in talking about anything else," I replied. "We'll need the real mask, if we're going to rule... but we can probably imprison Atropos without it."

"What are you saying?" He furrowed his brow.

"We'll need it, if we're going to rule. We find it and keep it."

Melchior digested this shift in strategy. It wasn't as if I'd had much luck finding the Eternal Slumber so far.

"Could we manage that? It hasn't exactly gone as planned," he said quietly.

Our eyes met. The understanding that passed between us was familiar, yet different. Unguarded.

I wanted to try, though, and I told him so.

"I sat in that throne room at eight, nine, ten years old and watched as she gleefully massacred my nursemaid; then when I was fourteen, my best friend. The only way to make her stop was to promise her that I would join her, that I would *entice* people to come here, just so she could toy with them."

He pressed his hand over his eyes and I noticed an almost imperceptible tremble. "She – my mother – is jealous. She doesn't feel love, doesn't care, but she hates to have others get close to me. Anything I loved, she took away."

What a terrible life. He'd been stuck since then, trying to find a path forward. Alone.

"So, when Lachesis came, when she said you could help me defeat my mother, help me be rid of her forever..." Melchior closed his eyes. "But I'm afraid my mother will take you away from me too. Torture you and kill you right in front of me, and I won't be able to do anything about it."

After a moment, he pressed his forehead to my shoulder, repeating the words as if they were a prayer. "It'd be so much easier if you'd leave."

"If you could go back, would you change anything?" I asked. "About how we met? And what happened after?"

He considered the question for a long while. "No. Although it's something I think a lot about."

"Because Lachesis made you do it?"

"No, because... she'd told me so much by then, I felt like I already knew you. I couldn't discover you, as I might have, if I wouldn't have known."

She. Lachesis.

I despised her. Yet I was a little grateful she'd directed him to me. That she'd safeguarded him and ensured he saved my life, more than once.

"In the history books I've read, the Chronos is only for the Fates to read and write in. Meant to be kept a secret. Yet you said Lachesis gave it to you?"

Melchior rubbed his lips across my shoulder. "Mm. She did."

I knew - knew - for Lachesis to give him the book was a grave violation of her role as a Fate. It was just as bad as Atropos refusing to kill Tassos.

"So you know everything that's going to happen in your life?"

"Not nearly. I skipped some...the boring parts. Some things I didn't want to know. And she didn't inspect everything; it's nearly impossible to see all of it. There's no point. She can't inspect every time thread, nor every decision."

"Did you ever notice her listening after that?"

"Of course. Once I knew what to look for, I realized she was doing it all the time. It makes a sound when she arrives, most don't notice it. It's a click, like a ticking clock or a door softly shutting. And it smells a little like firerose."

For a moment I was dumbfounded. I couldn't believe he hadn't told me before. I'd had that happen at least a dozen times since I'd been here. And I could remember times when I'd been in Fidelisgrove... Lachesis had been watching us, watching *me,* far more than he knew.

I gritted my teeth. It would do no good to attack her. He'd think me jealous, and that wouldn't accomplish anything.

"You think she shouldn't have?" he asked.

I decided right then I would lie.

About my feelings, about my thoughts and plans. Mostly because I didn't know if Lachesis would someday listen in on this conversation. "No. I think it was wise of her. It helped you see your path. I only wish we had a Chronos for me."

Melchior made a humming sound. "I suppose that's true. If we had yours, we would know whether you retrieve the mask, and I'd know if you leave me once you get those ten thousand gold coins... or decide to stay."

He looked at me, perhaps inviting me to share my feelings for him.

But I was too surprised. "You didn't read the whole thing?"

"I only read up until our wedding. Like I said, I hadn't even met you yet. Plus, it was in her tone of voice. Her observation of events. On our wedding night, she said we had sex, that she heard part of it, that it broke her heart. I didn't read any after that. I didn't believe such a thing was possible. I threw it into the fire while we were arguing."

That had been three years ago. We hadn't even met, and he'd been here fighting with Lachesis about our future wedding.

"You can see how, when we were there, in that bed, and I put the sheet between us... I was thinking both of what I'd read and I was looking at your face, but then you turned your head and kissed me, and it felt like..."

"Like what?"

"All those years in between reading my Chronos and then it happening, I thought I would feel indifferent. I'd convinced myself that she misinterpreted it somehow. But then when I was with you, I felt your skin and tasted your mouth..."

He kissed me again.

"You wanted me?"

"Couldn't you tell?" His mouth drifted to the juncture of my neck and shoulder and he kissed and sucked along my collarbone until I arched against him.

"Yes," I admitted, sliding my hands across his back.

"I hoped there would be nothing between us. But then when there was, I didn't know what to do. Or what would happen if I tore that sheet away. If it would scare you or insult you."

I digested this. "And why were you so upset earlier tonight? When you came to find me?"

"Because I woke up and you weren't there. Because I can't keep you safe. I curse myself daily for throwing that Chronos into the fire, because if I had it, I would have known what would happen with Julian. I would know where you'd gone."

I supposed it was true. If he knew what would happen, he would have found me faster in the crypts...He'd be better at planning our future...He'd know where to find the mask.

If *we* knew.

The words rattled inside my mind; it was a stunning realization. What we needed was another Chronos - the book of fate that would tell us everything. Only then could I be confident of our plans, because I'd be able to read what would happen.

He'd seen his own - at least a little bit of it, before he'd foolishly thrown it into the fire. We needed Lachesis to *give* us another Chronos, ideally one for me. Then we'd know exactly what to do and when, if his plan would ultimately fail. We'd know what the outcome of Atropos' experiments would be. If we could somehow persuade Lachesis to help, then we'd have a fighting chance.

"Could you ask her?" I said finally, studying his face in the candlelight. "Ask Lachesis for another Chronos, to help us?"

"She wouldn't do it."

"Why not? She loved you. She's protected you all these years. She helped save me, more than once." My voice rang with hope and optimism. I had to persuade him first, and damn her, I needed her to hear me.

I sat up and gave him a serious look. "This is how we do it. We read the Chronos. We follow our futures, like a map. No deviations."

Melchior ran his thumb down my cheekbone. “Having the Chronos doesn’t solve everything. After all, I knew so much about you and our future and I still made mistakes. It was far from smooth.”

“But it could work.”

“It could... Certainly it would be better than nothing.”

“You say it like you’re agreeing with me.”

The corner of his mouth twitched. “Not at all. I think this is a fool’s errand.”

I smiled and snuggled closer. “Then let’s be fools.”

Melchior chuckled. “Fine, but I don’t want you to have the wrong idea. Destinies are fixed, it is only our journey that’s flexible. And even with the Chronos, it will be a dark road.” His black eyes reflected the last of the dying candles.

“Not if we walk it together.” I threaded my fingers through his. “Not if Lachesis will help us.”

23

Because we were otherwise occupied, Melchior and I missed breakfast, then lunch, with Atropos. Hours simply slipped by, unnoticed, and all efforts to summon or find us failed. Julian, now dead in the crypts, was also curiously missing.

When neither of her sons showed up for meals, Atropos was very unhappy. Death, it turned out, did not appreciate being ignored.

Melchior and I appeared at dinner, and we immediately knew it was going to go poorly. Atropos, obviously in an ill-temper, glared at us. Her dark eyes reminded me of the maw of an angry beast, yawning open to devour its victims.

"It's nice to see you two. I'm so glad you could join me."

My hand was clasped firmly in his; Melchior squeezed it to reassure me. My heart gave a pang as we took our seats, which now seemed terribly far apart.

One servant, a girl with lank brown hair and a terrified expression, brought our food, her hands shaking slightly as she placed the plates of nearly raw meat in front of us.

Some of the food was burnt.

Some was undercooked.

The diced fruit was uneven.

"I missed you terribly these last few days," Atropos said to Melchior. "You know I expect you at meal times."

He moved the food around with his fork, then bared his teeth in the semblance of a smile.

"Apologies, mother. Malinda and I were busy."

"You didn't even inform me. It's an intolerable slight, don't you think? Death invites you to dine, and you don't even have the courtesy to decline?"

The meat on her plate was bloody; it sat in a pool of itself, essentially raw, and she speared it with her fork.

"I know it's not *your* fault, Melchior. You know the rules of this house well." She sipped her wine. "But your wife, no. And she *must* learn a lesson. We can't let her disrespect continue, can we?"

"Certainly not," he said, after a brief silence.

I was shocked.

"So we agree then. Your wife should be punished. Will you expect her to bear it, or will you be doing that in her place?" Atropos looked back and forth between the two of us.

Punishment? What was she talking about?

I studied Melchior, eyes narrowed and calculating.

Melchior steadfastly refused to look at me. Instead, he nodded slowly. "I'll do it."

Atropos smiled. "I thought you might."

The corner of his mouth quivered.

"Melchior?"

Something–I didn't know what was happening.

He swallowed his food carefully, calmly, and laid down his fork.

I kept expecting him to say something. Confused, I watched as my husband stood from his chair, and then tucked it neatly back into the table. With a deep, uneven breath, he walked around the edge of the room, until he came to my side.

He hesitated.

"Now, Melchior. Like a good boy."

Melchior held out his knife. For lack of knowing what else to do, I accepted it, taking it by the handle from him.

"What are you doing?" I whispered.

"I have to kneel," he said, cutting me off sharply. "Unless you want her to kill you, you will do as she says." Every word was clipped, as if he said them through clenched teeth.

Much to my complete shock, my husband took off his shirt. Drawing it over his head, revealing his chest and stomach, the ridges of muscles like carved marble.

His eyes were dull. Calm. He knelt next to my chair, bowing his head. Waiting.

It slowly occurred to me what she wanted me to do.

Frozen, the knife slipped from my fingers and clattered onto the floor. Melchior picked it up and silently handed it back to me.

I tried to understand it. This... missing piece of their relationship. Certain I was misunderstanding, I looked at Atropos.

"Do as he says."

Transfixed, I stared at the knife he'd handed to me, at the silver handle with the embedded onyx stone. Then I gazed down at his broad shoulders, and noted his quick, involuntary shudder. The scars that crisscrossed his back. They were cuts, a hundred tiny wounds. All from *Atropos.* She made him sit here while she ate her dinner. And she carved him up. Some of the scars were old, but some were not.

The room was so quiet.

"No," I said, shaking my head slowly.

"Malinda." Melchior squeezed my ankle. Begging me to play along.

My heart was pounding, faster and faster. "No," I repeated. "I won't."

I had killed before. This was so much less than that. I stared down at my plate, at the knife in my hand. She was going to force me.

Cold rage filled my throat, so much that I could barely breathe. I swallowed, and felt it settle into my belly. My mind was crystal clear, and when I raised my face to Atropos, my emotions were carefully guarded, trapped in a stone box where they clawed the walls and screamed.

I'm going to use this knife to carve the lips off her face.

I'm going to bury her alive.

However she has treated him, I will be a thousand-fold worse.

I gave Atropos my cruelest, coldest smile.

"Ah. There you are. I knew my son would not choose a weak girl for a wife. I had my doubts, but he assured me that underneath, you're no stranger to violence."

"Not too much," I said briefly, my tone cool. "I don't like blood on my sheets."

Atropos laughed. "You'll get over that."

I gave his mother the most cunning, feminine smile in my arsenal. "So tell me–" I murmured, as I held up the knife. "How deeply do I need to cut before he screams?"

"You should have told me," I said, as I dressed his wounds.

Melchior was sitting in my desk chair, his head buried in his arms so his voice was muffled. "What good would that have done?"

"I don't know."

They weren't deep, but the cuts I made *would* scar him. And it was enough– enough to make me feel ill and guilty. I wiped the blood away and placed a cleansing potion onto his skin, touching him as lightly as possible. Still he winced. Silently, I counted his scars and I promised myself I would repay each one with equal violence.

Especially the ones I'd been forced to make.

The memory of our first day together came back to me. Not of him rescuing me, nor carrying me, but how gentle his hands were as they tended my wounds. He'd bandaged my torn flesh, talking to fill the silence. It must have reminded him of how Atropos had tortured him, of how she'd scarred his shoulders. That touch had been the first kindness I'd known in years. The first time he'd touched a woman's skin since Lachesis left him years before.

"The first time I saw you," Melchior said, "you were fighting the Keres in the alley. I couldn't decide if you were really smart, or just very stupid."

I waited for him to go on.

"Now that I know you better, I still can't decide. If you were smart, you'd go."

"Is that what you want?"

"Want has nothing to do with it."

"Then what?" I pressed. It felt as if we were teetering on the edge of a precipice, using the silence between us like a thin rope to keep us from falling.

"I wish I'd never brought you here," he finally said.

"You needed a thief. I was available." I looked at the ceiling.

"That's not true. I already knew I would fall for you and marry you. Lachesis told me. So when we met, when I left you at the cottage, I told myself I must never come back. Because if what she said was true, it was better to never see you again. So that I might spare you. The thief… was just something I said."

Under my hands, Melchior flinched again. "Let me get you out. I'll give you the money anyway."

"You can't ask me to give up while you stay here." Again I recalled the events at dinner. My time in the crypt. If he wanted to be Death, so be it. I didn't care why he wanted the mask or what he planned to do with it.

Atropos killed the innocent at random. She tortured and maimed. She did not bring peace or understanding, only blood and suffering.

I didn't want her to have anything, not the power of Death and not the will of the Gods, not the Eternal Slumber.

I wanted her to die slowly. Painfully.

Repeatedly.

"All done," I said at last.

Melchior flexed his shoulders, lifted his head, then gingerly put his black shirt back on. "Thanks."

Awkwardly, the two of us stood there, unsure what to say. "Let's get some sleep."

We laid down in my bed, the light of the fire casting a glow over us. Considering each other, and how things had shifted between us. I'd been keeping too many secrets of my own, and that had done nothing but cause confusion. It had made things more difficult, not less.

He closed his eyes and, within seconds, he was softly breathing. I was not so lucky. Instead I was reliving the crypt, the dinner, the days in between. Faintly, so faint I might have been imagining it, I heard a soft *click.* I sniffed the air and besides him, it was there... firerose. The room was dark, the fire low, but I was sure Lachesis was here.

Spying.

His former lover was watching him, watching us. How many times had she done that and I hadn't noticed? I sat up in bed and glanced toward the balcony. Carefully, I eased myself off the mattress and walked toward the door, tiptoeing, praying that Melchior wouldn't open his eyes and ask where I was going.

Taking a deep breath, I gripped the handle and turned it slowly. "Come on," I whispered to the empty room. "I want to talk to you."

I stepped out onto the snow-covered stones in my bare feet, the blue-black sky overhead littered with bright white stars. It was a quiet night, the sort I had always loved and would always remind me of him. When they said, *Prince of Darkness,* it was nights like these I thought of. Not his shadows, not Death, just this beautiful clear midnight.

Lachesis did not appear.

"Help me save him," I said anyway. "If you love him, or ever loved him. Help me get rid of Atropos. I'll do anything - I'll follow your instructions exactly. I won't be like him. I will believe anything you say. Everything you say. I know it is not allowed. But you've made an exception before, and I'm begging you to make one again. I swear on my life, I will do anything."

Far off, an owl hooted in the evergreens. The field of snow was a blank canvas, not a single hoofprint marring its pale surface.

I repeated the words like a litany. I wept silently, and asked her again. Pleaded with the most powerful Fate.

But she did not come.

Time watched, and waited, and planned to take everything from me. I, who never had much of anything, would be left with nothing after all. Finally, I was too cold, my feet too numb, to stand there any longer.

"Fine," I said aloud, my frozen fingers gripping the stone rail. "I'll do it alone."

I started to turn.

Click.

Inhuman, immortal arms closed around me.

Lachesis shoved me forward, over the rail and off the balcony.

24

"See how strong she is." I rub my face against the girl's small fist, marveling at her golden hair and dark eyes. Shadows wreathed the baby, tendrils curling around the shell of her ear, around her chubby thighs, and my daughter laughed. It's the most beautiful sound.

"Don't rile her up. It's bedtime," I coo.

Melchior chuckles. He is the shadows, noncorporeal. He makes a shape with his hands, a Pegasus made of inky black, and flaps it over her head.

"Get it, Morena. Grab it," he says.

She extends her little fist and smashes through it.

It was our future. Our family. My eyes were soft, my hands were gentle. I had a daughter who looked just like me.

"What is this? Where are we?" I asked Ilya—or rather, Lachesis, the Controller of Time. Bright white light stretched in all directions, as if we were inside a cloud.

"Your destiny. That's your daughter, Morena." With her flat gaze and deadpan tone, it was clear that Lachesis had watched this scene many times - that it bored her.

I kept my eyes on the baby. *A little girl. And her name is Morena.*

It was a revelation. Me, a mother. I'd never imagined such a thing. Riveted, I watched as Melchior and I played with the child. We were happy- truly happy—a feeling I'd always found to be just beyond my reach. And here it was, delivered, by her.

"We're in the Now'here, the in between. We're not really with them, we're looking into their time. Like a window."

"Could I talk to them? Could you?"

"I could, yes."

"Have you talked to them before?"

Lachesis blinked her bottomless sky blue eyes at me. "She is Atropos' undoing, and I have watched much of her life, wondering how she was able to succeed. Of course I've talked to her."

"Melchior and I don't defeat Atropos with the forged mask?"

"It keeps her imprisoned, but only for a while."

It took me a beat to process this.

"If Morena is her undoing, does that mean there is no Death, or no controller of Death?

"Your daughter *is* Death. She is Atropos' replacement." *Atropos' replacement.* My blood ran cold.

"How is that possible? There are already Three Fates."

"Our descendants can be granted Fates' powers. Hypothetically, there can be more than three at any given time."

It didn't seem believable to look at the little bundle and imagine that she would grow up to be anything like Atropos.

"Is she bloodthirsty and terrible?"

"Eventually. At first she was kind. Naive. In the beginning."

"And what of us? Melchior and I?" I feared I already knew the answer.

"You die. He becomes a ruthless monster who lives in misery."

I swallowed hard.

"Why are you showing me this?"

Lachesis was perturbed. "So you don't get any rash ideas. Now you know what to expect."

"Rash ideas?" It felt like I was walking on a razor's edge, in this strange place with the Controller of Time.

"It's inevitable that you end up here, just as it is inevitable that *she* ends up *there*."

I looked back at the scene, but now it was only a tall woman in black, wearing the Eternal Slumber. She was standing on a pile of bodies, a scythe in hand.

The girl hung her head. Her shoulders were slumped. Her long blonde hair - the same shade as mine - was tangled and matted, as if she hadn't bathed in weeks.

I'd never seen anyone who appeared to be more miserable.

"Will she ever be happy?"

"She's Death. Do you feel that a woman who will kill everyone she ever loves would be *happy*?"

My eyes returned back to the scene before us, where another version of me was now humming to a lullaby.

"It's only one moment in time," Lachesis told me, sensing my doubt. "It won't last."

"Couldn't you intervene?" I asked. "Couldn't you help me get her away?"

"Why would I do that?"

"Because you are my friend. Because you love Melchior."

Lachesis laughed. She had a deep, rich, lovely laugh. "We are not friends. And I have not loved Melchior for a long, long time."

She leaned close. "He betrayed me. He chose *you,* and fell in love with you. A useless, fragile, insignificant mortal. Even when I showed him how *ordinary* you were, how poor and unfit."

I closed my eyes, a sharp pang in my chest.

"You die here. In this castle, by his hand. Which is more than you ever deserved."

Somehow I'd walked into the lion's den; I'd made an enemy of Time without even knowing I was doing so.

"It's laughable, really. Melchior wants to remove Atropos from power, only to have his daughter be much worse. And you, who wished so fervently to escape your life as a thief, a liar, a murderer... Your offspring will become first among all villains. Her name will strike fear in multiple worlds."

Lachesis gloated. "She is stronger than you, wiser than you, more ruthless than you. She is the true Death, not the self-centered, arrogant, lazy version that Atropos became. As the Gods intended for us to be."

"Impossible," I said. "That is *not* who she will become."

"She will, Malinda. Everything you'll do is for nothing."

The blood drained from my face. "How do I know you aren't lying?"

"It's not the sort of thing I'd lie about."

"She's not a *thing.*" Protectively, I touched my stomach as I frowned, as though she were already there.

Lachesis smirked. "Fine. I have no reason to lie because your future is so awful that I couldn't possibly make it sound any worse than it already is."

"I don't want her to be a Fate."

Lachesis laughed. "There's no way around that. She's descended from Atropos."

"Can't Melchior and I choose differently?"

Lachesis smiled faintly. "The two of you are sacrifices to the Gods, tied to a rock in the sea. Doomed to drown over and over."

"Then we'll make that not true somehow."

"No. You only make it worse for yourself."

My heart sank. She had dug into both my past and my future, and was with me in my present. She'd given Melchior a Chronos of his own life. There was no way for her to be wrong, when she'd been there as a witness.

And yet...

Zeph always told me that nothing was inevitable. That the Gods rewarded those who fought, that victory came after many defeats. That there was always a choice, if we were brave enough to make it. That destiny, even if it seemed carved in stone, was always flexible.

"Accept it. She'll never know you; she'll hate him." Her harsh, unfeeling words were out of place with her beautiful face. It gave her pleasure to say the words; she waited for my reaction with relish.

"Why are you telling me this?" I asked again. "If you hate me so much, why tell me my future?"

"Ironically, me telling you just how doomed you truly are guarantees that you'll try even harder to change your future. It's quite entertaining. I don't believe I've ever seen so much misery."

Lachesis smiled, her eyes sharp, haunted.

She wants me to throw me in with the wolves, and then watch as I'm torn apart. That's why she's showing me this.

I decided to see what else the Controller of Time might reveal. "When does Melchior kill me?"

"A few months from now. You don't even make it to your anniversary."

"And then what happens?"

"Atropos raises your daughter. Remakes her and molds her, corrupts her mind until there's nothing left but a ruthless killer."

I studied Lachesis, clearly skeptical, questioning her intentions. Very likely, this was all complete fabrication, a story meant to manipulate me into leaving Melchior. Then she could put herself forward to console him in my absence.

"Prove it," I said. "Prove all of this is not some wild imagining."

Much to my surprise, Lachesis started talking. Revealing, one sentence at a time, my terrible destiny. I barely spoke, only nodding to show I was still listening. Occasionally, I asked her to repeat herself. It was all there, laid out cleanly, and Lachesis had it sorted and organized in her mind. It took over an hour, and through it all, she spoke with obvious relish. She truly, deeply hated me— had hated me, it seemed, for years.

"How do you remember it all?" I asked at last, genuinely impressed.

"I've seen so many versions of her future, and all their consequences. Sometimes, I observe for hours, days, weeks. They don't even know I'm there."

"The click as you come and go doesn't give it away?" I said wryly.

Lachesis chuckled. "Strangely, no. They have a lot of loud clocks. Morena often thinks it's a Cullen snapping its jaws, or a window blowing open."

But it wasn't. It was Lachesis. Watching my daughter and gloating over her misfortune. Laughing as she suffered. My emotions were a chaotic mix of worry, doubt...and pure, blind fury. Carefully masking that took every ounce of willpower I possessed, and silently I thanked Zeph for all the late night card games, for teaching me how lie so flawlessly.

"Why bother watching, if you know exactly what will happen?"

"In case they get off course. I might have to intervene, here and there. Rewind time, force them to do the right thing."

The right thing. It took me a moment to realize that this meant she was interfering with destiny, that she was manipulating my Morena's life. Possibly often. To make things worse, to ensure she suffered, Lachesis was altering destiny.

In small, little bites, she was devouring my daughter's goodness. Leaving a deathly skeleton behind. And she was so confident, so *sure* that I wouldn't be able to change anything about our future, that she was thrilled to tell me about it in explicit, excruciating detail. In her mind, telling me ensured that the future was even worse, because she could watch me try and fail to change it.

I suddenly felt much better about my decision to trick her.

Killing her slowly also sounded appealing.

In her arrogance, Lachesis had forgotten something. Or rather, someone. After all, at least one person had managed to defy Death and trick Time– Tassos. The only question was whether I could do the same. If I could *win* against her.

Lachesis studied me, her blue eyes hard as crystal.

I clenched my fist and swallowed. Invoking the ire of Time would be foolish, especially considering she could help me defy Death.

"I'm not sure I can remember everything you've said." I cracked my knuckles, worriedly. "I should have taken notes."

"Did you keep a Chronos for me? I'd like to have it." Instead of pretending or faking, flattering her, or trying to steal it from her, I simply asked.

Lachesis threw back her head and laughed. "Weren't you listening to anything I've said?"

"If you're right, then you have nothing to lose by giving it to me." I paused. "No matter what I do, I'm doomed, and so is Morena. Watching us fail should give you years of enjoyment."

Lachesis shook her head in disbelief, but pulled a book from her pocket. It was a small volume, bound in royal blue silk, marked with *XIII - Chronos y Kairos.*

"This is the only one you have?"

"It's all I'm willing to give." She held it up. "You should know that I already knew you would ask, which is why I have it with me. You reading this changes nothing."

Fair enough, I thought.

Lachesis waited impatiently as I opened it, while I read the first few pages.

It was not what I expected. It was not *mine,* or Morena's. It was Melchior's. Melchior's, when he'd said he'd thrown his into the fire.

I didn't understand how that could be. If Lachesis gave him a Chronos and Melchior read it and then burned it to ash... how could she have handed this one to me?

I flicked through another few pages. "You must have loved him very much," I murmured.

She blinked. "Why would you think that?"

Because hate is always born from a broken heart. Because I can see it in your eyes.

"Just a guess," I said, with a small shrug.

The scene around us began to dissolve, as we materialized again on the balcony of the Grace, standing in the snow.

"Which would bother you more? If I never loved him at all, or if he was the only man I ever loved?"

"I–I don't know."

It didn't really matter what my answer might have been. Either way, her motivations were very clear.

She wanted me to suffer.

25

I stayed up all night reading.

In broad strokes, The Chronos outlined exactly what would happen next. Line by line, in neat, precise print–

Melchior saves Malinda from the Keres;

They stand on the bridge watching a body in a river;

They have their first kiss;

Melchior and Malinda hide under a bed;

They marry;

They make love;

She becomes pregnant;

Their daughter is born.

It did not dwell on emotions or motivations. It did not say why. Rather, it was a list of tensely articulated facts and dates. Our future reduced to a few pages, a list meticulously annotated by his former lover Lachesis.

I was disbelieving. The Chronos stated it all, exactly as she described... And yet, I doubted the words of the Controller of Time. What guarantee did I have that her outlandish words were true? That she'd recorded it all faithfully?

According to her notes, I would give birth to a daughter who would become Death, who humans would refer to as *The Grim Reaper.* I mulled it over, turning it back and forth in my mind, trying to understand.

I could be pregnant already. If I was, then the daughter she described was already growing inside me. Though she'd be born innocent, our child would wreak havoc on the world, destroying Moirai. This was not the worst revelation, either. I stared down at the words, feeling sick.

Melchior kills Malinda before their first wedding anniversary.

The book of Fate must be wrong.

I squinted at the finely printed words in the moonlight, and carefully, thoughtfully, committed every word to memory. I watched Melchior as he slept, studying his face, looking for any sign I'd missed. Any stray frown or word out of place. If the words were true, he was a far, far better liar than I ever had been. If his affection for me was a grand ruse, it was the best played game I had ever witnessed.

But I strongly suspected that Lachesis was lying. She could be attempting to fool me, so that I would do something rash. Maybe she hoped that I would kill him first, or be disloyal and sell him out to Atropos.

Alone with all these secrets, adrift in what could be a sea of lies, I felt lost. I didn't know what was true. Melchior, despite his flaws, had been the one thing I'd trusted in this house. I wanted to tell him everything.

Yet I couldn't do it. Whether it was or wasn't my destiny, I couldn't quite bring myself to casually ask my new husband if he was planning to murder me. Thinking of his own past experience, it could very well be that he had no plans to kill me, but he would - maybe even by accident. Unhelpfully, Lachesis hadn't indicated whether he'd killed me *on purpose.*

She'd been very careful to leave out those sorts of details.

Burying my head in my hands, I tried to think through this strategically. To carefully control and put aside my emotions, to absolve myself of any guilt. After all, Melchior knew everything that would happen up until our wedding. He hadn't told me, and now I understood why.

Because I wouldn't have believed him.

He'd watched his entire life unfold exactly as the Chronos described, so perhaps he would believe me. Maybe, even if Melchior cared for me, he might just accept the idea of killing me as fact. Inevitable.

What sort of person was Lachesis, I wondered, to observe all this? If she loved him, if she'd seen it all–

It would have driven me insane to watch him with another woman. Maybe that was why she was so bitter... so hell bent on seeing our destruction. If she could not have him, she would not allow him to be happy with anyone else.

She'd watched all his life, then written a book about it. With straight, neat handwriting, she catalogued our kisses, places we'd had sex. I turned the pages and kept reading, my expression horrified.

Malinda attempts to leave him.

Melchior kills Malinda before their first wedding anniversary.

Atropos raises Morena to become a monster; holding her captive in the tower.

Morena kills the other descendants of the Fates, one by one.

Melchior disappears, assumed to be murdered by his daughter.

Moirai becomes a land of the dead, with the Grim Reaper as its queen.

The end.

The end.

As I read the words, it felt like a boulder had been placed on each of my shoulders. Like I might never pull myself out of the mire I was swimming in.

But I'd never been one to wallow in self-pity, I surely wasn't going to start now. I considered the options while drumming my fingers on the desk.

What if I left Melchior before our daughter was born and he never knew she existed?

What if I found the mask, and then killed Atropos?

What if I simply told him what was going to happen? Would that avoid everything?

This future couldn't possibly become true if any of the pieces were altered, could it?

I flipped back several pages. *I attempt to leave him. So he kills me.*

The *leaving him* plan sounded outlandish. Leave and go where? I wasn't even sure I knew which direction to go in. There were days of travel in a land of freezing temperatures. Why would I ever try to leave?

And yet, it also occurred to me that if I altered my destiny, everything in the Chronos would be void.

They have a lot of loud clocks. Morena thinks it's a Cullen snapping its jaws, or a window blowing open. I'm making sure they do the right thing.

... Lachesis could travel backwards in time and intervene. She'd already confessed to doing exactly that. Therefore it was entirely possible that even if I succeeded in altering our destiny, she'd appear and undo my handiwork. Especially if she had an interest in the outcome.

Control of time was a much more powerful ability than Death, and the idea that she might go back and undo any of the work I'd already done made me even more paranoid.

On the other hand, interfering, for one's own selfish purposes... that sort of behavior is what got Atropos' powers revoked by Nyx. Surely, what Lachesis was doing was nearly the same thing. And I'd heard clicks throughout my time here at Grace Castle. Not every day, certainly, but often enough to have thought it was strange.

No, you stupidly thought there were many loud clocks. Just like she said.

With a feeling of intense discomfort, I realized that the Controller of Time watched me regularly.

"This is so much worse than before," I said aloud, to myself. Now I had not one, but two all-powerful beings hanging over my shoulder. And of the two Fates, I feared Time much more.

I paced the room, back and forth, back and forth. If only I hadn't left the Nightingale. If only I hadn't accepted Melchior's offer. If only I hadn't married him, or had sex with him. It was all wishful thinking, and would do nothing to help me avoid a ruinous destiny. I thought and thought, until the fire was nothing but a sad pile of ash, the last two embers stubbornly glowing. In the end, I realized that only two things were certain.

First, I couldn't handle this alone.

Second, Lachesis wasn't done playing her game. I, the pawn, wasn't either.

26

The Gods underestimated how much I wanted to live. And the lengths to which I would go to free my child from their chains.

I paused all searching for the Eternal Slumber, and then re-read every grimoire in Grace Castle. Somewhere, I was sure, was the answer to this problem. I was going to defy my destiny, no matter what it took.

If Melchior was supposed to kill me, then what I needed was a spell for immortality.

If Lachesis was my enemy, then I needed a more powerful ally.

And if my daughter was doomed, then I needed to change her future.

It was as simple, and as complicated, as that.

Nilensi herself had told me that I didn't need a witch, or to become one– I simply needed the correct ingredients, and to pronounce the incantations properly. Thanks to Zeph, I could read and write as well as any lady. There was no reason not to research it all myself.

Of course, I knew that at any moment, if Lachesis didn't like what we were doing, she could rewind time by ten minutes and simply change things. The fact that she found my attempts to undo my destiny entertaining did nothing to make me feel better.

I reassured and distracted myself with Melchior, falling for him so completely and thoroughly that both of us were bewildered by it. I couldnt get enough of his body, his obsidian eyes. His hands, strong, rough, gentle, grasping.

With every kiss, with every touch, he whispered the words I most needed to hear.

I'll take care of you. You're mine. I love you.

He kissed me and kissed me, his mouth sealing his vow.

I won't let anything happen to you.

Of course, I didn't have the luxury of believing it. If I did, if I let down my guard, then we were all lost. So I moved with extreme caution, trying my best not to arouse his suspicions, reading the grimoires as he slept.

I wasn't accustomed to feeling such strong emotions. Whether it was pregnancy or the dark destiny looming over my head, I was tearful and tired, exhausted and angry. My outlook and confidence were both at an all time low.

It took me a week to formulate a plan of action, a ridiculous, risky theory that if unsuccessful would mean certain death. But I thought maybe– maybe– it might be possible. As I stared at the sea, and reviewed all the steps that I would take, my eyes welled again and I blinked the tears away.

The wind from the sea brushed my hair back, teased its ends. I stood outside on my balcony, with six layers of clothes – and still wretchedly cold. But the view of the sea was beautiful, and today the sun shone through the clouds here and there, making a patchwork across the water of light and dark, dark and light.

Ironically, the first time I ever liked Grace Castle was the day I decided to leave it.

Melchior stepped out onto the balcony, then came and put his arms around my waist, drawing me to his chest. I leaned into his warmth, grateful for his steady presence. I hoped his strength would help me to follow through.

"Still looking south I see."

I chuckled. "Where else is there to look?"

"You can hardly run a kingdom by daydreaming over the waves." Melchior balanced his chin on the top of my head.

"I think you'll manage it."

I turned to him. I wanted to see his face. Had to. I was his, and he was mine, and it was important that I look him in the eye.

His gaze met mine, and then, when he saw what lingered there, narrowed.

"What's wrong?" he asked.

I stepped back. "Our relationship has run its course." It felt as if I was cutting into my own veins as I said the words.

"And you've decided to leave me afterall." He waited for a beat. "Anything else?"

"There's quite a bit more, actually. But that should cover the essential points."

He shifted, puzzled, thrown off course. He hadn't expected this. "What if I don't want to let you go?"

"Is that a demand or a preference?"

"Malinda." He reached for me.

"Don't do that." I brushed his hands aside. It had to sound like I was out of his life for good, that I truly meant it. *Had to.* Just in case Lachesis was watching again.

"Fifty thousand." Melchior swallowed, his throat working. "Fifty thousand pieces of goblin gold if you stay and be my queen."

Something cracked painfully in my chest. "Surely you don't think this is still about the money."

"I don't know what it's about. I only want you to stay. Please stay."

He was begging. Without an ounce of pride.

Fifty thousand gold pieces. There was no way I'd ever spend that much, not even in a hundred lifetimes. The great irony being that I didn't care about the money. I only cared about us, and our daughter.

"We've been over this," I said. "I can't get you what you want. Now it's time for what I want. My freedom. I have my own life to think about."

"Give it a few more days. You came here to find the Eternal Slumber. And there's so few places left where it could be."

I started to shake my head. "It's impossible–"

"Nothing is impossible. And if we had a child..."

I froze. He wasn't supposed to know yet. I had said nothing, I wasn't even showing, my stomach still flat. He only meant *if*.

Hastily, I corrected him. "If we had a child, they'd be part of this bloody, awful legacy. What then? Would we let your mother poison them, steal their soul, force them into servitude the way she has you?"

"Of course not." I could see the thoughts spinning wildly behind his eyes. "I wouldn't let that happen. I'd kill her first."

"Only a Fate can kill another Fate. And if your lover Lachesis was going to do that, she would have done it already."

"We'll figure it out as we go."

"Or we'll just end up dead," I said, suddenly tired.

"Don't go," Melchior pleaded.

I sighed. "You're the Prince of Darkness. Raised by Death. Son of a dark wizard. Wielder of Shadows. No wife of yours could ever be happy."

The pain in his face gripped me so tightly I almost took it back. Almost.

Behind us, the sea crashed against the rocks and pilings, capped with white froth. If I'd wanted, this was the time to spew out all the anger and bitterness, to blame him for everything that had happened thus far. But I didn't want to hurt him.

I couldn't stand to wound him anymore than he already had been.

I only wanted to give our daughter what she needed. If that wasn't going to be a loving father, nor a loving mother, what was it?

"I have to go," I murmured. "You know I do. You told me so many times to go."

This was the split in the road, and I must force us both down it. All our lives depended on this moment, on how convincing I could be.

His shadows wrapped around my wrist. Cold, tight as an iron band. Chaining me to him and this wretched place.

My heart ached. All I wanted was to stop this, to not argue, to go inside and curl up together, to fall asleep on his chest as he read in the lamplight. Instead I had to go through with this. It felt like my heart was a series of rooms, and the ceilings were falling, crumbling and tumbling, caving in on themselves. I closed my eyes.

He cradled my face in his hands as he kissed me. Unable to resist, I traced my fingers up his chest, trying to memorize every detail of him: the warmth of his skin, the darkness of his eyes, the solid comfort and protection he made me feel.

"I would never hurt you. I would never betray you," he said.

Our eyes met. "I know. I know you wouldn't." I meant it.

His forehead was pressed against mine, and he whispered to me. "I have stored your gold at a castle called Rose Hall. It can only be reached via dragon. It's heavily guarded. If you go there, you will have both your fortune and a safe haven. Pirate and merchant ships often stop there, so it should be less than a week before you are able to sail toward Kinseamair."

He said it all as if it were a secret.

My mouth was as dry as a ball of wool. "How will they know to give me the money?"

"Because I told them your name." Melchior kissed me softly. "Two years ago."

Shock pinged through me, like a stroke of lightning. "Two years ago, we hadn't even met."

Clenching his jaw, he released me, and then turned toward the sea.

"Two years ago, I went to see a man named Zephyros Castan. We talked in his study. I offered him ten thousand gold coins just to see you. My destiny. My mate. He called me a fool, but he took my money anyway. He told me that if I went upstairs to the attic, I'd find you sleeping. He warned me if I touched you, I'd end up dead - that you'd put a knife in my chest before I could try anything, and that if you failed to kill me, he would."

Covering my mouth with my hand, I simply stared at him.

"You were nothing like how I thought you'd be. You were wearing all black - pants, even. You had blood on your clothes and the sheets, and your hair was braided. There were three knives on your nightstand."

I blinked repeatedly.

"But I knew you were my destiny. Just like Lachesis said. Not small, not shy, not soft. A dirty, lying thief. You were only seventeen, terrifying and real and raw, and I wanted–I wanted to wake you up and tell you everything, but... It didn't seem like the right thing to do. Dumping my entire sordid life and awful mother onto your shoulders. No matter how capable you were. I found myself hoping that I could change our destiny. If I did, maybe you would become someone else."

"I went back downstairs and told Zeph that I hoped I'd never see him again. That I would do my best to make sure we never met." Melchior sighed. "I sent a letter to Clotho, asking her if I might send part of my fortune to Rose Hall, to be kept there for you, should you ever choose to come claim it. You can't imagine how angry I was to have to save you from the Keres."

The knowledge shouldn't make a difference. We were still doomed. I needed to leave him before I ended up dead. It shouldn't make me want to hold him, console him, and apologize.

"I don't want to lose you. Not to my mother, not to a Fae, and not to some pirate ship heading south."

I would have to act as if I didn't care. So I rolled my eyes. "Lose me. How's that work? Our marriage was fake. Our wedding night, also fake. Your lover haunts my every footstep. Still here, in this house, whenever you want her. All I am is... an imitation."

"An imitation?" Melchior chuckled grimly. "If you were, I could have left you in the crypt. I would have left you to die from the Keres without another thought. An imitation wouldn't have me spinning every time I hear your voice, or worried whenever you're out of my sight. Or feeling like my heart is being ripped apart every time you take a bath and sit in there crying, because you think I can't hear."

He pulled me back into his arms. "I love you. If I have to die to prove it, I will."

My breath caught. He didn't mean it. "Let go."

He wouldn't. Instead, Melchior and his shadows gripped me tighter. "I married you. Healed you with my own blood, multiple times. That meant something. The symbolism can't be lost on you."

"If I meant so much to you, why did you leave? Why keep so many secrets? Why are you kind one moment, and cruel the next? You're the one lying, pushing me away at every turn."

"Because she killed them!" he exploded. "She killed *every* friend, any maid I became close to! Atropos killed my father. She even killed my dog, just because it was *meaningful* to me. Because that's who she is!"

"She tortured them right in front of me, until they begged *me* to end them." He swallowed. "So yes. Sometimes I can barely stand to be in a room with you. Because I know—" he wiped a tear away. "I *know* how this story ends."

He closed his eyes. "But you keep saying, and I keep thinking, that maybe destiny could be changed. Maybe."

The rest of his words were lost on the wind. He pushed me away because I mattered. Because he loved me. He didn't want to let me go. The way his intense gaze gripped me... Lachesis' words suddenly made sense. He'd kill me, *because he was forced to.*

Unless we could find a way to change our future.

"What do I have to do? Take the mask? Chain her in a cave? Kill her? I would do it, if I just knew it would work. That you'd be safe." He cleared his throat. Looked away. "All the while I'm hating myself, knowing I'm not worth the risk."

Gently, I took his face in my hands. "You are," I said simply. I cupped the stubbled jaw, and stared up into his dark eyes. His vulnerable frown tore at my heart, and I sighed heavily.

"I'm glad we met, and glad I married you. I don't regret any of it. I would do it all again."

He leaned his forehead against mine and exhaled slowly, brushing his lips over mine as he wrapped his arms around me. "Give me a few more days. Come inside. And be with me."

My resolve collapsed, like a boat made of parchment placed in the sea. Later – I'd leave later. I kissed him again, and then followed him back into the bedroom.

Sometime later, a random night, I dreamed that I stood on the edge of a vast obsidian sea. Melchior was next to me, only shadows, but I could feel his presence. I could scent him on the wind. *How do you kill a God?* he asked, his words carrying on the briny breeze. I didn't know; I didn't know. I was cold, the sea was dark, and I was afraid.

Click.

I woke up. My eyes flew open. The room seemed empty, but for us two... yet I knew she was there. Watching. Waiting.

His chest was pressed against my spine, and his movements were slow, a long stroke across my hip and stomach. His breath was warm on the back of my neck, in my hair. He slid his hand beneath my nightgown to cup my breast.

"Go back to sleep. I didn't mean to disturb you."

"You've been disturbing me for a long time," I muttered. "Why stop now?"

He smiled against my shoulder, then his thumb drifted over my nipple. It pebbled against his fingertips.

I turned over to face him.

"I love you," he murmured, his obsidian gaze still unfocused and sleepy. He meant it. I felt it down to the marrow of my bones– he loved me.

But did it even matter if he did? Wouldn't he just kill me anyway?

I kissed him, long and lingering. I hoped it made Lachesis miserable. I hoped she'd see us making love and die of a broken heart. I slid my hands over his chest. Mine to touch, mine to hold. *Until we are parted.*

Melchior gave a low sigh, a hum of satisfaction.

He preferred slow, intimate, thorough. He called it mating, or making love. Never sex, never fucking. He was not that sort of man. It never failed to surprise me.

I want her gone, I want her out of our lives. I want Time and Death both locked in a cave at the bottom of the sea, never to resurface. It was a litany inside my head.

Distantly, I heard the sound of the ocean. She'd left the balcony door open, again. To inconvenience me into getting out of bed. Like always, Melchior told me to ignore her. That we had bigger problems. He kissed my neck as I whispered to him, sweet nothings, random things, nothing notable, in case she got closer and decided to truly listen.

I prayed that Lachesis was wrong, or mistaken, or that I could successfully change our future just enough to make a difference. Knowing that if I didn't play this game carefully, perfectly... I would die. My eyes welled up. I started shaking - not a gentle tremble, but breath hitching, shoulders rattling. I covered my face with my hands.

"Malinda...?"

"I'm just cold," I lied.

Melchior stroked my hair gently, letting me weep on his chest. "We're going to win," he assured me. "You'll see."

We can't win. Only a Fate can kill a Fate. And only an immortal could survive them.

I sat up suddenly, pulling away from his touch.

"What?" he demanded. "What is it?"

Our eyes met in the dark. "I have an idea."

27

"They aren't alive," I insisted as Nilensi peered over the edge of the stone balcony, down into the courtyard below. "They don't care if we leave."

"What if they do? What if they chase us?"

Then they'll rip us apart. Just like they do everything else.

"I'm not sure it's a good idea," Nilensi began, but I cut her off.

"Atropos will kill you if you don't leave. And eventually, Nico too. You have to come with me." My eyes pleaded with her. I simply had to convince her. Otherwise, it would all fall apart.

"We are out of options," I told her. "Melchior thought we would be able to kill her, and we can't. She's managed to murder multiple people in the castle. It's only a matter of time until you and Nico are next."

"And you're sure it's in that book of yours? We escape, we live?"

"Yes. I'm sure." This was a lie.

She would go with me, even if she felt hesitant. I just had to be patient, convincing.

"We'll go north, to the elven villages and covens," I said. I knew Nilensi had family there, she could seek refuge with them - if we made it that far. Of course, I had no idea how long it would take to get there, or how many Cullen we would encounter along the way.

"I'm not sure they'd welcome me," Nilensi said. "My mother left as a teenager. I've never even met any of my cousins. What about the west? Doesn't Caerwyn know the way?"

"That's a good idea," I said. "We steal Melchior's horse. Then we won't have to go on foot."

Every route was full of peril, and most of them had Cullen along the way. As if she could read my thoughts, Nilensi spoke.

"I'd rather not be out there in the dark with those things."

"They aren't any friendlier in the daytime, you know."

She sighed. "Why are you pressuring so much? Why is it so urgent to leave now?"

"Because we're running out of time."

Nilensi blinked her large brown eyes. "Are you confident we will make it?"

Of course I wasn't. In fact, I was quite confident that we wouldn't.

"If we take the horse, if we go during the day, then they'll think we're just going on a ride. Getting fresh air. They won't come after us if we aren't running and panicking."

She was unconvinced. "We wear our warmest cloaks and gloves, and then hope we find shelter?"

I gritted my teeth. "Yes."

"What about Melchior?" she asked. "Won't he notice you missing from bed? Or wonder why you're suddenly interested in horseback jaunts around the grounds?"

I shrugged. "I told him I'm leaving. He knows."

The Chronos was in the bottom of my bag. Mentally, I thought of the page, of the words written in Lachesis' neat, precise handwriting.

Malinda attempts to leave him.

Atropos insists he punish her for it, so he kills her.

My idea was subtle, perhaps, but I hoped it was clever enough to defy destiny.

I would attempt to leave him now. If Melchior killed me, then Morena would die inside me. She would never become the grim reaper, never be a servant to Atropos, and Melchior would never be her captor.

But I did not think I would die. Too much of the future was on my shoulders. So I planned to go far, far away from here. Neither Melchior nor Atropos need ever know of her existence. If I succeeded, I'd be free, and so would she.

The castle corridors were so quiet I could hear the sound of myself buttoning my long gloves. It was normal that the usual bustle of court life was dimmed by the heavy snowfall; but now Grace Castle was almost completely silent. The mood was somber; so many had gone missing.

I slipped into my cloak, the thick black wool a welcome barrier against the chill that seeped through the stone walls of Grace Castle. Outside, the world was a blanket of white, snowflakes steadily falling.

Nilensi wrapped Nico in a bundle of furs. Her eyes met mine, a spark of determination flickering in their depths.

"We're just going for a walk," I murmured to her. "If anyone should ask. It's just for a bit of fresh air."

Her fingers deftly secured the last of Nico's wrappings. "Right," she echoed.

Cullen guards chattered as we passed, their gazes lingering just a moment too long. They didn't look at us with suspicion, but rather as if we were slabs of meat to gnaw upon. My heart thudded against my ribcage, and it was everything I could do not to run down the corridor.

Though it seemed like it took forever, soon we emerged through the side door into the courtyard. Frigid air bit at my cheeks and neck, and I drew my hood up, shielding my face from the cold.

"Did you leave a note for Fenix?" I asked.

"I did. But there's no hope of him receiving it. The best I can expect is that he'll sneak out after dark and come find us."

Nico shivered, his hand tucked in Nilensi's, oblivious to the dangers of our deceit. We trudged through the snow, our path meandering but purposeful. I kept my gaze forward, focused on the stables.

"Are you really sure we should be doing this?" Nilensi asked, for at least the tenth time.

"Yes," I said briefly, my gaze flickering to the western balcony that was ours. I half-expected him to still be standing there, watching me go.

We saddled Caerwyn, Nilensi with shaking hands, and then set out from the stable courtyard. Nico and I sat on the horse, all smiles, as Nilensi led us. Toward the gate, then out, then northwest. The edge of the wood seemed impossibly far.

Behind us, Grace Castle rose like a monster from the bed of white, its dark windows like empty eye sockets. I kept my focus on the distant line that marked the edge of the castle grounds. Freedom, or something like it, waited at the edge of the wood.

Wordless, we carried on, and I argued internally with myself about turning back. Wind whistled in my ears and I pulled my coat tighter around my body. With each step, I felt my resolve harden. I would not turn back. I couldn't. The only destiny that awaited me within those walls was Death - at least leaving, I had some measure of control.

Eventually, Caerwyn stepped beneath the dark boughs and I heaved a small sigh of relief. Evergreens loomed above us, blocking out the sun and casting us into an eerie darkness. I shivered, even though I was wrapped up tightly in my coat. I couldn't shake the feeling that something was watching, waiting to pounce. It was deadly quiet, but for Nilensi's ragged breathing. She had practically waded through the field, the snow above her knees.

Pausing for a moment, I rubbed my stomach with one hand. There'd been no sign of pursuit so far.

"Are you sure this is the best way to go?" she said, breaking the silence.

North. Toward the witches and goblins, toward the Elven villages. Toward all the darkest creatures in Moirai. Shuddering, I licked my cracked lips.

"Let's keep going. We'll walk until you and the horse are tired, then switch."

Nilensi didn't argue, so we continued.

Soon frost coated my eyelashes. Nilensi stumbled, tiring in the deep drifts of snow, both her hands bleeding from the sharp edges of ice as she pulled herself up. Her gloves were soft cloth, woven, and soaked through. The air was freezing, carrying the sharp scent of pine.

"Here," I said, pausing Caerwyn. "Take the horse. And my gloves."

I slid down from the horse, careful of my stomach and my footing. Breaking my ankle would definitely ruin our plans. Here the snow was deep, but powdery, like feathers.

Waiting patiently, I watched as Nilensi mounted the horse.

Then I gave her my only pair of gloves, thick hide and lined with fur. The ones Melchior had given me shortly after we arrived at Grace Castle. It seemed so long ago. As I watched Nilensi pull on those gloves, it felt as if my heart was breaking.

If not for *the Fates,* his devouring mother and soulless lover, none of this would be happening. If there had been any chance he would leave with me, I would have taken it. But I knew our future. It was unfair, it was terrible, and this was the best way for me to do something about it.

"I know what you did," I said at last, glancing up at Nilensi.

"What do you mean?" Her tone was sharp.

"That spell."

"I've done all sorts of spells. You'll have to be more specific."

I had no doubt that she knew exactly what I was referring to. "Demitra. The Cullen. That was you, was it not?"

Nico was listening intently to our conversation, meanwhile Nilensi's jaw worked as she stared stonily ahead. "How do you know about that?"

"It doesn't really matter how I know. It only matters why you did it."

"She threatened Nico. She said she just wanted me to try something, that her goal was to bring back her lover Tassos. A 'little experiment'. No real harm done."

"I suppose that was when Demitra said she was leaving?" I fought to keep up with Caerwyn, struggling through the knee deep snow.

"Yes."

Disbelieving, I glared up at her. Of all people, Nilensi should know how terrible this was. Why did she seem so calm?

"If you want to blame anyone, blame yourself. Atropos read the spells inside that grimoire you gave her and decided that I should test them on the other servants. On my *friends*."

"I didn't know–"

"No one could have. But we'll be paying for that mistake, as will the rest of Moirai, for hundreds of years."

My fingers were numb, my face felt frozen. Behind us, a branch cracked as the heavy weight of snow broke it, and flurries crashed to the ground. I heard a low growl in the distance.

We were being followed. Nilensi still hadn't noticed.

"Once she saw how useful the Cullen were, she wanted more. Then more. Atropos realized she could enslave them, and make an entire army."

"So you cast another spell to do just that?" I was shocked.

Nilensi huffed, her breath creating a puff of fog in the cold. "It's over all of Moirai. She made me — I couldn't say no. I did it to *save* my son's life."

I wrung my hands and tried to process this new, terrible information. It was so much worse than I'd originally thought. "You cursed *all* of the kingdom. Everyone is doomed."

Before she could reply, there was a low growl behind us. Guttural, high. Not a wolf, nor a bear, nor a mountain lion.

Nilensi looked over her shoulder. "Oh my god," she said.

I turned. It was nothing on my list. It was a child. A child - a servant child. A footman, perhaps, or one of the group who put away dishes. He had curling brown hair, and he snarled as he stumbled through the deep snow.

"Ride as fast and far as you can," I told her. "I'll catch up."

"We won't leave you behind," Nilensi replied.

"I said go!" I slapped the horse on her hind quarters, fully expecting her to take off in a run.

This is where the plan began to fall apart.

Caerwyn would not abandon me. She stood stock still, blinking, refusing to budge.

Loyal.

"Damn you horse, go on!" I shouted, to no avail.

More Cullen emerged from between the trees, drawn by the Cullen boy's shrieks. Nilensi leapt down from the back of the mare, her knife drawn.

"What are you doing?" I demanded.

"Saving you," she replied.

I'd never told her that such a thing wasn't possible. That the Chronos said Melchior would kill me.

I'd planned for her and Nico to run - if I could do nothing else, I could get them out.

One of the zombies leapt, gnashing their teeth, red eyes rolling, toward the two of us.

Punching and slashing, she stabbed the first Cullen six or seven times before the second, third, and fourth Cullen reached us. Nilensi fought hard.

One grabbed me around the waist and began dragging me back toward the castle.

"Run!" I heard Nilensi scream. "Nico, run!"

The boy slid down the horse and ran. Quick as a jackrabbit, he disappeared between the trees.

Caerwyn's neigh sounded more like a scream as Cullen leapt onto her back. The horse whinnied with fury, bucking and straining. The reins Nilensi dropped, however, tangled in the limbs of a tree. Two, then three more Cullen lurched forward, teeth gnashing and eyes rolling. Caerwyn kept fighting, lashing at them with her head and her hooves.

She was alive, and they were not.

She could tire, and they could not.

Nilensi beat several away from her with a short sword, but even with their ribs partially hacked away, the Cullen simply rose again. It was no use. There were too many.

There was a resounding crack that echoed through the trees as the beautiful mare fell to her knees. I strained to see, fighting against the Cullen's iron grip. I saw the moment they overpowered Nilensi, as the decaying bodies pressed her down into the snow, smothering her, ripping her cloak open, exposing her skin.

I screamed and struggled as I was dragged back toward Grace Castle. Behind us, Nilensi and Caerwyn were opened, ravaged, snow falling onto the backs of the Cullen as they feasted.

28

The Cullen dumped me in a heap at Melchior's feet. Protectively, I cradled my stomach. His tall figure was silhouetted against the flames of a fireplace, and in its red orange light, his face was terrifying. More like a demon's head than a man, and he stared down at me.

Cullen stepped back to the edges of the room, softly clicking their jaws. A movement caught my eye, and I glanced around the room.

"I suppose this wasn't included on your little tour. Welcome, wife, to the laboratory." Melchior struck a match, and lit several of the tall black candles along the table.

I'd never been here before. There was a long low table and a cauldron that bubbled in a corner. It smelled strongly of medicines, herbs, and ashes. Fenix hung from the ceiling, his throat cut, blood all down his chest, pooling at his feet. He'd been stabbed dozens of times, his penis and feet removed. Somehow - somehow - he was still alive.

Vomit rose up in my throat and I heaved.

In the corner, Atropos stood, a mountain of malice. The only thing more terrifying than her expression was her silence.

I pulled at the rope binding my wrists. They were too tight, and the golden fibers cut into my skin.

"Don't worry about those," Melchior said. "A little chafing is the least of your worries."

A muscle feathered in his jaw as our eyes met. The coldness on his face shocked me.

"I suppose that was a goodbye fuck this morning?" he asked.

We hadn't made love this morning. He was pretending, trying to signal me. Hope flared in my chest.

"No, I – it wasn't."

"How *dare* you try to leave my son." Atropos came close and spit in my face.

"Why couldn't you just let me handle things?" That part, he meant. "Since the moment you arrived, I've taken care of you. I'm the only reason you're not a rotting corpse downstairs in the dungeon."

"Unlike Demitra, you mean?" I demanded, glaring at Atropos. "An innocent woman who your mother tortured to death?"

"You don't know what you're talking about." Melchior took a long, bracing gulp of wine from a goblet before he reached for me, touched my golden hair. "I bowed to you. I got on my knees *for you.* A girl from nowhere."

Melchior was silent. He pressed his lips together into a thin line, as if he were trying to calm himself. "And you thought you could marry me and flee?"

"*You* should kill her for her treachery," Atropos hissed.

"No," he said forcefully. "I want to keep her."

"You can have another plaything. More beautiful. I'll find one for you."

"No!" Melchior shouted. "I want *her*!"

He was acting like a spoiled child. Much to my amazement, Atropos seemed to respond favorably to this.

"We could punish her," he said. "Make her unable to leave. Bind her to me."

Atropos raised an eyebrow. "What do you have in mind?"

I stared dully into the fire as the two of them conferred in low whispers. *The witch showed me a spell...she could... what if we...* their plan came to me in incomplete fragments.

Finally they both returned, Atropos with a cruel smile, Melchior looking determined. "My mother has been perfecting her resurrection spell, making Cullen. I've convinced her that *your* punishment should be to become one as well."

"What?" my mouth fell open.

Melchior held up a finger. "With one small change. You will be forever tied to me, forever *loyal* to me, forever a servant. Mine."

His maniacal grin chilled me to the bone. Confused, my gaze pinged back and forth between Melchior and Atropos. According to the Chronos, he would kill me. Certainly that seemed likely. And yet, he was signaling me that he had *something* planned.

"You won't be able to leave this house, ever, until I say. Until I choose to cast you out."

Our eyes met, and I know we were both thinking of the same night - the night Atropos forced him to kneel beside my chair so I could cut his shoulder. When he'd squeezed my ankle. *Go ahead. Do it.* He'd trusted me then. I could trust him now.

Surely he wouldn't actually kill me. Though, I supposed if he did, I wouldn't be around to complain about it. I squeezed my eyes shut, then gave a small, almost imperceptible nod. I grasped his wrist, which was just next to my hand. I squeezed it.

I trust you. I will always trust you.

"Hold her," he said to the Cullen. They came, eager to do his bidding. Their rotting hands dragged me to the table, then forced me down upon it.

"I'm sorry," I pleaded. "I'll stay. I won't try to get away again." Although I was putting on a show for Atropos, my words rang with truth.

"Too late for apologies now, girl." She hissed at me, hovering above my face. "You have disgraced this house."

From a shelf along the wall, Melchior retrieved a large ceremonial urn. Intricate ivory swirls decorated every inch of its surface, with a lid carved in the shape of a skull.

"What's that? What's it for?" Imagining it full of poison, I was relieved when he opened it to reveal nothing inside - it was empty.

"It's a canopus. A canopic jar, and this one has a powerful curse on it."

Melchior brought the urn to the table. In one hand he held a knife with a curved blade, made from the finest silver. Both of these, he sat next to me.

"You once said to never use dark magic," I said. "That it exacts too high a price."

Atropos laughed. "He told you that? My son has been learning dark magic since he was a boy. He knows more than the leader of the north coven."

Melchior turned the knife, inspecting it, and its wicked blade glinted in the firelight.

"I'm going to take something from you, Malinda. Something that is already mine, I think. If it's mine, you have nothing to worry about."

"What do you mean?" I whispered with horror. I wasn't pretending anymore. "What are you talking about?"

This was not in the Chronos. If he wasn't going to kill me, then I had no idea what he planned to do.

"If your heart is mine, *mine to hold,* it will continue to beat once I remove it."

"Melchior." The vague sense of panic was now a stampeding herd, and I nearly couldn't breathe from the fright.

"It's a trade. I'll take your heart, and you'll stay here. The magic will bind us - you won't be able to leave me. You can't leave, but you'll live."

"I thought you said I'll be a Cullen."

"You will. But I have no desire to be married to a corpse. So unlike them, your heart will be mine... and every so often, you'll have to get a new one to keep your body alive."

A new what? He couldn't possibly mean a new heart. There weren't any living people left in Grace Castle.

"Meanwhile, I'll keep your heart here, perfectly preserved, in this urn." He tapped it with one finger.

"The magic only works if your love is real. Otherwise, me holding your heart will force it to wither into nothing. I suppose it's a more powerful version of a truth potion."

I began to worry. "Melchior."

"Drink this," he demanded. Then he pressed a goblet to my lips. I tried to twist away, but he forced the foul-smelling mixture down my throat.

Atropos was watching.

I gave a stifled sob and turned my face away. A moment later, Melchior's hand brushed my cheek, wiping away a tear.

"We'll know once and for all whether this was a grand ruse to become queen. My mother thinks you want power and her position. I say you don't. We'll find out who is right."

"Please don't do this."

I'll protect you. I'd kissed his scars, just as he'd kissed mine.

I love you. Now he had me bound and tied, and there was a knife in his hand.

"I'm afraid," I whispered, so low I didn't know if he heard.

Our eyes met, green and black, black and green. Thieves. Liars. Murderers. Husband and wife. *Until we are parted.*

"You swore to me," he murmured. "You're mine, and I'm yours. You gave me your body and your blood and your soul. Didn't you?"

His fingers ghosted over my collarbone. Reassuring me.

"Yes," I admitted, a broken whisper.

Do you trust me? He'd asked, as he led me up to our wedding chamber.

In the corner, Atropos stirred the cauldron and sneered at me. "She won't live through it. Her heart will dry up and we'll pound it into dust."

Melchior glared at his mother. "You're wrong. She loves me."

Her smile was malicious, malevolent. "Then you have nothing to worry about, do you?"

He raised the knife.

"No," he said. Then he slammed the blade down upon my chest.

29

I woke slowly, like a nereid from the deep, emerging on the blue-green surface of the ocean. My eyesight was different, and everything was strangely fuzzy. As if I stared at the world through a thin tapestry, torn and poorly mended. Above me was a large, arching window in shades of red glass. Recognition pinged through me.

The chapel. I'm in the chapel. I'm alive.

Melchior sat in a chair next to me, his head buried in his hands. His clothes were rumpled. He looked... beaten. Broken. And I wondered what could have happened while I'd been gone.

Alive, laying in the chapel next to Melchior. Not in a crypt, not under the dirt, not on the table with a knife in my chest. I inhaled slowly, counting to five. I was alive.

He could be a little happier about it.

When I shifted, his head popped up, eyes wide and worried. Warm hands grasped mine a moment later - burning hot against my skin.

"Thank Zeus you're awake." His arms wrapped around me, tugged me upward, close to him. "I thought I failed. That the potion didn't work. That somehow I'd made a mistake." Melchior lifted his head, his grip on my hand almost painful. "Don't say anything. Let me have a moment."

He kissed my forehead, then my mouth. Desperate, urgent kisses that immediately sent a shockwave through my system. Hungrily, I kissed him back, wanting–

Wanting to bite him.

Wanting to *eat* him in great, huge chunks so my stomach didn't feel quite so empty.

I jerked backward, shocked at the impulse. The feeling was very unpleasant, not at all welcome, and I smothered it immediately.

"What happened?" I said.

"I removed your heart, and you died...exactly as planned." He swallowed hard. "But when you didn't wake up within a few hours, I thought I'd miscalculated."

Miscalculated.

He meant that if the spell didn't work, it was because I didn't love him after all. That he'd removed my heart and murdered me, or at least doomed me into being one of Atropos' undead army because his dark magic would only work if I *truly* loved him.

Lucky for both of us, my feelings were one of the few things I'd been honest about.

I sat up. *The baby.* Reflexively, I put my hand on the stomach. Would she still be there? I prayed to Nyx that she was alright.

"What did you do with my heart? Where is it?"

"Hidden. I've put it somewhere I hope it'll never be found."

Hopefully not the library, I thought wryly. That hadn't worked out so well with the grimoires.

"I'm sorry," he said. "I did everything by the book."

The book?

At my questioning gaze, Melchior flushed. "I read the Chronos. And the grimoire that you made. I wasn't exactly sure what your plan was, but on the balcony... I could tell you were lying."

Full of gratitude, I kissed him. He'd figured out, or guessed, that I was going to try and defy destiny..

I hugged Melchior tightly. "So you killed me, but before you did, you gave me a potion that would make me nearly immortal."

"Correct." He gave a small laugh. "I had no idea if it would work, but... here you are."

We had defied our destiny. Perhaps it was only temporary, but still, it was a success.

"So I'm a Cullen now?"

"Yes, but more aware. Able to feel and speak and think."

Puzzled, I glanced at my hands, which were paler, but otherwise the same. I wouldn't act like them, I wouldn't think like them, but I was still one of them. Dead.

I listened, and realized he was right. In fact, I could feel some things more, such as the heart beating in my chest.

I tilted my head quizzically.

"What is that?" I paused and listened again. "If you cut out my heart, what's thumping inside my ribs right now?"

"Fenix. I gave you his heart."

I froze, the blood draining from my face. "You did what?"

"Atropos was going to kill him anyway. At least with me, he wouldn't be tortured. And you needed a heart."

Fenix was the only person in our team who could replace the mask, or create another, or fix it if ours was somehow faulty.

Melchior shook his head. "If there had been any other option, I would have taken it."

"If Fenix is dead, where's the forgery?"

"Hidden in my armoire." Melchior gave me a sheepish look. "It made sense to keep it close."

I touched his chest. "I wasn't criticizing."

Melchior placed his hand over mine, warming it. "To look normal, you'll need a new heart. Regularly."

"From whom?"

Melchior rubbed the back of his neck, as if trying to massage away the tension. "Whomever we can find."

"You mean, whomever we can kill." *Whatever poor, innocent fool wanders across our path.*

"Right." He rolled his shoulders in a half-shrug. "I don't know how soon. It could be minutes; could be weeks."

I would have to think about that later- it was a problem for another day, after I had space and time to process all that had happened.

Gingerly, I got to my feet. They felt unsteady, wooden. As if I'd slept folded up in a box for a very long time. It wasn't only my legs, it was all of me. My hands were cold, my face felt... more solid, somehow. As if the blood in my veins no longer pulsed and beat, but instead moved at a sluggish crawl through narrowed veins.

Confused, I touched a hand to my cheek as if expecting to find rot. Yet my skin felt normal. Cold to the touch, of course, a chill there that hadn't been present before—as if I'd fallen asleep in the shadows on a long autumn day.

"It was the best I could do." He reached over and grasped my waist. Sudden warmth flooded me. I remembered the words of Lachesis on the balcony, the ones I'd written with shaking hands in the Chronos.

He'll kill you. A truth... and we'd manipulated it. Twisted our destiny despite the two Fates who wanted us dead.

We'd won.

No one mourned my death, including me.

I viewed it as a victory, unprecedented. I had managed to defy my destiny, no matter how slightly. Because of our manipulation, it was now obvious to both Melchior and I that the rules could be bent. The Chronos was a guide, a map, but it didn't tell us everything. We couldn't have blind trust in the words on its pages. Even if the major plot points were there, the details were obscured. Unknown.

As the witness to my death, Lachesis had already seen the chain of events. She'd known that my attempt to leave would fail catastrophically, but she'd also known that it would end Nilensi's life... and yet she made no mention of that in the Chronos.

Very likely, she didn't care. Nilensi was collateral damage, an unfortunate soul in the wrong place at the wrong time. Expressionless, I drew a skull in the dust with my index finger. I watched through the windowpane as the Cullen shuffled across the open expanse, toward the carcass of a stag with ribs cracked open. Something had killed it, and now half a dozen corpses huddled around it, devouring its insides. I was a little envious.

My gaze fixed on a Cullen dressed in an indigo cloak that hung in ragged strips. She was ripping off the jaw. Long black braids swirled, and her once dark skin now gray and sunken. Shocked, I realized that it was Nilensi–or some version of her. Digging my nails into my palm until I carved small half-moons into it, I continued to watch. Growling, grasping and lurching, Nilensi dragged herself across the snow.

My stomach churned with disgust, even though I was no better than she.

Click click Click.

At first, I thought it was Lachesis. Then, I realized that the sound was me. Clicking my jaw again, biting at imaginary food. Involuntary, it was unconscious. A horrifying reminder that I was now one of the Cullen. I willed myself to stop, massaging my chin in annoyance.

I was so terribly, terribly hungry. I wanted to rip something apart, make something *suffer*. In the bathroom was a plate with raw, still bloody, meat. Whenever the craving became too strong, I would gnaw on it. In secret. Just to... help.

Without this new heart in my chest I'd be down there, limping through the snow.

Up in the castle, I stared at my reflection in the window. I was other and neither, a *thing*. Something new.

Baring my teeth, I growled at my reflection in the glass. Cullen.

There was no shame in it. Though Time tricked me and Death stalked me...

I was still here.

Melchior and I, through sheer cunning, had manipulated Death.

Click. Lachesis appeared, her face full of fury. With otherworldly grace, she moved toward me like water flowing over stones. Her dress, sky blue silk, fluttered around her; her chestnut hair fell in soft waves around her porcelain skin. Like any creation of the Gods, she was both beautiful and terrifying.

"You tricked me," she hissed, grabbing my arm and savagely twisting it behind my back.

"Me? What did I do?" I tried to scramble away from her, but Lachesis had been gifted with immortality and inhuman strength–it was more likely I'd break my own arm than escape her grasp.

"What haven't you done? You have trespassed against the fabric of time. You have modified your future." Her voice shook with indignation.

In my chest, my new heart beat steadily, defiant and unafraid.

"I followed the script you provided." I folded my arms across my chest. "I attempt to leave him, he kills me—they were all part of the Chronos, and I did nothing differently."

Her fingers, elegant and pale like porcelain, twitched. As if she wanted to wring my neck. "Your actions will have consequences far beyond your comprehension."

"Consequences?" I laughed softly, the sound sharp as shattered glass. "I *died.* What worse consequence could there possibly be?"

Lachesis' lips formed a thin line of displeasure. "If you died, then how exactly are you here? Speaking with me?"

"Ask Atropos." I shrugged, unconcerned. "She's the one bringing the dead back to life. She's cursed all of Moirai, and I'm now stuck here... an aberration just like Demitra and the rest."

Lachesis studied me, her gaze piercing. Assessing.

"Look," I placated her. "I'm just as confused as you are. The last thing I remember is Melchior stabbing me. He killed me, just as you saw him do. Then, I woke up later, alive again. Although, *alive* might be a generous term... here I am. What do you expect me to do?"

I dragged in a deep breath and waited while the Controller of Time grappled with her thoughts.

Lachesis continued to frown, but I could see my words had settled and made sense to her. Exactly as I hoped. She could lay the blame on her enemy Atropos, blinding her to my actions.

I was thrilled. She believed me.

"Nevertheless. Your destiny has been changed. And not only yours, but Melchior and your daughter too. I no longer know what will happen to them. It is a mystery." Framed by the gossamer threads of time that swirled around her, for a brief moment I worried that she would undo it all, and have me go through it again.

"At least it'll be entertaining?"

"Indeed. Despite this change, your tale does not have a happy ending. Destiny won't be swayed by such a small thing as this."

You don't know that. I bit back the words, holding them captive in my mouth until they faded. Lachesis examined the silver bracelet upon her wrist. As if she were expecting it to be tarnished. Her callousness took my breath away.

Masking my fury, I considered Melchior's former lover. She'd pretended to be my friend while in disguise, she'd gladly ruin my daughter's life for her petty vengeance.

She was a cruel, vicious creature.

And I was going to make sure she didn't wreak any more havoc.

Briefly, I recalled the words of the Chronos - the one that was now void. There was precious little information between Morena's birth and my death, but I'd now changed everything by trying to escape *before* her birth. Still, even if I'd subverted destiny, that didn't mean I knew what to do next. It didn't mean I'd saved her from her terrible destiny of becoming the Grim Reaper, and murdering all of the descendants of the Fates.

Shortly after this thought, I realized that if Lachesis did already have a child, I would not know if it were Melchior's. That Morena might one day kill her own sibling, unknowingly–

Suddenly, I had an idea. A stunning, magnificent idea. I whirled toward Lachesis.

"I've read that only a Fate can kill another Fate. Why didn't you ever try to kill Atropos?"

"It's forbidden."

"You mean Nyx would punish you for it, and take your powers?"

"Precisely."

"Still, if you wanted her gone, why didn't you help Melchior before now?"

"I did help. I *gave* him the Chronos, an act which is also forbidden."

"Shouldn't you have tried harder? In the Chronos, it says that Morena kills all of the other Fates, and their descendants. I assume that means you, and whatever children you have stashed somewhere."

"I don't have any–"

I barreled on.

"If you care about your own offspring, or your future offspring, it's in your best interest to ensure Morena *doesn't* become the grim reaper. Because then she'll kill your child, as well as Clotho's. Won't she?"

I paced as I spoke, clicking my teeth with excitement. "If Atropos raises Morena, your children and grandchildren are doomed, right? That's what you saw?"

Now, surely the Controller of Time was aware that she was intended to be an objective, fair, neutral weapon of the Gods. That changing the future was frowned upon. That changing Morena's destiny, and her descendants' destinies, was forbidden.

From the corner of my eye I watched as she examined the possibility. I saw her face grow worried, then sad, then angry by turns.

"With your help, we may succeed in getting rid of Atropos forever. I'll leave Melchior, you can have him. All I want is my daughter." My green eyes were wide, guileless as I looked at her. "Who knows. Maybe your descendants are *his* children."

Her gaze flickered. "...I– I've never considered that."

I was actually surprised. "Really? Why not?"

Lachesis frowned. "Because he married you."

"So? He told me that you were the only woman he'd ever *truly* loved." Our eyes met. "So how do you know? Maybe you and he..."

"It's against the rules to see my own future, I refuse to look... but I could check his."

"You should," I told her. "I would like to know."

The Controller of Time inspected me until I thought I might wither from her gaze.

"Fine. I'll go now. Don't do anything stupid while I'm gone."

"I won't. I'll stay right here." I assured her. "But when you come back, you'll help us kill Atropos?"

Lachesis' blue eyes narrowed. "Maybe."

Maybe. It wasn't a yes. But it was better than a no.

30

I was nearly breathless with glee. I wrote Zeph a letter telling him he was right, and signed my name as *Princess Malinda of Kinver'i.*

Of course, I knew it was possible that I'd be dead - truly deceased - by the time he received it. That I most certainly shouldn't take my victory as anything other than temporary.

Melchior assured me this wasn't the case. "Dark magic fills your blood, courses in your veins. You're faster, you don't feel pain. As long as your heart is safe, you are nearly as immortal as the Fates."

Nearly being the key caveat. *Nearly immortal* was not good enough.

"I thought you said that if I don't replace the heart regularly, I rot away one piece at a time."

Melchior grimaced. "I didn't say the situation was perfect."

Almost immediately, I lost weight. I became pale, as if my face had never seen sunlight. My features lost their softness, my cheekbones protruded. Whether it was stress or my own death, it looked as if I were a prisoner to a cruel master, one who dressed me well but otherwise tormented me. And when my heart grew tired, which was often, it felt as if I hadn't slept for a week.

The servant he brought to me was only the second person I'd ever killed, and it was awful. I buried Fenix's heart in the field outside our window, marking it with a cross. Out of guilt, or out of gratitude, I didn't know. But I was still here, still alive enough to fight for us, because of him.

I turned to see Melchior sitting in bed. My husband's long, tapered fingers flicked through page after page of the Chronos, his black eyes skimming each quickly.

It was now useless, and held no valuable information. Since we'd already altered all our futures, it was likely that everything in it was no longer true. This was the theory, at least.

I watched his face, studying him in the lamplight.

"What do you think?" I sat down next to him.

"This is all bad news," Melchior murmured.

"I know." I could tell by his expression, his furrowed brow.

"Mmm." He turned another page, then paused, bent down its corner. This was something he wanted to come back to later.

"When did you realize that Nilensi betrayed us?" he asked.

"I first suspected it when I found Atropos coming out of her bedroom. Then, while you were gone. She knew far too much about Atropos' thoughts about the Cullen, and that was before they started crawling all over the castle."

"So everyone who dies, *anyone in all of Moirai*, will reawaken as Cullen? It's not just here at Grace Castle?"

"Yes."

He exhaled, then scratched the top of his head. "I don't suppose we stumble across the antidote?"

"We aren't that lucky."

He continued, re-reading the words. I continued to wait, holding my breath, until he got to the page where I started leaving notes in the margin.

Melchior shook his head faintly, then thumbed forward - to the end of the Chronos. To *my* writing. More notes I'd taken based on what Lachesis said. He went back again.

After a long pause he laid the book down.

"I've been meaning to ask...A baby?"

I gave him a tentative smile.

His tense exterior cracked. "*Our baby,*" he whispered, sweeping me into his arms.

It was exactly the reaction I hoped for. My eyes filled with unshed tears. "You're happy?"

"More than you could ever guess."

He kissed me, and placed his hand on my belly. "A little girl."

"A grim reaper," I corrected him, snuggling against his shoulder. "And apparently she has quite the rough time of it."

Melchior chuckled. "What did you expect? She *is* our daughter."

He rubbed slow circles on my back as he held me. "How are you feeling?"

Like I could easily kill a dozen men without blinking. Being dead had intensified my cunning, made me more ruthless. Since my heart was locked away in a jar, cursed with dark magic, I supposed that made sense.

"Worried, mostly. We have to protect her. From Atropos. From the other Fates and their descendants."

My eyes met his, the rest of the sentence unsaid. *From ourselves.*

He'd already read how Atropos kept our daughter in the tower, and taught her how to kill. How she would eventually become numb to it. How he'd helped her do it.

"I would never keep my own daughter prisoner."

"Yet, you do. That's what the Chronos said."

"The Chronos doesn't tell us everything."

"I know that. It's only what Lachesis observes, and only from her point of view. And, well… I've started to think those omissions are intentional."

Melchior sighed. "There's no reason for her to do that." He still had trust and faith in his old flame. I, on the other hand, had no reason to believe her.

Melchior's eyes met mine. "I had my own Chronos. And at the time, I couldn't see how it could possibly be true. I argued and fought against it… and look where we are. I met you. Saved you from the Keres. Brought you here. Married you. I don't see any reason to believe Lachesis would omit details from the Chronos."

"The real question is, now that we've diverged from destiny," I said, "is anything in the Chronos accurate?"

"Probably not."

I tried to reassure the both of us. "Well. She'll be strong. Smart. If we play our cards right, and we are careful, we can bend the rules just enough to give Morena the edge."

"I don't want to give her *an edge*, Malinda. I want to get her out. I want my daughter to have love and family. Friends. I don't want her to be one of us."

I moved to my side to face him, propping myself up on one elbow. "One of us? What's so wrong with being a prince? Of having wealth beyond all imagining? She shouldn't have to live out her days in a hovel, stealing to keep her belly full."

"I wasn't suggesting that. I simply meant that if we had to choose between being poor and eating dinner next to Death for hundreds of years, I know which I would choose."

"It can't be that those are our only choices."

Melchior digested this, then spoke. "What if we leave? We'll go to Rose Hall and have a normal life," he said.

"What happens to Moirai? And all its citizens, who are dying and becoming Cullen?"

"Moirai can go to hell, and the Gods can deal with Atropos' mess."

I massaged the line between my eyebrows. I was getting a headache. "We can't leave things like this."

"Why not? Why is it *our* problem?" Melchior folded his arms across his chest. "We should look out for ourselves. For our family."

"It was my fault. I showed Atropos the spell. None of this would have happened if I hadn't done that."

"So?" Melchior shrugged, his expression obstinate.

"All we have to do is kill Atropos or contain her until our daughter is old enough to defend herself. And undo the spell."

"That would require enchanting the kingdom. Do you know how to do that?"

"No, of course not."

"I don't either. And Nilensi is dead."

We were silent for a full minute.

"What about Nico?" I asked.

"He's just a boy. He could never—"

"A boy whose mother and father were some of the most powerful witches in Moirai."

"He's too young, not ready."

I rubbed my eyebrows with one hand, frowning. "Our daughter can't end up on the blood throne, commanding an undead army. I don't want that."

"Me neither," he agreed.

"The only solution we have is for Lachesis to help us. We *need* her to kill Atropos. Nilensi told me that Cullen will obey the Queen of the Blood Throne, so as long as she sits upon it, Moirai is doomed."

I squeezed his wrist. "You have to be the one to convince her."

Melchior was skeptical. "Convince her how?"

I pursed my lips. "I don't know. Think of something."

I might have guessed that he would be violently opposed to the idea.

Melchior cursed at me and paced the room. He mumbled to himself and then shouted like a mad king. He worried and swore and drank, then buried his head in his hands and refused to speak to me.

Through most of it, I sat as still as a stone. Letting him think it through. Letting him cycle through anger, resentment, fear, denial, and all the rest.

"How many years?" he asked again. "In the original Chronos, how many years passed until our daughter killed Atropos?"

"About twenty."

When he finally spoke, he didn't say what I thought he would.

"You don't know what it was like being raised in this house. A slave to Death, pressured to either die or spend your entire life murdering people.

Without ever being told why, and having nothing make sense... and then, finding out that the reason for all of it - the reason that your life is so awful, so terribly empty and unbearable is simply because the Gods were *too lazy* to do anything themselves."

"That although it was sold to you as incredible power and wealth, that you're almost a God... the reality is that you, your mother, your offspring, are nothing more than cosmic exterminators. Trapped for all time."

He closed his eyes as if he were in pain. "So if there's any chance we can avoid that fate for our daughter, I'll take it."

It was nearly dinner time. Another exciting meal with Atropos.

With a gentle finger, Melchior traced the diamond beading on the shoulder of my gown. As he did, shadows slid from his palms. Down the bodice, swirling over my hips, falling like water toward my feet.

"Atropos says if you always wear black, no one can see the bloodstains."

"Smart," I muttered. "I'll have to do that."

I took a small, shallow breath as one of his shadows caressed my throat. With them cloaking me, it did look like I was wearing a moving sea of ink.

"You're going to make us late again."

"I don't care," he said roughly, seemingly fascinated by the shadows sliding over me.

"Well I do. I have no desire to carve you up again because we arrive at seven o' four."

Melchior's shadows tugged at the bodice of my gown. "I'll be quick."

"You don't know the meaning of the word."

He laughed and slid his hands down to my hips, then began lifting the fabric of my dress. "Quicker than usual?"

His shadows began the work of stripping me naked.

Melchior slid into me a moment later in one delicious, fast thrust. All the way inside, as deeply as he could get.

I drew in a shuddering breath at the wild sensations that ricocheted through me, then glanced up to find him watching me in the mirror. His dark eyes crinkled at the corners as he gave a small, knowing smile. My head swimming from his scent, I bent towards the mirror.

"Don't close your eyes," he growled.

So I didn't. I watched, helpless, as he pushed in and pulled out of me, mind-numb and dumb with pleasure. Every rasp of his flesh against mine was like the waves crashing upon the shore. All the sensations burst through me: the ever-tightening clasp of his hands, his breathless words in my ear, the way my borrowed heart wrenched at each kiss.

I felt strong. Powerful. More than anything, I felt *him,* and he was everything. As he retreated and then sank deep again, I moaned. *His.*

With quick, harsh strokes, he filled me.

Later that night, at dinner, I sat across from Atropos, looked into in those cold, black eyes. She was Death, but I was already dead. Why should I fear her now?

I smiled, a cruel cunning sneer, and silently dared her to stand against me.

Under the table, I rubbed small circles over my stomach, and I whispered to my daughter.

We're going to take their power, darling. Destroy them one by one, until the only Fate left is you.

SUMMONING A GOD

Note that warm goat's blood is highly preferred by most deities. With the left index finger, draw a wheel using blood, ideally on stone. Say the name of the God you wish to summon, drawing also the half-moon of supplication upon the forehead.

Incantation

Te voco, Invoco te.
Tvam gratiam peto.

~~[illegible]eat thric[illegible]~~

31

Once Melchior knew about the baby, he worried. Just as I imagined he would, he over-prepared and imagined every bad scenario. He hovered over me and slept poorly. His shadows erupted at every strange noise, primed to defend us from Death.

"We have to give Lachesis a reason to help," I told him. "She won't want to see you die."

"It's been years since we were together. If she ever loved me, she surely doesn't now." His expression was tired.

"True love never dies. It changes, but it doesn't fade."

Melchior frowned. "I would not have thought you were such a romantic."

"I'm not," I insisted. "But you have to talk to her, and win her over. Convince her."

"Are you expecting me to sleep with her for it?"

I sputtered. "Of course not! No! That's not what I was saying. But if you could just–make her feel like a future with you is possible. A hint."

He exhaled slowly, weighing my words. "If I go - if I do this - you will not be involved. You'll stay upstairs, and let the two of us handle it."

I felt myself pale. "You can't shut me out."

I tried to touch him, but he jerked away from the contact. Silently, I begged him to look at me. "We do this together. We're partners, remember?"

"Are we?" he finally said, turning to look at me, his eyes intent. "You're pregnant. You can't have a knife fight with Atropos. You shouldn't use dark magic, because it could harm our baby. How will you help me?"

His eyes were calculating. "If you love me, if you're serious about saving our child, the best thing you could do is *stay here,* in this room. Surely it's occurred to you that even though you are Cullen, Atropos could still dismember you, behead you, or any other number of painful, irreversible outcomes?"

"I know, but–"

"How do you expect me to feel if something happens to you, *again?* If something happens to you and the baby, all of this is for nothing."

His voice was firm. Unyielding. "Let me handle it. I'm not asking you; it isn't negotiable. You and the baby need to stay safe. If you're there, I'll only be more worried and distracted."

I'll take care of you. I love you. He'd said that just a few hours ago.

"Besides... Lachesis is more likely to say yes if it's just her and me."

Every fiber of me screamed with impotent rage. I knew that I should not accept this. But I also knew that if we didn't have Lachesis, the chances we could kill Atropos were zero. Only a Fate could kill another Fate.

"I agree," I said, my voice wavering. "I'll stay–right here. I won't even open the door."

He didn't believe me. Melchior studied me, his eyes narrowed. "You swear?"

"I swear."

"Then I'll go now. I'll be back within a few hours."

I tried to ignore the pang in my chest. "How will you–"

"I'll summon her. We have a spell."

That was all he said before he walked out of our room.

So I waited. My stomach churning, I pressed the heels of my hands to my eyes, ordering myself not to cry. Not to panic. Not to be jealous. He was going to her, because she was the only option we had. Would he kiss her? I'd told him to do whatever it took... would he?

Of course he won't. But maybe... I was slowly going insane.

To keep myself occupied, I read the grimoires, forcing myself to focus. Just in case things went wrong, it would be useful to have another protection in place. If Lachesis and Atropos fought, it was possible that Lachesis would lose – then what would we do? I needed to make sure that Melchior was protected, especially if I wasn't going to be there. I no longer worried about myself. Being Cullen and having my heart hidden away, I was essentially immortal...

But Melchior wasn't.

He had his own dark magic, however I didn't know exactly what would happen if Atropos tried to kill him. If he'd considered that possibility and prepared for it.

My hands shook as I flipped through the pages, as my eyes scanned through the jumble of words. *Invincibility. I need a spell so that he cannot lose.*

Vaguely, I recalled seeing spells like that. Meant for war, they often invoked Achilles and Ares. Perhaps the cover had a ruby embedded in it... There was nothing like that in the grimoires in either of our rooms. If it was the book I was thinking of, it was still in Nilensi's bookcase.

I glanced at the clock. Melchior had been gone an hour already; I promised him that I wouldn't leave our room. But, if I was only leaving to get the book, I would be right back. He wouldn't know that I'd gone.

So I would have to hurry.

Shelf by shelf, I scanned the titles and pulled down any book that seemed like it might contain something useful. The pile was nearly waist high already, and I realized that I wouldn't have nearly enough time to read them all. I opened the largest, skimmed the table of contents, then set it aside.

The problem was, I didn't exactly know what I was looking for.

□*Click click click click.* I clenched my jaw. I was clicking my teeth again, like one of them. Wringing my hands, I stared at the half-hazard pile and cursed.

"What are you doing?" said a small voice.

I nearly jumped out of my skin.

"I'm looking for a spell. Remember how we're going to try and defeat Atropos? I need something that will help us win."

"Oh." The boy watched me with large, untrusting hazel eyes.

"Do you know if there's anything like that in any of these books?" I asked. "It would really help me."

Since his mother's death, the boy had aged beyond his years. His face was solemn as he peered over my shoulder at the bookcases.

He was silent so long I turned away, assuming that he'd either gone mute or was refusing to speak to me.

"The silver one," said a small voice from behind me. "It has a discorporation spell."

I wasn't even familiar with the word. But I hunted through the books with my eyes, desperately seeking until I spotted a grimoire bound with light gray fabric.

"What's discorporation?" I took it down from the shelf and opened the book. It was full of spells, incantations, and ingredient lists. No different than any of the others I'd read.

"It takes the soul out of a person so you can hide it somewhere else. Like he did with your heart."

"Thanks," I said brightly. "I'm sure it will help."

I wasn't sure, not at all.

"Did your mother tell you the plan?"

The boy crossed his arms over his chest and scowled. "The Prince said I should stay out of the way. That I'm too little to do anything."

He's only trying to protect you. I swallowed. "Well. I don't think that's true. In fact, I want you to be right there watching, and if I call for you, you come. You know what to do?" I leaned close to him, kneeling so our faces were level.

"Definitely." Nico brightened. "Mother had me do lots of things, and go in Atropos' room when she wasn't there."

"I know she did. You're a proper thief, just like me."

He smiled.

I glanced at the clock on the desk. *Two hours.*

"I have to leave now. I'll take this one with me, alright?" I held up the silver grimoire.

Nico nodded. "I won't forget. And I won't get scared."

Suddenly, I had a thought. "Are your mother's protection charms still in place? All the wards she put on you?"

Nico smiled widely. Then he held up one hand toward me, and after a moment, the boy began to glow. Gold, brilliant, like a star falling through the night. "She said they'd always be with me."

I nodded slowly. "Good."

He was going to need them.

32

"She said no."

Incredulous, I furrowed my brow. "What do you mean?"

"Exactly what I said. She refused to help. Said that we're on our own. So I suppose we are back to the original plan." Melchior shrugged, casual and unbothered.

I tried to argue; I shouted and told him he had to go back, and explain everything to her again.

He sighed. "I will. Tomorrow. For tonight, let's just get some sleep?"

In a huff, full of rage, I pulled the covers up to my neck and scowled at the ceiling. "How could she possibly *say no?*"

"It will be fine. We'll handle it." He seemed utterly unconcerned. "I have a backup plan. You don't have to worry about me dying."

Very quickly, he was asleep, his breathing deep and even.

I hate Lachesis almost as much as Atropos.

The sound of the door woke me, and I immediately realized I was alone. Melchior's space in the bed next to me was empty, the covers still warm to the touch. He was trying to sneak away. Too bad he hadn't been quieter.

I leapt from the wide bed, sheets tangled and rumpled, and quickly yanked on a white dress. I bound my hair just to keep it out of my face-there wasn't time to braid it. I kept my feet bare, so they'd be soundless on the stairs. I grabbed all three knives from my dresser. The cold steel of the dagger felt heavier than it should have been, and I gripped its hilt tightly.

I hesitated. With my hand on the door handle. He had all but begged me to stay here, in this room. He didn't want to be distracted. Would me being there save him, or doom him? All our plans, all our schemes—they had led us here, to this final moment. What was the right thing to do?

I decided that I couldn't let him face Death without me. This wasn't just about him anymore, it was about our family. I had the right to defend it.

Racing down the hall, I hurtled toward the throne room. Toward him.

Even though I expected their confrontation, I still wasn't prepared when I skidded around a corner and found Melchior and Atropos facing each other, faces twisted with fury, like two vipers poised to strike. Melchior, cloaked in shadows that writhed and danced. The air reeked of firerose, and they both shouted incantations and curses at each other.

"Atropos!" I shouted, my voice slicing through the chaos.

She turned slowly, her eyes gleaming with unnatural light, the corners of her mouth twitched into a smirk.

"You," she said, her tone dripping with disdain, "you've turned my son against me."

Atropos sent a dark cloud toward me, and the gargoyles near the ceiling dived at me, screeching. I threw myself under a table, drawing my knives. One stuck its face toward me, hissing with its pointed teeth bared, and I kicked it squarely in the face, launching it into the wall — where it shattered.

It was only the slightest of distractions, but while she was focused on me, Melchior took the opportunity and lunged forward, a glowing light between his hands which resembled the line of a lightning bolt. This, he wrapped around her throat, easily maneuvering behind her. Then he snapped it tight, a guillotine, and wrenched it backward with all his strength.

I felt a dull, pulsing horror as I watched the blinding white wire cut through the skin and bone like a hot blade, easily slicing all the way backward to her platinum hair.

Her head *should* have toppled to the floor.

She *should* have been dead, at least temporarily.

But instead, Atropos laughed—a hollow, mirthless sound that echoed off the ancient stones– and with a crack of her neck, the wound immediately sealed back together.

"You've forgotten the rules," she told Melchior, whirling to face him and drawing her razor-sharp nails across his face. Instantly, four deep claw marks appeared on his cheek, blood welling as if she'd called for it. "Only a Fate can kill another Fate."

Her fingers closed around his neck and she squeezed, lifting him off the ground with one hand. Easily, as if he weighed no more than a puppy.

"Such a disappointment," she hissed. "I should have killed you years ago."

"Why didn't you?" he demanded, his face red as he struggled to breathe.

"I needed the entertainment."

She threw him down to the stone and the sickening thud made me wince.

"Sentimentality has always been your weakness, Melchior," she continued, her voice laced with venom. "You cling to hope when there is none. You fight the inevitable."

She loomed over him like a black cloud of smoke rising toward the sky.

Her eyes full of malice, she plucked a scythe from the wall. Tall, with a wickedly sharp silver blade, it was as tall as she was.

"How could you think you would defy Death?" She took the scythe's handle in her pale, long hands.

Melchior's shadows rose from the blue-black stone and covered him, forming a shield of night between them, cocooning his chest.

Atropos raised the blade over her head.

That was when I struck. Sliding out into the middle of the floor, I threw two poisoned knives at her chest in quick succession. Then another. The thief in me surfaced, the one who slithered through darkness and fought in silence. Like extensions of my will, the daggers were a last bid to carve a path to our survival.

All three embedded deep in her chest.

Atropos did not even flinch. Instead, she grinned, a horrifying Death's head, and ran her tongue across her teeth. "Pathetic, but amusing nonetheless."

She dropped the scythe and drew the blades out of her own body. Smoke-colored liquid seeped from the wounds. With a knowing smile, she flipped the knives, agile and quick, and then sent them sailing across the room with deadly precision –

Straight toward my face.

I hit the ground with a crack, throwing myself out of their path, the air forced out of my lungs in a loud whoosh. Melchior crawled to my side, wrapping his shadows and arms around me, protecting me from the third, which she launched an instant later.

Atropos loomed above us, a figure robed in black, her silhouette cut from the fabric of night. In her hand, the scythe again gleamed.

"I'll kill you both for this treachery," she hissed. And then brought the blade down with all her furious might.

The shadows protected us. Her scythe clanged against them, bouncing off as if they were made of iron. Meanwhile, the inky fog wrapped around Melchior and me, forming a bubble of safety.

"Why are you here? I told you to stay upstairs!" he whispered furiously.

Lachesis wasn't coming. Without her, we had no way to kill Atropos. Melchior was a fool – she couldn't be killed.

She was beating upon the shadows, hammering at them with her scythe. I didn't know how long Melchior's shadows would protect us, but my face paled as I watched Atropos trying to reach us. We were doomed. Everything we had fought for, everything we had cherished, slipping through our fingers like grains of sand in an hourglass.

A few more seconds.

A few more ticks of the clock. Atropos hacking and chopping at his shadows, that silver hooked blade wrenching them away. Inescapable, irrevocable Death was just moments away.

I screamed for Nico.

The boy launched across the room, darting past the three of us as if he were carried by the wind itself. Before Atropos could even react, his fingers closed upon the mask. *Her* mask, which he grabbed from a bag at his side and held up in the candlelight.

"Malinda!" he shouted. "I have brought the mask!" Nico wore a gleeful, impish grin as he withdrew the forgery.

Atropos whirled toward him, forgetting us entirely. "How did you get that?! You sneaky thief! That's mine!"

She was too caught up in her fury to pause and wonder how he'd gotten it.

Nico grasped The Eternal Slumber firmly, acting as if he planned to settle it onto his face.

"You can't do that!" Atropos threw down the scythe and lurched toward him.

Melchior's shadows grabbed the hem of her black gown and held on tightly, trying to slow her. She whirled and kicked him in the face. "Let go! He has the Eternal Slumber!"

Her eyes were wide and as black as an abyss, mad with rage. "Who gave it to you?!"

"GIVE IT BACK!"

She grabbed the boy by his dark curls. Nico was helpless, caught in Death's grasp, but he tore himself free, unscathed. He lunged away, darting through her pale fingers like a fish in the brook.

Dropping the forgery within her reach.

He made a show of thinking about going back for it.

"Nico, go!" I cried out. "Get away from her!"

He looked back at me just before he ran up the stairs. Atropos was bent over, reaching for the forgery of the Eternal Slumber. Nico had convinced her it was real, he had pretended to be stealing it. It was a masterful performance, and she suspected nothing.

The forgery was now in her hands.

"I've had enough of this," Atropos said. Glaring at Melchior and I, she lifted the Eternal Slumber, and its obsidian sparkled, its bones of pearl glinted. The power it promised pulsed through the room, a dark heartbeat that echoed her own.

Holding it in both hands, Atropos slowly fitted the mask to her face, sighing in ecstasy as it molded itself to her features.

Falling straight into our trap.

I watched as it molded to her, as its black skin split and expanded, wrapping itself around her skull, hiding her hair. It fit perfectly; custom-made by the Fae, built to last for eternity.

Fenix had done his job well.

"Ah," she whispered, her voice caressing the ancient stone walls, "That's so much better."

As its dark magic rolled down her in waves, shadows fell like waterfalls over her chest and back, down her thighs and between her knees to the stone floor.

Atropos laughed, childlike and full of wonder. "The power sings in my veins."

For one terrifying moment I thought Fenix had missed something. Or that the poison Nilensi has dosed the mask with was flawed somehow. I almost made myself believe it, so strong was my doubt.

Tilting her head, she studied Melchior and me. "Now you'll know the force of my fury. You'll writhe at my feet and beg for Death... to whom should I bestow the honor?"

"Start with yourself," I said.

She cackled. "Always a witty retort. I think it shall be you, Malinda. My son can watch and know it's all his fault for bringing you here."

But even as Atropos reveled in her might, a hint of doubt crept into her face, a tiny whisper that something was amiss.

Fenix said that at first, the mask would merely seem cold, then it would begin to burn. Then as the poison took hold, a tingling pain would claw at her essence. Her skin would begin to melt.

"What trickery is this?" Atropos let out a strangled gasp.

She began tearing at the mask. She tried to pull it away, digging her long fingernails into her temples. But it clung to her like a parasite, its poison sinking into her skin. Was it a numbness that slowly spread past her jaw? I wondered what it felt like to have your eyes burned out and poison seep into your skin. Hopefully it was excruciating.

I began to laugh.

Her knees buckled, the strength fleeing her body as the venom spread its roots through her veins. Every convulsion thrilled me, each shudder a welcome note and a sign of her undoing.

"What have you done?" The question tore from her lips, raw and desperate. She was asking Melchior. "How could you choose her instead of me?"

He owed his mother no mercy; she'd never given him any. Of course he would believe the woman who had been the only person to ever show him love and kindness. Yet Atropos was strangely surprised.

She fell face first onto the stone, deaf to whatever Melchior might have answered.

"Is she...dead?" Melchior and I studied the prone form of Atropos, whose chest rose and fell with shallow breaths.

Click. "Of course she's not dead. She's immortal. We must move quickly." Lachesis was suddenly at Melchior's side. "She won't sleep for long. The dose was not nearly enough."

"What are you doing here?" I demanded, as I picked up my knives from the stone floor. "Aren't you a little late?"

She scowled at me. "I'm exactly on time, actually."

Melchior ignored our squabbles. "What now?" he asked her.

"We take her to the tower. We'll bind her to the stone. Pick her up. Hurry."

Bind her to the stone? "What does that mean?"

"You aren't going to kill her?" I asked her in disbelief, I looked over at Lachesis as Melchior hoisted Atropos into his arms.

"Not right now."

Together the three of us hastened from the throne room, Melchior carrying Atropos, her limbs dangled as we proceeded.

I followed them, confused, our footsteps echoing through the corridors. As quickly as we could, we ascended the spiral staircase. Up and up, into the north tower, until we reached the topmost floor.

This was the place Lachesis chose to keep her – a door painted with blood, pulsing with dark magic. Inside, there was a stone table, meant for sacrifices to the Gods. It was an ideal place; she must have scouted it beforehand.

"Place her there," Lachesis directed, her hands weaving patterns in the air, tendrils of light coiling around her fingers. Melchior obeyed, laying Atropos down as though she were a sacrificial offering to some forgotten deity.

"I'll bind her to the stone with a blood curse, then I will slow time in this room only. It will hold her."

I drew my dagger, and she held out her palm. I made a long slice across the line of her heart. This, Lachesis drew across the table, her blood draining readily into it, almost as if the stone were sucking it from the wound. Its surface was grooved with channels designed to cage Atropos.

As the three of us watched, the blood snaked underneath Atropos, contracting until it outlined her sleeping form, and then was consumed - absorbed into her skin through her black gown.

"Blood of the Fates binds thee to this stone," Lachesis intoned, her voice slow and quiet, full of power. "I curse you to be held fast, to sleep without end. By my will, let it be so. And only shall another Fate unbind you."

Her eyes shot open, and Atropos stared at the ceiling, her veins suddenly pulsing black. I leapt backward with a small scream, but before we could do anything—

Her eyes closed again, and Death slept.

33

Lachesis inspected the body of Atropos. "Well done," she murmured. A soft smile ghosted her lips.

His eyes met hers. "Thanks."

It was not the right moment for the flash of jealousy that streaked through me, nor was it appropriate that I would suddenly recall that they'd spent years together, having trysts in this castle, rolling around in his bed.

After a beat, Melchior glanced at me, breaking the spell between them. "Are you alright?" he asked.

"Of course. Why wouldn't I be?" I sounded defensive. We had succeeded. Now we would find out if Lachesis' blood would hold. Half-disbelieving, I very much expected Atropos to pop up from the stone table, her hair streaming and black eyes livid–

"She'll be bound to the stone forever, hopefully."

"I don't understand why you can't just kill her," I said. "If a Fate can kill another Fate... I have a knife. If you would only do it, and we can all be done with her."

Lachesis waved me away. "It's not meant to be. There are rules of Time and we must not interfere with her future again."

"That never stopped you before. You interfered in my future, and Melchior's, and Morena's. Multiple times. If you weren't going to kill her, why are you here?"

Lachesis eyes narrowed. "I checked my future, as you suggested. I saw my grandchild. Since I would rather your daughter *not* murder her, I decided to assist."

"We should go," Melchior interrupted. "This isn't the time or place for this conversation."

I glanced down at Atropos on the stone. He was right. It really wasn't.

"Do we leave the mask on her?" Lachesis asked.

"I'll take it." Careful to only touch the face and not the interior, Melchior hooked his finger under the jaw, and lifted.

The forgery released its hold easily. Back it went into the velvet bag, and I hoped fervently to never see it again.

When I looked up, Lachesis was already in the hallway. "Let's go."

Back in the corridor, the door shut behind us with a soft click that echoed like the telltale heartbeat of our crime. Draughts that carried the faint scent of snow and sea whispered through the halls, brought in from an open window.

Melchior ran his hands over the wooden door, sealing Atropos inside. Hiding my surprise, I started down the stairs, trailing the two of them.

It had all gone smoothly. *Like when a door was left unlocked to entice you in, so you walk willingly into the trap.*

In the Now'here, Lachesis claimed that Melchior would kill me and give our daughter over to Atropos. *He will always betray you. The only path forward for you is with him dead.*

"I will accept your payment now," Lachesis said to Melchior. "The deed is done, as I promised."

"What payment?" I asked, a bit too loudly.

"Malinda." Melchior grasped my hands. "Stay here."

"What do you mean? Where are you going?"

"It's going to be alright," Melchior vowed, suddenly tense. "You and our daughter will be fine—" Melchior's shadows gathered, then wrapped around me.

In one swift motion, Lachesis twisted - I saw one of my poisoned knives in her hand. Silver light pulsed from her skin, and Melchior stilled. His shadows stuck fast, unable to move.

Stuck in time. I could neither shift nor scream, I could only stare at Lachesis in cold horror. She'd paused me, freezing me in place to watch.

Chuckling, Lachesis held up my knife. "You should have made sure you had all three."

She stepped close to Melchior. Leaned in, and kissed him on the lips. Slowly, deeply. Then she shook her head. "You were never very good at lying, you know. The moment I saw you, I knew you weren't there because you still loved me. No matter what you said or what promises you made."

Melchior barely looked at her. Instead, his eyes found mine. Anguish. Guilt.

Lachesis traced her index finger down his chest. "And I realized something."

"Gods. don't. like. being. used."

Too quick for him to protect himself, she stabbed him in the throat. His eyes were unblinking, his mouth unable to scream.

Lachesis sneered. "You thought I'd kill your little thief, when what I want is for her to live. Now her life is mine, and I'll do as I see fit. Killing her would be a mercy. And I'm afraid I'm just not in the giving mood."

Inside I was raging.

Gripping the hilt in both hands, she twisted the knife free. Her pulsing light vanished, abruptly gone, and Melchior grabbed his neck, then fell to his knees. His blood streamed out, a dark bloom spreading from the wound. She'd struck true; directly into his throat. He wouldn't live another two minutes.

"Meanwhile," Lachesis said. She wiped my blade clean on her blue gown and tossed the knife down. "I'm not going to kill you, because that child in your belly will do it for me. It's poetic, don't you think?"

Shocked, I knelt by Melchior, pressing my hands to the wound on his throat, trying to staunch the flow. Slumped against the wall, Melchior blinked. Blood ran onto his pants, then the indigo stone floor.

"Why did you do that?" I pleaded with her. "We imprisoned Atropos. There was no reason..."

"I'm a Fate. I can do whatever I want."

Aghast, I stared up at her. "What? You can't—"

"Enjoy your new future. This time, you're a widow. And Queen."

But you're not Death, I thought. Lachesis wasn't Death, she controlled Time. She couldn't just *arbitrarily* change how someone died, nor could she abruptly kill them; that power rested with Atropos. She was violating the rules flagrantly now.

"Zeph will be pleased. Didn't he say, *if you play your cards right?*" She laughed. "You're now the Queen of the Blood Throne. Atropos is imprisoned. You're immortal. You're free to do as you like, a woman of great wealth and power. Isn't that what you always wanted?"

What I wanted was to rip her apart, slowly. One limb at a time. Until she went blind from the agony.

"He thought he could break my heart and get away with it. That he could choose *you* instead of me. Now you both know better."

Lachesis started to walk away, and then paused on the topmost stair. "One other thing. Not that you asked for my advice, but you shouldn't leave him there. Throw his body into the sea. You don't want him coming back as Cullen."

"Lachesis." I raised my eyes to hers. "I'm going to kill you."

She smirked. "As much as I'd love to stay and watch what happens next... I have to get going. I will check in on you soon."

Lachesis vanished with a loud click that sounded like another tick of the clock.

I stared at the place where she had been. *No you won't.*

The moment she was gone, I grasped Melchior. I curled against his shoulder, putting my hand on his chest, over his heart. Just as I often did, as if he were reading in bed.

"Lachesis betrayed us." Just as I'd thought she would. Her Chronos had been a lie, as I'd suspected. There was no joy in being right.

He exhaled slowly, then leaned his face down and pressed his cheek to the top of my head. Stroking my hair, there we sat. His breathing became shallower and more ragged as the minutes passed, but he seemed unhurried. Unworried.

He squeezed my wrist, and I glanced up at him. His eyes were closed, anguish etched onto his features.

"Hurry up, use your magic. Heal yourself. What's the backup plan?"

He guided my hand toward his pocket. I reached in and pulled out a crumpled piece of parchment.

The greatest threat to your happiness has always been me.

I read, then re-read the words.

"What does this mean?" I held up the paper.

He looked at me, his expression sad. Regret-filled. Resigned. As if he were saying goodbye.

Panic coursed through me.

The corridor was completely silent, as if all the light and sound had been sucked away.

"No."

I grabbed at his shirt. "You are not doing this. You are not just *giving up* and leaving me here."

As his heart slowed; my borrowed heart thudded far too fast, wearing itself out.

"We had a plan. We defeated Death. We're going to have a baby and be a real family. Remember? That's our plan."

I held onto him tightly, as if my grip could keep him in place. "Our daughter needs a father."

The greatest threat to your happiness has always been me. "You spent years learning dark magic so you could stay alive— now *stay alive.*"

It felt as if my life were folding in upon itself, a smaller and smaller square, until it was a dot too tiny to see.

"You are not leaving now that we've *won.*" My voice trembled.

But under that sadness, that despair, was a lake of fire– of pure rage. How could he do this to me?

Melchior closed his eyes again.

I, always on the alert for lies, had fallen for his. I'd believed in our love so much that it hadn't occurred that he didn't. That he read the Chronos and saw its words about him killing me, raising our daughter, and accepted them as written in stone.

I steeled myself. "You're not the only one capable of dark magic, Melchior. Not the only one who made plans."

I'd read every grimoire in this house. I knew what to do; I had prepared. Just in case he failed. He might be barely breathing, and he was still mine. Resolved, my face expressionless, I took the edges of his shirt in both fists and ripped it open.

"Didn't you hear her? I'm the Queen of the Blood Throne— and I say you're staying."

I looked up and down the corridor and called out for the only person in Grace Castle who could help me. "Nico! Come here!"

As expected, the boy emerged from the shadows, his hazel eyes worried. "She stabbed him."

I flinched. "Your mother said we should never trust the Fates."

Solemn, he came forward and knelt beside me. "You read the spells? You know what to do?"

Of course I had. Nilensi had helped me. I'd read the silver grimoire, memorizing its instructions, mouthing the names written there. Preparing for the possibility that I might fail, that something inside that book would save him. If I could say the incantation correctly.

I didn't know if Melchior would come back exactly as he was. He might be different... Dead. Still. I was not in any position to expect a man who was perfect, or even alive. Determined to be brave, to accept any outcome, I squared my shoulders.

Nico Ecclesiastes, a witch's son, the last of his line, guided my hand to Melchior's chest. "Then say it."

"And you'll help me?" I asked. "If he's... not right?" If we failed, my only ally in an entire kingdom would be a boy who was less than ten years old. I refused to think about it. I could worry about it later, some other time.

"I will."

Together, we said the incantation. White light exploded from my palm, making Melchior gasp. His skin glowed like a thousand candles, and his body– his body simply melted away, lost in the brilliance of stars.

34

"How much longer do you think it will be?" I asked Nico, for the third time, as I paced the throne room.

"I don't know."

I couldn't bear the thought that my spell might have failed. That one small mispronunciation might have doomed my husband. It had taken me hours to wake, but that had been a different spell than the one I'd used on him. In truth, it didn't matter how long it took, as long as Melchior returned.

His body had vanished. Had it worked at all? I couldn't be sure.

"I need him here, Nico. Decisions have to be made, and I–I'm not sure. These were all his plans, not mine. I don't want to be queen. Don't know how to be one."

Overhead, the stone gargoyles growled. One glared down at me, baring its teeth. *If I can get my hands on those, they will be the first things to go. I can't have those ghastly beasts in my house.*

The boy went to stand by the window. The grounds were veiled in fog, the soft gray light of dawn just beginning to touch the eastern sky. "It's okay," he said after a long pause. "We'll find more servants."

"And what about hearts?" I asked dully. "You know I'll have to—"

"Yeah."

35

I didn't forget about Lachesis.

When Melchior did not appear, I went to find his green silk grimoire, the one with the pages I'd marked. I went to Nilensi's room, to the stables and the kitchens. Gathering all the necessary ingredients. It did not take long.

Barefoot and dressed in a black glittering gown, I clenched the frayed rope of a goat in one hand. It bleated, knowing full well that it was too cold and too late for it to be roaming outside the stable.

"Be quiet," I told him. "Or the Cullen will come to rip you apart, which is a far worse thing than what I'm planning."

I took the silver knife from my pocket and said a quick prayer. It was not the first, nor the last, terrible thing I would have to do.

I cut its throat, quick and clean, draining its blood into my hands. I worked fast. Time was not on my side. I drew a circle in the sand and stood in the center, then traced a crimson moon on my forehead.

"Te voco, Nyx."

"Invoco te."

"Tuam gratiam peto."

I said it three times. If Nyx was listening, and I hoped she was, she would come.

The night was quiet, waves breaking softly on the shore. I bit my lip and waited.

The blood began to dry on my forehead.

I cracked my knuckles.

Then I glanced down at my feet. Was I exactly in the center of the circle? It said to make the circle on stone, but wasn't the sand on this beach just pieces of stone?

Perhaps it wasn't good enough.

The sky above was black as pitch, clear and starry. I looked up and up, the dark castle behind me.

"Come *on,* "I pleaded. I couldn't even imagine what would happen if Lachesis discovered me out here; it would be nothing good. I fidgeted and played with the fur on the edge of my cloak.

"Waiting for someone?" asked a pleasant voice, making me jump.

"Oh god!" I cursed, jerking away.

When I looked over, my mouth fell open. It was as if the twilight itself had formed into a cloak, the stars and universes embedded in its cloth. Her skin glowed white, like the surface of the moon, and her black hair cascaded down like rivers of night.

It was her. The Goddess Nyx. Ethereal. Endless. Intangible as the shadows that lurked in the corners of my room.

"You're here," I said, reverent.

"You summoned me." Her voice was like the memory of a mother's lullaby. Comforting.

Though I should have, I did not drop to one knee. I did not weep or tear my hair. I was in fact so awed that I could do nothing more than openly stare at her.

"Lachesis gave me this." I extended my hand to her, giving her the Chronos.

Nyx, keeper of dreams and nightmares, studied the cover, then opened it. Curious, she skimmed some of its pages. A breeze drifted over the two of us, and snowflakes swirled around her flowing cloak. Her hands moved with the sureness of a celestial who had never been challenged, a being of eternal grace and patience.

"She has defied the laws of the Gods," Nyx said finally. "Just as Atropos once did."

"I know." I bit my lip. I dared not ask her for anything, nor demand anything.

"What is it you want?"

"That Lachesis no longer interfere in my life, or the lives of my children."

"She had offspring. There will be another Controller of Time."

My heart sank. Still, there was nothing I could do about that. Having Lachesis herself out of the picture was still an improvement on our futures, even if her offspring would eventually show up and make my life a hell.

"I shall revoke her powers, as I took those of Atropos and Clotho. Her past selves and future selves will be destroyed."

On the next gust of wind, the Chronos crumbled into glimmering blue dust, gently shining. This she held up and blew upon gently, and the fine powder drifted out into the heavens, eventually forming stars in the sky.

"Will you tell my daughter what really happened?"

Nyx was absolute stillness, alive yet not breathing. "What really happened?"

"That her father and I loved each other, that the Fates were selfish and petty and cruel, and not to be trusted. That I died."

"Why don't you tell her yourself?" she asked.

"Because she'll hate me. Maybe even kill me."

"Didn't Lachesis explain the threads of time?" Nyx interrupted. "How each version of ourselves co-exists, also happening, and that there are many possible futures for each of you?"

"No... she didn't."

"There are many outcomes for Morena, not all of them bleak."

"She won't be a Grim Reaper? She won't be Death?" I felt suddenly hopeful, like a weight lifted from my shoulders.

Nyx softened. "That one, I'm afraid, is irrevocable."

My heart crumbled. "So it was all for nothing."

"Not for nothing. You've made her future so very, very different. You'll make *her* very different." Nyx gave me a sad smile.

"I just want her to be able to choose. I never could, neither could her father."

"You chose each other."

"And we both died for it."

Nyx bowed her head in agreement. "It is true that your destiny has not been kind."

Not kind. I gave a hoarse laugh. *Abandoned by my parents. The only person who saved me was killed. Raised as a liar and thief. Nearly murdered multiple times before I was even of age. Then a fake, forced marriage, followed by a baby who is doomed. Now an immortal existence, where, if I want to survive, I must murder the innocent regularly. If all that wasn't enough, I made an enemy of both Death and Time.*

It was unspeakable. If I opened my mouth, I might scream at her.

Nyx studied me. "I won't deny that my creations have punished you. I am not blind to your pain. You may ask for a favor from me."

"Two." The words were out of my mouth before I had a chance to take them back. "Two favors. One for me, and one for Melchior."

Nyx frowned. "Ask."

There were so many things I could request. I wrung my hands, unsure. What if I asked for the wrong things? What if I only made her life worse? I didn't want to overthink it; and I had only my instincts – and my own bloody past– to guide me.

"Love," I said suddenly. "I want my daughter to have love. Someone who will always fight for her."

Nyx gave a small smile and looked back at the castle. "She has that already."

"I mean a great love. Something too deep to ever cleave apart. A mate. A partner."

She considered it for far too long, her gaze unfocused. "Done, although—"

"Don't tell me anything. I've heard far too much about her destiny already."

The Goddess of Night chuckled. "And your second favor?"

This one took longer for me to verbalize. I knew what I wanted immediately, but once the words came to me, I had trouble saying them.

"I want him back. One day she will need her father. I don't know– I don't know if the spell worked. But I need him, our daughter needs him. She doesn't have to know. But he and I..." my voice cracked.

I had to finish in a whisper. "He would want to be here."

Nyx did not react.

Blinking back tears, I swallowed hard. "If that's too difficult, maybe—"

I glanced up at the space where Nyx had been, and the Goddess of Night had already gone.

Nico was waiting for me by the front door. I should have known he would be – now that it was just us two in the castle, he followed me everywhere. Three of the Cullen stood in the shadows just behind him, and another stood guard at the door.

"What's this?" I asked wearily.

"They answer to the Queen of the Blood Throne," Nico muttered. "That's you now."

Warily, we watched the Cullen, and they watched us.

"I don't like it," he said at last.

"Me neither," I agreed.

But internally, however, I acknowledged that it wasn't such a terrible outcome. I'd gained an undead army that answered only to me. With every death in Moirai, my army would grow larger. The Cullen would protect me and my child, and when the other descendants of the Fates came, which they surely would, they would tear them apart.

I glanced over at Nico. He was still so small. His hair needed cutting and his clothes were barely better than rags. He was an orphan, just as I had been.

"We won't tell anyone what happened. That you and I have dark magic."

"I know. I won't."

Clicking my jaw in annoyance, I stepped over a rotting arm that was on the floor. "Clean this up," I said to the Cullen. "It looks like a slaughterhouse in here."

Immediately, all three snapped to attention, and the taller one stepped forward, retrieving the stray arm and hurrying away with it.

With another long-suffering sigh, I inspected the throne room.

The House of Atropos was now mine.

The black banners that hung on the walls, the indigo stone, the silver floors that writhed with prayers, the army of the undead. All of it, mine.

To the victor shall go the spoils of war, and somehow, impossibly, I had won. I had beaten both Time and Death at their own game.

Instead of feeling joyful, all I felt was tired. Exhausted. My back and head ached, my throat was parched, my golden hair was matted with blood. My emotions were spent.

My legs and hands trembled as I climbed the dais toward Atropos' throne. Drawing a ragged breath, I sat down. Dimly, I heard a small sucking sound, and looked down with horror as the throne sought blood from the folds of my gown.

Carefully schooling my features into a neutral expression, I stroked the knobby armrest carved in the shape of skulls. All the months of living in the House of Atropos had taught me well enough the value of pretending to be calm when you felt like screaming.

I leaned my head back against the chair – bone-tired. I needed to lay down. I was wearing out this new heart far too quickly.

Uncomfortable, I twitched and shifted on the blood throne, wondering what exactly I should do with myself. With Nilensi dead, Fenix dead... Atropos bound to the stone, and most of the servants of the castle now roaming the forests as Cullen, I had nothing to do. No one but Nico to talk to. I'd been queen for less than an hour and I'd already decided it was lonelier than being a street rat or a thief.

But there was one thing I was sure of. No matter how far I had to go, or how ruthless I had to be, no one was going to take my daughter from me. No one was going to make her weak, or manipulate her. I would hone her into a weapon, teach her just as Zeph taught me. She wouldn't go out into their world like a lamb for slaughter.

Nico and I were all that was left, but we would both watch out for her.

Twitching uncomfortably, I cursed. It felt like I was sitting on the edge of a book rather than a chair. Placing my hands on the seat of the Blood Throne, I moved forward, and realized that indeed, the surface of the chair was not completely even. Almost as if something were hidden underneath. Just like the one by the fire in Melchior's room.

I leapt to my feet and considered.

The seat was a simmering pool, bubbling, undulating. Crimson waves lapped at the arms, spilled over the sides and down to the dais.

With a grimace, I closed my eyes and made a face... then plunged my hand into the blood.

Immediately, my fingers brushed against something hard and cold. A face - probably obsidian, with bones of pearl. In disbelief, I drew my hand from the pool.

Firmly holding the Eternal Slumber.

Dripping red and glittering with dark magic, the mask of Death stared up at me.

Nervous, hesitant, I held it in my palms. After all that searching, it'd been here. Hidden inside her chair, right underneath her. It had never occurred that, in order to take her throne, I'd merely need to sit on it. Gently, I stroked the pearlescent bones, the shimmering obsidian.

With the Eternal Slumber, I would have the power of a Fate. One day, when Morena was old enough, I would give it to my daughter. Melchior might be gone, but I could do it alone.

I took a deep breath, then pressed the mask to my face. I was the Queen of the Blood Throne. I would protect her.

EPILOGUE

I did not miscarry, despite constant paranoia that I would. Instead, my daughter grew strong inside me, along with her dark power. Power she shared, at least for a little while.

She was a double-edged weapon, a blade whose hilt was poison to its bearer. I was so excited to be her mother, to see if she resembled her father or me.

Thanks to Melchior's magic, I remained myself. Paler, more beautiful than before. And considerably less fearful. Thanks to the Eternal Slumber, I could kill whomever I wished, walk without being seen. I did, in fact, hire more servants… though most of these were devoured by Cullen, or fled once they saw the working conditions.

For much of my days, I paced the throne room, clicking my teeth. Chewing my fingers until they bled.

As indicated by the grimoire, my emotions were more volatile, harder to control or mask. My dreams were all of bloodshed and vengeance and burning the castle to ashes. That, I guess, was not so different than before.

I counted the days until my daughter arrived. It was the only thing I had to look forward to. Then, during an otherwise unremarkable snowy night, she was born dead.

I wept and screamed until my voice was gone, my grief so overwhelming that the new heart I'd taken burst... In a fit, I killed the midwife, stealing hers.

Lachesis, Atropos, Melchior, me– all of it was for nothing.

I buried my daughter in the snow with my bare hands, in the same row where I'd buried all the innocent hearts I'd already used up. I buried her next to my true heart, still snug in its jar, still beating which... honestly, I wanted to smash on the cliffs. I dragged myself back inside and drank poison, praying it would kill me.

It didn't.

Somehow–and I did not know how– the next day Nico brought me Morena. Rosy cheeked and alive. I felt peace as soon as he settled her into my arms, with hair soft and white-blonde as Atropos. She was sound asleep.

He said he dug her up, that he heard her crying. I suspected he was lying, and couldn't bring myself to care. It didn't matter at all because I had her. Finally.

"She's beautiful," I whispered, nuzzling the tiny bundle.

Enthralled, I watched as she frowned and smacked her little lips.

Nico hovered. "I can take her back to the tower, if you like."

"No!" I said sharply, shocking him.

"You can go." My eyes were glued to her face. "I'll hold her. Take care of her."

Reluctantly, the boy looked around the room. "Are you sure?"

"Yes." I gave him a brief smile. "I can protect her. Atropos is bound to the stone. Rest easy."

"What about the Cullen?" he said.

"I'll lock them outside. She won't be in any danger."

"What about you?" Nico gave me a skeptical look. "You know how you are."

"It's fine," I insisted. "I feel good today. I have—I have control."

Sometimes, I didn't. Then I would kill anything within reach. Animals. People. Fae. Nico kept the doors locked, or chained me in a cell in the dungeon, during those times.

"Call if you need me." Clearly unconvinced, the boy retreated. He trudged up the stairs, his footsteps heavy, and disappeared into the darkness of the castle.

Shadows gathered behind me, formed, expanded, until they made a column. They wreathed around my neck, around her head.

"Come and see," I said quietly.

The shadows touched me, stroked through my gown. Black, ice cold, Melchior was not so much a man, but a silhouette carved from night itself. His form shifted and swirled, composed entirely of shadows and mists that flickered with each of my breaths. My gift from Nyx.

The baby mewled, and I smiled. Our girl. "This will take some getting used to," I said.

Melchior chuckled, and the sound might have been mistaken for a breeze, or a hint of the waves breaking upon the shore. Still powerful, still the Prince of Darkness, but different. So very different. All that remained of him was shadow. Unnoticed and undetected, watching from afar.

We'd beaten Death and Time, and the price was high.

It was the best we could do, and it wasn't nearly good enough.

"You'll have better luck," I told the baby. "We'll make sure of it."

Melchior traced her fingers with his shadows.

"She has a strong grip," I murmured, then kissed her nose. "She knows how to hold onto the people she loves."

Melchior made a hmm'ing sound.

"Maybe she gets that from her father." I smiled down at our daughter, and his shadows slid over my shoulder. Tomorrow, I would look for a spell that would help him find a human body to possess. He'd need strength for what was to come.

After all, it was just us four now.

The boy, the reaper, the queen, and the shadows. Now we would wait.

NICO

Snow fell on the graves of the children. Here it was always winter, white and knife-cold, and the boy hated it. Hated the castle of dark-blue stone. Hated the handsome king and hated the sounds and the smells and the guards and the food.

The boy longed for fire.

He longed for his cozy bed and the view of the blue river and green, rolling hills... but the boy knew he would die in this bleak place, far from warmth. For the Queen must stay, and she was all he had left.

"It's not the fairytales that lie to us, but the people we love." His mother had always said that. As if that would explain things.

It was before dawn when the boy heard the insistent knocking at the door. Half asleep, dead tired, he wanted nothing more than to ignore it. "Go away," he mumbled into his pillow.

Around him the other servants slept hard, exhausted from long days and nights working in the castle.

The hand knocked again, harder this time. As the youngest, and the person whose cot was nearest to the door, it was his responsibility to check. Nico knew that, yet it was so tempting to ignore.

"Open the door!" a female voice demanded.

"Sure, sure, I'm coming!" he grumbled, as he lurched out of the low cot and wrapped his threadbare blanket tightly around himself. The room was bitterly cold, and he rubbed his hands together as he went to open the door. He yanked hard, hard enough to make his hands ache. He was not quite big enough to work around the Castle—he could not carry the swords, the axes, or the other weapons—but the queen put him to task anyway.

A woman in a heavy cloak stood in the snow and moonlight, her blue eyes capturing him.

"May I help you?" He didn't recognize her, but the cloth of her gown and robe were quite fine. He hoped this meant she was one of the new priestesses.

Her brow knit together. "You're just a boy."

Offended, Nico puffed out his chest. "I'm eight, and the fastest in the castle with a blade."

"I'll bet you are. I wanted to see if you would help me with something. Something very important."

"Of course." He couldn't believe she was asking so politely. Most of the others ordered him about as if he were a field hand, or else ignored him completely. He didn't pause to wonder why she was asking in the dead of night; everyone knew the priestesses walked at midnight.

"Do you know where the children are buried?"

He shuddered. That Gods' forsaken field of snow was dotted with tiny graves. The other servants said that the babies were still reeking of blood, pulled from the Queen's warm womb. Then they were tossed into holes in the snow, left to freeze to death. All because the Queen didn't want children in her castle.

That's what they said. They'd never *seen it,* of course. Rumors and lies, the servants thought what they wanted. Whatever *she* made them believe.

At one point even he had nightmares about it; that the priestesses dug holes in the snow and tossed the children in, still alive, leaving them to die. Even though he knew what they really were; even though the truth was so much worse.

His skin crawled. "Yes," he mumbled. "I know the place."

"One of them is alive. I've marked it in the snow. Can you do that? Can you bring her here, keep her warm, and give her milk?" She held out her hand and it was full of goblin gold, more than Nico had ever seen.

Still, he hesitated. It was impossible to survive outside in the midst of this snowstorm—he would only last minutes. And the prospect of going out there in the dark, with them, terrified him. But it was true that a single coin would feed the entire house for a month, and there were at least twenty in her palm, enough to buy himself whatever he wanted.

"Why?" he asked. "Atropos has killed so many already." He gave the woman a look of disgust.

She leaned close. "This baby is special, Nico. She'll rid us of the plague of undead and reunite Moirai one day ... if you and I can help her."

Fair-skinned, the woman's hair was soft brown and waved around her face. Her blue eyes were like a piece of the sky that had been tugged from Heaven. She was beautiful, in the same way that angels and princesses were. She smelled just a little bit like flowers.

"Will you save her? And keep her safe? Can you be her hero?"

If he wasn't decided before, that single word did him in. Nico puffed out his chest again. "Of course I will." He fixed his chin, and gave a firm nod. "I'll go right now."

"You'll keep her next to you? You won't let her get cold?"

"Never. I can take care of a baby." He didn't know how, but he didn't want the beautiful lady to doubt him. Perhaps she'd come back and bring more coins, if he did a good job.

"Thank you," she murmured. "I can always count on you."

Later, the boy would regret his words. He couldn't know, not then, how much work it would be to raise the infant, how many years he would need to lie and kill to keep her safe. He didn't know who the girl would become or that there would be other babies, a burden that lay heavy on his small shoulders.

Nico strode through the killing fields with purpose, the snow spilling over the top of his boots with every step. Trembling and anxious to be done with his errand, he scanned the ground. Maybe she was mistaken, he thought. Maybe the baby was already dead. Then he saw it, just as she said: two sticks, stark and black, laid in a simple cross on top of the snow.

Nico stared down at it for only a moment, just one, then he began to dig.

It was years before he saw her again, the woman in blue with eyes of sky. She came to him in the tower. *Just to say hello, she said.* Nico showed her the crib, the milk, the blanket, and how he brought firewood up the circular stairs.

"And you've taken good care of her?" The expression in her eyes was somehow complicated, and not entirely happy.

"Day and night. Her mother is not here half as much as I am."

"Of course not." She brushed a strand of her brown hair back from her temple, tucking it behind her ear.

"Are you a goddess?" he asked. "Like Athena or Aphrodite?"

She laughed, and the sound was like a tinkling bell, or a brook in a sunny glade. "Not quite."

"Tell me your name then."

"Well..." The lady hesitated, and Nico, who was well accustomed to the House of Atropos by now, hastily reassured her.

"I won't tell anyone else. I swear."

"No one at all? Not ever?"

"Never."

She considered him. He was old enough now that if she did tell him, he might remember it. But she didn't plan to see him again for many, many years. And in all the times they'd spoken, he'd never mentioned this specific memory. Never shown any indication at all that he knew her, that she'd been part of his childhood.

His witch hazel eyes were wide, hopeful, and glued to her face.

So young. So different from who he became. Unable to resist, she reached forward and tousled his hair.

"My name is Vitess. It's nice to meet you."

Vitess. He committed the name to memory. Her blue eyes, her soft brown hair– even without her abilities, he recognized that she was a descendant of Lachesis. And while he didn't know if she was a threat, he knew by nature of her power and her bloodline, he should be wary.

Fate gives and it takes, and it always takes more than you want to give.

Queen Malinda taught him that. Of course he would tell her the woman's name. She would want to know.

Once Vitess left, satisfied, Nico examined Morena. The princess was sleeping in her crib, sucking her thumb. He stroked her pale cheek, eyed her hair. White as moonlight, it was the exact shade of Atropos', only soft and downy as a bird. He hoped she'd sleep soundly for a few more hours. He had errands to do.

Nico left his ward alone, and eased the door closed. Locked it. Then he crept, silent as a shadow, down the circular stairs.

From an alcove, he grabbed a jug that sloshed as he lifted it, heavy with clear liquid. Its scent was thick, oily, and he tried hard not to breathe as he lugged it toward the door.

Saying a prayer to Nyx, Nico stepped out of the castle, then made his way toward the graveyard, toward the crypts. It wasn't far, but by the time he reached the stone minotaur he was panting, winded from stomping through the deep snow and the weight of what he carried.

"A little further."

It wouldn't take long. He was nearly there, and then it would be done.

A few more steps.

Straining, he made his way into the crypt, then shut the heavy iron door behind him, sealing himself inside.

There was thudding, dragging, and immediate shrieking from downstairs. The sounds were a relief - Nico had feared that he hadn't tied it up properly, that the thing would get away. Freshly determined, he picked up the jug again, his arm muscles straining.

When he entered the room, she lunged, jaws snapping, desperate to rip him apart. Rotting, gray fingers clutched the air, just a few steps from where he stood. Heavy ropes still held her, even though they'd obviously been chewed in his absence.

Nico faced her. His jaw clenched, eyes cold, he looked much older than his years.

Raising a child, living in a castle of the dead, having his mother murdered in front of him - it forces a boy into becoming a man rather quickly. And Malinda, on her part, had been training him as promised. *Knives. Thieving. Lying. Stealth. Bluffing.*

By now, he knew quite a bit about deception.

Still... his expression wobbled. His jaw trembled.

The thing screamed. Not pain - he hadn't done anything yet - but pure rage. It wanted to eat him, and had tried to do just that many times already.

Today he would be done with it. He would see if this spell his mother taught him would work.

Not wanting to get too close, he pulled a slab of meat from his pocket. Raw. He tossed it near the wall, and the monster threw herself after it, like a dog following a bone. That done, Nico got as close as he dared, and then threw the jug directly at her.

It crashed at her feet, the liquid soaking the entire area.

Unbothered, she continued gnawing, chattering at him now and then, unintelligible.

"You can stop that. I'm not fooled. The Queen says you can speak, but I've never seen anything but murder from your lot."

Nico stared hard, looking for any sign - *even the smallest, most inconsequential signal* - that the thing understood him.

There was nothing.

They never reasoned. They never spoke. They only killed. Anything they came near, the Cullen destroyed with their ravenous appetites and superhuman strength.

Closing his eyes with a long sigh, Nico held up his left hand.

"Fieren lumin, encanta."

A blaze appeared in his palm. It wasn't a gift from the Gods. It was a gift from his mother, the only person who had ever loved him. She'd taught him everything she knew, and told him that if she hadn't left the north, she would have been leader of the coven. She would be proud, if she knew how strong his magic was now. How patient he could be.

If she knew what he meant to do.

"You are not my mother. So I'm not sorry to see you go." Nico stretched his fingers open and light streaked across the room, like a comet, landing at the monster's feet.

Transfixed, with an expression that strangely resembled disbelief, the Cullen studied the fire at her feet. Then, what was left of her clothing caught, like dry kindling. The Cullen called Nilensi began to scream.

Nico, never one to leave a job unfinished, stayed to watch.

He did not cry.

AFTERWORD

Here we are, continuing on this journey with Morena, Malinda, and all the other characters of Moirai! For all of those who have reached out to me with encouragement, questions, corrections, enthusiasm... all of it, thank you. You have no idea how thrilling it is to be a writer, to have *readers,* to put this story out in the world. I started writing about Morena and the Fates in 2020. Like any first time author, I was full of enthusiasm and ideas, but they needed editing and polishing, they needed reader feedback. You're part of my journey, part of making me better, and it is you that keeps me writing. I have two small kids, and when it was midnight and I didn't want to finish a chapter, it was messages from my readers that made me buckle down and do it.

If you liked this book, please review it and recommend it! As an indie author with a full time job and two small kids, it is hard to find time to write and even harder to find time to do *marketing,* things like make instagram posts and reels and ads. Every review helps, even if it's not a five-star one. Please feel free to message me anytime!

To continue the story, please order QUEEN OF MAZES AND MIRRORS,

We'll pick up again with Morena as she continues her fight against a grim destiny.

You can also join my mailing list THE UNDERGROUND at queensofmoirai.com for dark fantasy and dark romance reads, giveaways, fan art, and more.

Thank you again for reading.

Printed in Great Britain
by Amazon

57662523R00178